PENGUIN  CLASSICS

JOHN DONNE: SELECTED PROSE

John Donne was born into a Catholic family in 1572. After a conventional education at Hart Hall, Oxford, and Lincoln's Inn, he took part in the Earl of Essex's expedition to the Azores in 1597. He secretly married Anne More in December 1601, and was imprisoned by her father, Sir George, in the Fleet two months later. He was ordained priest in January 1615, and proceeded to a Doctorate of Divinity at Cambridge in April of that year. In 1621 he was made Dean of St Paul's in London, a post that he held until his death in 1631. He is famous for the sermons he preached in his later years as well as for his poems.

•

Neil Rhodes was a Scholar of St Catherine's College, Oxford, from 1971 to 1974; he won the Newdigate Prize and took the degrees of M.A. and D.Phil. He was a Lecturer in the Department of English Studies at Strathclyde University from 1977 to 1979 and is currently a lecturer in English at St Andrews University. He is the author of *Elizabethan Grotesque* (1980).

JOHN DONNE

SELECTED PROSE

EDITED WITH AN INTRODUCTION AND
NOTES BY NEIL RHODES

PENGUIN BOOKS

Penguin Books Ltd, Harmondsworth, Middlesex, England
Viking Penguin Inc., 40 West 23rd Street, New York, New York 10010, U.S.A.
Penguin Books Australia Ltd, Ringwood, Victoria, Australia
Penguin Books Canada Limited, 2801 John Street, Markham, Ontario, Canada L3R 1B4
Penguin Books (N.Z.) Ltd, 182–190 Wairau Road, Auckland 10, New Zealand

First published in Penguin Classics 1987

Introduction copyright © Neil Rhodes, 1987
All rights reserved

Made and printed in Great Britain by
Richard Clay (The Chaucer Press) Ltd,
Bungay, Suffolk
Typeset in 10 on 12 pt Monophoto Bembo

CONTENTS

INTRODUCTION

Donne expected to be remembered as a great preacher rather than a great poet, and one of the aims of this book is to show why. Another is to enlarge the very partial image of Donne which is formed by an isolated reading of the *Songs and Sonnets* – to enlarge it not by pointing to a different, drabber Donne, but by illustrating the considerable imaginative and intellectual continuity in his writing as a whole. *Paradoxes and Problems* was the title given to his earliest prose works, and it is one which could serve equally well for his poetry: it would embrace not only the engagingly flimsy argumentation of 'The Flea', but also the delicate probing of love's mysteries in 'Air and Angels' and 'The Ecstasy' or the extravagant bleakness of 'A Nocturnal upon S. Lucy's Day'. Paradox and problem form the knotty fabric of *Biathanatos*, as Donne ponders whether suicide can ever be justified; it is through paradox and problem that he explores the relationship between the self and the world in the moving account of his near-fatal illness, *Devotions*; and paradox and problem permeate the Sermons, emerging in such typical expressions of wonderment as that the angels are the 'Riddles of Heaven'.

The *Paradoxes* themselves were probably composed in the early 1590s when Donne was a law student, so they are roughly contemporary with the *Elegies*, *Satires* and the earliest of the *Songs and Sonnets*. (The *Problems* were written between 1603 and 1610, the 'dead' period of his career.) Donne himself described them in a letter as 'swaggerers' and 'pretily guilt', as if to acknowledge the bluster and showiness of some of these pieces. Certainly the *Paradoxes* are highly volatile compositions, and the reader is frequently sprayed with arguments which have little overall consistency and which are sometimes based on no more than verbal sleight of hand; as in 'A Defence of Womens Inconstancy', where he claims, 'I would you had your Mistresses so constant that they would never change, no not so much as their *Smocks*, then should you see what a sluttish virtue Constancy were'. But even his most flippant offerings can be attractively sharp; on the virtue of cosmetics, for instance, he points out that 'If in kissing or breathing upon her, the painting fall off, thou art angry: wilt thou be so, if it stick on?' As far as women were concerned, the swagger of the *Paradoxes* becomes more menacing in the *Problems*, which are generally gloomier than the earlier pieces, and we are invited to consider whether females even have souls; after all, they have the edge on the apes only because they can speak. The absurdity of this proposition was sternly rebuked by Donne himself in a late sermon (51), and it would indeed be absurd to suppose that the *Paradoxes and Problems* represent what he actually believed about the subjects he investigates. But as so often in the love poetry, flippancy and seriousness mingle, and some of his subjects are ones with which he was profoundly concerned. The argument that the gifts of the body are better than those of the mind, for example, is not so much an exercise in cynical materialism as an honest affirmation of the sensitivity of our physical faculties, mixed with regret for the helplessness of the soul: 'But alas my Soule cannot make any part, that is not of it selfe disposed, to see or heare'. The first part of this Paradox seems genuinely troubled, and its theme was to reappear in his religious prose. Similarly, the contradictory arguments of Paradoxes 1 and 5, that all things kill themselves, and that only cowards dare die, suggest a real conflict about the legitimacy of killing oneself which he was later to explore in *Biathanatos*.

Conflict is the essence of the *Paradoxes*, whether within Donne himself or between Donne and the reader. Wit is dynamic, he asserts, and discord creative: 'While I . . . feele the contrary repugnances and adverse fightings of the Elements in my body, my body increaseth; and whilst I differ from common opinions, by this discord the number of my Paradoxes encreaseth.' The connection he makes might seem arbitrary, but it is entirely characteristic of Donne that he should associate his sense of internal, physical conflict with an intellectual position of sceptical antagonism. It is this last quality which he identifies in his letter about the *Paradoxes*; their object, he says, is to make the reader 'find better reasons against them' and in themselves they are 'nothings'. In this respect the *Paradoxes* are what the critic Stanley Fish has called 'self-consuming artifacts' (a term which he in fact applies to Donne's sermons); that is to say, they are dialectical works whose meaning is not intrinsic, but is generated by their argumentative relationship with the reader. How seriously we should take them, then, is a question of how serious we make them.

Biathanatos, Donne's treatise on suicide, was probably written in 1608, at a time when he was engaged in knotty religious controversy and the regular augmentation of his family. The latter does not seem to have provided a cheerful respite from his intellectual labours, and it is clear from his letters of this period that Donne was in fact extremely miserable. Whether or not that is reflected in his choice of subject, *Biathanatos* could hardly be described as an emotional work; it is a long and tortuously legalistic answer to the question: 'Is self-homicide inevitably sinful?' (Donne does not use the term 'suicide'). With the exception of the preface, the work is apparently so drained of personality that it is easier to see it as a masochistic rather than a therapeutic exercise, though given the nature of the topic these may not be entirely distinct. At any rate, Donne was proud of his achievement and did not repudiate it after he had been ordained. Before going to Germany in 1619 he sent a copy to his friend Sir Robert Ker, boasting that various Oxbridge dons had told him that 'there was a false thread in it, but not easily found'; he asked Ker not to destroy it, but not to publish it either, as the subject was 'misinterpretable'. In fact, *Biathanatos* was eventually published in 1647 by Donne's less scrupulous son, who was busy capitalizing on his father's literary estate.

The real interest in the work lies in the fact that it is the first book about suicide to be written in English. It is a symptom of the Jacobean mood, an enormous footnote to Hamlet's anguished question, and a product, too, of the scepticism which had been encouraged by Florio's translation of Montaigne in 1603. 'The voluntariest death is the fairest. Life dependeth on the will of others, death on ours', Montaigne had asserted (*Essays*, II.3). Donne had certainly read Montaigne, and the individualism of this position may have appealed to him, as he reflected in his preface that 'I have the keyes of my prison in mine owne hand'. But it would be misleading to associate the two writers too closely. Montaigne's arguments derive in part from Stoic and therefore pagan philosophy, which has little place in *Biathanatos* outside the preface. A Roman might do the decent thing and retrieve his honour without fear of damnation, but this would be a very dangerous course of action for a Christian to take; the evil angel who offers Dr Faustus a dagger knows that he is jeopardizing Faustus's soul by tempting him to the sin of despair, but no such considerations apply to the suicide of Brutus in *Julius Caesar*. (The moral aspect of suicide, as of revenge, becomes more confused when classical and Christian conventions are mixed, as they are in *The Spanish Tragedy*, for instance.) For Donne, however, the context of the debate is almost exclusively Christian, and he is concerned in particular with the arguments put forward by St Augustine (*City of God*, I.17–27) and codified by Aquinas: that suicide is unnatural, because every creature naturally loves itself and therefore tries to keep itself alive; that suicide is a crime against the community of which every man is a part; and that since life is a gift from God a person who takes his own life sins against God (*Summa*, II, 2.64.5). By dividing his book into three parts, dealing with the law of nature, the law of reason, and the law of God, Donne is attempting to meet this threefold argument.

The result is a work of rather doubtful character, and *Biathanatos* is in fact both a paradox and a problem. It is a paradox, as its full title declares, because it sets out to defend a seemingly untenable thesis, and it is a problem in that it is casuistical, i.e. it grapples with a morally problematic 'case' of conscience. But it is also a problem in the more straightforward sense that it is not entirely clear whether or not Donne means us to take his arguments seriously – a familiar enough experience to the reader of the *Songs and Sonnets*. The mere physical appearance of the book might suggest a satire on casuistry, as each page in the original edition is so festooned with brackets and indices and marginalia that it resembles a computer program as much as a literary text. The style, too, with its bloated parentheses and meandering subordinate clauses is of a kind that Donne himself might have described as 'riddling and per-plexed'. Not surprisingly, then, modern writers have questioned the intentions of the work, suggesting that it is basically ironic or 'a paradox about paradoxy' (Rosalie Colie); but if this is so Donne gives us re-markably few clues, and the tone of *Biathanatos* is too often earnest for the dismissive judgement on its sincerity to be very convincing. The volume and ingenuity of the argumentation and the abstruseness of the learning are quite in character with the kind of mental habits which his poetry reveals. Besides, however dreary his circumstances at the time, the notion of Donne compiling a gigantically learned spoof among the damps of Mitcham, in order to defer conversation with his wife (see Letter 2), seems mildly improbable.

In the first part of *Biathanatos* Donne tries to show that suicide does not contravene any law of nature, and as a preliminary to this he severs the traditional association between suicide and despair. There are plenty of instances, he points out, where people have done away with themselves with great gusto, a theme to which he frequently returns. The real problem in this section is to define what is meant by 'the law of nature', and, of course, it helps Donne's case to fog the issue sufficiently to dispense with it altogether: 'I confesse I read it a hundred times before I understand it once.' The range of interpretation is certainly enormous – from the libertine and decidedly un-Christian principle of following one's own instincts to the definition of Aquinas that the law is implanted in nature by God, and carries with it moral imperatives which can be discerned by the light of human reason. Donne's position is not libertine, but it is a good deal more sceptical and individualistic than that of Aquinas: 'he whose conscience well tempred and dispassion'd, assures him that the reason of selfe-preservation ceases in him, may also presume that the law ceases too', he claims with characteristic self-assertiveness. But the apparent reasonableness of this argument is belied by the main thrust of part I, which is to show that, *pace* Aquinas, so far from naturally striving to preserve themselves, human beings have a 'natural desire' for death. From the opening words of the preface, through the long list of classical suicides (not reprinted here), to the grand theatre of the early Christian martyrs, Donne describes us as a race of lemming-like creatures raring for an orgy of self-destruction, and he notes with aphoristic relish that in the early Church 'many were baptised onely because they would be burnt'. As an argument for the naturalness of suicide this has considerable originality, as well as imaginative appeal; if it were not for the fact that the martyrs were expecting re-birth, Donne would seem to be anticipating Freud's theory of the death-wish.

It is in part II that the central ambivalence of *Biathanatos* emerges. This section deals with the law of reason, which means in effect the laws laid down by Church and State. In 'The Relique' a more libertine Donne had claimed that this 'late law' injured nature, but here his position is quite different and he seems to be thoroughly in favour of the horrifying legal penalties which exist to deter suicide. Such laws do not imply that suicide is a particularly heinous crime, he adds, but only that people are very prone to it, which is a bad thing for society. In particular, slaves who lead miserable lives would be bound to take the easy way out, if given half a chance. Partly what Donne objects to here is the thought that suicide may proceed from slothfulness; death is fine, provided that it is sufficiently strenuous, as he observes of his own imagined demise in a letter of 1608 (see Letter 3). He shifts to an even more authoritarian position when he considers whether it is permissible for the relatives of condemned men to speed their execution by, say, pulling on the legs of those being hanged. No, because the law which has 'appointed a painfull death to deterre others' would then be 'defrauded'. These sentiments fit awkwardly with the more liberal line of argument in part I, and it is clearly not the case that in *Biathanatos* Donne is standing up for the individual against tyrannical governments. He was at heart an authoritarian, and a firm supporter of firm government, but one who felt that, as far as he was concerned, authority resided in himself.

In his third section, on the law of God, Donne produces what he evidently intends to be his clinching argument: Christ himself committed suicide. While he does not make this shocking claim entirely explicit, 'This actuall emission of his soule, which is death, and which was his own act, and before his naturall time' is an unequivocal account of an entirely voluntary death, and the reader is left to decide whether or not this amounts to suicide. The point is central, because Apollonia and others, whose martyrdoms are graphically described earlier in the book, are now shown to be imitating Christ, and it may well be that underlying the baffling intricacies of *Biathanatos* is the argument that 'self-homicide' is permissible only in so far as it conforms to the pattern of Christ himself. The law of God, as revealed in the Bible, carries a good deal more weight than that of nature or reason, but as Donne points out at the opening of this section, the meaning of the Scriptures is almost infinitely malleable, so even here one is left in doubt as to his true purposes. The problem of *Biathanatos* lies not so much in its irony, of which there is little evidence, but in the fact that Donne's scepticism seems so complete that it is almost as self-annihilating as the object of its inquiry.

In *Devotions upon Emergent Occasions* (1624) we find Donne contemplating his own dissolution in a much less hypothetical way. He had been a priest for nearly nine years when he fell dangerously ill of relapsing fever, and assumed that he was dying. It was a momentous opportunity for him to record the process of his own death, and he worked with literally feverish activity to do so, having the book ready for publication before he had left the sickroom. The casual yet obsessive intimations of mortality in his poetry – 'When I am dead, and doctors know not why . . .' – are here focussed upon the actual disintegration of his body: 'I have cut up mine own *Anatomy*, dissected my selfe', he writes in Meditation 9. The prospect of death became an intellectual challenge, and something of the morbid intensity with which Donne met that challenge is indicated by the fact that at the time of the book's publication he was still under doctor's orders not to read, let alone write. *Devotions* was composed, as so many of his poems appear to be composed, from within the turmoil of the experience it records.*

The book is divided into twenty-three sections or 'stations', each of which concerns a particular phase in Donne's illness, and each section consists of three parts, a Meditation, an Expostulation, and a Prayer. The number of sections may correspond to the actual days of the illness, but in stopping at the 'hour before midnight' Donne may also be re-minding himself, and us, that death was still to come. While the Meditations do form a coherent sequence by themselves they must inevitably give a rather one-sided impression of the character of the work as a whole. For one thing, they are predominantly secular, and the physical experiences which they explore are related to the physical world, rather than placed in a Christian context. The Expostulations which follow, with their anguished, lurching rhythms and insistent repetitions, have the hectoring quality of many of the *Holy Sonnets*: 'My God, my God, why is not my *soule*, as sensible as my *body*?' is a familiar Donneian *cri de cœur*. The Expostulations are in a sense the panic at the centre of each phase of the illness, and it is the function of the concluding Prayers to control and subdue that panic; if the Expostulations reflect the mood of the *Holy Sonnets*, the Prayers share the calmness and resolution of his last poems, the three great *Hymns*.

To say that the Meditations are secular is to say that they do not much resemble anything in the Christian meditative tradition, either Catholic or Protestant. Erudite controversy has raged over the extent of Donne's debt to the *Spiritual Exercises* of the Spanish Jesuit, St Ignatius Loyola (1491–1556), but despite his use of the term *stationes* in his Latin 'list of contents' – suggesting the familiar subject of Catholic meditation, the stations of the cross – the Meditations in no way contemplate the life of Christ, which is an essential part of St Ignatius's *Exercises*. On the

---

* C. S. Lewis makes this a point against Donne (see 'Donne and Love Poetry in the Seventeenth Century'), but the tension between the emotional agitation and the studied formal control seems to me a source of strength.

other hand, a contemporary Protestant view of meditation is given by Paul Baynes in *Briefe Directions unto a Godly Life* (1618), and it is equally remote from Donne: 'Meditation . . . is when we doe of purpose separate our selves from all other things, and consider as we are able, and think of some points of instruction necessary to leade us forward to the Kingdome of Heaven.' Donne's earthbound and egocentric exercises could hardly be less orthodox.

In its insistence upon the separation of the self from the world Baynes's statement does, however, point up an essential quality of the Meditations in *Devotions*, a quality which C. S. Lewis, in describing Donne's poetic imagination, called 'centripetal'. The world converges on the patient; as Donne said in a very different context, 'all here in one bed lay'. Geography and cosmology, politics and alchemy, are ransacked for analogies with his suffering body in the hope that they will provide a universal meaning for the particular features of his physical experience: fevers are like earthquakes, 'insensible' diseases are like secret political agitators, the body is like a swamp-ridden farm. When the doctors decide to apply dead pigeons to the soles of his feet in order to 'draw the vapors from the Head', Donne thinks of himself as a well, an oven and a mine, replete with noisome gases and fumes. When he is finally able to get out of bed he totters giddily, and reflects that he is 'a *new Argument* of the *new Philosophie*, That the *Earth* moves round'. These kinds of correspondence stem from an all-pervasive application of the analogy between microcosm and macrocosm, the favourite Renaissance notion that the human being is like a little world. Donne took this quite literally and followed Paracelsus (1493–1541), the Swiss alchemist and physician, in believing that the human body actually contained everything that could be found in the animal, vegetable and mineral world outside it: 'the whole world hath nothing, to which something in man doth not answere', he observes in Meditation 4. But even that is an understatement: 'so hath man many pieces, of which the whol world hath no representation'. In less lugubrious circumstances Donne might have seen this in a humanist light as being a token of man's dignity and importance, as he does frequently in the Sermons, but here his likening the body to a container only emphasizes the reverse. If the universe resembles a nest of boxes with man at the centre, then man is the centre of decay: 'This is *Natures nest of Boxes*; The Heavens containe the *Earth*, the *Earth*, *Cities*, *Cities*, *Men*. And all these are *Concentrique*; the common *center* to them all, is *decay, ruine*' (Meditation 10). Throughout the Meditations we are reminded of the paradox that, while the 'carcass' of the physical body is confined within the 'close prison' of the sickbed, the decaying centre of the world, the mind may soar at will through the universe, vigorously discovering analogies for the human condition which nevertheless point relentlessly to its impotence and self-destructiveness. The intellectual energy of *Devotions* is directed towards a gloomy inversion of the exuberant aim in 'The Good Morrow' of 'making one little room an everywhere'.

What this suggests is that *Devotions* is above all a metaphysical prose work, and more completely so than most of Donne's poetry. It takes to extreme lengths the principle of the metaphysical conceit that human experience can be explored through an infinitely complex system of correspondences, which link the self with the world and various parts of the world with various parts of the self. But whereas in Donne's love poetry intellectual excitement feeds on emotional excitement, and the global fantasies of 'The Sun Rising' or 'The Good Morrow' result from the celebration of a shared experience, in *Devotions* the opposite is the case. The sense of constant mental agitation in the metaphorical structure of the work, as he snatches at one analogy after another, betrays the terror of isolation and disintegration which prompts such analogies. '*Solitude* is a torment which is not threatned in *hell* it selfe', he says in Meditation 5, and 'the height of an infectious disease of the body, is *solitude*, to be left alone: for this makes an infectious bed, equall, nay worse than a *grave*, that thogh in both I be equally alone, in my bed I *know* it, and *feele* it, and shall not in my *grave*'. The correspondences which Donne forges in the loneliness of his sickbed, in order to re-establish his sense of being in the world, have the effect of negative feedback; each comparison, each metaphysical conceit, only compounds the feeling that his predicament is uniquely wretched. We are presented with a series of macabre paradoxes in which eventually even the possibilities of self-help or mutual aid provoke morbid reflections:

. . . I have taken a *farme* at this *hard rent*, and upon those *heavie covenants*, that it can afford it selfe no *helpe*; (no part of my *body*, if it were cut off, would *cure* another part; in some cases it might *preserve* a sound part, but in no case *recover* an infected) and, if my *body* may have any *Physicke*, any *Medicine* from another *body*, one *Man* from the flesh of another *Man* (as by *Mummy*, or any such *composition*,) it must bee from a man that is dead . . . (Meditation 22)

Personally cut off from the society of the living, Donne considers the possibility of returning to physical wholeness through actual physical dismemberment. Impossible, he admits, but it is a paradox which highlights a central anxiety in the Meditations, which is the way that bodily disintegration seems to image a separation of the individual from human society, and even from God himself. Donne's constant attempts to establish connections between his personal condition and the wider world, so as to conquer his sense of isolation, are the precise opposite of Protestant recommendations of contemplative un-worldliness.

The function of the Expostulations and Prayers is to battle with and quell such anxieties, but the psychological tension in the Meditations derives chiefly from Donne's feeling that his plight is self-inflicted. Physical sickness has always been a convenient metaphor for other kinds of failure, and at a time when outbreaks of the plague were thought to be caused by people's wickedness, it is not surprising to find Donne attributing his condition to moral backsliding. 'I fall sick of *Sin*, and am bedded and bedrid, buried and putrified in the practise of *Sin*', he tells us in the first Expostulation, and the sense that he is, as it were, stewing in his own juice is made grotesquely literal by the fact that the first symptom of the disease is a violent sweat. Later he reflects that cleansing himself of sin would be more like trying to drain a moat than a marsh. This powerfully tactile sense of being steeped or 'macerated' (a favourite word) in wickedness is not peculiar to Donne. It is typically present in St Augustine's *Confessions*, though elsewhere Augustine cautions, 'We have exaggerated the disease, let us also praise the Physician'. Spiritual sickness is a fact of the human condition, but Donne's peculiarly elaborate pessimism seems to come from the feeling that it is also his own over-intellectual temperament which has laid him low. The first Meditation closes with the observation that man is a little world chiefly in that he contains the wherewithal to destroy himself, and that hypochondria is a form of suicide. The final Meditation returns to the same theme. As soon as he has recovered, he becomes terrified of relapsing, and the terror of relapsing is increased by the belief that relapses are usually self-induced: 'wee are not onely *executed*, (that implies *guiltinesse*) but wee are *executioners*, (that implies *dishonor*) and *executioners* of *our selves*, (and that implies *impietie*)'. There is a neurotic circularity, not only in the arguments of the individual Meditations, but in the sequence as a whole. In fact it is at the mid-point of the sequence, in Meditation 12, that this particular anxiety is explored most fully. It transpires that he is suffering from melancholic 'vapours', the intellectual's disease: 'They tell me it is my *Melancholy*; Did I infuse, did I drinke in *Melancholly* into my selfe? It is my *thoughtfulnesse*; was I not made to *thinke*? It is my *study*; doth not my *Calling* call for that?' Again the monstrous thought arises that thinking is suicidal, and the despairing cry, 'was I not made to *thinke*?' poignantly exposes the quite obsessive intellectuality of *Devotions*. He finally reports that 'my *meditation* is fearefully transferred from the *body* to the *minde*'.

This is not to say that in *Devotions*, or even in the sequence of Meditations, Donne emerges as self-indulgent or self-pitying. Indeed, it is the intensity of the intellectual activity which prevents the work from becoming a merely lugubrious exercise in breast-beating. Not only that, but he is constantly alert to what is going on around him: when the doctor arrives, Donne sharply observes the man's mounting trepidation, which he tries to disguise; the more he tries to disguise it the more worried Donne becomes. But he is strikingly objective about his own fear: the doctor 'knowes that his *feare* shall not disorder the practise, and exercise of his *Art*, but he knows that my *fear* may disorder the effect, and working of his practise'. This alertness, this watchfulness, is apparent in a different way in the Meditations on time. Lying sleeplessly in bed, he is acutely aware of the fact that while his own experience as a patient is one of distressing timelessness, in which hours and days flow ceaselessly into one another, the disease itself, which took hold 'in a minute', has fallen on 'critical dayes'. In this way the highly formal structure of the book (Donne talks of past, present and future as three 'stations' in Meditation 14) suggests that he is making a deliberate effort to discipline that sense of time as meandering flux, as '*Imaginary halfenothing*', which is so much a part of his melancholy. What concentrates his mind at this point is the sound of the neighbouring church bells, tolling for the deaths of others, and it is the three Meditations on the bells which form the climax of *Devotions*. Bells count the hours; they may, indeed, have kept him awake; but these bells are both recorders of time and heralds of eternity, 'where there shall bee no more distinction of *houres* . . . where I shall wake continually and never sleepe more'. The sound of the bells translates his insomnia into a positive image of everlasting wakefulness.

But the bells also effect a kind of psychological release in Donne in a different way. He opens Meditation 16 with a reference to a man who had written a book about bells while in prison, and comments, 'How would hee have enlarged himselfe if he had beene my *fellow Prisoner* in this *sicke bed*'. 'Enlarged' in this context means 'released'; what does Donne mean? The point, I think, is that the bells have enabled him to transfer his meditations from himself to others, and, more importantly, to share in the fate of another, so as to release himself from the state of corrosive introspection in which his body and soul seemed to sum up everything that is corrupt and self-defeating in human nature. Meditation 16, on the funeral bell, is concerned with the deaths of others; Meditations 17 and 18, however, on the passing bell and the death knell, concentrate on a single individual, and it is through his particular identification with the plight of another man that Donne achieves a sense of his spiritual reintegration in the body of the Church. This leads in the first place to a marvellous image of the heavenly community: '*Gods* hand is in every *translation*; and his hand shall binde up all our scattered leaves againe, for that *Librarie* where every *booke* shall lie open to one another' (17). The lines seem to echo Dante's vision at the end of the *Paradiso*: 'Within its depths I saw ingathered, bound by love in one volume, the scattered leaves of all the universe' (X X X III.85–7), and while Dante's 'scattered leaves' refer solely to the pages of a book, it is difficult to resist the autumnal associations of Donne's lines. 'In heaven it is alwaies Autumne', he wrote in a sermon preached later that year (27). In the second part of the Meditation he returns quite literally to earth with the famous assertion of our common humanity:

No man is an *Iland*, intire of itselfe; every man is a peece of the *Continent*, a part of the *maine*; if a *Clod* bee washed away by the *Sea*, *Europe* is the lesse, as well as if a *Promontorie* were, as well as if a *Mannor* of thy *friends*, or of *thine owne* were; Any Mans *death* diminishes *me*, because I am involved in *Mankinde*; And therefore never send to know for whom the *bell* tolls; It tolls for *thee*.

It has to be said that this most famous passage of Donne's prose writings expresses uncharacteristically hopeful sentiments about his ability to integrate himself with his fellow human beings, and, if it is the climax of *Devotions*, it is by no means the conclusion of the work. Listening to the death knell of another seems to have been cathartic because it is at this point that Donne begins to recover, but as he does so he lapses again into morbid introspection, and ends, as we have seen, by worrying about the dangers of physical relapse: 'It is not in *mans body*, as it is in the *Citie*, that when *the Bell* hath rung, to cover your *fire*, and rake up the *embers*, you may lie downe, and sleepe without feare' (Meditation 23). The comfortingly domestic image is invoked only to be rejected. Relapses, we are told, are even more likely to be self-inflicted than the original disease, and we return inexorably to the subject of the first Meditation. *Devotions* is Donne's most self-revealing work, so it may not be out of place finally to notice its affinities with a Romantic poem – *The Ancient Mariner*. Coleridge's account of a self-inflicted crisis of despair, of guilt-ridden self-absorption, broken by a spontaneous act of benediction which apparently restores the sufferer's sense of harmony with the world, is remarkably similar to the pattern of Donne's work. So too is the final absence of reconciliation: both Donne and the mariner have to go on telling their tales.

We must now turn to the Sermons. Donne had been ordained in 1615; he became chaplain to King James, Reader at Lincoln's Inn and, from 1621, Dean of St Paul's. It may be difficult to imagine the highly self-conscious and strong-willed individualist of the love poems in the submissive and self-effacing role of God's servant. Isaak Walton, his first biographer, saw him as a modern St Augustine, sinner turned saint, but the division is much less abrupt. Donne never reached a calm plateau from which he could survey the spiritual anxieties of his earlier life with equanimity, and the sense of struggle continued. 'Scatter thy thoughts no farther then, contract them in thy self', he advises his congregation in one of the earliest sermons (1), but Donne himself found such acts of pious concentration difficult: 'I throw my selfe downe in my Chamber, and I call in, and invite God, and his Angels thither, and when they are there, I neglect God and his Angels, for the noise of a Flie, for the ratling of a Coach, for the whining of a doore' (38.3). Elsewhere he castigates such wanderers as 'self-Excommunicators'. Throughout Donne's writing there is clearly a tension between his need to assert his sceptical, inquiring personality and his greater need to submerge that personality, with all its fretfulness, in an all-embracing Divinity. In Paradox 5 he had scorned 'those men which dye that Allegoricall death of entring into Religion' as cowards, yet later, in 'A Hymn to Christ, at the Author's last going into Germany', he imagined his journey towards God as a death by drowning, a total immersion. The conflict is perhaps

expressed most succinctly in the letter which he wrote to Sir Henry
Goodyer (3) where he feels that a shipwreck would be the preferable
way to go, as it would at least give him the opportunity of struggling
against the waves.

Another, quite different way in which Donne's sermons may be
related to his earlier self is to see them as the product of a literary
intelligence. They are in some measure works of literary criticism. Like
other sermons of the time, and some today, they are based upon the
close verbal analysis of biblical texts – exercises in 'practical criticism',
but with moral and spiritual application. Although he maintained that
his preaching was directed towards the consciences rather than the 'affections' (emotions) of his listeners, he was less equivocal than St
Augustine in finding a literary eloquence in the Bible: 'The Holy Ghost
in penning the Scriptures delights himself, not only with a propriety,
but with a delicacy, and harmony, and melody of language; with height
of Metaphors, and other figures, which may work greater impressions
upon the Readers' (24.2) and, appropriately enough for a poet, his
favourite book of the Old Testament was the Psalms. But we should
not suppose that his insistence upon the figurative nature of the Scriptures entails a rejection of their literal interpretation. What the word
'Bible' basically means is *ta biblia*, 'the little books', and these books are
written in different genres (Donne calls Job a tragicomedy, for instance),
which must be read in different ways: the danger with Genesis lies in *not*
taking it literally, with Revelation in the failure to see that the literal
sense is to be discerned through figures and metaphors. 'The literall
sense is alwayes to be preserved; but the literall sense is not alwayes to be
discerned', he writes in an Easter sermon (25.1). But more important
than the precise nature of Donne's scriptural exegesis is the fact that the
sermons themselves are alive with metaphor, much of which reflects the
imagery and method of his poetry. One to which he frequently returns,
and which does not occur in the Bible, is the image of the world as a
book: 'The world is a great Volume, and man the Index of that Booke;
Even in the body of man, you may turne to the whole world; This
body is an Illustration of all Nature; Gods recapitulation of all that he
had said before' (38.4). This is the Paracelsian notion of *Devotions* 4, that
man is a microcosm, but here it is placed in a wider context. The world,
the 'Book of the Creatures', is a universal system of signs inscribed by
God: if the Bible is the language of the Holy Spirit, the world is the

language of God. Reading the world, then, is a parallel activity to reading the Bible, for both lead us to knowledge of the divine author, and Donne's sermons refer constantly from one book to the other.

While this may indicate a peculiarly verbal experience of the world, Donne is not, like his near contemporary Lancelot Andrewes, a philological pedant. T. S. Eliot reckoned this a disadvantage and described Donne with lurid distaste as 'the religious spellbinder ... the flesh-creeper, the sorcerer of emotional orgy'. Certainly his sermons are dramatic, and here too there is a continuity with the poet who boasted of his 'words' masculine persuasive force' in Elegy 16. In one sense the preacher's role is passive, that of medium – 'a blessed hermaphrodite', as he puts it in the poem on Mr Tilman's ordination – but he is also a powerful transmitter for God's stentorian oratory: 'this is not Gods ordinary way, to be whispering of secrets ... his Ordinance of preaching batters the soule, and by that breach, the Spirit enters', he declares (42.1), perhaps remembering his Holy Sonnet, 'Batter my heart, three-personed God'. And he was also highly conscious of the theatrical possibilities of the pulpit. The hourglass which stood at his side to mark the duration of the sermon was also a stage-prop, serving as a potent symbol of the brevity of life, the moment of judgement, and the eternity into which the soul would be launched. 'But we are now in the work of an houre, and no more. If there be a minute of sand left, (There is not) If there be a minute of patience left, heare me say, This minute that is left, is that eternitie which we speake of; upon this minute dependeth that eternity' (40.4). The passage follows a spine-chilling account of the midnight terrors of the guilty soul – no wonder then, as contemporaries record, that during Donne's sermons women fainted and brave men wept. In contrast with the academic Andrewes, Donne is live, immediate and frequently personal, not merely in publicly confessing his own delinquencies, but also in using the pulpit to enact a personal spiritual drama. The eloquent sermon on St Stephen, the first Christian martyr, is a case in point; the histrionic gesture of self-sacrifice prompted by Donne's identification with Stephen, 'I will give God a Cup, a cup of my blood', blends submission with self-assertion (45.2). In suffering, the martyr returns the communion chalice to his Saviour. Donne's interest in martyrdom is, of course, intimately connected with his interest in suicide, and his final appearance in the pulpit was an attempt to consummate his desire of being master of his own death. 'This is my play's last scene . . .' he had written in one of the Holy Sonnets, and *Deaths Duell* revitalizes (if that is the right word) the tired metaphor of the world as a stage. He had expressed a wish that he 'might die in the Pulpit'. He failed to achieve this, but the dramatic effect of this last performance was not lost upon his audience. As Isaak Walton remarked, 'Dr Donne had *preach't his own Funeral Sermon*'.

All this may suggest that Donne regarded his sermons primarily as a vehicle for self-expression, for a vulgar exhibitionism even, and that indeed is what Eliot's stricture seems to imply. But this is misleading. What Donne does is to offer himself symbolically in roles which drama- tize for his audience basic spiritual truths: his 'I' is also a 'we'. The masterful amplification on the possibility of damnation, which begins, 'That God should let my soule fall out of his hand, into a bottomlesse pit, and roll an unremoveable stone upon it, and leave it to that which it finds there' is an expansive invitation to the congregation to contem- plate, in the person of the speaker, the moment of their own judgement (18.2). Earlier in the sermon he had confessed his personal weaknesses – 'I bend all my powers, and faculties upon God, as I think, and suddenly I finde my selfe scattered, melted, fallen into vaine thoughts, into no thoughts' – but in the later passage the 'I' modulates into the subject of a shared experience, an experience of terror punctuated by priestly reassur- ances, and moves finally to the universal 'we'. This is not showmanship, but a rhetorical strategy for engaging the consciences of the congrega- tion. Where the reader today is more likely to feel uneasy is in the passages which divide 'us' and 'them'. Part of the latter category are atheists, about whom Donne is particularly blood-curdling; in a late sermon, for instance, he imagines the unbeliever begging the mountains, like Dr Faustus, to fall and hide him from the wrath of God. 'Is there a God now?' he asks the man gloatingly (48). Another passage that may seem less than charitable is that beginning, 'When the Holy Ghost hath brought us into the Ark from whence we may see all the world without, sprawling and gasping in the flood' (36.1). If this suggests to the modern reader the *schadenfreude* of the nuclear bunker, it is worth pointing out that medieval theologians had claimed that viewing the sufferings of the damned would be one of the features of heavenly bliss. According to Aquinas, to feel pity would be wrong because that would imply a criticism of God's judgement. Still, theological explanation may not alter our response to Donne's more fearsome imaginings. He is not a gentle preacher, like Jeremy Taylor. What does seem true of these passages is that their emotional power springs not so much from a crude thrill, on his own part, of terrorizing his audience, as from their representing a genuine struggle within Donne himself to evoke and subdue shared spiritual anxieties. 'Exorcist' might be a better term than Eliot's 'sorcerer'.

This is one reason why he rarely exploits the more sensational imagery of hell, the flaming spits and pools of molten lead, which had stoked up many an Elizabethan sermon. Indeed, his reminders of damnation are always counterbalanced by an insistence upon God's infinite mercy, and it is not mere accident that perhaps the most celebrated passage in all his Sermons is the one which ends, 'God comes to thee, not as in the dawning of the day, not as in the bud of the spring, but as the Sun at noon to illustrate all shadowes, as the sheaves in harvest, to fill all penuries, all occasions invite his mercies, and all times are his seasons' (27.1). What *may* seem untypical here is the marvellously sensuous quality of the lines, in which the autumnal image is perfectly reflected in the rich laxity of the rhythms themselves. It is certainly true that the imagery of the sermons, like that of the poems and *Devotions*, tends to derive from man's intellectual endeavours such as map-making and navigation, geometry or chemical refinement, rather than from the visual beauties of nature. But paradoxically, Donne is at his most lush when describing what is most completely unimaginable, i.e. what it is like in heaven: 'I shall finde my self, and all my sins enterred, and entombed in his wounds, and like a Lily in Paradise, out of red earth, I shall see my soule rise out of his blade, in a candor, and in an innocence, contracted there, acceptable in the sight of his Father' (5.3). This kind of baroque decoration suggests a Counter-Reformation sensibility which we might associate more readily with Crashaw than with Donne. It may suggest that he was visually excited more by things which could not actually be seen. Hell is a good deal easier to visualize than heaven, yet in speaking of damnation Donne concentrates primarily on the more abstract (though worst) torment of being eternally separated from God. In fact, he frequently disproves the literary truism that heaven is more boring than hell because heaven is less physical: 'I shall see nothing but God, and what is in him; and him I shall see *In carne, in the flesh*' (8.2); the joy of the martyrs was such 'as would worke a liquefaction, a melting of my bowels' (49.3), but the joy of heaven is even greater.

The physicality of Donne's heaven points us to what is possibly the central preoccupation in his writing as a whole, that is, the relationship between matter and spirit, body and soul. The shifts of mood from elation to disgust in the love poetry suggest a sensibility acutely concerned with the value which may be placed upon the flesh, and Donne's estimates veer wildly from the 'lovely glorious nothing' of the body etherealized by love in 'Air and Angels' to the contemptuous 'mummy, possessed', where the body is likened to dead flesh preserved in bitumen ('Love's Alchemy'). But many of these poems reflect his struggle to mediate between body and soul, and the most celebratory of the *Songs and Sonnets*, such as 'Love's Growth', assert the vital interdependence of body and soul in consummated love. And this, Donne insists again and again in his Sermons, is the essence of heaven: 'the Kingdome of Heaven hath not all it must have to a consummate perfection, till it have bodies too' (13.1); 'A man is not saved, a sinner is not redeemed, I am not received into heaven, if my body be left out' (*Sermons*, ed. Potter and Simpson, VII.103). Unlike Milton, Donne believed that angels were entirely incorporeal, and for that reason he claimed that 'Man cannot deliberately wish himselfe an Angel, because he should lose by that wish, and lacke that glory, which he shall have in his body' (31). But whereas in 'Air and Angels' Donne handles the distinction between matter and spirit with agility and delicacy, he can also be absurdly leaden (as well as inconsistent), as when he claims that if we stuff ourselves with 'wittie sawces' we will lose that wonderfully slim resemblance to the angels in heaven, who are, of course, completely weightless (34.1). The clumsiness here testifies to the obvious difficulties involved in expressing a transition from matter to spirit, or indeed in imagining what a glorified body might be like; in heaven 'Bodies are purer, than best souls are here', he remarks in the 'Elegy on Mistress Boulstred'.

Donne persistently wrestled with such paradoxes, and both his poetry and prose hanker after new images of refinement 'Like gold to aery thinness beat' – which is one reason why alchemy so much appealed to him. Renaissance alchemy was not merely a crackpot scheme for making money, despite a tradition of caricature from Breugel to Ben Jonson. The possibility of transmuting base metals into gold was certainly a part of the alchemist's dream, but to the more high-minded devotee such as Paracelsus it was an all-embracing philosophy of regeneration and purification. The 'spiritual alchemist' combined the roles (in theory, at any rate) of chemist, doctor and priest, and set out a universal programme of refinement in which souls and bodies, as well as minerals, could be purged of their imperfections and resurrected as 'gold'. Donne takes up this idea in a sermon on the penitential Psalms: 'David . . . was metall tried seven times in the fire, and desired to be such gold as might be laid up in Gods Treasury', he explains, and then launches into the mysteries of 'calcination', 'Ablution' and 'Fixion' (19). Despite the whiff of charlatanry, at the heart of alchemical 'philosophy' was the earnestly optimistic belief that body and soul, matter and spirit, could somehow be reconciled, and it is this which explains why Donne was so ready to exploit its imagery in a religious context.

The spiritual alchemy of Donne's Sermons, then, offers a vision of resurrection and refinement. It is directed above all to the Last Day, on which body and soul will be reunited in a glorified state and their mutual antagonisms triumphantly healed. But Donne himself admitted that the resurrection of the body was 'the hardest Article of the Creed', and while the mechanics of this operation clearly fascinated him, his descriptions of it hardly suggest a process of refinement. It has become a cliché to call Donne's Sermons 'macabre', implying, no doubt, that they are full of the Gothic lumber of worms and winding-sheets. While there is a fair amount of this, Donne dwells upon the features of bodily decay not so much to instil a fear of death as to impress his audience with the miraculousness of bodily resurrection. 'Between that excrementall jelly that thy body is made of at first, and that jelly which thy body dissolves to at last; there is not so noysome, so putrid a thing in nature.' How wonderful, then, that a glorified body can emerge from such putrescence! The same sermon continues, 'Shall I imagine a difficulty in my body, because I have lost an Arme in the East, and a leg in the West? because I have left some bloud in the North, and some bones in the South?' (8). In visualizing the Last Day his fondness for geographical metaphor becomes grotesque; we are asked to admire an astonishing feat of reconstruction, in which 'legions of Angels, millions of Angels' hurry round the globe collecting severed limbs and scattered dust (14.1). While the aim is to press home a divine miracle, what we get is something much more disconcertingly earthbound and physical. Disconcerting, too, is Donne's habit of reserving his more macabre performances for weddings: 'Where be all the splinters of that Bone, which a shot hath shivered and scattered in the Ayre? Where be all the Atoms of that flesh, which a *Corrasive* hath eat away, or a *Consumption* hath breath'd, and exhal'd away from our arms, and other Limbs?' he ponders at the marriage of the Earl of Bridgewater's daughter (44.1). On such an occasion one might have thought that the bland abstractions of alchemy would have been more decorous, but this image of bodily disintegration, and its corollary of reintegration, is not entirely gratuitous. As an attempted joining of two distinct selves, marriage looks forward to the ultimate marriage of Christ and his Church, and to the perfect reunion of body and soul. The fragmented body awaiting its resurrection is, perhaps, an extreme image of the imperfections and divisions within an earthly marriage, and the impossibility of overcoming separateness this side of heaven. The connection may seem awkward, but it is entirely typical of a poetic sensibility which was so concerned with the difficulties of 'we two being one'.

To draw attention to the grotesque elements in Donne's Sermons is not to invite mockery of an apparent ineptitude. His fascination with the subject of bodily resurrection may be quirky from the standpoint of a theologian, but such passages are as imaginatively powerful and revealing as his more lyrical visualizations of heaven. What they reveal, or at any rate suggest, is that Donne's mystic impulses were burdened by an acute sense of the dualism of things, in particular the seeming irreconcilability of spirit and matter. His compulsive attention to the physical details of disintegration and resurrection marks the strain of trying to overcome that dualism. As John Carey has pointed out,* throughout Donne's writing, from the love poems to the late sermons, there runs a tremor of anxiety about separation and disjunction – limb and limb, body and soul, man and woman, self and others – and his search for ways of reconciling these divisions provides the imaginative thrust to both his secular and religious work. Terms such as 'reingrafted', 'redintegration' and 're-incorporated' are frequent in the Sermons. What they point to is not simply a quest for wholeness within the self, a glorious reunion of body and soul, but a desire for reconciliation between self and others. The Church is the body of Christ: the image of physical integrity is an image of social integrity, of the society of heaven and the communion of saints. '. . . we would consider the joy of our

---

* See John Carey, *John Donne: Life, Mind and Art* (1981), especially chapter 9.

society, and conversation in heaven, since society and conversation is one great element and ingredient into the joy, which we have in this world . . . all soules shall be so intirely knit together, as if all were but one soule' (35); 'Our first step . . . is the *sociablenesse*, the *communicablenesse* of God; He loves holy meetings, he loves the *communion of Saints*, the *houshold of the faithfull*' (26). These passages return us to the theme of both the letters from Mitcham and of *Devotions* – the misery of solitude and the fear of being 'cut off'. But Donne's view of solitude is moral as well as emotional: he talks of 'cowardly solitariness' in an early paradox, and in a late sermon, 'solitude is one of the devils scenes' (51.2). While a love of solitude and a belief in individualism are not, of course, the same thing, in disapproving the first Donne seems to be conscious of the limitations of the second. There is a nagging tension here which directs us, still further, to the conflict between individualism and social cohesiveness in *Biathanatos*, and, more generally, to his ambivalence about the drowning of personal identity in entering the Church. The letter to Goodyer already referred to in this context puts the matter tersely: 'To chuse, is to do: but to be no part of any body, is to be nothing'. The oddly modern, existentialist ring to the first part of the sentence, coupled with the corporatism of the second, produces a characteristically Donneian dilemma.

It is the underlying desire to resolve such dilemmas which accounts for the most persistent image in Donne's sermons, that of the circle. Circles are symbols of wholeness and eternity, pledges of continuity; in circles, beginning and ending are seamlessly joined, and they allow no angles or interruptions: 'God hath made all things in a *Roundnesse* . . . God hath wrapped up all things in Circles, and then a Circle hath no *Angles*' (42.1). The assertion shows a splendid disregard for the 'new philosophy' which Donne is sometimes supposed to have embraced with enthusiasm, but while he undoubtedly found the earth-centred model of the universe, with its concentric spheres, more imaginatively satisfying, his purpose here is not to fight a rearguard action against Copernicus. In fact, his immediate point is that there can be no such thing as 'Corner Divinity': Christian worship is public and sociable, bringing the solitary from his study and re-integrating him with his fellow human beings. The connection Donne makes between circles and the 'openness' of religion is in keeping with his emphasis on the body of the Church, and it is not difficult to see how his fondness for the image stems from his fear of separateness and fragmentation. Another kind of circle is presented by the earth itself. For Donne, globes have the marvellous effect of joining opposites and making all things whole: 'Take a flat Map, a Globe *in plano*, and here is East, and there is West, as far asunder as two points can be put: but reduce this flat Map to roundnesse, which is the true form, and then East and West touch one another, and are all one' (5.2). The point he goes on to make is that this images the way in which birth and death are miraculously joined, 'So death doth touch the resurrection', as he writes in 'Hymn to God my God, in my Sickness'.

Perhaps the most famous of Donne's circles is the one described by the compasses in 'A Valediction: forbidding Mourning'. Originally, and with some justice, regarded by Dr Johnson as an absurdly strained conceit, it is an image which nevertheless acquires a particular resonance in the Sermons. (The poem, of course, is about the impending separation of two lovers.) In the sermon at the Bridgewater wedding (44.1) Donne declared:

First then, Christ establishes a Resurrection, *A Resurrection there shall be*, for, that makes up *Gods circle*. The *Body* of Man was the first point that the foot of Gods Compasse was upon: First, he created the body of *Adam*: and then he carries his Compasse round, and shuts up where he began, he ends with the *Body of man* againe in the glorification thereof in the Resurrection.

In the love poem the compasses had been a figure of the indivisbility of two souls; here in the sermon they emphasize the continuation of the body and, by implication, the reunion of body and soul. The perfect circle which they make ought then to resolve, in a suitably abstract image, the problem of all those grotesque bits and pieces, arms in the East and legs in the West, which haunt Donne's vision of the Last Day. But that circle, which the passage of the compass point through time describes, can only be perceived from the vantage point of eternity, and in this life we remain aware of the apparent disjointedness of the journey itself. The depth of the problem is starkly illustrated by the fact that, in the Bridgewater sermon, Donne passes almost immediately from the circle to the passage on the dismembered body.

So if physical separation and geographical divisions are one kind of discontinuity which Donne's circles attempt to heal, the 'rags of time', the hours, days and months in which human experience is pieced out, are another pressing source of anxiety. Indeed, the relationship between time and eternity is similar to that between flat maps and round globes. As we have seen, the baffling nature of time had been a conspicuous problem in *Devotions*, where Donne presented it as 'a short *parenthesis* in a longe *period*' (Meditation 14), and even in the Sermons he resorts to analogies of millions of grains of sand, as though time were a series of disconnected moments. But in the second Prebend sermon (33) the sense of time as mere flux is triumphantly overcome. Here, circle and globe are not incidental images, but are subsumed into the structure of the entire sermon. In Donne's text, 'Because thou hast been my help, Therefore in the shadow of thy wings will I rejoyce' (Psalm 63.7), we have 'the whole compasse of Time, Past, Present, and Future', and he claims that its theme, that of spiritual reassurance for the future in the remembrance of God's mercies in the past, is the theme of the whole book of Psalms. 'Fixe upon God any where, and you shall finde him a Circle; He is with you now, when you fix upon him; He was with you before, for he brought you to this fixation; and he will be with you hereafter . . .' Accordingly, he divides the sermon into three parts, of which the last is future joy: 'If you looke upon this world in a Map, you find two Hemisphears, two half worlds. If you crush heaven into a Map, you may find two Hemisphears too, two half heavens; Halfe will be Joy, and halfe will be Glory'. What this sermon so eloquently presents is the divine equivalent of the imagined conquering of time and space in the great trio of secular love poems, 'The Anniversary', 'The Sun Rising' and 'The Good Morrow' – the equivalent, that is, without such conditions as '*If* our two souls be one'. It climaxes in a vision of sublime continuity, of an ecstatic melting into the Divinity, 'for all the way to Heaven is Heaven . . . [we] goe by Heaven to Heaven'. Time rolls effortlessly into a joyous eternity, an abyss of reconcilement.

Deaths Duell, Donne's final sermon, implies by its title a more strenuous translation, and centres on the paradox that birth is death and death rebirth. Wombs and tombs are reversible images of confinement. It is a classic early seventeenth-century topic, which appears in the prose of Sir Thomas Browne or the poetry of George Herbert, and in El Greco's painting 'The Burial of Count Orgaz',★ where the dead man's

---

★ The painting offers an interesting comparison with *Deaths Duell*. The soul of the dead man is shown as a new-born baby which is being delivered back

soul is assumed into the womb of heaven through a spiralling vaginal entrance in the clouds. In Donne's sermon the maternal womb is a 'close prison', dark and putrid, a potential death-trap, while at the end of life we are brought to 'the lippes of that whirlepoole, the grave'. His text, 'And unto God the Lord belong the issues of death' (Psalm 68.20), puns on 'issue' as birth, while God himself is presented in the first two parts of the sermon as a midwife who 'delivers' us: '*God* . . . hath delivered me from the *death* of the *wombe*, by bringing mee into the *world*, and from the manifold *deaths* of the *world*, by laying me in the *grave*'. In the last part of the sermon Donne brings together the two great mysteries of Christianity, the Incarnation and the Resurrection, as he focusses upon our deliverance from death by Christ's death. For Christ 'this *Baptisme* was *his death*', and '*Moses* . . . in his *Exodus* had *prefigured* this *issue of our Lord*, and in passing *Israel* out of *Egypt* through the *red Sea*, had foretold in that actual *prophesie*, *Christs passing* of *mankind through* the *sea* of his *blood*'. This favourite piece of typology, our safe passage to eternal life through the sea of Christ's blood, is a theme which simultaneously evokes birth and death, 'And makes me end, where I begun'. Donne's sermon is indeed a valediction forbidding mourning. And while he is perhaps too fully conscious of the impending moment of his own physical dissolution to repeat the soaring climax of the second Prebend sermon, its theme is present none the less, and he states it with a fitting glance towards his own eloquence: 'As the first part of a sentence peeces wel with the last, and never respects, never hearkens after the *parenthesis* that comes betweene, so doth a *good life* here flowe into an *eternall life*, without any consideration, what *manner* of *death* we dye'.

---

into the womb of heaven by an angel who acts as midwife. The painting was completed in 1586 and still hangs in its original place in the church of Santo Tomé in Toledo.

FURTHER READING

EDITIONS

Paradoxes and Problems, ed. Helen Peters (Oxford, 1980).

Biathanatos, ed. Michael Rudick and M. Pabst Battin (New York, 1982). A modern-spelling edition.

Letters to Severall Persons of Honour (*1651*), introd. M. Thomas Hester (New York, 1977). A facsimile reproduction.

Devotions upon Emergent Occasions, ed. A. Raspa (Montreal and London, 1975).

The Sermons of John Donne, ed. George R. Potter and Evelyn M. Simpson, 10 vols. (Berkeley and Los Angeles, 1953–62).

CRITICISM

General

Carey, John, *John Donne: Life, Mind and Art* (London and Boston, 1981).

Simpson, Evelyn M., *A Study of the Prose Works of John Donne* (2nd edn, Oxford, 1948).

Webber, Joan, *Contrary Music: The Prose Style of John Donne* (Madison, 1963).

Paradoxes, Problems and *Biathanatos*

Colie, Rosalie L., *Paradoxia Epidemica: The Renaissance Tradition of Paradox* (Princeton, 1966).

Malloch, A. E., 'The Techniques and Function of the Renaissance Paradox', *Studies in Philology* 53 (1956), 213–29.

Ornstein, Robert, 'Donne, Montaigne and Natural Law', *Journal of English and Germanic Philology* 55 (1956).

Williamson, George, 'The Libertine Donne', *Philological Quarterley*, 13 (1935), 276–91. Takes an opposite line from Ornstein.

Letters

Carey, John, 'John Donne's Newsless Letters', *Essays and Studies* (1981), pp. 45–65.

Devotions

Harding, D. W., 'The *Devotions* Now' in *John Donne: Essays in Celebration*, ed. A. J. Smith (London, 1972).

Webber, Joan, 'Donne and Bunyan: The Style of Two Faiths' in *The Eloquent "I": Style and Self in Seventeenth-Century Prose* (Madison, 1968); reprinted in Stanley Fish, ed., *Seventeenth-Century Prose: Modern Essays in Criticism* (New York, 1971).

Winny, James, 'Devotions upon Emergent Occasions' in *A Preface to Donne* (2nd edn, London and New York, 1981).

Sermons

Fish, Stanley, 'The Aesthetic of the Good Physician' in *Self-Consuming Artifacts: The Experience of Seventeenth-Century Literature* (Berkeley and Los Angeles, 1972). On *Deaths Duell*.

Gardner, Dame Helen, 'Readers and Reading' in *In Defence of the Imagination* (Oxford, 1982). A critique of the above.

Mahood, M. M. 'Donne: The Baroque Preacher' in *Poetry and Humanism* (London, 1950).

Merchant, W. Moelwyn, 'Donne's Sermon to the Virginia Company' in *John Donne: Essays in Celebration*, ed. A. J. Smith (London, 1972).

Quinn, Dennis, 'Donne's Christian Eloquence', *English Literary History* 27 (1960), 276–97; reprinted in Fish (1971).

Rooney, William J. J., 'John Donne's "Second Prebend Sermon" – A Stylistic Analysis', *Texas Studies in Literature and Language* 4 (1962), 24–34; reprinted in Fish (1971).

Schleiner, Winfried, *The Imagery of John Donne's Sermons* (Providence, R. I., 1970).

A NOTE ON THE TEXTS

As there is no standard edition of Donne's prose works the texts presented here are necessarily eclectic. For the Sermons I have used the text established by Potter and Simpson, and I am most grateful to the University of California Press for permission to excerpt so fully from their edition. The text of *Devotions* is that of the first edition of 1624 with a few minor emendations. Letters 2, 3 and 4 are taken from the first edition of 1651; Letter 1 is based on the transcript by Evelyn Simpson in *A Study of the Prose Works of John Donne* (2nd edn, Oxford, 1948), and Letter 5 comes from *A Collection of Letters made by Sir Tobie Matthew* (1660). The text of *Biathanatos* is based on the first edition of 1647, but I have admitted readings from MS. e Musaeo 131 in the Bodleian Library, Oxford, by kind permission of the Librarian. I have also removed the cumbersome apparatus of marginalia and parentheses, and corrected the punctuation at points where it seems to be positively misleading. For the selections from *Devotions*, the *Letters* and *Biathanatos* I have used copies of first editions in St Andrews University Library, and I am grateful to Mr Geoffrey Hargreaves for his help in preparing these texts. The first sound text of the *Paradoxes and Problems* has been established by Helen Peters (1980) and I have based my text on that edition. However, since Peters derives her text from manuscripts (the early printed texts have no authority), I have considerably revised the spelling in order to bring it into line with that of the other texts reproduced here, and I have also occasionally altered the punctuation to aid the sense.

The selection which follows includes the complete series of Paradoxes and six of the nineteen Problems. The selection from *Devotions* gives the complete sequence of Meditations, and I have also given the first section entire (Meditation, Expostulation and Prayer) in order to show the form of the work as a whole. The following Sermons are also given entire: A Sermon of Valediction at my going into Germany; A Sermon Preached to the Honourable Company of the Virginian Plantation; the second Prebend Sermon; Deaths Duell.

PARADOXES

1. THAT ALL THINGS KILL THEMSELVES

To affect, yea to effect their owne deaths, all living are importun'd. Not by Nature only which perfects them, but by Art and education which perfects her. Plants quickned and inhabited by the most unworthy Soule,[1] which therefore neither will, nor worke, affect an end, a perfection, a Death. This they spend their Spirits to attaine; this attained, they languish and wither. And by how much more they are by Mans industry warm'd, and cherisht, and pamper'd, so much the more early they climbe to this perfection, this Deathe. And if between men, not to defend be to kill, what a heinous selfe murder is it, not to defend it selfe? This defence, because beasts neglect, they kill themselves: because they exceede us in number, strength, and lawless liberty. Yea, of horses, and so of other beasts, they which inherit most courage by beeing bred of galantest parents, and by artificiall nursing are bettered, will run to their own Deathes, neither sollicited by spurs, which they neede not, nor by honor which they apprehend not. If then the valiant kill himselfe, who can excuse the coward? Or how shall man be free from this, since the first man taught us this? Except we cannot kill our selves because he kill'd us all. Yet lest some thing should repaire this common ruine, we kill daily our bodies with Surfets, and our Minds with anguishes. Of our Powers, remembring kills our Memory. Of affections, lusting our Lust. Of Vertues, giving kills Liberality. And if these things kill themselves, they do it in their best and supreme perfection: for after perfection immediatly follows excess: which changes the natures and the names, and makes them not the same things. If then the best things kill themselves soonest (for no perfection indures) and all things labor to this perfection,[2] all travaile to their owne Death: Yea the frame of the whole World (if it were possible for God to be idle) yet because it begun must dye: Then in this idleness imagind in God, what could kill the world but it selfe, since out of it nothing is.

2. THAT WOMEN
OUGHT TO PAINT THEMSELVES[3]

Foulness is lothesome; can that be so too which helpes it? Who forbids
his beloved to gird in her wast, to mend by shooing her uneven lameness,
to burnish her teethe, or to perfume her breathe? Yet that the face be
more precisely regarded it concernes more. For as open confessing
Sinners are allwayes punished, but the wary and conceald, offending
without witness, do it allso without punishment, so the secret parts
neede less respect; but of the Face discoverd to all Survayes and ex-
aminations there is not too nice a jealousy. Nor doth it only draw the
busy eye, but allso is most subject to the divinest touche of all, to
kissing, the strange and misticall union of Soules.[4] If She should prostitute her selfe to a more Worthy Man than thy selfe, how earnestly
and how justly wouldst thou exclaime? Then for want of this easy and
ready way of repairing, to betray her body to ruine and Deformity, the
tirannous ravishers and sodain deflowrers of all Women, what a hainous
adultery is it? What thou lov'st most in her face is color, and this
painting gives that. But thou hat'st it not because it is, but because thou
knowest it: Foole, whome only ignorance makes happy. The Stars, the
Sun, the Skye, whom thou admirest, alas have no color, but are faire
because they seeme color'd; If this seeming will not satisfy thee in her,
thou hast good assurance of her color, when thou seest her lay it on. If
her face be painted upon a boord or a wall, thou wilt love it, and the
boord and the wall. Canst thou lothe it then, when it smiles, speekes,
and kisses, because it is painted? Is not the earths face in the most
pleasing season new painted? Are we not more delighted with seeing
fruits, and birds, and beasts painted, than with the Naturalls? And do we
not with pleasure behold the painted Shapes of Devills and Monsters,
whom true we durst not regard? We repaire the ruines of our houses,
but first cold tempest warns us of it, and bites us through it: We mend
the wracke and washe the staines of our apparell, but first our eye and
other body is offended: But by this providence of women this is prevented. If in kissing or breathing upon her, the painting fall off, thou art
angry: wilt thou be so, if it stick on? Thou didst love her: if thou beginst
to hate her then it is because she is not painted. If thou wilt say now,
thou didst hate her before, thou didst hate her and love her together. Be

constant in some thing; and love her who shewes her great love to thee, by taking this paines to seeme lovely to thee.

3. THAT OLD MEN ARE MORE FANTASTIQUE[5] THAN YOUNGE

Who reads this Paradox but thinks me more fantastique than I was yesterday when I did not think thus? And if one day make this sensible change in me, what will the burden of many yeares? To be fantastique in young men is a conceitfull distemperature, and a witty madness: but in old men whose senses are withered, it becomes naturall, therfore more full and perfect. For as when we sleepe our fancy is most strong, so is it in Age, which is a slumber of the deepe sleepe of Deathe. They taxe us of inconstancy, which in themselves young they allow'd; So that reproving that which they did approve, their inconstancy exceeds ours, because they have changd once more than we. Yea, they are more idly busied in conceiting[6] apparell than we, for we when we are melancholy, weare black; when lusty, greene; when forsaken, tawny; pleasing our owne inward affections, leaving them to others indifferent. But they prescribe Laws, and constraine the Noble, the Scholler, the Marchant, and all estates to certaine habits. The old men of our time have chang'd with patience their own bodies, much of their Lawes, much of their Language, yea their Religion, yet they accuse us. To be amorous is proper and naturall in a young man, but in an old man most fantastique. And that ridling humor of Jealousy, which seekes and would not find, which inquires and repents his knowledg, is in them most common yet most fantastique. Yea that which falls never in young men, is in them most fantastique and naturall; that is Coveteousness; even at their journeys end to make great provision. Is any habit in young men so fantastique as in the hottest Seasons to be double gownd and hooded, like our elders? Or seemes it so ridiculous to weare long haire as to weare none? Truly, as amongst Philosophers, the Sceptique which doubts all is more contentious than either the Dogmatique which affirmes, or Academique which denyes all, So are these uncertaine elders, which both call them fantastique which follow others inventions, and them allso which are led by their owne humors suggestion, more fantastique than either.

4. THAT NATURE IS OUR
WORST GUIDE

Shall she be guide to all creatures which is herselfe one? Or if she allso
have a guide, shall any creature have a better guide than we? The
affections of Lust and Anger, yea even to erre is naturall: shall we follow
these? Can she be a good guide to us which hath corrupted not us only
but her selfe? Was not the first man by desire of knowledg corrupted,
even in the white integrity of Nature? And did not Nature, if Nature do
any thing, infuse into him this desire of knowledg, and so this corruption
in him, in her selfe, in us?[7] If by Nature we shall understand our essence,
our definition, our reasonableness, then this, beeing alike common to all
men (the ideot and wisard beeing equally reasonable) why shall not all
men, having one nature, follow one course? Or if we shall understand
our inclinations, Alas, how unable a guide is that which follows the
temperature of our slimy bodies? For we cannot say that we derive our
inclinations, our minds, our soules, from our parents by any way. To
say it, as All from All, is error in reason, for then with the first nothing
remaines; or as part from all is error in experience, for then this part
equally imparted to many children, would (like Gavelkind[8] lands) in
few generations become nothing. Or to say it by communication is
error in Divinity; for to communicate the ability of communicating
whole essence with any but God is utter blasphemy. And if thou hast
thy fathers nature and inclination, he allso had his fathers, and so
climbing up, all come of one man, all have one nature, all shall embrace
one course. But that cannot be. Therfore our complexions[9] and whole
bodies we inherit from parents, our inclinations and minds follow that.
For our mind is heavy in our bodies afflictions, and rejoyceth in the
bodies pleasures: How then shall this nature governe us, which is
governd by the worst part of us? Nature, though we chase it away, will
returne. Tis true: but those good motions and inspirations which be our
guides, must be wooed and courted, and wellcomed, or else they
abandon us. And that old *Tu nihil invita etc.*[10] must not be said, thou
shalt, but thou wilt do nothing against nature: so unwilling he notes us
to curbe our naturall appetites. We call our bastards allwayes our naturall
issue, and we designe a foole by no name so ordinarily as by the name of
naturall.[11] And that poore knowledg wherby we but conceive

what raine is, what wind, what thunder, we call Metaphisique, supernaturall. Such small things, such nothings, do we allow to our plaine
natures comprehension. Lastly by following her, we lose the pleasant
and lawfull commodities of this life, for we shall drinke water, and eate
akornes and rootes, and those not so sweete and delicate as now by mans
art and industry they are made. We shall lose allso the necessities of
Societyes, Lawes, Arts, and Sciences, which are all the workmanship of
man. Yea, we shall lack the last best refuge of Misery, Deathe: because
no deathe is naturall; for if yee will not dare to call all Deaths violent
(though I see not why Sicknesses be not violences), yet confess that all
deaths proceede of the defect of that which nature made perfect and
would preserve, and therefore are all against Nature.

5. THAT ONLY COWARDS DARE DYE

Extreames are equally removed from the meane: So that headlong
desperatness as much offends true valor as backward cowardice.[12] Of
which sorte I reckon justly all unenforced deathes. When will your
valiant man dye? necessited? So cowards suffer what cannot be avoided.
And to run to death unimportun'd is to run into the first condemn'd
desperatness. Will he dye when he is riche and happy? Then by living
he might do more good. And in afflictions and misery death is the
chosen refuge of cowards. *Fortiter ille facit qui miser esse potest.*[13] But it is
taught and practisd amongst our Valiants, that rather than our reputation
suffer any maime, or we any misery, we shall offer our breasts to the
cannons mouthe, yea to our swords points. And this seemes a brave, a
fiery sparkling, and a climbing resolution, which is indeed a cowardly,
an earthly, and a grovelling Spirit. Why do they chaine these Slaves to
the gallies, but that they thirst their deathes, and would at every lashe
leap into the Sea? Why do they take weapons from condemnd men, but
to bar them of that ease which Cowards affect, a speedy death? Truly
this life is a tempest, a warfare; and he that dares dye to escape the
anguishes of it, seemes to me but so valiant, as he which dares hang
himselfe, lest he be prest to the wars. I have seene one in that extremity
of melancholy, which was then become madness, strive to make his
owne breath an instrument to stop his breath, and labor to choke
himselfe: but alas he was mad. And we knew another, that languished

under the oppression of a poore disgrace so much, that he tooke more paines to dye than would have servd to have nourish'd life and spirit enough to have outlivd his disgrace; what foole will call this cowardliness, valor, or this baseness, humility? And lastly of those men which dye that Allegoricall death of entring into Religion, how few are found fit for any shew of valiancy, but only of soft and supple metall, made only for cowardly solitariness.[14]

6. THAT THE GIFTS OF THE BODY ARE BETTER THAN THOSE OF THE MIND OR OF FORTUNE

I say againe that the body makes the mind. Not that it created it a mind, but formes it a good or bad mind. And this mind may be confounded with Soule, without any violence or injustice to Reason or philosophy, then our Soule (me seemes) is enabled by our body, not this by that.[15] My body licenceth my Soule to see the Worlds beauties through mine eyes, to heare pleasant things through mine eares, and affords it apt Organs for conveyance of all perceiveable delights. But alas my Soule cannot make any part, that is not of it selfe disposed, to see or heare: though without doubt she be as able and as willing to see behind as before. Now if my Soule would say, that she enables my parts to tast these pleasures, but is her selfe only delighted with those riche sweetnesses which her inward eye and senses apprehend, she should dissemble, for I feele her often solaced with beauties which she sees through mine eyes, and Musicke which through mine eares she heares. This perfection then my body hath, that it can impart to my mind all her pleasures, and my mind hath this maime, that she can neither teach my indisposd parts her faculties, nor to the parts best disposd shew that beauty of Angels or Musicke of Spheares, wherof she boasts the contemplation. Are Chastity, Temperance, or Fortitude gifts of the mind? I appeale to phisicians whether the cause of these be not in the body. Healthe is a gifte of the body, and patience in sickness, of the mind; then who will say this patience is as good a happiness as health, when we must be extreamly miserable to have this happiness? And for nourishing of Civil Societies and mutual Love amongst men, which is one chiefe end why we are men, I say the beauty, proportion, and presence of the body hath a more masculine force in begetting this Love than the vertues of the mind. For it strikes us sodainly, and possesseth us immediatly, when to know these vertues requires sound judgement in him which shall discerne, and a long triall and conversation betweene them. And even at last, alas how much of our faithe and beleefe shall we be driven to bestow, to assure our selves that these vertues are not counterfeited? For it is the same to be and to seeme vertuous. Because he that hath no vertu can dissemble none. But he that hath a little may guild, and enamell, yea and transforme much vice into vertu. For allow a man to be discreete and flexible to companies, which are great vertues and gifts of the mind, this discretion wil be to him the Soule and Elixar [16] of all vertue. So that touch'd with this, even pride shal be made civil humility, and cowardice, honorable and wise valor. But in things seene there is not this danger. For the body which thou lovst and esteemst faire is faire certainly, and if it be not faire in perfection, yet is is faire in the same degree that thy judgment is good. And in a faire body I do seldome suspect a disproportiond mind, or expect a good in a deformed. As when I see a goodly house I assure my selfe of a worthy possessor, and from a ruinous witherd building I turne away, because it seemes either stuffd with varlets as a prison, or handled by an unworthy negligent tenant, that so suffreth the wast thereof. And truly the gifts of fortune which are riches are only handmaids, yea pandars of the bodies pleasure; with their service we nourish health, and preserve beauty, and we buy delights. So that vertue which must be lovd for her selfe and respects no further end, is indeede nothing; and riches, whose end is the good of the body, cannot be so perfectly good as the end wherto it levells.

7. THAT A WISE MAN
IS KNOWNE BY MUCH LAUGHINGE

Ride si sapis o puella ride; [17] if thou beest wise laugh. For since the powers of discourse, and reason, and laughter, be equally proper to only man, why shall not he be most wise which hath most use of laughing, as well as he which hath most of reasoning and discoursing. I allwayes did and shall understand that Adage,

per risum multum possis cognoscere stultum,

that by much laughing thou mayst know there is a foole, not that the laughers are fooles, but that amongst them there is some foole at whome wise men laugh. Which mov'd *Erasmus* to put this as the first argument in the mouthe of his Folly, that she made beholders laughe.[18] For fooles are the most laughed at, and laugh least themselves of any. And Nature saw this faculty to be so necessary in man, that she hath beene content that by more causes we should be importun'd to laughe than to the exercise of any other power. For things in themselves utterly contrary beget this effect. For we laugh both at witty and absurd things. At both which sorts I have seene men laugh so long and so ernestly, that at last they have wept that they could laugh no more. And therfore the poet, having describ'd the quietness of a wise retired man, saith in one what we have said before in many lines,

Quid facit Canius tuus? ridet.[19]

We have receaved that even the extremity of laughing, yea of weeping allso hath beene accoumpted wisdome: and *Democritus* and *Heraclitus*[20] the lovers of these extremes have beene called lovers of wisdome; Now amongst our wise men, I doubt not, but many would be found, who would laughe at *Heraclitus* his weeping, none which would weep at *Democritus* laughing. At the hearing of Comedies or other witty reports, I have noted some, which not understanding the jests, have yet chosen this as the best meanes to seeme wise and understanding, to laugh when their companions laughe, and I have presumd them ignorant, whom I have seene unmovd. A foole if he come into a Princes Court, and see a gay man leaning at the wall, so glistering and so painted in many colors that he is hardly discernd from one of the pictures in the Arras hangings,[21] his body like an Ironbound chest girt in, and thicke ribd with broad gold laces, may and commonly doth envy him, but alas shall a wise man, which may not only not envy this fellow, but not pity him, do nothing at this monster? Yes: let him laugh. And if one of these hot colerique firebrands, which nourish themselves by quarelling and kindling others, spit upon a foole but one sparke of disgrace, he like a thatchd house quickly burning, may be angry. But the wise man as cold as the Salamander,[22] may not only not be angry with him, but not be sory for him. Therfore let him laughe. So shall he be knowne a man, because he can laughe: a wiseman that he knowes at what to laughe; and a valiant man, that he dares laughe. For who laughs is justly reputed

more wise than at whome it is laughed. And hence I thinke proceeds
that which in these later formall times I have much noted. That
now when our superstitious civility of manners is become but a
mutuall tickling flattery of one another, allmost every man affects an
humor of jesting, and is content to deject and deforme himselfe, yea to
become foole, to none other end that I can spy, but to give his wise
companions occasion to laughe, and to shew themselves wise. Which
promptness of laughing is so great in wise men, that I thinke all wise
men (if any wise men do read this paradox) will laugh both at it and
me.

8. THAT GOOD IS MORE COMMON
THAN EVILL

I have not beene so pitifully tired with any vanity as with silly old mens
exclaiming against our times and extolling their owne. Alas they betray
themselves. For if the times be chang'd, their manners have chang'd
them, but their senses are to pleasure as sick mens tasts to Liquors. For
indeed no new thing is done in the world. All things are what and as
they were; and good is as ever it was, most plenteous, and must of
necessity be more common than evill, because it hath this for Nature,
and end, and perfection, to be common. It makes love to all creatures
and all affect it. So that in the worlds early infancy, there was a time
when nothing was evill; but if this world shall suffer dotage in the
extremest crookedness thereof, there shal be no time when nothing shal
be good.[23] It dares appeare and spred and glister in the world, but evill
buries it selfe in Night and darkness, and is supprest and chastis'd, when
good is cherished and rewarded. And as Embroderers, Lapidaries, and
other Artisans can by all things adorne their works, for by adding better
things they better them so much, by equall things they double their
goodness, and by worse they encrease their Shew, and Lustre, and
eminency, So good doth not only prostitute her owne amiableness to
all, but refuseth no aid, no, not of her utter contrary evill, that she may
be more common to us. For evill manners are parents of good Lawes.
And in every evill there is an excellency, which in common speech we
call good. For the fashions of habits, for our movings in gestures, for
phrases in our speech, we say they were good as long as they were usd,

that is as long as they were common: and we eate, we walke, we sleepe only when it is, or seemes good to do so. All faire, all proffitable, all vertuous is good. And these three things I thinke embrace all things but their utter contraries, of which allso foule may be riche and vertuous, poore may be vertuous and faire, vicious may be faire and riche. So that Good hath this good meanes to be common, that some subjects she can possesse entirely; and in subjects poysond with evill, she can humbly stoope to accompany the evill. And of indifferent many things are become perfectly good only by beeing common; as Customes by use are made binding Lawes; but I remember nothing that is therfore ill because it is common but women; of whom allso they which are most common are the best of that occupation they profess.

9. THAT BY DISCORD THINGS INCREASE

Nullos esse Deos, inane caelum
Affirmat Selius, probatque, quod se
Factum, dum negat haec, videt beatum.[24]

So I assever this the more boldly, because while I maintaine it, and feele the contrary repugnances and adverse fightings of the Elements in my body, my body increaseth; and whilst I differ from common opinions, by this discord the number of my Paradoxes encreaseth. All the riche benefits which we can faine in concord is but an even conservation of things; in which evenness we may expect no change nor motion; therfore no encrease or augmentation, which is a member of motion. And if this unity and peace can give increase to things, how mightily is Discord and war to this purpose, which are indeed the only ordinary parents of peace. Discord is never so barren that it affords no fruit, for the fall of one State is at worst the increase of another; because it is as impossible to find a discommodity without any advantage as corruption without generation. But it is the nature and office of Concord to preserve only; which property when it leaves, it differs from it selfe, which is the greatest Discord of all. All Victories and Emperies gain'd by war, and all judiciall decidings of doubts in peace, I claime chilldren of Discord. And who can deny that Controversies in religion are growne greater by Discord; and not the controversies only but even Religion it selfe. For in a troubled misery men are allwayes more religious than in a secure peace. The number of good men (the only charitable harbourers of Concord) we see is thin, and daily melts and waines; but of bad and discording men it is infinit and growes hourely. We are acertaind of all disputable doubts only by arguing and differing in opinion, and if formal disputation which is but a painted, counterfeit, and dissembled Discord, can worke us this benefit, what shall not a full and maine discord accomplish? Truly, methinks I owe a devotion, yea a Sacrifice to Discord for casting that ball upon *Ida*,[25] and for all the business of Troy, whom ruind I admire more than *Rome* or *Babylon* or *Quinzay*. Nor are removd corners fullfilld only with her fame, but with Cities and thrones planted by her fugitives. Lastly betweene cowardice and despaire valor is ingendred, and so the Discord of extreames begets all vertues; but of the like things there is no issue without miracle.

> *Uxor pessima, pessimus maritus,*
> *Miror tam male convenire vobis.*[26]

He wonders that betweene two so like there could be any discord, yet for all this discord perchance there was nere the lesse increase.

10. THAT IT IS POSSIBLE TO FIND SOME VERTUE IN SOME WOMEN

I am not of that sear'd impudency that I dare defend women, or pronounce them good: yet when we see phisitians allow some vertu in every poyson, alas why should we except women? Since certainly they are good for phisick:[27] at least so as wine is good for a fever. And though they be the occasioners of most Sins, they are allso the punishers and revengers of the same Sins. For I have seldome seene one which consumes his substance or body upon them escape diseases or beggery. And this is their justice. And if *Suum cuique dare*[28] be the fullfilling of all civil justice, they are most just: for they deny that which is theirs to no man.

> *Tanquam non liceat, nulla puella negat.*[29]

And who may doubt of great wisdome in them, that doth but observe with how much labor and cunning our Justices and other dispencers of the lawes study to imbrace them:[30] and how zealously our Preachers dehort men from them, only by urging their Subtelties and policies and wisdome which are in them, yea in the worst and most prostitute sorte of them. Or who can deny them a good measure of fortitude, if he consider how many valiant men they have overthrowne, and beeing them selves overthrowne, how much and how patiently they beare? And though they be all most intemperat, I care not: for I undertooke to furnish them with some vertu, not all. Necessity which makes even bad things good, prevailes allso for them: and we must say of them as of some sharpe punishing lawes; If men were free from infirmities, they were needlesse: but they are both good scourges for bad men. These or none must serve for reasons: and it is my great happiness that Examples prove not rules, for to confirme this opinion the World yields not one Example.

11. A DEFENCE OF
WOMENS INCONSTANCY[31]

That *Women are inconstant*, I with any man confess, But that *Inconstancie* is a bad Qualitie I against any man will maintaine; for every thinge, as it is one better than another, so is it fuller of Chaunge. The Heavens themselves continually turne, the Stars move, the Moone changeth, fire whirleth, Air flyeth, water ebbs and flowes, the Face of the earth altereth her lookes, time stayes not, the colour that hath most light will take most dyes; So in Men, they that have the most reason are the most alterable in their designes, and the darkest and most ignorant do seldomest change. Therfore Women changing more than men have also more reason, they cannot be immutable like stockes, like stones, like the earths dull Center. Gold that lyeth still rusteth, water corupteth, and Aire that moveth not poysoneth. Then why should that which is the perfection of other things be imputed to women as greatest Imperfection? Because thereby they deceive men? Are not your wits pleased with those Jests which cozen your Expectation? You can call it pleasure to be beguiled in Trifles, and in the most excellent Toye in the world you call it Treacherie. I would you had your Mistresses so constant that they would never change, no not so much as their *Smocks*, then should you see what a sluttish virtue Constancy were. *Inconstancy* is a most

commendable and cleanly qualitie; and *Women* in this quality are far
more absolute than the *Heavens*, than the *Stars*, than *Moone*, or any thing
beneath it, for longe observation hath pickt certainty out of this *Muta-*
bility. The learned are so well acquainted with the *Stars* Signes and
Plannets, that they make them but *Characters* to read the meaning of the
heaven in his owne forhead. Everie simple fellowe can bespeake the
Change of the Moone a great while before hand. But I would faine
have the learnedst man so skilfull as to tell when the simplest *woman*
meaneth to *varie*. Learninge affords no rules to knowe, much lesse
knowledge to rule the minde of *A Woman*. For as *Philosophie* teacheth
us, that light things doe always tend upwards, and heavy things decline
downwards, *Experience* teacheth us otherwise, That the disposition of a
Light *Woman* is to fall downe; the Nature of *Women* being contrary to
all art and Nature. Women are like Flyes which feed amongst us at our
Table, or Fleas sucking our verie blood, who leave not our most retired
places free from their Familiaritie. Yet for all their fellowship will they
never be tamed, nor commanded by us. *Women* are like the Sun which
is violently carried one way, yet hath a proper Course Contrary.[32] So
though they (by the Mastery of some over-rulinge churlish husbands)
are forced to his Bias, yet have they a motion of their owne, which their
Husbands never knowe of. It is the nature of nice and fastidious mindes
to know things only to be weary of them. *Women* by their sly-chang-
ableness, and pleasing doubleness, prevent even the Mislike of those, for
they can never be so well knowne, but that there is still more unknowne.
Every *Woman* is *A Science*, for he that plods upon a woman all his life
longe shall at length find himselfe short of the knowledge of her. They
are borne to take down the pride of *wit* and Ambition of wisdome,
making fooles wise in the adventuring to win them, wise men fooles
with conceit of losing their labour, wittie men starke mad being confounded with their uncertainties. *Philosophers* write against them for
spite, not desert, that having attained to some knowledge in all other
things, in them only they know *nothing but are merely ignorant*. Active
and experienced men raile against them because they love in their live-
lesse and decrepite Age, when all goodness leaves them. These envious
Libellers ballad against them because having nothinge in them selves
able to deserve their love, they maliciously discommend all they cannot
obtaine; thinking to make men believe they know much because they
are able to dispraise much, and rage against *Inconstancy* when they were

never admitted into so much favor as to be forsaken. In mine opinion such men are happie that women are *Inconstant*, for so they may chance to be beloved of some excellent Woman (when it comes to their turne) out of their Inconstancy, and Mutability, though not out of their owne desert. And what reason is there to clog any woman with one Man be hee never so singular? *Women* had rather (and it is far better, and more *Judiciall*) to enjoy all the virtues in severall men, than but some of them in one, for otherwise they lose their tast like divers sorts of Meat minced together in one dish. And to have all Excelencies in one Man (if it were possible) is confusion, not diversitie. Now who can deny, but such as are obstinately bent to undervalue their worth, are those that have not Soule enough to comprehend their Excellencie, Women being the most excellent Creatures, in that Man is able to subject all things else, and to growe wise in every thinge, but still persists a Foole in *Woman*. The greatest Scholler, if he once take a wife, is found so unlearned that he must begin his hornbooke,[33] and all is by *Inconstancie*. *To conclude*, therfore, this name of *Inconstancie* which hath bene so much poysoned with Slanders ought to be chaunged into *variety*, for the which the world is so delightfull, and a woman for that the most delightfull thinge in the World.

PROBLEMS

1. WHY DOE YOUNG LAYMEN SO MUCH
STUDY DIVINITY?

Is it because others, tending busily Church preferment, neglect the study? Or had the church of *Rome* shut up all our wayes till the Lutherans broke downe their uttermost stubborne dores and the Calvinists pick'd their inwardest and subtillest locks? Surely the Devill cannot bee such a foole to hope that hee shall make this study contemptible by making it common, Nor, as the Dwellers by the river *Ougus* [1] are said (by drawing infinite ditches to sprinkle their barren country) to have exhausted and intercepted the maine channell, and so lost their more profitable course to the sea: so wee, by providing every ones selfe divinity enough for his owne use, should neglect our teachers and fathers. Hee cannot hope for better Heresies than hee hath had, nor was his kingdome ever so much advanced by debating religion (though with some Aspersions [2] of Errour) as by a dull and stupid security in which many grosse things are swallowed. [3] Possibly out of such an Ambition as wee now have to speake plainly and fellowly of Lords and Kings, wee thinke also to acquaint our selves with Gods secrets. Or perchance when wee study it by mingling humane respects, it is not divinity.

2. WHY HATH THE COMMON OPINION
AFFORDED WOEMEN SOULES? [4]

It is agreed that wee have not so much from them as any part of either of our mortall soules of sense or growth; And wee denye soules to others equall to them in all but Speeche, for which they are beholding onely to their bodily instruments, for perchance an Apes heart or a Goates or a Foxes or a Serpents, would speake just so if it were in the breast and could move the tongue and jawes. Have they so many Advantages and meanes to hurt us (for even their loving destroyes us) that wee dare not displease them, but give them what they will, and so, when some call them Angels, some Goddesses, and the Peputian

Heretikes[5] made them Bishopes, wee descend so much with the streame to allow them soules. Or doe wee somwhat, in this dignifying them, flatter Princes and greate Personages that are so much governd by them? Or doe wee, in that easinesse and prodigality wherein wee daily lose our owne soules, allow soules to wee care not whome, and so labour to perswade our selves that sith a woman hath a soule, a soule is no great matter? Or doe wee but lend them soules and that for use, since they for our sakes give their soules againe, and their bodies to boote? Or perchance because the Devill who doth most mischeefe is all soule, for conveniency and proportion, because they would come neere him, wee allow them some soule. And so as the *Romans* naturalized some Provinces in revenge, and made them *Romans* onely for the burden of the common wealth: so wee have given woemen soules onely to make them capable of damnation.

3. WHY ARE THE FAIREST FALSEST?

I meane not of false Alchimy[6] beauty, for then the question should bee inverted, why are the falsest fairest? It is not onely because they are much sollicited and sought for, so is Gold, yet it is not so coming, And this suite to them should teach them their value and make them more reserved. Nor is it because delicatest bloud hath best spirits,[7] for what is that to the flesh? Perchance such constitutions have the best wits, and there is no other proportionable subject for woemens wits but deceipt. Doth the mind so follow the temper of the body that because these complexions are aptest to change, the mind is therefore so too? Or as Bells of the purest mettall retaine the tinkling and sound longest: so the memory of the last pleasure lasts longer in these, and disposes them to the next? But sure, it is not in the complexion, for those that doe but thinke themselves faire are presently enclined to this multiplicity of loves, which beeing but faire in conceipt are false indeed. And so perchance when they are borne to this beauty, or have made it or have dreamt it, they easily beleeve all Addresses and Applications of every man, out of a sense of their owne worthinesse, to bee directed to them, which others lesse worthy in their owne thoughts apprehend not or discredit. But I thinke the true reason is, that beeing like Gold in many properties, (as that all snatch at them, that all corruption is by them, that

the worst possesse them, that they care not how deepe wee dig [8] for
them, and that by the Law of Nature, *Occupanti conceditur* [9]) they would
bee also like in this, that as Gold to make it selfe of use admits Allay,
so they, that they may bee tractable and malleable and currant, have for
their Allay Falshood.

4. WHY VENUS STAR
ONELY DOTH CAST A SHADOWE?

Is it because it is neerer the earth? But they whose profession it is to see
that nothing bee done in heaven without their consent (as *Kepler* [10] says
in himselfe of all Astrologers) have bid *Mercury* to bee nearer. Is it
because the workes of *Venus* neede shadowing, covering and disguising?
But those of *Mercury* neede it more. For eloquence, his occupation, is all
shadowes and colours. [11] Let our life bee a sea, and then our reason, and
even passions, are wind enough to carry us whither wee should goe, but
Eloquence is a storme and tempest that miscarries us. And who doubts
that Eloquence (which must perswade people to take a yoke of Sover-
aignty and then beg and make lawes to tye them faster, and then give
monny to the Invention, repair and strengthen it) needes more shadowes
and colourings than to perswade any man or woman to that which is
naturall. And Venus markets [12] are so naturall, that when wee sollicite
the best way (which is by marriage) our perswasions worke not so
much to drawe a woman to us, as against her nature, to drawe her from
all others besides. And so when wee goe against nature and from *Venus*
workes (for Marriage is chastity) wee neede shadowes and colours, but
not else. In *Senecas* time it was a coarse and *un-Romane* and a contemptible thing, even in a matron, not to have had a love besides her husband,
which though the Lawe required not at their hands, yet they did it
Zealously, out of the counsell of the custome and fashion, which was
Venery of Supererogation.

Et te spectator plus quam delectat Adulter, [13]

sayth *Martiall*: And *Horace*, because many lights would not shewe him
enough, created many Images of the same Object, by wainscotting his
chamber with looking glasses. [14] So then *Venus* flyes not light so much
as *Mercury*, who creeping into our understanding in our darknesse, were

defeated if hee were perceaved. Then either this Shadowe confesseth that same darke Melancholly repentence which accompanies it, Or that so violent fires neede some shadowy refreshing and intermission, Or else Light signifying both day and youth, and shadowe both Night and Age, shee pronounceth, by this, that shee professeth both all times and persons.

5. WHY DOTH THE POXE SO MUCH AFFECT TO UNDERMINE THE NOSE?

Paracelsus [15] perchance saith true, that every disease hath his exaltation in some certaine part, but why this in the nose? Is there so much mercy in this disease that it provides that one should not smell his owne stinke? Or hath it but the common fortune that beeing begot and bred in the obscurest and secretest corner, because therefore his Serpentine crawlings and Insinuations bee not suspected nor seene, hee comes sooner to great place, and is abler to destroy the worthiest Member than a disease better borne. Perchance as mice defeate Elephants by gnawing their Proboscis, which is their nose, this wretched Indian Vermine practises to do the same upon us. [16] Or as the Ancient furious custome and connivence of some Lawes (that one might cut off their noses whome hee deprehended in Adultery) was but a type of this, and now that more charitable Lawes have taken away all revenge from particular hands, this common Magistrate and executioner is come to doe the same office invisibly. Or by withdrawing this conspicuous part, the nose, it warnes from adventuring on that coast (for it is as good a marke to take in a flag, as to hang out one [17]). Possibly heate, which is more potent and active than cold, thought her selfe injurd, and the harmony of the world out of tune, when cold was able to shewe [18] the high wayes with noses in *Muscovy*, except shee found the meanes to doe the same in other countries. But because, by consent of all there is an Analogy and proportion and Affection betweene the nose and that part where this disease is first contracted, (And therefore *Heliogabalus* chose not his Minions in the Bath but by the nose, and *Albertus* had a knavish meaning when hee preferrd great noses, and the Licentious Poet was *Naso Poeta* [19]) I think this reason is neerest truth, that the Nose is most compassionate with that part. Except this bee neerer, that it is reasonable that this disease should in particular men affect the most eminent and conspicuous part, which amongst men in generall doth affect to take hold of the most eminent and conspicuous men.

6. WHY PURITANS MAKE LONG SERMONS?[20]

It needes not for perspicuousnesse, for God knowes that they are plaine enough. Nor doe all of them use the long Sembriefe Accent, some of them have Crotchets enough.[21] It may bee they pretend not to rise like glorious Tapers or Torches, but like long thinne wretched and sick watch candles, which languish and are in a dimme consumption from the first Minute, yet spend more time in their glimmering, yea in their snuff and stinke, than others in their more profitable glory. I have thought sometimes that out of conscience they allow large measure to coarse ware, and sometimes that usurping in that place a liberty to speake freely of Kings and all, they think themselves Kings then and would raigne as long as they could. But now I thinke they doe it out of a zealous Imagination that it is their duty to preache on till their Auditory wake againe.

BIATHANATOS

A Declaration of that Paradoxe, or Thesis,
that Selfe-homicide is not so Naturally Sinne,
that it may never be otherwise.[1]

Beza,[2] A man as eminent and illustrious, in the full glory and Noone of Learning, as others were in the dawning, and Morning, when any, the least sparkle was notorious, confesseth of himself, that only for the anguish of a Scurffe, which over-ranne his head, he had once drown'd himselfe from the Millers bridge in *Paris*, if his Uncle by chance had not then come that way; I have often such a sickely inclination. And, whether it be because I had my first breeding and conversation with men of a suppressed and afflicted Religion, accustomed to the despite of death, and hungry of an imagin'd Martyrdome;[3] Or that the common Enemie find that doore worst locked against him in mee; Or that there bee a perplexitie and flexibility in the doctrine it selfe; Or because my Conscience ever assures me, that no rebellious grudging at Gods gifts, nor other sinfull concurrence accompanies these thoughts in me, or that a brave scorn, or that a faint cowardlinesse beget it, whensoever any affliction assailes me, mee thinks I have the keyes of my prison in mine owne hand,[4] and no remedy presents it selfe so soone to my heart, as mine own sword. Often Meditation of this hath wonne me to a charitable interpretation of their action, who dy so: and provoked me a little to watch and exagitate[5] their reasons, which pronounce so peremptory judgements upon them.

A devout and godly man hath guided us well, and rectified our uncharitablenesse in such cases, by this remembrance, *Scis lapsum, &c. Thou knowest this mans fall, but thou knowest not his wrastling; which perchance was such, that almost his very fall is justified and accepted of God.* For, to this end, saith one, *God hath appointed us tentations, that we might have some excuses for our sinnes, when he calles us to account . . .*

If therefore, of Readers, which *Gorionides* observes to be of foure sorts, Spunges which attract all without distinguishing; Howre-glasses, which receive and powre out as fast; Bagges, which retaine onely the dregges of the Spices, and let the Wine escape; and Sives, which retaine the best onely, I find some of the last sort, I doubt not but they may bee hereby enlightened. And as the eyes of *Eve* were opened by the taste of the Apple, though it bee said before that shee saw the beauty of the tree, So the digesting of this, may, though not present faire objects, yet bring them to see the nakednesse and deformity of their owne reasons, founded upon a rigorous suspition, and winne them to be of that temper, which *Chrisostome* commends, *He which suspects benignly would faine be deceived, and bee overcome, and is piously glad, when he findes it to be false, which he did uncharitably suspect.* And it may have as much vigour (as one observes of another Author) as the Sunne in *March*; it may stirre and dissolve humors, though not expell them; for that must bee a worke of a stronger power.

Every branch which is excerpted from other authors, and engrafted here, is not written for the readers faith, but for illustration and comparison. Because I undertooke the declaration of such a proposition as was controverted by many, and therefore was drawne to the citation of many authorities, I was willing to goe all the way with company, and to take light from others, as well in the journey as at the journeys end. If therefore in multiplicity of not necessary citations there appeare vanity, or ostentation, or digression my honesty must make my excuse and compensation, who acknowledg as *Pliny* doth, *That to chuse rather to be taken in a theft, than to give every man his due is obnoxii animi, et infelicis ingenii.*[6] I did it the rather because scholastique and artificiall men use this way of instructing; and I made account that I was to deale with such, because I presume that naturall men are at least enough inclinable of themselves to this doctrine.

This is my way; and my end is to remove scandall. For certainly God often punisheth a sinner much more severely, because others have taken occasion of sinning by his fact. If therefore wee did correct in our selves this easines of being scandalized, how much easier and lighter might we make the punishment of many transgressors? for God in his judgements hath almost made us his assistants, and counsellers, how far he shall punish; and our interpretation of anothers sinne doth often give the measure to Gods Justice or Mercy.

If therefore, since *disorderly long haire which was pride and wantonnesse in* Absolon, *and squallor and horridnes in* Nebuchodnozor, *was vertue and strength in* Samson, *and sanctification in* Samuel, these severe men will not allow to indifferent things the best construction they are capable of, nor pardon my inclination to do so, they shall pardon me this opinion, that their severity proceeds from a self-guiltines, and give me leave to apply them that of *Ennodius*, *That it is the nature of stiffe wickednesse, to think that of others, which themselves deserve, and it is all the comfort which the guilty have, not to find any innocent.*

OF THE LAW OF NATURE

I. i. 2–3

They who pronounce this sinner to be so necessarily damnable, are of one of these three perswasions. Either they mis-affirme that this act alwaies proceeds from desperation;[7] and so they load it with all those comminations with which from Scriptures, Fathers, Histories, that common place abounds. Or else they entertaine that dangerous opinion, that there is in this life an impenitiblenesse, and impossibilitie of re-turning to God, and that apparent to us (for else it could not justifie our uncharitable censure); Or else they build upon this foundation, that this act being presum'd to be sinne, and all sinne unpardonable without repentance, this is therefore unpardonable, because the very sin doth preclude all ordinary wayes of repentance.

To those of the first Sect, if I might be as vainly subtile, as they are uncharitably severe, I should answer that all desperation is not sinnefull. For in the devill it is not sinne, nor doth hee demerit by it, because he is not commanded to hope. Nor in a man which undertook an austere and disciplinary taming of his body by fasts or corrections, were it sinfull to despaire that God would take from him *stimulum carnis*.[8] Nor in a Priest employ'd to convert infidels were it sinfull to despaire that God would give him the power of miracles; If therefore to quench and extinguish this *stimulum carnis*, a man should kill himselfe, the effect and fruit of this desperation were evill, and yet the root it selfe not necessarily so. No detestation nor dehortation against this sinne of desperation (when it is a sinne) can be too earnest. But yet since it may be without infidelitie, it cannot be greater than that. And though *Aquinas* there calls it sinne truly, yet he sayes hee doth so, because it occasions many sinnes. And if it bee as others affirme, *Poena peccati*,[9] it is then *involuntarium*, which will hardly consist with the nature of sinne: Certainly, though many devout men have justly imputed to it the cause and effect of sin, yet as in the penitentiall Cannons, greater Penance is inflicted upon one who kills his wife, than one who kills his mother; and the reason added, not that the fault is greater, but that otherwise more would commit it; So is the sinne of desperation so earnestly aggravated, because springing from Sloth, and Pusillanimity, our nature is more slippery and inclinable to such a descent, than to presumptions, which yet without doubt do more wound and violate the Majesty of God than desperation doth.[10] But howsoever, that none may justly say that all which kill themselves have done it out of a despaire of Gods mercy (which is the onely sinnefull despaire) we shall in a more proper place, when we come to consider the examples exhibited in Scriptures, and other Histories, finde many who at that act have been so far from despaire, that they have esteemed it a great degree of Gods mercy to have been admitted to such a glorifying of his name, and have proceeded therein as religiously as in a sacrifice.

I.i.7

This terme the law of Nature is so variously and unconstantly deliver'd, as I confesse I read it a hundred times before I understand it once, or can conclude it to signifie that which the author should at that time meane. Yet I never found it in any sence which might justifie their vociferations upon sinnes against nature. For the transgressing of the Law of nature in any act doth not seeme to me to increase the haynousnesse of that act, as though nature were more obligatory than divine Law: but only in this respect it aggravates it, that in such a sin we are inexcusable by any pretence of ignorance since by the light of nature we might discern it. Many things which we call sin, and so evill, have been done by the commandment of God; by *Abraham* and the *Israelites* in their departing from *Ægypt*. So that this evill is not in the nature of the thing, nor in the nature of the whole harmony of the world, and therefore in no Law of nature, but in violating, or omitting a Commandement; All is obedience or disobedience. Whereupon our Country-man *Sayre* confesseth that this SELF-HOMICIDE is not so intrinsecally ill as to Ly. Which is also evident by *Cajetan* where he affirmes that I may not to save my life accuse my self upon the Racke. And though *Cajetan* extend no farther herein, than that I may not bely my self: Yet *Soto* evicts[11] that *Cajetan's* reasons with as much force forbid any accusation of my self, though it be true. So much easier may I depart with life than with truth, or with fame, by *Cajetan*. And yet we find that of their fame many holy men have been very negligent. For not onely *Augustine*, *Anselm*, and *Hierome*, betray themselves by unurged confessions, but St *Ambrose* procur'd certain prostitute women to come into his chamber, that by that he might be defamed, and the People thereby abstaine from making him Bishop. This intrinsique and naturall evill therefore will hardly be found. For God, who can command a murder, cannot command an evill, or a sinne, because the whole frame and government of the world being his, he may use it as he will. As, though he can doe a miracle, he can do nothing against nature, because that is the nature of everything which he works in it. Hereupon, & upon that other true rule, whatsoever is wrought by a superior Agent upon a patient who is naturally subject to that Agent is naturall, we may safely infer that nothing which we call sinne is so against nature, but that it may be sometimes agreeable to nature.

On the other side, nature is often taken so widely and so extensively, as all sinne is very truely said to be against nature. Yea, before it come to be sinne. For *S. Augustine* sayes, Every vice, as it is a vice, is against nature. And vice is but habite which being produced to act, is then sinne. Yea the parent of all sinne, which is hereditary originall sin, which *Aquinas* calls a languor and faintnesse in our nature, and an indisposition, proceeding from the dissolution of the harmony of originall Justice, is by him said to be in us, *quasinaturale*,[12] and is, as he saith in another place, so naturall that it is propagated with our nature in generation, though it be not caused by the principles of nature. So as if God would now miraculously frame a man, as he did the first woman, of another's flesh and bone, and not by way of generation, into that creature all infirmities of our flesh would be derived, but not originall Sin. So that originall sinne is traduced[13] by nature onely, and all actuall sinne issuing from thence, all sinne is naturall.

I. ii. 2

Our safest assurance, that we be not mislead with the ambiguity of the word Naturall Law, and the perplex'd variety thereof in Authors, will be this, that all the precepts of Naturall Law result in these, Fly evill, seek good; that is, doe according to Reason . . .

No law is so primary and simple, but it foreimagines a reason upon which it was founded: and scarce any reason is so constant, but that circumstances alter it. In which case a private man is Emperor of himselfe; for so a devout man interprets those words, *Faciamus hominem ad imaginem nostram,* id est, *sui juris.*[14] And he whose conscience well tempred and dispassion'd, assures him that the reason of selfe-preservation ceases in him, may also presume that the law ceases too, and may doe that then which otherwise were against that law.

And therefore if it be true that *it belongs to the Bishop of* Rome *to declare, interpret, limit, distinguish the law of God,* as their Doctors teach, which is, to declare when the reason of the Law ceases: it may be as true which this Author, and the Canons affirme, that he may dispense with that Law: for hee doth no more than any man might doe of himselfe, if he could judge as infallibly. Let it be true that no man may at any time doe anything against the law of nature, yet, *as a dispensation workes not thus, that I may by it disobey a law, but that that law becomes to me no law in that case wher the reason ceases,* so may any man be the Bishop & Magistrate to himselfe, and dispense with his conscience, where it can appeare that the reason which is the soule and forme of the law is ceased. Because, as in Oathes and Vowes, so in the Law, the necessitie of dispensations proceedes from this, that a thing which universally considered in it selfe is profitable and honest, by reason of some particular event becomes either dishonest or hurtfull, neither of which can fall within the reach or under the Commandement of any law; and in these exempt and privileged cases the privilege is not *contra jus universale,* but *contra universalitatem juris.*[15] It doth onely succor a person, not wound, nor infirme a law. No more, than I take from the vertue of light, or dignitie of the Sunne, if to escape the scortching thereof, I allow my selfe the reliefe of a shadow.

I. iii. 2

God forbid any should be so malignant so to mis-interpret mee, as though I thought not *the blood of Martyrs to be the seed of the Church,*[16] or diminished the dignity thereof; yet it becomes any ingenuity to confesse that those times were affected with a disease of this naturall desire of such a death; and that to such may fruitfully be applyed those words of the Good B[lessed] *Paulinus, Athleta non vincit statim, quia exuitur: nec ideo transnatant, quia se spoliant.*[17] Alas! we may fall & drown at the last stroke; for to sayle to heaven it is not enough to cast away the burdenous superfluities which we have long carried about us, but we must also take in a good frayte. It is not lightnesse, but an even-reposed stedfastnesse, which carries us thither.

But *Cyprian* was forced to find out an answer to this lamentation, which he then found to be common to men on their death beds, *Wee mourne because with all our strength we had vowed our selves to Martyrdome, of which we are thus deprived, by being prevented by naturall death*. And for them who before they were called upon offered themselves to Martyrdome, he is faine to provide the glorious and satisfactory name of Professors.

From such an inordinate desire, too obedient to nature, proceeded the fury of some Christians who when sentence was pronounced against others standing by, cryed out, *Wee also are Christians*.

And that inexcusable forwardnesse of *Germanus* who drew the beast to him, and enforced it to teare his body; And why did he this? *Eusebius* delivers his reason, that he might bee the sooner delivered out of this wicked and sinfull life. Which acts *Eusebius* glorifies with this prayse, that they did them *mente digna Philosophis*.[18] So that it seemes wisest men provoked this by their examples, as at the burning of the temple at Jerusalem, *Meirus* and *Josephus*, though they had way to the Romans, cast themselves into the fire. How passionately *Ignatius* solicites the Roman Christians not to interrupt his death. *I feare, saith he, your charity will hurt me, and put me to beginne my course again, except you endeavour that I may be sacrified now. I professe to all Churches,* quod voluntarius morior. *And after,* Blandiciis demulcete feras;[19] *entice and corrupt the Beasts to devoure me, and to be my sepulchre,* fruar bestiis, *Let me enjoy those beasts, whom I wish much more cruell than they are; and if they will not attempt, I will provoke and draw them by force.* And what was *Ignatius* reason for this, being a man necessary to those Churches, and having allowable excuses of avoiding it? *quia mihi utile mori est*.[20] Such an intemperance urged the woman of *Edissa*, when the Emperour *Valens* had forbidden the Christians one temple to which particular reasons of devotion invited them, to enrage the Officers with this Contumely, when they asked her why thus squallid and headlong she dragg'd her sonne through the streets; *I do it least when you have slaine all the other Christians, I and my sonne should come too late to partake that benefit.* And such a disorderly heate possessed that old wretched man, which passing by after the execution of a whole legion of 6666, by iterated decimation, under *Maximianus*, although he were answered that they dyed not onely for resisting the Roman Religion, but the State, for all that wish't that he might have the happines to be with them, and so extorted a Martyrdome. For that age was growne so hungry and ravenous of it, that many were baptized onely because they would be burnt, and children taught to vexe and provoke Executioners, that they might be thrown into the fire.

And this assurednesse that men in a full perswasion of doing well would naturally runne to this made the proconsul in *Africk* proclaime, Is there any more Christians which desire to dy, and when a whole multitude by generall voice discovered themselves, he bid them *Goe hang and drown your selves and ease the Magistrate*. And this naturall disposition afforded *Mahomet* an argument against the *Jews, if your Religion be so good, why doe you not dy?* for our primitive Church was so enamored of death, and so satisfied with it, that to vex and torture them more, the Magistrate made lawes to take from them the comfort of dying, and encreased their persecution by ceasing it, for they gloried in their Numbers.

I. iv. I

Amongst the *Athenians* condemned men were their own executioners by poyson. And amongst the *Romans* often by bloodlettings. And it is recorded of many places that all the *Sexagenarii* were by the lawes of wise States precipitated from a bridge. Of which, if *Pierius* his conjecture be true, that this report was occasioned by a custome in *Rome*, by which men of that age were not admitted to suffrage, and because the way to the Senate was *per pontem*,[21] they which for age were not permitted to come thither were called *Depontani*, yet it is more certaine that amongst the *Ceans* unprofitable old men poysoned themselves, which they did crownd with garlands, as triumphers over humane misery.[22] And the *Ethiopians* loved death so well that their greatest Malefactors being condemned to banishment escaped it Ordinarily by killing themselves. The civill law, where it appoints no punishment to the delinquent in this case, neither in his estate nor memory, punishes a keeper if his prisoner kill himselfe, out of a prejudice that if meanes may be afforded them, they will all doe so.

And do not we see it to be the custome of all Nations now to manacle and disarme condemned men, out of a sore assurance that else they would escape death by death? Sir *Thomas Moore* [23] (a man of the most tender and delicate conscience that the world saw since Saint *Augustine*) not likely to write any thing in jest mischievously interpretable, sayes that in *Utopia* the Priests and Magistrates did use to exhort men afflicted with incurable diseases to kill themselves, and that they were obeyed as the interpreters of Gods will; But that they who killed themselves without giving an account of their reasons to them, were cast out unburied. And *Plato* [24] who is usually cited against this opinion, disputes in it, in no severer fashion, nor more peremptory than thus, *What shall we say of him, which kills his nearest and most deare friend? which deprives himselfe of life, and of the purpose of destiny? And not urged by any Sentence, or Heavy Misfortune, nor extreame shame, but out of a cowardlinesse, and weaknesse of a fearfull minde, doth unjustly kill himselfe? What Purgatory, and what buriall by law belongs to him, God himselfe knowes. But let his friends inquire of the Interpreters of the law, and doe as they shall direct.* You see nothing is delivered by him against it, but modestly, limitedly, and perplexedly.

OF THE LAW OF REASON

II. iii. 1–4

Since therefore, to my understanding, it hath no foundation in Naturall nor Emperiall Law, nor receives much strength from those reasons, but having by custome onely put on the nature of law, as most of our law hath,[25] I beleeve it was first induced amongst us because we exceeded in that naturall desire of dying so. For it is not a better understanding of nature which hath reduc'd [26] us from it, but the wisedome of Lawmakers and observers of things fit for the institution and conservation of states.

For in ancient Common-wealths, the numbers of slaves were infinite, as ever both in *Rome* and *Athens*, there were 10 slaves for one Citizen; and *Pliny* sayes that in *Augustus* time, *Isidorus* had above 4000. And *Vedius Pollio* so many that he alwayes fed his fish in ponds with their blood; and since servitude hathe worne out, yet the number of wretched men exceeds the happy (for every labourer is miserable and beastlike in respect of the idle abounding men); It was therefore thought necessary by lawes, and by opinion of Religion, as *Scaevola* is alleged to have said, *Expedit in Religione Civitates falli*,[27] to take from these weary and macerated wretches, their ordinary and open escape, and ease, voluntary death . . .

For wheresoever you finde many and severe Lawes against an offence it is not safe from thence to conclude an extreame enormity or hainousnesse in the fault, but a propensenesse of that people, at that time, to that fault . . .

That reason which is grounded upon the Edict of *Tarquinius Priscus*, who when this desire of Death raigned amongst his men like a contagion, cured it by an opprobrious hanging up their bodies, and exposing them to birds and beasts. And upon that way of reducing the Virgins of *Milesium*, who when they had a wantonnesse of dying so, and did it for fashion, were by Decree dishonourably exhibited as a spectacle to the people naked . . . proves onely a watchfull solicitude in every State by all meanes to avert men from this naturall love of ease, by which their strength in numbers would have been very much empaired.

II. iv. 8–11

There are many Metaphoricall and Similitudinarie Reasons, scattered amongst Authors, as in *Cicero* and *Macrobius*,[28] made rather for illustration, than for argument or answer; which I will not stand to gleane amongst them, since they are almost all bound up in one sheafe, in that Oration of *Josephus* . . . *Josephus* then in that Oration hath one Reason drawen from the custome of an Enemy. We esteeme them enemies, who attempt our lives, and shall wee bee enemies to our selves? But besides that, in this place, *Josephus* speaks to save his owne life, and may justly be thought to speak more *ex animo*,[29] and dispassioned, where in the person of *Eleazar* he perswades to kill themselves, there is neither certaine truth in the Assertion, nor in the Consequence. For do we esteeme God, or the Magistrate our enemy, when by them death is inflicted? And do not Martyrs, in whose death God is glorified, kisse the Executioners, and the Instruments of their death? Nor is it unlawfull, unnaturall, or unexpedient for us, in many cases, to be so much our owne Enemies as to deny our selves many things agreeable to our sensitive nature, and to inflict upon our selves many things repugnant to it, as was abundantly shewed in the first part.

In the same Oration he hath another allusorie argument, *That a Servant which runnes away, is to be punished by the Law, though his Master bee severe; much more if we runne away from so indulgent a Master as God is to us.* But not to give strength or delight to this reason, by affording it a long or diligent answer, wee say, In our case the Servant runnes not from his Master, but to him, and at this call obeys his voyce. Yet it is as truely, as devoutly sayd, *The devill is overcome by resisting, but the world and the flesh by running away.* And the farther, the better.

His last, which is of any taste, is *That in a tempest, it were the part of an idle and treacherous Pylot, to sinke the Ship.* But I say, if in a Tempest we must cast out the most precious ware aboard to save the lives of the Passengers, and the Marchant who is damnified thereby cannot impute this to any, nor remedie himselfe, how much more may I, when I am weather-beaten, and in danger of betraying that precious soule which God hath embarqued in me, put off this burdenous flesh, till his pleasure be that I shall resume it? For this is not to sinck the ship but to retire it to safe Harbour, and assured Anchor.

II. vi. 7

Though amongst *Italian* relations, that in *Sansovine* concerning *England* have many marks and impressions of malice, yet of that custome, which hee falsely sayes to bee observed here, *That men condemned to be hanged are ever accompanied to their Executions by all their kinred, who then hang at their feet, to hasten their ende; And that when a Patient is abandoned by the Physicians, his neerest kinsman strangles him with a pillow.* Of this, I say, that Author had thus much ground, that ordinarily at Executions, men, out of a Charitie, as they thinke, doe so; and women which are desperate of sicke persons recovery use to take the pillow from under them, and so give them leave to dye sooner. Have they any more the Dominion over these bodies than the person himselfe? Or if a man were able to doe these Offices to himselfe, might he not doe it? Or might he not with a safe conscience put so much waights in his pockets as should countervaile their stretchings? I speake but comparatively; might not he doe it as well as they?

For to my understanding such an act, either in Executioner or by-stander, is no way justifiable; for it is both an injury to the party, whom a sudden pardon might redeeme; and to the Justice, who hath appointed a painfull death to deterre others. The breaking of legs in Crucified men, which was done to hasten death, was not allowed but upon Petition. And the Law might be much defrauded, if such violence might be used, where the breaking of the halter delivered the Prisoner from death, as in some places it doth; and good opinions concurre, that it is to doe ever without doubt, whatsoever is for ease, or escaping painfull passage out of this life; in such cases a man may more allowably doe by his owne act than a stranger may, for Law of Nature enclines and excuses him; but they are by many Lawes forbidden to hasten his death, for they are no otherwayes interested in it than as parts of the whole body of the State, and so it concernes them that Justice be executed. Yet we see this, and the other of withdrawing the pillowes, is ordinarily done, and esteemed a pious office.

II. vi. 8

The Church whose dignity and constancy it becomes well that that Rule of her owne Law be ever justly said of her self, *Quod semel placuit amplius displicere non potest*,[30] where new reasons do not interpose, celebrates upon the 9 of *February* the Birth, that is the death, of the Virgin and Martyr *Appollonia*;[31] who, after the persecutors had beat out her teeth, and vexed her with many other tortures, when she was presented to the fire, being inflamed with a more burning fire of the Holy Ghost, broke from the Officers hands, and leapt into the fire.

For this act of hers many Advocates rise up for her, and say, that either the History is not certain, (yet the Authors are *Beda*, *Usuardus*, *Ado*, and as *Barronius* sayes, *Latinorum caeteri*[32]) Or else, says *Sayr*, you must answer that she was brought very neer the fire, and as good as thrown in: Or else that she was provoked to it by divine inspiration. But, but that another divine inspiration, which is true Charity, moved the beholders then to beleeve, and the Church ever since to acknowledge, that she did therein a Noble and Christian act, to the speciall glory of God, this act of hers, as well as any other, might have been calumniated to have been done but of wearinesse of life, or fear of relapse, or hast to Heaven, or ambition of Martyrdome.

The memory of *Pelagia*, as of a virgin and Martyr, is celebrated the ninth of *June*. And though the History of this woman suffer some perplexity, and give occasion of doubting the truth thereof, (for *Ambrose* says that she and her Mother drownd themselves, and *Chrysostome* that they flung themselves downe from a house top; and *Baronius* saw this knot to be so hard to unentangle, that he says, *Quid ad hac dicamus, non habemus*[33]) yet the Church, as I said, celebrates the Act, as though it were glad to take any occasion of approving such a courage in such a cause, which was but preservation of Chastity. *Their Martyrdome,* saith Saint Augustine, *was ever in the Catholique Church frequented* Veneratione Celeberrima.[34]

And Saint *Ambrose*, when his sister *Marcellina* consulted him directly upon the point, what might be thought of them who kill themselves in such cases, (and then it is agreed by all that the opinions of the Fathers are especially to be valued when they speake of a matter, not incidently or casually, but directly and deliberately) answers thus, *We have an example of such a Martyrdome in* Pelagia. And then he presents her in this religious meditation, *Let us die, if we may have leave, or if we be denied leave, yet let us die. God cannot be offended with this, when we use it but for a remedy,* and our faith takes away all offence. Here is no difficulty: for who is willing to dye, & cannot, since there are so many waies to death? I will not trust my hand least it strike not home: nor my breast, least it withdraw it selfe: I will leave no escape to my flesh, for we can dye with our own weapons, and without the benefit of an Executioner.

And then having drest her selfe as a Bride, and going to the water, Here, sayes she, let us be baptized; this is the Baptisme where sinnes are forgiven, and where a kingdome is purchased: and this is the baptisme after which none sinnes. This water regenerates; this makes us virgines, this opens heaven, defends the feeble, delivers from death, and makes us Martyrs. Onely we pray to God that this water scatter us not, but reserve us to one funerall. Then entred they as in a dance, hand in hand, where the torrent was deepest and most violent. And thus dyed, (as their mother upon the bank called them) *These Prelates of virginitie, Captaines of Chastitie, and companions in Martyrdome.*

OF THE LAW OF GOD

III. i. 1

That light which issues from the Moone doth best represent and expresse that which in our selves we call the light of Nature; for as that in the Moone is permanent and ever there, and yet it is unequall, various, pale, and languishing, so is our light of Nature changeable. For being at the first kindling at full, it wayned presently, and by departing further and further from God, declined by generall sinne to almost a totall Eclipse: till God comming neerer to us, first by the Law, and then by Grace, enlightned and repayred it againe, conveniently to his ends, for further exercise of his Mercy and Justice. And then those Artificiall Lights, which our selves make for our use and service here, as Fires, Tapers, and such, resemble the light of Reason, as wee have in our Second part accepted that Word. For though the light of these Fires and Tapers be not so naturall as the Moone, yet because they are more domestique and obedient to us, wee distinguish particular objects better by them than by the Moone; so, by the Arguments, and Deductions, and Conclusions, which our selves beget and produce, as being more serviceable and under us, because they are our creatures, particular cases are made more cleare and evident to us; for these we can behold withall, and put them to any office, and examine and prove their truth or likeliehood, and make them answere as long as wee will aske; whereas the light of Nature, with a solemne and supercilious Majestie, will speake but once, and give no Reason, nor endure Examination.

But because of these two kindes of light, the first is too weake, and the other false, (for onely colour is the object of sight, and we do not trust candlelight to discerne Colours) we have therefore the Sunne, which is the Fountaine and Treasure of all created light, for an Embleme of that third best light of our understanding, which is the Word of God. *Mandatum lucerna, & Lex lux,* sayes *Solomon.*[35] But yet, as weake credulous men think sometimes they see two or three Sunnes, when they see none but Meteors or other apparances, so are many transported with like facilitie or dazeling, that for some opinions which they maintaine, they think they have the light and authority of Scripture, when, God knowes, truth, which is the light of Scriptures, is Diametrally under them, and removed in the farthest distance that can bee. If any small place of Scripture mis-appeare to them to bee of use for justifying any opinion of theirs, then (as the Word of God hath that precious nature of gold, that a little quantity thereof, by reason of a faithfull tenacity and ductilenesse, will be brought to cover 10000. Times as much of any other Mettall,) they extend it so farre, and labour and beat it to such a thinnesse,[36] as it is scarce any longer the Word of God, only to give their other reasons a little tincture and colour of gold, though they have lost all the waight and estimation.

But since the Scripture it self teaches, *That no Prophecie in the Scripture is of private interpretation,*[37] the whole Church may not be bound and concluded by the fancie of one, or of a few, who being content to enslumber themselves in an opinion and lazy prejudice, dreame arguments to establish and authorize that.

A professed interpreter of Dreames tells us, *That no Dreame of a private man may be interpreted to signifie a publike businesse.* This I say because of those places of Scriptures which are aledged for the Doctrin which we now examine, scarce any one, (except the Precept, *Thou shalt not kill*) is offered by any two Authors. But to one, one place, to another, another seemes directly to governe in the point, and to me (to allow Truth her naturall and comely boldnesse) no place but that seems to looke towards it.

III. ii. 8

The most proper, and direct, and strongest place is the Commandement, for that is of Morall Law, *Thou shalt not kill*; and this place is cited by all to this purpose.

But I must have leave to depart from S. *Augustines* opinion here, who thinks that this Commandement is more earnestly bent upon a mans selfe, than upon another, because here is no addition, and in the other, there is, *Against thy Neighbour*; for certainely I am as much forbid by that Commandement to accuse my selfe falsely as my Neighbour, though onely he be named. And by this I am as much forbid to kill my neighbour as my selfe, though none be named. So, as it is within the circuit of the Command, it may also bee within the exceptions thereof. For though the words be generall, *Thou shalt not kill*, we may kill beasts; Magistrates may kill men; and a private man in a just warre may not onely kill, contrary to the sound of this Commandement, but hee may kill his Father, contrary to another.

When two naturall Lawes contrary to one another occurre, we are bound to that which is *strictioris vinculi*,[38] as all Lawes concerning the Honour of God, and Faith, are in respect of the second Table, which is directed upon our Neighbour by Charitie. If therefore there could be a necessity that I must doe an act of Idolatry, or kill, I were bound to the later.

By which Rule, if perchance a publique, exemplary person, which had a just assurance that his example would governe the people, should be forced by a Tyrant to doe an act of Idolatry, (although by circumstances he might satisfie his owne conscience that he sinned not in doing it) and so scandalize and endanger them, if the matter were so carried and disguised, that by no way he could let them know that he did it by constraint, but voluntarily, I say perchance he were better kill himselfe.

It is a safe Rule, *Juri Divino derogari non potest, nisi ipsa derogatio juri Divino constet*.[39] But since it is not thought a violating of that Rule, *To kill by publique Authority, or in a just Warre, or defence of his life, or of anothers*, why may not our case be as safe and innocent?

If any importune me to shew this Priviledge, or exemption of this case from the Commandement, I may with *Sotus* retort it, and call for their priviledge to kill a Day-thiefe, or any man in defence of another.

And as these Lawes may be mediately and secondarily deduced from the conformity of other Lawes, and from a generall Authority which God hath afforded all Soveraignes to provide as necessities arise, so may our case bee derived as well from that necessary obligation which lyes alwayes upon us of preferring Gods glorie above all humane respects. So that we cannot be put to shew or pleade any exemption, but, when such a case arises, wee say that that case never was within the reach of that Law. Which is also true of all the other which we called exemptions before.

For, whatsoever might have beene done before the Law, (as this might if it be neither against Nature nor Justice, from both which we can make account that wee have acquitted it,) upon that, this Commandement never fell, nor extended to it.

III. iii. 3

Of the evils which seeme to us to bee of punishment, of which kind Death is, God ever makes others his executioners; for the greatest of all, though it be spirituall, which is Induration,[40] is not so wrought by God himselfe immediately, as his spirituall comforts are, but Occasionally, and by Desertion.

Sometimes in these God imployes his Angels, sometimes the Magistrate, somtimes our selves. Yet all which God doth in this life by any of these is but Physicke: for even excaecation[41] and induration is sent to further Salvation in some, and inflicted medicinally. And these ministers and instruments of his are our Physitians, and wee may not refuse any bitternesse, no not that which is naturally poyson, being wholesomely corrected by them. For as in Cramps which are contortions of the Sinewes, or in Tetans, which are rigors and stiffenesses in the Muscles, wee may procure to our selfe a fever to thaw them, or we may procure them in a burning feaver to condense and attemper our bloud againe, so in all rebellions and disobediences of our flesh, wee may minister to our selves such corrections and remedies as the Magistrate might, if the fact were evident. But because, though for prevention of evill wee may doe all the offices of a Magistrate upon our selves in such secret cases, but whether we have that authority to doe it after or no, especially in Capitall matters, is disputable, and at this time wee need not affirme it precisely, I will examine the largenesse of that power no farther now, but descend to that kind of evill, which must of necessity be understood in this place of *Paul*:[42] which is that we account naturally evill. And even in that, the Bishops of *Rome* have exercised their power to dispence with *Bigamy*, which is in their doctrine directly against Gods Commandement, and therefore naturally evill. So did *Nicholas* the fifth dispense with a Bishop in *Germany* to consult with Witches for recovery of his health, and it were easie to amasse many cases of like boldnesse.

In like manner the Imperiall Law tollerates Usurie, Prescription[43] *Malae fidei*, and Deceit *ad Medium*,[44] and expressely allowes Witchcraft, to good purposes. *Conformably to which Law*, Paracelsus *sayes, It is all one whether God or the Devill cure, so the Patient be well.*

And so the Canons have prescribed certain rules of doing evill, when we are overtaken with perplexities, to chuse the least, of which S. *Gregory* gives a naturall example, *That a man attempted upon a high wall,*

and forced to leape it, would take the lowest place of the wall. And agreeably
to all these, the *Casuists* say, *That in extreame necessitie, I sinne not if I
induce a man to lend me mony upon usury; And the reason is, because I incline
him to a lesse sinne, which is usury, when else he should be a homicide, by not
relieving me.* And in this fashion God him selfe is said to work evill in us,
because when our heart is full of evill purposes, he governs and disposes
us rather to this than to that evill, wherein though all the vitiousnesse be
ours, and evill, yet the order is from God, and good. Yea, he doth
positively encline one to some certain evill thus, that he doth infuse into
a man some good thoughts, by which he, out of his vitiousnesse, takes
occasion to thinke he were better doe some other sinne than that which
he intended. Since therefore all these lawes and practises concurre in
this, that we sometimes doe such evill, not onely for expresse and
positive good, but to avoid greater evill, all which seems to be against
this doctrine of S. *Paul.*

And since, whatsoever any humane power may dispence withall in
us, we, in extream necessity, in impossibility of resource to better
counsell, in an erring conscience, and in many such cases, may dispence
with our selves, (for that Canon of *duo mala* [45] leaves it to our naturall
reason to judge, and value, and compare, and distinguish betweene
those two evills which shall concurre.)

And since for all this it is certaine that no such dispensation from
another, or from my selfe, doth so alter the nature of the thing that it
becomes thereby the more or the lesse evill, to mee there appeares no
other interpretation safe but this, that there is no externall act naturally
evill; and that circumstances condition them, and give them their nature;
as scandall makes an indifferent thing hainous at that time, which, if
some person go out of the roome, or winke, is not so.

III. iii. 4–5

Our body is so much our owne, as we may use it to Gods glory; and it is
so little our owne, as when hee is pleased to have it, we doe well in
resigning it to him by what Officer soever he accept it, whether by
Angell, Sicknesse, Persecution, Magistrate, or our selves. Onely bee
carefull of this last lesson, in which hee amasses and gathers all his
former Doctrine, *Glorifie God in your body, and in your spirit, for they are
his.*

The place of the *Ephesians* hath some affinity with this, which is, *But let us follow the truth in love, and in all things grow up into him which is the head, that is Christ, till we are all met together, unto a perfect man.*[46] By which wee receive the honour to be one body with Christ our head, which is after more expressely declared, *We are Members of his body, of his flesh, and of his bone.* And therefore, they say, that to withdraw our selves which are limmes of him, is not onely homicide of our selves, who cannot live without him, but a Paricide towards him, who is our common Father.

But as in Fencing, Passion layes a man as open as unskilfulnesse, and a troubled desire to hitt, makes one not onely misse, but receive a wound, so out of an inordinate fervour to strike home, hee which alledgeth this place overreacheth to his owne danger; for onely this is taught herein, that all our growth and vegetation flowes from our head, Christ. And that he hath chosen to himselfe for the perfection of his body, limmes proportionall thereunto, and that, as a soule through all the body, so this care must live and dwell in every part, that it be ever ready to doe his proper function, and also to succour those other parts for whose reliefe or sustentation it is framed and planted in the body. So that herein there is no litterall construction to be admitted, as though the body of Christ could be imperfited by the removing of any man. For, as from a tree, some leaves passe their naturall course and season, and fall againe being withered by age, and some fruits are gathered unripe, and some ripe, and some branches which in a storme fall off, are carryed to the fire, so in this body of Christ, the Church, (I meane that which is visible) all these are also fulfilled and performed, and yet the body suffers no maims, much lesse the head any detriment.

III. iv. 5

A Christian nature rests not in knowing thus much, That we may doe it, That Charitie makes it good, That the good doe it, and that wee must alwaies promise, that is, encline to doe it, and doe something towards it, but will have the perfect fulnesse of doing it in the resolution and doctrine, and example of our blessed Saviour, who saies, *de facto, I lay down my life for my sheepe.*[47] And saith *Musculus,* hee useth the present word, because hee was ready to doe it: and as *Paul and Barnabas,* men yet alive, are said to have laid downe their lives for Christ. But I rather thinke, (because exposing to danger is not properly call'd a dying,) that Christ said this now because his Passion was begun; for all his conversations here were degrees of exinanition.[48]

To expresse the abundant and overflowing charitie of our Saviour all words are defective; for if we could expresse all which he did, that came not neere to that which he would doe, if need were. It is observed by one, (I confesse, too credulous an Authour, but yet one that administers good and wholesome incitements to Devotion) that Christ going to *Emaus* spake of his Passion so sleightly, as though he had in three dayes forgot all that he had suffered for us.

And that Christ in an apparition to Saint *Charles* sayes that he would be content to dy againe, if need were.

Yea, to Saint *Brigit* he said, *That for any one soule he would suffer as much in every limme, as he had suffered for all the world in his whole body*.

And this is noted for an extreame high degree of Charity, out of *Anselme*, that his B[lessed] Mother said, *Rather than he should not have been Crucified, shee would have done it with her owne hands*.

And certainly his charity was not inferiour to hers; he did as much as any could be willing to doe. And therefore, as himself said, *No man can take away my soule* and *I have power to lay it down*; so without doubt, no man did take it away, nor was there any other than his own will the cause of his dying at that time, many Martyrs having hanged upon Crosses many days alive: And the theeves were yet alive, and therefore *Pilate* wondred to heare that Christ was dead. *His Soule, saith S. Aug*[ustine], *did not leave his body constrained, but because he would, and when he would, and how he would*. Of which S. *Thomas* produces this symptome, that he had yet his bodies nature in her full strength, because at the last moment he was able to cry with a loud voice. And *Marlorate* gathers it upon this, that whereas our heads decline after our death by the slacknesse of the sinews and muscles, Christ did first of himself bow downe his head, and then give up the ghost. So, though it be truly said, *After they have scourged him, they will put him to death*, yet it is said so because malitiously and purposely to kill him they inflicted those paines upon him, which would in time have killed him, but yet nothing which they had done occasioned his death so soone.

And therefore S. *Thomas*, a man neither of unholy thoughts, nor of bold or irreligious or scandalous phrase or elocution (yet I adventure not so farre in his behalfe as *Sylvester* doth, *that it is impossible that hee should have spoken any thing against faith or good manners,)* forbeares not to say *That Christ was so much the cause of his death, as he is of his wetting, which might and would not shut the windowe, when the raine beats in.*[49]

This actuall emission of his soule, which is death, and which was his own act, and before his naturall time,[50] (which his best beloved Apostle could imitate, who also died when he would, and went into his grave, and there gave up the Ghost, and buried himselfe, which is reported but of very few others, and by no very credible Authors,) we find thus celebrated, That that is a brave death, which is accepted unconstrained; and that it is an Heroique Act of Fortitude, if a man when an urgent occasion is presented, expose himselfe to a certaine and assured death, as he did.

And it is there said that Christ did so as *Saul* did, who thought it foule and dishonourable to dye by the hand of an Enemy. And that *Apollonia* and others, who prevented the fury of Executioners and cast themselves into the fire, did therein immitate this act of our Saviour of giving up his soule before hee was constrained to do it. So that if the act of our blessed Saviour, in whom there was no more required for death but that he should wil that his soule should goe out, were the same as *Sauls* and these Martyrs actuall furtherance, which could not dye without that, then wee are taught that all those places, of *Giving up our bodies to death*, and of *Laying downe the soule*, signifie more than a yeelding to death when it comes.

III. v. 7

Of *Judas*, the most sinnefull instrument of the most mercifull Worke, the common, though not generall, opinion is that he killed himselfe; but whether by hanging, or no, is more controverted.

For from the words in the *Acts, That he threw himselfe down headlong, and burst asunder, and his bowels gushed out,*[51] *Euthymius* thinks that he was rescued whilst he hanged, and carryed away, and that after that hee killed himselfe by throwing himselfe headlong.

And *Brentius* leaves that indifferent to us, to thinke what we will thereof. But it seemes by *Oecumenius* that he did not only overlive this hanging, but that he grew to so enormous a bignesse and burden to himselfe that he was not able to withdraw himselfe out of a Coaches way, but had his guts crushed out so; which he receives from *Papias* the

Disciple to Saint *John*, whose times cannot be thought ignorant or incurious of *Judas* History.

And it is there said further that by others it was said that being swolne to that vastnesse, and corrupted with vermine, hee laid himselfe down upon his field, and there his guts broke out. And this *Theophilact* followes.

And it falls out very often that some one Father, of strong reputation and authority in his time, doth snatch and swallow some probable interpretation of Scripture: and then digesting it into his Homilies, and applying it in dehortations, and encouragements, as the occasions and diseases of his Auditory or his age require, and imagining thereupon delightfull and figurative insinuations, and setting it to the Musique of his stile (as every man which is accustomed to these Meditations shall often finde in himselfe such a spirituall wantonnesse and devout straying into such delicacies), that sense which was but probable growes necessary, and those who succeed had rather enjoy his wit than vexe their owne; as often times we are loath to change or leave off a counterfeit stone, by reason of the well setting thereof.

By this meanes, I thinke, it became so generally to be beleeved that the fruit which *Eve* eat was an Apple; And that *Lots* wife was turned to a pillar of Salt; And that *Absalon* was hanged by the haire of the head; And that *Jephthe* killed his daughter; And many other such, which grew currant, not from an evidence in the Text, but because such an acceptation was most usefull and applyable. Of this number *Judas* case might be.

But if it were not, that act of killing himselfe is not added to his faults in any place of Scriptures; no not in those two Psalmes [52] of particular accusations and bitter imprecations against him, as they are ordinarily taken to be Prophetically purposed and directed.

And even of this man, whose sinne, if any can exceed mercy, was such, *Origen* durst hope, not out of his erronious compassion and sinnefull charity, by which he thinks that even the Devill shall be saved, but out of *Judas* repentance. He says, *The Devill led him to the sinne, and then induced him to that sorrowfulnesse which swallowed him*. But speaking of his repentance, he says, *Those words,* when *Judas* saw that he was condemned, *belong to* Judas *himselfe, for Christ was not then condemned*. And upon this conscience and consideration began his repentance. *For, it may be, saith* Origen, *that Satan which had entred into him, staid with him*

till Christ was betray'd, and then left him, and thereupon repentance followed.
And perchance, sayes he, he ment to prevent, and goe before his Master,
who was to dye, and so to meet him with his naked soule that he might
gaine Mercy by his confession and prayers.

And *Calvine*, though his purpose be to enervate and maime (or at
least declare it to be so defective) that repentance which is admitted for
sufficient in the *Romane Church*, says that *In Judas there was perfect contrition of heart, Confession of the mouth, and satisfaction for the money.*

But *Petilian*, against whom Saint *Augustine* writes, proceeded further
in justification of *Judas* last act, than any. For hee said, *That in suffering
death when hee repented, and so was a Confessor, hee became a Martyr.*
Which opinion being pronounced singularly and undefensibly, Saint
Augustine answers as choleriquely, *Laqueum talibus reliquit.*[53] Yet Saint
Augustine himselfe confesseth that an innocent man, should more have
sinned in such an act than *Judas* did, because in his execution there were
some degrees of justice.

But of his actuall impenitence I purposed not to speake, nor of his
repentance, but onely to observe to you that this last fact is not imputed
to him, nor repentance said to be precluded thereby.

CONCLUSION

And this is as farre as I allowed my discourse to progresse in this way,
forbidding it earnestly all darke and dangerous Secessions and divertings
into points of our Freewill and of Gods Destiny: though allowing many
ordinary contingencies to be under our Election, it may yet seem reasonable that our maine periods, of Birth, of Death, and of chief alterations
in this life be more immediately wrought upon by Gods determination.
It is usefully said, and appliable to good purpose (though by a wicked
man, and with intention to crosse *Moses*), *That man was made of shadow,
and the Devil of fire.* For as shaddow is not darknesse, but grosser light,[54]
so is mans understanding in these mysteries, not blind but clouded. And
as fire doth not always give light (for that is accidentall, and it must
have aire to work upon), but it burneth naturally, so that desire of
knowledge which the Devill kindles in us, (as he doth as willingly bring
bellows to inflame a heart curious of knowledge, as he doth more ashes
to stupifie and bury deeper a slumbering understanding) doth not alwaies

give us light, but it always burnes us, and imprints upon our judgement stigmaticall marks, and at last seares up our conscience.

If then reasons which differ from me and my reasons be otherwise equall, yet theirs have this disadvantage, that they fight with themselves and suffer a Civill Warre of contradiction. For many of their reasons incline us to a love of this life, and a horror of death, and yet they say often that wee are too much addicted to that naturally. But it is well noted by *Alcuinus*, (and I thinke from Saint *Augustine*) *That though there bee foure things which wee must love, yet there is no precept given upon any more than two, God and our neighbour*. So that the other which concernes our selves may be pretermitted in some occasions.

But because of the benefits of death, enough hath beene occasionally interserted before, having presented *Cyprians* encouragement to it, who out of a contemplation that the whole frame of the world decayed and languished, cries to us, *Nutant parietes, The walls and the roofe shake, and would'st not thou goe out? Thou art tyred in a pilgrimage, and would'st thou not goe home?* I will end with applying *Ausonius* thanks to the Emperour, to death, which deserveth it better, *Thou providest that thy benefits and the good which thou bringest shall not be transitory; and that the ills from which thou deliverest us shall never returne*. Since therefore because death hath a little bitternes, but medicinall, and a little allay, but to make it of more use, they would utterly recline & avert our nature from it, as *Paracelsus* says of that foule contagious disease[55] which then had invaded mankind in a few places, and since overflowes in all, that for punishment of generall licentiousnes God first inflicted that disease, and when the disease would not reduce us, he sent a second worse affliction, which was ignorant, and torturing Physitians; so I may say of this case, that in punishment of *Adams* sinne, God cast upon us an infectious death, and since hath sent us a worse plague of men, which accompanie it with so much horrour and affrightment that it can scarce be made wholsome and agreeable to us. That which *Hippocrates*[56] admitted in cases of much profit, and small danger, they teach with too much liberty, *That worse meat may be given to a patient, so it be pleasanter, and worse drink, so it be more acceptable*. But though I thought it therefore needfull to oppose this defensative, as well to re-encourage men to a just contempt of this life, and to restore them to their nature, which is a desire of supreame happines in the next life by the losse of this, as also to rectify and wash again their fame, who religiously assuring themselves that in some cases, when wee were destitute of other meanes, we might be to ourselves the stewards of Gods benefits and the Ministers of his mercifull Justice, had yet, being, as *Ennodius* says, Innocent within themselves, incurred *damnum opinionis*,[57] yet (as I said before) I abstained purposely from extending this discourse to particular rules or instances, both because I dare not professe my self a Maister in so curious a science, and because the limits are obscure, and steepy, and slippery, and narrow, and every errour deadly, except where a competent dilligence being fore-used, a mistaking in our conscience may provide an excuse.

As to cure diseases by touch, or by charme, (both which one excellent Chirurgian, and one excellent philosopher,[58] are of opinion may be done, because what vertue soever the heavens infuse into any creature, man, who is Al, is capable of, and being borne when that vertue is exalted, may receive a like impression, or may give it to a word, or character made at that instant, if he can understand the time) though these, I say, be forbidden by divers Lawes, out of a Just prejudice that vulgar owners of such a vertue would misimploy it, yet none mislikes that the Kings of *England & France* should cure one sicknesse by such meanes, nor that the Kings of *Spaine* should dispossess Daemoniaque persons so, because Kings are justly presumed to use all their power to the glory of God; So is it fit, that this priviledge of which we speak should be contracted and restrained.

For that is certainly true of this, which *Cassianus* saith of a ly, *That it hath the nature of* Ellebore, *wholsome in desperate diseases, but otherwise poyson*; though I dare not averre with him, *That we are in desperate diseases, whensoever we are in ingenti lucro, aut damno, et in humilitate, ad evitandam gloriam*.[59] Howsoever if *Cassianus* mistake that, and we this, yet as he, and *Origen*, and *Chrysostome*, and *Hierome*, are excused for following *Platoes*[60] opinion that a ly might have the nature of medicine and be admitted in many cases, because in their time the church had not declared her self in that point, nor pronounced that a ly was naturally ill, by the same reason am I excusable in this Paradox. Against the reasons whereof, and against charity, if prejudice, or contempt of my weaknes, or mis-devotion have so precluded any that they have not beene pleased to tast and digest them, I must leave them to their drowsines still, and bid them injoy the favour of that indulgent Physitian, *Qui non concoxit, dormiat*.[61]

LETTERS

1. ADDRESSEE UNKNOWN
[? 1600]

Sir,

I am no great voyager in other mens works: no swallower nor devourer of volumes nor pursuant of authors. Perchaunce it is because I find borne in my self knowledg or apprehension enough, (for without forfeiture or impeachment of modesty I think I am bond to God thankfully to acknowledg it) to consyder him and my self: as when I have at home a convenient garden I covet not to walk in others broad medows or woods, especially because it falls not within that short reach which my foresight embraceth, to see how I should employ that which I already know; to travayle for inquiry of more were to labor to gett a stomach and then find no meat at home. To know how to live by the booke is a pedantery, and to do it is a bondage. For both hearers and players are more delighted with voluntary than with sett musike.[1] And he that will live by precept shal be long without the habite of honesty: as he that would every day gather one or two feathers might become brawne with hard lying before he make a feather bed of his gettings. That Erle of Arundell[2] that last dyed (that tennis ball whome fortune after tossing and banding brikwald[3] into the hazard) in his imprisonment used more than much reading, and to him that asked him why he did so he answerd he read so much lest he should remember something. I am as far from following his counsell as hee was from Petruccios:[4] but I find it true that after long reading I can only tell you how many leaves I have read. I do therfore more willingly blow and keep awake that smale coale which God hath pleased to kindle in mee than farr off to gather a faggott of greene sticks which consume without flame or heat in a black smoother: yet I read something. But indeed not so much to avoyd as to enjoy idlenes. Even when I begun to write these I flung away Dante the Italian, a man pert enough to bee beloved and too much to bee beleeved: it angred me that Celestine a pope [so] far from the manners of other popes, that he left even their seat, should by the court of Dantes witt bee attacked and by him throwne into his purgatory.[5] And it angred me as much, that in the life of a pope he should spy no greater fault, than that in the affectation of a cowardly securyty he slipt from the great burthen layd upon him. Alas! what would Dante have him do? Thus wee find the story related: he that thought himself next in succession by a trunke thorough a wall whispered in Celestines eare counsell to remove the papacy: why should not Dante be content to thinke that Celestine tooke this for as immediate a salutacion and discourse of the holy ghost as Abrahim did the commandment of killing his sonn? If he will needs punish retyrednes thus, what hell can his witt devise for ambition? And if white integryty merit this, what shall *Male* or *Malum* which Seneca[6] condems most, deserve? But as the chancellor Hatton[7] being told after a decree made that his predecessor was of another opinion, he answered hee had his genius and I had myne: So say I of authors that they thinke and I thinke both reasonably yet possibly both erroniously; that is manly: for I am so far from perswading yea conselling you to beleeve others that I care not that you beleeve not mee when I say that others are not to bee beleeved: only beleeve that I love you and I have enough.

2. A. V. *MERCED*.[8]

Sir,

I write not to you out of my poor Library, where to cast mine eye upon good Authors kindles or refreshes sometimes meditations not unfit to communicate to near friends; nor from the high way, where I am contracted, and inverted into my self; which are my two ordinary forges of Letters to you. But I write from the fire side in my Parler, and in the noise of three gamesome children; and by the side of her, whom because I have transplanted into a wretched fortune,[9] I must labour to disguise that from her by all such honest devices, as giving her my company, and discourse, therefore I steal from her, all the time which I give this Letter, and it is therefore that I take so short a list, and gallop so fast over it; I have not been out of my house since I received your pacquet. As I have much quenched my senses, and disused my body from pleasure, and so tried how I can indure to be mine own grave, so I try now how I can suffer a prison. And since it is but to build one wall more about our soul, she is still in her own Center, how many cir-

cumferences soever fortune or our own perversnesse cast about her. I
would I could as well intreat her to go out, as she knows whither to go.
But if I melt into a melancholy whilest I write, I shall be taken in the
manner: and I sit by one too tender towards these impressions, and it is
so much our duty, to avoid all occasions of giving them sad apprehensions, as S. *Hierome* accuses *Adam* of no other fault in eating the Apple,
but that he did it *Ne contristaretur delicias suas*.[10] I am not carefull what I
write, because the inclosed Letters may dignifie this ill favoured bark,
and they need not grudge so course a countenance, because they are
now to accompany themselves. My man fetched them, and therefore I
can say no more of them than themselves say. Mistress *Meauly*[11] in-
treated me by her Letter to hasten hers; as I think, for by my troth I
cannot read it. My Lady was dispatching in so much haste for *Twicknam*,
as she gave no word to a Letter which I sent with yours; of Sir *Tho.
Bartlet*, I can say nothing, nor of the plague, though your Letter bid
me: but that he diminishes, the other increases, but in what proportion I
am not clear. To them at *Hammersmith*, and Mistress *Herbert* I will do
your command. If I have been good in hope, or can promise any little
offices in the future probably, it is comfortable, for I am the worst
present man in the world; yet the instant, though it be nothing, joynes
times together, and therefore this unprofitableness, since I have been,
and will still indevour to be so, shall not interrupt me now from
being

> *Your servant and lover*
> J. Donne

3. TO SIR HENRY GOODYER
[SEPTEMBER 1608]

Sir,
    Every tuesday I make account that I turn a great hour-glass, and
consider that a weeks life is run out since I writ. But if I aske my self
what I have done in the last watch, or would do in the next, I can say
nothing; if I say that I have passed it without hurting any, so may the
Spider in my window. The primitive Monkes were excusable in their
retirings and enclosures of themselves: for even of them every one

cultivated his own garden and orchard, that is, his soul and body, by meditation, and manufactures; and they ought the world no more since they consumed none of her sweetnesse, nor begot others to burden her. But for me, if I were able to husband all my time so thriftily, as not onely not to wound my soul in any minute by actuall sinne, but not to rob and cousen her by giving any part to pleasure or businesse, but bestow it all upon her in meditation, yet even in that I should wound her more, and contract another guiltinesse: As the Eagle were very unnaturall if because she is able to do it, she should pearch a whole day upon a tree, staring in contemplation of the majestie and glory of the Sun, and let her young Eglets starve in the nest. Two of the most precious things which God hath afforded us here, for the agony and exercise of our sense and spirit, which are a thirst and inhiation [12] after the next life, and a frequency of prayer and meditation in this, are often envenomed, and putrefied, and stray into a corrupt disease: for as God doth thus occasion, and positively concurre to evill, that when a man is purposed to do a great sin, God infuses some good thoughts which make him choose a lesse sin, or leave out some circumstances which aggravated that; so the devill doth not only suffer but provoke us to some things naturally good, upon condition that we shall omit some other more necessary and more obligatory. And this is his greatest subtilty; because herein we have the deceitfull comfort of having done well, and can very hardly spie our errour because it is but an insensible omission, and no accusing act. With the first of these I have often suspected my self to be overtaken; which is, with a desire of the next life: which though I know it is not meerly out of a wearinesse of this, because I had the same desires when I went with the tyde, and enjoyed fairer hopes than now: yet I doubt worldly encombrances have encreased it. I would not that death should take me asleep. I would not have him meerly seise me, and onely declare me to be dead, but win me, and overcome me. [13] When I must shipwrack, I would do it in a Sea, where mine impotencie might have some excuse; not in a sullen weedy lake, where I could not have so much as exercise for my swimming. Therefore I would fain do something; but that I cannot tell what, is no wonder. For to chuse, is to do: but to be no part of any body, is to be nothing. At most, the greatest persons, are but great wens, and excrescences; men of wit and delightfull conversation, but as moales for ornament, except they be so incorporated into the body of the world, that they contribute something to the sustentation of the whole. This I made account that I begun early, when I understood the study of our laws: but was diverted by the worst voluptuousnes, which is an Hydroptique[14] immoderate desire of humane learning and languages: beautifull ornaments to great fortunes; but mine needed an occupation, and a course which I thought I entred well into, when I submitted my self to such a service, as I thought might [have] imployed those poor advantages, which I had. And there I stumbled too, yet I would try again: for to this hour I am nothing, or so little, that I am scarce subject and argument good enough for one of mine own letters: yet I fear, that doth not ever proceed from a good root, that I am so well content to be lesse, that is dead. You, Sir, are farre enough from these descents, your vertue keeps you secure, and your naturall disposition to mirth will preserve you; but lose none of these holds, a slip is often as dangerous as a bruise, and though you cannot fall to my lownesse, yet in a much lesse distraction you may meet my sadnesse; for he is no safer which falls from an high tower into the leads, than he which falls from thence to the ground: make therefore to your self some mark, and go towards it *alegrement*.[15] Though I be in such a planetary and erratique fortune, that I can do nothing constantly, yet you may finde some constancy in my constant advising you to it.

Your hearty true friend
J. Donne

4. TO SIR HENRY GOODYER
[1609]

Sir,

It should be no interruption to your pleasures, to hear me often say that I love you, and that you are as much my meditations as my self: I often compare not you and me, but the sphear in which your resolutions are, and my wheel; both I hope concentrique to God: for me thinks the new Astronomie[16] is thus appliable well, that we which are a little earth, should rather move towards God, than that he which is fulfilling, and can come no whither, should move towards us. To your life full of variety, nothing is old, nor new to mine; and as to that life, all stickings and hesitations seem stupid and stony, so to this, all fluid slipperinesses, and transitory migrations seem giddie and featherie. In that life one is ever in the porch or postern, going in or out, never within his house himself: It is a garment made of remnants, a life raveld out into ends, a line discontinued, and a number of small wretched points, uselesse, because they concurre not: A life built of past and future, not proposing any constant present; they have more pleasures than we, but not more pleasure; they joy oftner, we longer; and no man but of so much understanding as may deliver him from being a fool, would change with a mad-man, which had a better proportion of wit in his often *Lucidis*.[17] You know, they which dwell farthest from the Sun, if in any convenient distance, have longer daies, better appetites, better digestion, better growth, and longer life: And all these advantages have their mindes who are well removed from the scorchings, and dazlings, and exhalings of the worlds glory: but neither of our lives are in such extremes; for you living at Court without ambition, which would burn you, or envy, which would devest others, live in the Sun, not in the fire: And I which live in the Country without stupefying, am not in dark-nesse, but in shadow, which is not no light, but a pallid, waterish, and diluted one. As all shadows are of one colour, if you respect the body from which they are cast (for our shadows upon clay will be dirty, and in a garden green, and flowery) so all retirings into a shadowy life are alike from all causes, and alike subject to the barbarousnesse and insipid dulnesse of the Country: onely the emploiments, and that upon which you cast and bestow your pleasure, businesse, or books, gives it the tincture, and beauty. But truly wheresoever we are, if we can but tell our selves truly what and where we would be, we may make any state and place such; for we are so composed, that if abundance, or glory scorch and melt us, we have an earthly cave, our bodies, to go into by consideration, and cool our selves: and if we be frozen, and contracted with lower and dark fortunes, we have within us a torch, a soul, lighter and warmer than any without: we are therefore our own umbrella's, and our own suns. These, Sir, are the sallads and onions of *Micham*, sent to you with as wholesome affection as your other friends send Melons and *Quelque-choses*[18] from Court and *London*. If I present you not as good diet as they, I would yet say grace to theirs, and bid much good do it you. I send you, with this, a Letter which I sent to the Countesse.[19] It is not my use nor duty to doe so, but for your having of it, there were but two consents, and I am sure you have mine, and you are sure you have hers. I also writ to her Ladiship for the verses she shewed in the garden, which I did not onely to extort them, nor onely to keep my promise of writing, for that I had done in the other Letter, and perchance she hath forgotten the promise; nor onely because I think my Letters just good enough for a progresse, but because I would write apace to her, whilest it is possible to expresse that which I yet know of her, for by this growth I see how soon she will be ineffable.

5. TO SIR ROBERT KER [20]
[APRIL, MAY, OR JUNE 1623]

Sir,

Your way into *Spain* was Eastward, and that is the way to the land of Perfumes and Spices; their way hither is Westward, and that is the way to the land of Gold, and Mynes. The Wise men, who sought Christ, laid down both their Perfumes, and their Gold, at the feet of Christ, the Prince of Peace. If All confer all to his glory, and to the peace of his Church, *Amen*. But now I consider in Cosmography better; they and we differ not in East and West: we are much alike Easterlie. But yet, *Oriens nomen ejus*, the East is one of Christ's names, in one Prophet; And, *Filius Orientis est Lucifer*, the East is one of the Devill's names, in another: and these two differ diametrically. And so in things belonging to the worship of God, I think we shall, *Amen*. But the difference of our scituation is in North and South; and you know, that though the labour of any ordinary Artificer in that Trade, will bring East and West together, (for if a flat Map be but pasted upon a round Globe, the farthest East, and the farthest West meet, and are all one) [21] yet all this brings not North and South a scruple of a degree the nearer. There are things in which we may [meet]; and in that wherein we should not, my hope is in God, and in Him, in whom God doth so evidently work, we shall not meet, *Amen*. They have hotter daies in Spain than we have here, but our daies are longer; and yet we are hotter in our businesse here, and they longer about it there. God is sometimes called a Gyant, running a race; and sometimes is so slow-paced, as that a thousand years make but a day with God; and yet still the same God. He hath his purposes upon our noble and vehement affections, and upon their warie and sober discretions; and will use both to his glory. *Amen*.

   Sir, I took up this Paper to write a Letter; but my imaginations were full of a Sermon [22] before, for I write but a few hours before I am to Preach, and so instead of a Letter I send you a Homily. Let it have thus much of a Letter, That I am confident in your love, and deliver my self over to your service. And thus much of a Homily, That you and I shall accompanie one another to the possession of Heaven, in the same way wherein God put us at first. *Amen.*

> *Your very humble and very thankfull*
> *servant in Christ, &c.*

DEVOTIONS

I. INSULTUS MORBI
PRIMUS;[1]

*The first alteration,
The first grudging [2]
of the sicknesse.*

1. MEDITATION

Variable, and therfore miserable condition of Man; this minute I was well, and am ill, this minute. I am surpriz'd with a sodaine change, and alteration to worse, and can impute it to no cause, nor call it by any name. We study *Health*, and we deliberate upon our *meats*, and *drink*, and *Ayre*, and *exercises*, and we hew and wee polish every stone, that goes to that building; and so our *Health* is a long and a regular work; But in a minute a Canon batters all, overthrowes all, demolishes all; a *Sicknes* unprevented for all our diligence, unsuspected for all our curiositie; nay, undeserved, if we consider only *disorder*, summons us, seizes us, possesses us, destroyes us in an instant. O miserable condition of Man, which was not imprinted by *God*, who as hee is *immortall* himself, had put a *coale*, a *beame* of *Immortalitie* into us, which we might have blowen into a *flame*, but blew it out, by our first sinne; wee beggard our selves by hearkning after false riches, and infatuated our selves by hearkning after false knowledge. So that now, we doe not onely die, but die upon the Rack, die by the torment of sicknesse; nor that onely, but are preafflicted, super-afflicted with these jelousies and suspitions, and apprehensions of *Sicknes*, before we can cal it a sicknes; we are not sure we are ill; one hand askes the other by the pulse, and our eye asks our own urine, how we do. O multiplied misery! we die, and cannot enjoy death, because wee die in this torment of sicknes; we are tormented with sicknes, and cannot stay till the torment come, but pre-apprehensions and presages, prophecy those torments, which induce that *death* before either come; and our dissolution is conceived in these *first changes*, *quickned* in the *sicknes* it selfe, and *borne* in *death*, which beares date from these first changes. Is this the honour which Man hath by being a *litle world*,[3] That he hath these *earthquakes* in him selfe, sodaine shakings; these *lightnings*, sodaine flashes; these *thunders*, sodaine noises; these *Eclypses*, sodain offuscations, and darknings of his senses; these *blazing stars*, sodaine fiery exhalations; these *rivers of blood*, sodaine red waters? Is he a *world* to himselfe onely therefore, that he hath inough in himself, not only to destroy, and execute himselfe, but to presage that execution upon himselfe; to assist the sicknes, to antidate [4] the sicknes, to make the sicknes the more irremediable, by sad apprehensions, and as if hee would make a fire the more vehement, by sprinkling water upon the coales, so to wrap a hote fever in cold Melancholy, lest the fever alone shold not destroy fast enough, without this contribution, nor perfit the work (which is *destruction*) except we joynd an artificiall sicknes, of our owne *melancholy*, to our natural, our unnaturall fever. O perplex'd discomposition, O ridling distemper,[5] O miserable condition of Man.

1. EXPOSTULATION

If I were but meere *dust* and *ashes*, I might speak unto the *Lord*, for the *Lordes* hand made me of this *dust*, and the *Lords* hand shall recollect these *ashes*;[6] the *Lords* hand was the wheele, upon which this vessell of clay was framed, and the *Lordes* hand is the *Urne*, in which these *ashes* shall be preserv'd. I am the *dust*, and the *ashes* of the *Temple* of the *H. Ghost*; and what Marble is so precious? But I am more than *dust* and *ashes*; I am my best part, I am my *soule*. And being so, the *breath* of God, I may breath back these pious *expostulations* to my *God. My God, my God*, why is not my *soule*, as sensible as my *body*? Why hath not my *soule* these apprehensions, these presages, these changes, those antidates, those jealousies, those suspitions of a *sinne*, as well as my body of a *sicknes*? why is there not alwayes a *pulse* in my *Soule*, to beat at the approch of a *tentation* to sinne? why are there not always *waters* in mine eyes, to testifie my spiritual sicknes? I stand in the way of tentations, (naturally, necessarily, all men doe so: for there is a *Snake in every path*, tentations in every vocation) but I go, I run, I flie into the wayes of tentation, which I might shun; nay, I breake into houses, wher the plague is; I presse into places of tentation, and tempt the *devill* himselfe, and solicite and importune them, who had rather be left unsolicited by me. I fall sick of *Sin*, and am bedded and bedrid, buried and putrified in the practise of *Sin*, and all this while have no presage, no pulse, no sense of my *sicknesse*; O heighth, O depth of misery, where the first *Symptome* of the sicknes is *Hell*, and where I never see the fever of lust, of envy, of ambition, by any other light, than the darknesse and horror of *Hell* it selfe; and where the first Messenger that speaks to me doth not say,

Thou mayst die, no, nor *Thou must die*, but *Thou art dead*: and where the first notice, that my *Soule* hath of her sicknes, is *irrecoverablenes, irremediablenes*: but, O my God, *Job did not charge thee foolishly*, in his temporall afflictions, nor may I in my spirituall. Thou hast imprinted a *pulse* in our *Soule*, but we do not examine it; a voice in our conscience, but wee doe not hearken unto it. We talk it out, we jest it out, we drinke it out, we sleepe it out; and when wee wake, we doe not say with *Jacob, Surely the Lord is in this place, and I knew it not*:[7] but though we might know it, we do not, we wil not. But will *God* pretend to make a *Watch*, and leave out the *springe*? to make so many various wheels in the faculties of the Soule, and in the organs of the body, and leave out *Grace*, that should move them? or wil *God* make a *springe*, and not *wind* it up? Infuse his first *grace*, and not second it with more, without which, we can no more use his first *grace*, when we have it, than wee could dispose our selves by *Nature*, to have it? But alas, that is not our case; we are all *prodigall sonnes*, and not *disinherited*; wee have received our portion, and misspent it, not bin denied it. We are *Gods tenants* heere, and yet here, he, our *Land-lord* payes us *Rents*; not yearely, nor quarterly; but hourely, and quarterly; *Every minute he renewes his mercy*, but wee *will not understand, least that we should bee converted, and he should heale us.*[8]

1. PRAYER

O Eternall, and most gracious *God*, who, considered in thy selfe, art a *Circle*,[9] first and last, and altogether; but considered in thy working upon us, art a *direct line*, and leadest us from our *beginning*, through all our wayes, to our end, enable me by thy grace, to looke forward to mine end, and to looke backward to, to the considerations of thy mercies afforded mee from the beginning; that so by that practise of considering thy mercy, in my beginning in this world, when thou plantedst me in the Christian *Church*, and thy mercy in the beginning in the other world, when thou writest me in the *Booke of life*,[10] in my *Election*, I may come to a holy consideration of thy *mercy*, in the beginning of all my actions here: That in all the beginnings, in all the accesses, and approches of spirituall sicknesses of *Sinn*, I may heare and hearken to that voice, *O thou Man of God, there is death in the pot*,[11] and so refraine from that, which I was so hungerly, so greedily flying to. *A faithfull Ambassador is health*,[12] says thy wise servant *Solomon*. Thy voice received, in the beginning of a sicknesse, of a sinne, is true health. If I can see that light betimes, and heare that voyce early, *Then shall my light breake forth as the morning, and my health shall spring foorth speedily*.[13] Deliver mee therefore, O my God, from these vaine imaginations; that it is an overcurious thing, a dangerous thing, to come to that tendernesse, that rawnesse, that scrupulousnesse, to feare every *concupiscence*, every offer of *Sin*, that this suspicious and jealous diligence will turne to an inordinate dejection of spirit, and a diffidence in thy care and providence; but keep me still establish'd, both in a constant assurance, that thou wilt speake to me at the beginning of every such sicknes, at the approach of every such *Sinne*; and that, if I take knowledg of that voice then, and flye to thee, thou wilt preserve mee from falling, or raise me againe, when by naturall infirmitie I am fallen: doe this, *O Lord*, for his sake, who knowes our naturall infirmities, for he had them; and knowes the weight of our sinns, for he paid a deare price for them, thy *Sonne*, our *Saviour*, *Chr: Jesus, Amen*.

2. ACTIO LAESA

The strength, and the function of the Senses, and other faculties change and faile.

2. MEDITATION

The *Heavens* are not the less constant, because they move continually, because they move continually one and the same way. The *Earth* is not the more constant, because it lyes stil continually, because continually it changes, and melts in al the parts thereof. *Man*, who is the noblest part of the *Earth*, melts so away, as if he were a *statue*, not of *Earth*, but of *Snowe*. We see his owne *Envie* melts him, hee growes leane with that; he will say, anothers *beautie* melts him; but he feeles that a *Fever* doth not melt him like *snow*, but powr him out like lead, like yron, like brasse melted in a furnace: It doth not only *melt* him, but *Calcine* him, reduce him to *Atomes*, and to *ashes*; not to *water*, but to *lime*. And how quickly? Sooner than thou canst receive an answer, sooner than thou canst conceive the question; *Earth* is the *center* of my *Body*, *Heaven* is the *center* of my *Soule*; these two are the naturall places of those two; but those goe not to these two, in an equall pace: My *body* falls down without pushing, my *Soule* does not go up without pulling: *Ascension* is my *Soules* pace and measure, but *precipitation* my *bodies*: And, even *Angells*, whose home is *Heaven*, and who are winged too, yet had a *Ladder* to goe to *Heaven*, by steps.[14] The *Sunne* who goes so many miles in a minut, The *Starres* of the *Firmament*, which goe so very many more,[15] goe not so fast, as my *body* to the *earth*. In the same instant that I feele the first attempt of the disease, I feele the victory; In the twinckling of an eye, I can scarse see; instantly the tast is insipid, and fatuous; instantly the appetite is dull and desirelesse: instantly the knees are sinking and strengthlesse; and in an instant, sleepe, which is the picture, the copy of death, is taken away, that the *Originall*, *Death* it selfe may succeed, and that so I might have death to the life. It was part of *Adams* punishment, *In the sweat of thy browes thou shalt eate thy bread*:[16] it is multiplied to me, I have earned bread in the sweat of my browes, in the labor of my calling, and I have it; and I sweat againe, and againe, from the brow, to the sole of the foot, but I eat no bread, I tast no sustenance: Miserable distribution of *Mankind*, where one halfe lackes meat, and the other stomacke.

3. DECUBITUS SEQUITUR TANDEM.   *The Patient takes his bed.*

3. MEDITATION

Wee attribute but one priviledge, and advantage to Mans body, above other moving creatures, that he is not as others, groveling, but of an erect, of an upright form, naturally built, and disposed to the contemplation of *Heaven*. Indeed it is a thankfull forme, and recompences that *soule*, which gives it, with carrying that soule so many foot higher, towards *heaven*. Other creatures look to the *earth*; and even that is no unfit object, no unfit contemplation for *Man*; for thither hee must come; but because, *Man* is not to stay there, as other creatures are, *Man* in his naturall forme, is carried to the contemplation of that place, which is his *home*, *Heaven*. This is *Mans* prerogative; but what state hath he in this *dignitie*? A fever can fillip him downe, a fever can depose him; a fever can bring that head, which yesterday caried a *crown* of gold, five foot towards a *crown* of glory, as low as his own foot, today. When *God* came to breath into *Man* the breath of life, he found him flat upon the ground; when hee comes to withdraw that breath from him againe, hee prepares him to it, by laying him flat upon his bed. Scarse any prison so close, that affords not the prisoner two, or three steps.[17] The *Anchorites* that barqu'd themselves up in hollowe trees, and immur'd themselves in hollow walls; That perverse man, that barrell'd himselfe in a Tubb,[18] all could stand, or sit, and enjoy some change of posture. A sicke bed, is a grave; and all that the patient saies there, is but a varying of his owne *Epitaph*. Every nights bed is a *Type* of the *grave*:[19] At night wee tell our servants at what houre wee will rise; here we cannot tell our selves, at what day, what week, what moneth. Here the head lies as low as the foot; the *Head* of the people, as lowe as they, whome those feete trod upon; And that hande that signed Pardons, is too weake to begge his owne, if hee might have it for lifting up that hand: Strange fetters to the feete, strange Manacles to the hands, when the feete, and handes are bound so much the faster, by how much the coards are slacker; So much the lesse able to doe their Offices, by how much more the Sinewes and Ligaments are the looser. In the *Grave* I may speak thorough the stones, in the voice of my friends, and in the accents of those wordes, which their love may afford my memory; Here I am mine owne *Ghost*, and rather affright my beholders, than instruct them; they conceive the worst of me now, and yet feare worse; they give me for dead now, and yet wonder how I doe, when they wake at midnight, and aske how I doe, to morrow. Miserable, and, (though common to all) inhuman *posture*, where I must practise my lying in the *grave*, by lying still, and not practise my *Resurrection*, by rising any more.

4. MEDICUSQ; VOCATUR.   *The Phisician is sent for.*

4. MEDITATION

It is too little to call *Man* a *little World*; Except *God*, Man is a *diminutive* to nothing.[20] Man consistes of more pieces, more parts, than the world; than the world doeth, nay than the world is. And if those pieces were extended, and stretched out in Man, as they are in the world, Man would bee the *Gyant*, and the world the *Dwarfe*, the world but the *Map*, and the man the *World*. If all the *Veines* in our bodies, were extented to *Rivers*, and all the *Sinewes*, to *vaines of Mines*, and all the *Muscles*, that lye upon one another, to *Hilles*, and all the *Bones* to *Quarries* of stones, and all the other pieces, to the proportion of those which correspond to them in the *world*, the *aire* would be too litle for this *Orbe* of Man to move in, the firmament would bee but enough for this *star*; for, as the whole world hath nothing, to which something in man doth not answere, so hath man many pieces, of which the whol world hath no representation. Inlarge this Meditation upon this *great world, Man*, so farr, as to consider the immensitie of the creatures this world produces; our *creatures* are our *thoughts, creatures* that are borne *Gyants*: that reach from *East* to *West*, from *earth* to *Heaven*, that doe not onely bestride all the *Sea*, and *Land*, but span the *Sunn* and *Firmament* at once; My thoughts reach all, comprehend all. Inexplicable mistery; I their *Creator* am in a close prison, in a sicke bed, any where, and any one of my *Creatures*, my *thoughts*, is with the *Sunne*, and beyond the *Sunne*, overtakes the *Sunne*, and overgoes the *Sunne* in one pace, one steppe, everywhere. And then as the other *world* produces *Serpents*, and *Vipers*, malignant, and venimous creatures, and *Wormes*, and *Caterpillars*, that endeavour to devoure that world which produces them, and *Monsters* compiled and complicated of divers parents, and kinds, so this world, our selves, produces all these in us, in producing *diseases*, and *sicknesses*, of all those sorts; venimous, and infectious diseases, feeding and consuming diseases, and manifold, and entangled diseases, made up of many several ones.[21] And can the other world name so many *venimous*, so many consuming, so many monstrous creatures, as we can diseases, of all these kindes? O miserable abundance, O beggarly riches! how much doe wee lacke of having *remedies* for everie disease, when as yet we have not *names* for them? But wee have a *Hercules* against these *Gyants*, these *Monsters*; that is, the *Phisician*; hee musters up al the forces of the other world, to succour this; all Nature to relieve Man. We *have* the Phisician, but we *are not* the Phisician. Heere we shrinke in our proportion, sink in our dignitie, in respect of verie meane creatures, who are *Phisicians* to themselves. The *Hart* that is pursued and wounded, they say, knowes an Herbe, which being eaten, throwes off the arrow: A strange kind of *vomit*. The *dog* that pursues it, though hee bee subject to sicknes, even *proverbially*, knowes his *grasse* that recovers him. And it may be true, that the *Drugger* is as neere to *Man*, as to other *creatures*, it may be that obvious and present *Simples*,[22] easie to bee had, would cure him; but the *Apothecary* is not so neere him, nor the *Phisician* so neere him, as they two are to other creatures; Man hath not that *innate instinct*, to apply those naturall medicines to his present danger, as those inferiour creatures have; he is not his owne *Apothecary*, his owne *Phisician*, as they are. Call back therefore thy Meditation again, and bring it downe; whats become of mans great extent and proportion, when himselfe shrinkes himselfe, and consumes himselfe to a handfull of dust; whats become of his soaring thoughts, his compassing thoughts, when himselfe brings himselfe to the ignorance, to the thoughtlesnesse of the *Grave*? His *diseases* are his owne, but the *Phisician* is not; hee hath them at home, but hee must send for the Phisician.

5. SOLUS ADEST.   *The Phisician comes.*

5. MEDITATION

As *Sicknesse* is the greatest misery, so the greatest misery of sicknes is *solitude*; when the infectiousnes of the disease deterrs them who should assist, from comming; even the *Phisician* dares scarse come. *Solitude* is a torment which is not threatned in *hell* it selfe. Meere *vacuitie*, the first *Agent*, God, the first *instrument* of God, *Nature*, will not admit; Nothing can be utterly *emptie*, but so neere a degree towards *Vacuitie*, as *Solitude*, to bee but one, they love not. When I am dead, and my body might infect, they have a remedy, they may bury me; but when I am but sick, and might infect, they have no remedy, but their absence, and my solitude. It is an *excuse* to them that are *great*, and pretend, and yet are loth to come; it is an *inhibition* to those who would truly come, because they may be made instruments, and pestiducts,[23] to the infection of others, by their comming. And it is an *Outlawry*, an *Excommunication* upon the *patient*, and seperats him from all offices not onely of *Civilitie*, but of *working Charitie*. A long sicknesse will weary friends at last, but a pestilentiall sicknes averts them from the beginning. *God* himself wold admit a *figure* of *Society*, as there is a plurality of persons in *God*, though there bee but one *God*; and all his externall actions testifie a love of *Societie*, and *communion*. *In Heaven* there are *Orders* of *Angels*, and *Armies of Martyrs*, and *in that house, many mansions*;[24] in *Earth, Families, Cities, Churches, Colleges*, all *plurall things*; and lest either of these should not be company enough alone, there is an association of both, a *Communion of Saints*, which makes the *Militant*, and *Triumphant Church*, one *Parish*; So that *Christ*, was not out of his *Dioces*, when hee was upon the *Earth*, nor out of his *Temple*, when he was in our flesh. *God*, who sawe that all that hee made, was good, came not so neer seeing a *defect* in any of his works, as when he saw that it was not good, for man to bee *alone*, therefore *hee made him a helper*; and one that should helpe him so, as to increase the *number*, and give him *her owne*, and *more societie*. *Angels*, who do not propagate, nor multiply, were made at first in an abundant number; and so were starres: But for the things of this world, their blessing was, *Encrease*; for I think, I need not aske leave to think, that there is no *Phenix*; nothing singular, nothing alone: Men that inhere upon *Nature* only, are so far from thinking, that there is anything *singular* in this world, as that they will scarce thinke, that this world it selfe is *singular*, but that every *Planet*, and every *Starre*, is another *World* like this; They finde reason to conceive, not onely a *pluralitie* in every *Species* in the world, but a *pluralitie of worlds*;[25] so that the abhorrers of *Solitude*, are not solitary; for *God*, and *Nature*, and *Reason* concurre against it. Now, a man may counterfeyt the *Plague* in a *vowe*, and mistake a *Disease* for *Religion*; by such a retiring, and recluding of himselfe from all men, as to doe good to no man, to converse with no man. *God* hath two *Testaments*, two *Wils*;[26] but this is a *Scedule*, and not of his, a *Codicill*, and not of his, not in the body of his *Testaments*, but *interlind*, and *postscrib'd* by others, that the way to the *Communion of Saints*, should be by such a *solitude*, as excludes all doing of good here. That is a *disease* of the *mind*; as the height of an infectious disease of the body, is *solitude*, to be left alone: for this makes an infectious bed, equall, nay worse than a *grave*, that thogh in both I be equally alone, in my bed I *know* it, and *feele* it, and shall not in my *grave*: and this too, that in my bedd, my soule is still in an infectious body, and shall not in my grave bee so.

6. METUIT.   *The Phisician is afraid.*

6. MEDITATION

I observe the *Phisician*,[27] with the same diligence, as hee the *disease*; I see hee *feares*, and I feare with him: I overtake him, I overrun him in his feare, and I go the faster, because he makes his pace slow; I feare the more, because he disguises his fear, and I see it with the more sharpnesse, because hee would not have me see it. He knowes that his *feare* shall not disorder the practise, and exercise of his *Art*, but he knows that my *fear* may disorder the effect, and working of his practise. As the ill affections of the *spleene*,[28] complicate, and mingle themselvs with every infirmitie of the body, so doth *feare* insinuat it self in every *action*, or *passion* of the *mind*; and as *wind* in the body will counterfet any disease, and seem the *Stone*, and seem the *Gout*, so *feare* will counterfet any disease of the *Mind*; It shall seeme *love*, a love of having, and it is but a *fear*, a jealous, and suspitious feare of loosing; It shall seem *valor* in despising, and undervaluing danger, and it is but *feare*, in an overvaluing of *opinion*, and *estimation*, and a feare of loosing that. A man that is not afraid of a *Lion*, is afraid of a *Cat*; not afraid of *starving*, and yet is afraid of some *joynt of meat* at the table, presented to feed him; not afraid of the sound of *Drummes*, and *Trumpets*, and *Shot*, and those, which they seeke to drowne, the last cries of men, and is afraid of some particular *harmonious instrument*; so much afraid, as that with any of these the *enemy* might drive this man, otherwise valiant enough, out of the field. I know not, what fear is, nor I know not what it is that I fear now; I feare not the hastening of my *death*, and yet I do fear the increase of the *disease*; I should belie *Nature*, if I should deny that I feard this, and if I should say that I feared *death*, I should belye *God*; My weaknesse is from *Nature*, who hath but her *Measure*, my strength is from *God*, who possesses, and distributes infinitely. As then every cold ayre, is not a *dampe*,[29] every *shivering* is not a *stupefaction*, so every *feare*, is not a *fearefulnes*, every declination is not a running away, every debating is not a resolving, every wish, that it were not thus, is not a murmuring, not a dejection though it bee thus; but as my *Phisicians* fear puts not him from his *practise*, neither doth mine put me, from receiving from *God*, and *Man*, and *my selfe*, *spirituall*, and *civill*, and *morall* assistances, and consolations.

7. SOCIOS SIBI JUNGIER INSTAT.   *The Phisician desires to have*
others joyned with him.

7. MEDITATION

There is *more feare*, therefore *more cause*. If the *Phisician* desire help, the burden grows great: There is a grouth of the *Disease* then; But there must bee an *Autumne* too; But whether an *Autumne* of the *disease* or *mee*, it is not my part to choose: but if it bee of *me*, it is of *both*; My disease cannot *survive mee*, I may *overlive it*. Howsoever, his desiring of others, argues his *candor*, and his *ingenuitie*; If the danger be *great*, hee *justifies* his proceedings, and he *disguises* nothing, that calls in *witnesses*; And if the danger bee not *great*, hee is not *ambitious*, that is so readie to divide the thankes, and the honour of that work, which he begun alone, with others. It diminishes not the dignitie of a *Monarch*, that hee derive part of his care upon others; *God* hath not made many *Suns*, but he hath made many *bodies*, that *receive*, and *give* light. The *Romanes* began with *one King*; they came to *two Consuls*; they returned in extremities, to *one Dictator*: whether in *one*, or *many*, the *soveraigntie* is the same, in all *States*, and the danger is not the more, and the providence is the more, wher there are more *Phisicians*; as the State is the happier, where businesses are carried by more counsels, than can bee in one breast, how large soever. *Diseases* themselves hold *Consultations*, and conspire how they may multiply, and joyn with one another, and *exalt* one anothers force, so; and shal we not call *Phisicians*, to *consultations*? *Death* is in an olde mans dore, he appeares, and tels him so, and *death* is at a yong mans *backe*, and saies nothing; *Age* is a sicknesse, and *Youth* is an *ambush*; and we need so many *Phisicians*, as may make up a *Watch*, and spie every inconvenience. There is scarce any thing, that hath not killed some body; a *haire*, a *feather* hath done it; Nay, that which is our best *Antidote* against it, hath donn it; the best Cordiall hath bene *deadly poyson*; Men have dyed of *Joy*, and allmost forbidden their friends to weepe for them, when they have seen them dye laughing. Even that Tiran *Dyonisius*[30] (I thinke the same, that suffered so much after) who could not die of that sorrow, of that high fal, from a *King* to a *wretched private man*, dyed of so poore a *Joy*, as to be declard by the *people* at a *Theater*, that hee was a good *Poet*. We say often that a *Man may live of a litle*; but, alas, of how much lesse may a Man dye? And therfore the more assistants, the better; who comes to a day of hearing, in a caus of any importance, with one *Advocate*? In our *Funerals*, we our selfs have no interest; there wee cannot *advise*, we cannot *direct*: And though some *Nations*, (the *Egiptians* in particular) built themselves better *Tombs*, than *houses*, because they were to dwell *longer* in them; yet, amongst our selves, the greatest *Man of Stile*, whom we have had, *The Conqueror*, was left, as soone as his soule left him, not only without persons to assist at his *grave*, but without a *grave*.[31] Who will keepe us then, we know not; As long as we can, let us admit as much *helpe* as wee can; Another, and another *Phisician*, is not another, and another *Indication*, and *Symptom* of *death*, but another, and another *Assistant* and *Proctor of life*: Nor doe they so much feed the imagination with apprehension of *danger*, as the understanding with *comfort*; Let not one bring *Learning*, another *Diligence*, another *Religion*, but every one bring all, and, as many Ingredients enter into a Receit,[32] so may many men make the Receit. But why doe I exercise my Meditation so long upon this, of having plentifull helpe in time of need? Is not my Meditation rather to be enclined another way, to condole, and commiserate their distresse, who have *none*? How many are sicker (perchance) than I, and laid in their wofull straw at home (if that corner be a home) and have no more hope of helpe, though they die, than of preferment, though they live? Nor doe no more expect to see a *Phisician* then, than to bee an *Officer* after; of whome, the first that takes knowledge, is the *Sexten* that buries them; who buries them in *oblivion* too? For they doe but fill up the number of the dead in the Bill,[33] but we shall never heare their *Names*, till wee reade them in the Booke of life, with our owne. How many are sicker (perchance) than I, and thrown into *Hospitals*, where, (as a fish left upon the Sand, must stay the tide) they must stay the *Phisicians* houre of visiting, and then can bee but *visited*? How many are sicker (perchaunce) than all we, and have not this *Hospitall* to cover them, not this straw, to lie in, to die in, but have their *Grave-stone* under them, and breathe out their soules in the eares, and in the eies of passengers, harder than their bed, the flint of the street? That taste of no part of our *Phisick*, but a *sparing dyet*; to whom ordinary porridge would bee *Julip*[34] enough, the refuse of our servants, *Bezar* enough, and the off-scouring of our Kitchin tables, *Cordiall* enough. O my *soule*, when thou art not enough awake, to blesse thy *God* enough for his plentifull mercy, in affoording thee many *Helpers*, remember how many lacke them, and helpe them to them, or to those other things, which they lacke as much as them.

8. ET REX IPSE   *The King sends*
SUUM MITTIT.   *his owne Phisician.*

8. MEDITATION

Stil when we return to that Meditation, that *Man* is a *World*, we find new *discoveries*. Let him be a *world*, and him self will be the *land*, and *misery* the *sea*. His misery (for misery is his, his own; of the happinesses even of this world, hee is but *tenant*, but of misery the *free-holder*; of happines he is but the *farmer*, but the *usufructuary*,[35] but of misery, the *Lord*, the *proprietary*) his misery, as the *sea*, swells above all the hilles, and reaches to the remotest parts of this earth, *Man*; who of himselfe is but *dust*, and coagulated and kneaded into earth, by *teares*, his *matter* is *earth*, his *forme*, *misery*. In this *world*, that is *Mankinde*, the highest ground, the eminentest *hils*, are *kings*; and have they line, and lead enough to fadome this *sea*, and say, My misery is but this deepe? Scarce any misery equal to *sicknesse*; and they are subject to that equally, with their lowest subject. A *glasse* is not the lesse brittle, because a *Kings* face is represented in it; nor a King the lesse brittle, because *God* is represented in him. They have *Phisicians* continually about them, and therfore *sicknesses*, or the worst of sicknesses, continuall feare of it. Are they *gods*? He that calld them so, cannot flatter. They are *Gods*, but *sicke gods*; and *God* is presented to us under many human affections, as far as *infirmities*; *God* is called *angry*, and *sorry*, and *weary*, and *heavy*; but never a *sicke God*: for then hee might *die* like men, as our *gods* do. The worst that they could say in reproch, and scorne of the *gods* of the *Heathen*, was, that perchance they were *asleepe*; but *Gods* that are so sicke, as that they cannot sleepe, are in an infirmer condition. A *God*, and need a *Phisician*? A *Jupiter* and need an *Æsculapius*?[36] that must have *Rheubarbe* to purge his *Choller*, lest he be too angry, and *Agarick*[37] to purge his *flegme*, lest he be too drowsie; that as *Tertullian* saies of the *Ægyptian gods, plants* and *herbes, That God was beholden to Man, for growing in his garden*, so wee must say of these *gods, Their eternity,* (an eternity of three score and ten yeares) is in the *Apothecaryes* shop, and not in the *Metaphoricall Deity*. But their *Deitye* is better expressed in their *humility*, than in their *heighth*; when abounding and overflowing, as *God*, in means of doing good, they descend, as *God*, to a communication of their abundances with men, according to their necessities, then they are *Gods*. No man is well, that understands not, that values not his being well; that hath not a cheerefulnesse, and a joy in it; and whosoever hath this *Joy*, hath a desire to communicate, to propagate that, which occasions his happinesse, and his *Joy*, to others; for every man loves witnesses of his happinesse; and the best witnesses, are experimentall witnesses; they who have tasted of that in themselves, which makes us happie: It consummates therefore, it perfits the happinesse of *Kings*, to confer, to

transfer, honor, and riches, and (as they can) health, upon those that
need them.

9. MEDICAMINA   *Upon their Consultation,*
SCRIBUNT.   *they prescribe.*

9. MEDITATION

They have seene me, and heard mee, arraign'd mee in these fetters, and
receiv'd the *evidence*; I have cut up mine own *Anatomy*, dissected my
selfe, and they are gon to *read* upon me. O how manifold, and perplexed
a thing, nay, how wanton and various a thing is *ruine* and *destruction*?
God presented to *David* three kinds, *War, Famine,* and *Pestilence*; *Satan*
left out these, and brought in, *fires from heaven,* and *windes from the
wildernes.*[38] If there were no *ruine* but *sicknes,* wee see, the Masters of
that *Art,* can scarce *number,* nor *name* all sicknesses; every thing that
disorders a faculty, and the function of that is a sicknesse: The names wil
not serve them which are given from the *place affected,* the *Plurisie* is so;
nor from the *effect* which it works, the *falling sicknes*[39] is so; they cannot
have names ynow, from *what it does,* nor *where it is,* but they must
extort names from what *it is like,* what it *resembles,* and but in some one
thing, or els they would lack names; for the *Wolf,* and the *Canker,* and
the *Polypus*[40] are so; and that question, *whether there be more names or
things,* is as perplexd in sicknesses, as in any thing else; except it be easily
resolvd upon that side, that there are more *sicknesses* than *names.* If *ruine*
were reduc'd to that one way, that Man could perish noway but by
sicknes, yet his danger were infinit; and if *sicknes* were reduc'd to that
one way, that there were no *sicknes* but a *fever,* yet the way were infinite
still; for it would overlode, and oppress any naturall, disorder and
discompose any artificiall *Memory,* to deliver the *names* of severall *Fevers*;
how intricate a worke then have they, who are gone to *consult,* which of
these *sicknesses* mine is, and then which of these *fevers,* and then what it
would do, and then how it may be countermind. But even in *ill,* it is a
degree of *good,* when the *evil* wil admit *consultation.* In many *diseases,*
that which is but an *accident,* but a *symptom* of the main *disease,* is so
violent, that the *Phisician* must attend the cure of that, though hee
pretermit (so far as to intermit) the cure of the *disease* it self. Is it not so
in *States* too? sometimes the insolency of those that are *great,* puts the

people into *commotions*; the great disease, and the greatest danger to the *Head*, is the *insolency of the great ones*; and yet, they execute *Martial law*, they come to present executions upon the *people*, whose commotion was indeed but a *simptom*, but an *accident* of the maine *disease*; but this *symptom*, grown so violent, wold allow no time for a *consultation*. Is it not so in the accidents of the *diseases* of our *mind* too? Is it not evidently so in our *affections*, in our *passions*? If a *cholerick* man be ready to strike, must I goe about to purge his *choler*, or to breake the blow? But where there is room for *consultation*, things are not desperate. They *consult*; so there is nothing *rashly, inconsideratly* done; and then they *prescribe*, they *write*, so there is nothing *covertly, disguisedly, unavowedly* done. In *bodily diseases* it is not alwaies so; sometimes, as soon as the *Phisicians* foote is in the *chamber*, his *knife* is in the patients *arme*; the disease would not allow a *minutes* forbearing of *blood*, nor *prescribing* of other remedies. In States and matter of government it is so too; they are somtimes surprizd with such *accidents*, as that the *Magistrat* asks not what may be done by *law*, but does that, which must necessarily be don in that case. But it is a degree of *good*, in *evill*, a degree that carries hope and comfort in it, when we may have recourse to that which is *written*, and that the proceedings may be apert,[41] and ingenuous, and candid, and avowable, for that gives satisfaction, and acquiescence. They who have received my *Anatomy* of my selfe, *consult*, and end their *consultation* in *prescribing*, and in prescribing *Phisick*; proper and convenient remedy: for if they shold come in again, and chide mee, for some disorder, that had occasion'd, and inducd, or that had hastned and exalted this *sicknes*, or if they should begin to write now rules for my *dyet*, and *exercise* when I were well, this were to *antidate*, or to *postdate* their *Consultation*, not to give *phisicke*. It were rather a vexation, than a reliefe, to tell a condemnd prisoner, you might have liv'd if you had done this; and if you can get your pardon, you shal do wel, to take this, or this course hereafter. I am glad they know (I have hid nothing from them) glad they consult, (they hide nothing from one another) glad they write (they hide nothing from the world) glad that they write and prescribe *Phisick*, that there are *remedies* for the present case.

10. LENTÈ ET SERPENTI   *They find the Disease to*
SATAGUNT OCCURRERE MORBO.   *steale on insensibly, and*
                                   endeavour to meet with it so.

10. MEDITATION

This is *Natures nest of Boxes*; The Heavens containe the *Earth*, the *Earth*,
Cities, *Cities*, *Men*. And all these are *Concentrique*; the common *center* to
them all, is *decay*, *ruine*; only that is *Eccentrique*, which was never made;
only that place, or garment rather, which we can *imagine*, but not *de-
monstrate*, That light, which is the very emanation of the light of *God*, in
which the *Saints* shall dwell, with which the *Saints* shall be appareld,
only that bends not to this *Center*, to *Ruine*;[42] that which was not made
of *Nothing*, is not threatned with this annihilation. All other things are;
even *Angels*, even our *soules*; they move upon the same *poles*, they bend
to the same *Center*; and if they were not made immortall by *preservation*,[43] their *Nature* could not keepe them from sinking to this *center*,
Annihilation. In all these (the *frame of the hevens*, the *States upon earth*, and
Men in them, comprehend all) Those are the greatest mischifs, which are
least discerned; the most insensible in their *wayes* come to bee the most
sensible in their *ends*. The *Heavens* have had their *Dropsie*, they drownd
the world, and they shall have their Fever, and burn the world. Of the
dropsie, the flood, the world had a foreknowledge 120 yeares before it
came; and so some made provision against it, and were saved; the *fever*
shall break out in an instant, and consume all; The *dropsie* did no harm
to the *heavens*, from whence it fell, it did not put out those *lights*, it did
not quench those *heates*; but the *fever*, the fire shall burne the *furnace* it
selfe, annihilate those *heavens*, that breath it out; Though the *Dog-
Starre*[44] have a pestilent breath, an infectious exhalation, yet because we
know when it wil rise, we clothe our selves, and wee diet our selves, and
we shadow our selves to a sufficient prevention; but *Comets* and *blazing
starres*, whose effects, or significations no man can interrupt or frustrat,
no man foresaw: no *Almanack* tells us, when a *blazing starre* will break
out, the matter is carried up in secret; no *Astrologer* tels us when the
effects wil be acomplished, for thats a secret of a higher spheare, than
the other; and that which is most *secret*, is most *dangerous*. It is so also
here in the *societies* of men, in *States*, and *Commonwealths*. Twentie
rebellious drums make not so dangerous a noise, as a few *whisperers*, and

secret plotters in corners. The *Canon* doth not so much hurt against a wal, as a *Myne* under the wall; nor a thousand enemies that threaten, so much as a few that take an *oath* to say *nothing*. *God* knew many heavy sins of the people, in the wildernes and after, but still he charges them with that one, with *Murmuring, murmuring* in their *hearts*, secret disobediences, secret repugnances against his declar'd wil; and these are the most deadly, the most pernicious. And it is so to, with the *diseases* of the *body*; and that is my case. The *pulses*, the *urine*, the *sweat*, all have sworn to say *nothing*, to give no *Indication* of any dangerous *sicknesse*. My forces are not enfeebled, I find no decay in my strength; my provisions are not cut off, I find no abhorring in mine appetite; my counsels are not corrupted or infatuated, I find no false apprehensions, to work upon mine understanding; and yet they see, that invisibly, and I feele, that insensibly the *disease* prevailes. The *disease* hath established a *Kingdome*, an *Empire* in mee, and will have certaine *Arcana Imperii, secrets of State*, by which it will proceed, and not be bound to *declare* them. But yet against those secret conspiracies in the State, the *Magistrate* hath the *rack*; and against these insensible diseases, *Phisicians* have their *examiners*; and those these employ now.

11. NOBILIBUSQ; TRAHUNT, A CINCTO CORDE, VENENUM, SUCCIS ET GEMMIS, ET QUAE GENEROSA, MINISTRANT ARS, ET NATURA, INSTILLANT.

They use Cordials, to keep the venim and Malignitie of the disease from the Heart.

11. MEDITATION

Whence can wee take a better argument, a clearer demonstration, that all the *Greatnes* of this world, is built upon *opinion* of others, and hath in itself no *reall being*, nor power of subsistence, than from the *heart of man*? It is always in *Action*, and *motion*, still busie, still pretending to doe all, to furnish all the powers, and faculties with all that they have; But if an enemy dare rise up against it, it is the soonest endangered, the soonest defeated of any part. The *Braine* will hold out longer than it, and the *Liver* longer than that; They will endure a *Siege*; but an unnatural heat, a rebellious heat, will blow up the *heart*, like a *Myne*, in a *minute*. But howsoever, since the *Heart* hath the *birthright* and *Primogeniture*, and that it is *Natures eldest Sonne* in us, the part which is first borne to life in man, and that the other parts, as *younger brethren*, and servants in this family, have a dependance upon it, it is reason that the principall care bee had of it, though it bee not the strongest part; as the *eldest* is oftentimes not the strongest of the family. And since the *Braine*, and *Liver*, and *Heart*, hold not a *Triumvirate* in *Man*, a *Soveraigntie* equally shed upon them all, for his *well-being*, as the foure *Elements* doe, for his very *being*, but the *Heart* alone is in the *Principalitie*, and in the *Throne*, as *King*, the rest as *Subjects*, though in eminent *Place* and *Office*, must contribute to that, as *Children* to their *Parents*, as all persons to all kinds of *Superiours*, though often-times, those *Parents*, or those *Superiours*, bee not of stronger parts, than themselves, that serve and obey them that are weaker; Neither doth this Obligation fall upon us, by second *Dictates* of *Nature*, by *Consequences* and *Conclusions* arising out of *Nature*, or deriv'd from Nature, by *Discourse*, (as many things binde us, even by the Law of *Nature*, and yet not by the *primarie* Law of *Nature*; as all Lawes of *Proprietie* in that which we possesse, are of the Law of *Nature*, which law is, *To give every one his owne*, and yet in the *primarie* law of Nature there was no *Proprietie*, no *Meum & Tuum*, but an universall *Communitie* over all;[45] So the obedience of *Superiours*, is of the law of *Nature*, and yet in the *primarie* law of *Nature*, there was no *Superioritie*, no *Magistracie*;) but this contribution of assistance of all to the *Soveraigne*, of all parts to the *Heart*, is from the very *first dictates of Nature*; which is in the first place, to have care of our owne *Preservation*, to looke first to ourselves; for therefore doth the *Phisician* intermit the present care of *Braine*, or *Liver*, because there is a possibilitie that they may subsist, though there bee not a present and a particular care had of them, but there is no possibilitie that they can subsist, if the *Heart* perish: and so, when we seeme to begin with others, in such assistances, indeed wee doe beginne with ourselves, and wee ourselves are principally in our contemplation; and so all these officious, and mutuall assistances, are but *complements* towards others, and our true end is *ourselves*. And this is the reward of the paines of *Kings*; sometimes they neede the power of law, to be obey'd; and when they seeme to be obey'd *voluntarily*, they who doe it, doe it for their owne sakes. O how little a thing is all the *greatnes of man*, and through how false glasses doth he make shift to *multiply it*, and *magnifie* it to himselfe? And yet this is also another misery of this *King of man*, the *Heart*, which is also applyable to the *Kings* of this world, *great men*, that the venime and poyson of every pestilentiall disease directs itself to the *heart*, affects that, (pernicious affection,) and the *malignity* of ill men, is also directed upon the *greatest*, and the *best*; and not only *greatnesse*, but *goodnesse* looses the vigour of beeing an *Antidote*, or *Cordiall* against it. And as the noblest, and most generous *Cordialls* that *Nature* or *Art* afford, or can prepare, if they be often taken, and made *familiar*, become no *Cordialls*, nor have any extraordinary operation, so the greatest *Cordiall* of the *Heart*, patience, if it bee much exercis'd, exalts the *venim* and the *malignity* of the *Enemy*, and the more we suffer, the more wee are insulted upon. When *God* had made this *Earth* of *nothing*, it was but a little helpe, that he had, to make other things of this *Earth*: nothing can be neerer nothing, than this *Earth*; and yet how little of this *Earth* is the *greatest Man*? Hee thinkes he treads upon the *Earth*, that all is under his feete, and the *Braine* that thinkes so, is but *Earth*; his highest Region, the flesh that covers that, is but *Earth*; and even the toppe of that, that, wherein so many *Absolons* take so much pride,[46] is but a bush growing upon that *Turfe of Earth*. How litle of the world is the *Earth*? And yet that is all, that *Man hath*, or *is*. How little of a *Man* is the *Heart*, and yet it is all, by which he *is*; and this continually subject, not only to forraine poysons, conveyed by others, but to intestine poysons bred in ourselves by pestilentiall sicknesses. O who, if before hee had a beeing, he could have sense of this miserie, would buy a being here upon these conditions?

12. SPIRANTE COLUMBÂ
SUPPOSITÂ PEDIBUS, REVOCANTUR
AD IMA VAPORES.

They apply Pidgeons, to draw the vapors from the Head.[47]

12. MEDITATION

What will not kill a man, if a *vapor*[48] will? how great an *Elephant*, how small a *Mouse* destroyes! to dye by a *bullet* is the *Souldiers dayly bread*; but few men dye by *haile-shot*: A man is more worth, than to bee sold for *single money*;[49] a *life* to be valued above a *trifle*. If this were a violent shaking of the Ayre by *Thunder*, or by *Canon*, in that case the *Ayre* is condensed above the thicknesse of *water*, of *water* baked into *Ice*, almost *petrified*, almost made stone, and no wonder that that kills; but that that which is but a *vapor*, and a *vapor* not forced, but breathed, should kill, that our *Nourse* should overlay us, and *Ayre*, that nourishes us, should

destroy us, but that it is a *halfe Atheisme* to murmure against *Nature*,
who is *Gods immediate Commissioner*, who would not think himselfe
miserable to bee put into the hands of *Nature*, who does not only set
him up for a *marke* for others to shoote at, but delights herselfe to blow
him up like a *glasse*, till shee see him breake, even with her owne breath?
nay, if this infectious *vapor* were sought for, or travail'd to, as *Plinie*
hunted after the *vapor* of *Ætna*, and dard, and challenged *Death*, in the
form of a *vapor* to doe his worst, and felt the worst, he dyed;[50] or if this
vapor were met withall in an *ambush*, and we surprized with it, out of a
long shutt *Well*, or out of a new opened *Myne*, who wold lament, who
would accuse, when we had nothing to accuse, none to lament against,
but *Fortune*, who is lesse than a *vapour*: But when our selves are the
Well, that breaths out this exhalation, the *Oven* that spits out this fiery
smoke, the *Myne* that spues out this suffocating, and strangling *dampe*,
who can ever after this, aggravate his sorrow, by this *Circumstance*, That
it was his *Neighbor*, his *familiar friend*, his *brother* that destroyed him, and
destroyed him with a whispering, and a calumniating breath, when wee
our selves doe it to our selves by the same means, kill our selves with
our owne *vapors*? Or if these occasions of this selfe-destruction, had any
contribution from our owne *wils*, any assistance from our owne *intentions*, nay from our owne *errors*, wee might divide the rebuke, and chide
our selves as much as them. *Fevers* upon wilful distempers of drinke, and
surfets, *Consumptions* upon intemperances, and licentiousnes, *Madnes*
upon misplacing, or overbending our naturall faculties, proceed from
our selves, and so, as that our selves are in the plot, and wee are not
onely *passive*, but *active* too, to our owne destruction; But what have I
done, either to *breed*, or to *breath* these *vapors*? They tell me it is my
Melancholy; Did I infuse, did I drinke in *Melancholly* into my selfe? It is
my *thoughtfulnesse*; was I not made to *thinke*? It is my *study*; doth not my
Calling call for that? I have don nothing, wilfully, perversely toward it,
yet must suffer in it, die by it; There are too many *Examples* of men,
that have bin their own *executioners*, and that have made hard shift to
bee so; some have alwayes had *poyson* about them, in a *hollow ring* upon
their finger, and some in their *Pen* that they used to write with: some
have beat out their *braines* at the wal of their prison, and some have eate
the *fire* out of their chimneys: and one is said to have come neerer our
case than so, to have strangled himself, though his hands were bound,
by crushing his throat between his knees; But I doe nothing upon my

selfe, and yet am mine owne *Executioner*. And we have heard of *death* upon small occasions, and by scornefull *instruments*; a *pinne*, a *combe*, a *haire*, pulled, hath gangred, and killd; But when I have said, a *vapour*, if I were asked again, what is a *vapour*, I could not tell, it is so insensible a thing; so neere *nothing* is that that reduces us to *nothing*. But extend this *vapour*, rarifie it; from so narow a roome, as our *Naturall bodies*, to any *Politike body*, to a *State*. That which is *fume* in us, is in a State, *Rumor*, and these *vapours* in us, which wee consider here pestilent, and infectious fumes, are in a State *infectious rumors*, detracting and dishonourable *Calumnies*, *Libels*. The *Heart* in that *body* is the *King*; and the *Braine*, his *Councell*; and the whole *Magistracie*, that ties all together, is the *Sinewes*, which proceed from thence; and the *life* of all is *Honour*, and just *respect*, and due *reverence*; and therfore, when these *vapors*, these venimous *rumors*, are directed against these *Noble parts*, the whole body suffers. But yet for all their priviledges, they are not priviledged from our *misery*; that as the *vapours* most pernitious to us, arise in our owne bodies, so doe the most dishonorable *rumours*, and those that wound a *State* most, arise at home. What ill *ayre*, that I could have met in the street, what *channell*, what *shambles*,[51] what *dunghill*, what *vault*, could have hurt mee so much, as these home-bredd *vapours*? What *fugitive*, what *Almesman of any forraine State*, can doe so much harme as a *Detracter*, a *Libeller*, a scornefull *Jester* at home? For, as they that write of *Poysons*, and of creatures naturally disposed to the ruine of Man, do as well mention the *Flea*, as the *Viper*, because the *Flea*, though hee kill none, hee does all the harme hee can, so even these libellous and licentious *Jesters*, utter the venim they have, though sometimes *vertue*, and alwaies *power*, be a good *Pigeon* to draw this *vapor* from the *Head*, and from doing any deadly harme there.

13. INGENIUMQ; MALUM,	*The Sicknes declares*
NUMEROSO STIGMATE, FASSUS	*the infection and malignity*
PELLITUR AD PECTUS,	*thereof by spots.*
MORBIQ; SUBURBIA, MORBUS.	

13. MEDITATION

Wee say, that the world is made of *sea*, and *land*, as though they were equal; but we know that ther is more *sea* in the *Western*, than in the

Eastern Hemisphere: We say that the *Firmament* is full of *starres*, as though it were equally full; but we know, that there are more *stars* under the *Northerne*, than under the *Southern Pole*. We say, the *Elements* of man are *misery*, and *happinesse*, as though he had an equal proportion of both, and the dayes of man vicissitudinary,[52] as though he had as many *good daies*, as *ill*, and that he livd under a perpetuall *Equinoctiall*, *night*, and *day* equall, good and ill fortune in the same measure. But it is far from that; hee *drinkes misery*, and he *tastes happinesse*; he *mowes misery*, and hee *gleanes happinesse*; hee *journies in misery*, he does but *walke in happinesse*; and which is worst, his misery is *positive*, and *dogmaticall*,[53] his happinesse is but *disputable*, and *problematicall*; All men call *Misery*, *Misery*, but *Happinesse* changes the name, by the taste of man. In this *accident* that befalls mee now, that this sicknesse declares itself by *Spots*, to be a malignant, and pestilentiall disease, if there be a *comfort* in the declaration, that therby the *Phisicians* see more cleerely what to doe, there may bee as much *discomfort* in this, That the malignitie may bee so great, as that all that they can doe, shall doe *nothing*; That an enemy *declares* himselfe, then, when he is able to subsist, and to pursue, and to atchive his ends, is no great comfort. In intestine Conspiracies, *voluntary Confessions* doe more good, than Confessions upon the *Rack*; In these Infections, when *Nature* her selfe confesses, and cries out by these outward declarations, which she is able to put forth of her selfe, they minister *comfort*; but when all is by the strength of *Cordials*, it is but a *Confession upon the Racke*, by which though wee come to knowe the malice of that man, yet wee doe not knowe, whether there bee not as much malice in his heart then, as before his confession; we are sure of his *Treason*, but not of his *Repentance*; sure of him, but not of his *Complices*. It is a faint comfort to know the worst, when the worst is *remedilesse*; and a weaker than that, to know *much ill*, and not to know, that that is the worst. A woman is comforted with the birth of her *Son*, her body is eased of a burthen; but if shee could *prophetically* read his *History*, how *ill a man*, perchance how *ill a sonne*, he would prove, shee should receive a greater burthen into her *Mind*. Scarce any purchase that is not cloggd with secret *encumbrances*; scarce any *happines*, that hath not in it so much of the *nature* of false and base money, as that the *Allay* is more than the *Mettall*. Nay is it not so, (at least much towards it) even in the exercise of *Vertues*? I must bee poore, and want, before I can exercise the vertue of *Gratitude*; miserable, and in torment, before I can exercise the vertue of *patience*; How deepe do we dig, and for how course gold? And what other *Touch-stone* have we of our *gold*, but *comparison*? Whether we be as happy, as others, or as ourselvs at other times; O poore stepp toward being well, when these *spots* do only tell us, that we are worse, than we were sure of before.

14. IDQ; NOTANT CRITICIS,   *The Phisicians observe these*
MEDICI EVENISSE DIEBUS.   *accidents to have fallen upon*
                                            the criticall dayes.

14. MEDITATION

I would not make *Man* worse than hee is, Nor his Condition more miserable than it is. But could I though I would? As a man cannot *flatter* God, nor over prayse him, so a man cannot *injure* Man, nor undervalue him. Thus much must necessarily be presented to his remembrance, that those *false Happinesses*, which he hath in this World, have their *times*, and their *seasons*, and their *Critical dayes*, and they are *Judged*, and *De-nominated* according to the times, when they befall us. What poore *Elements* are our *happinesses* made off, if *Tyme*, *Tyme* which wee can scarce consider to be *any thing*, be an essential part of our *happines*?[54] All things are done in some *place*; but if we consider *place* to be no more, but the next hollow *Superficies* of the *Ayre*, Alas, how thinne, and fluid a thing is *Ayre*, and how thinne a *filme* is a *Superficies*, and a *Superficies* of *Ayre*? All things are done in *time* too; but if we consider *Tyme* to be but the *Measure of Motion*, and howsoever it may seeme to have three *stations*, *past*, *present*, and *future*, yet the first and *last* of these *are* not (one is not, now, and the other is not yet) And that which you call *present*, is not *now* the same that it was, when you began to call it so in this *Line*, (before you sound that word, *present*, or that *Monosyllable*, *now*, the present, and the *Now* is past,) if this *Imaginary halfe-nothing*, *Tyme*, be of the Essence of our *Happinesses*, how can they be thought *durable*? *Tyme* is not so; How can they bee thought to be? *Tyme* is not so; not so, considered in any of the *parts* thereof. If we consider *Eternity*, into that, *Tyme* never Entred; *Eternity* is not an everlasting flux of *Tyme*; but *Tyme* is as a short *parenthesis* in a longe *period*;[55] and *Eternity* had bin the same, as it is, though time had never beene; If we consider, not *Eternity*, but *Perpetuity*, not that which had no *tyme* to beginne in, but which shall

out-live *Tyme* and be, when *Tyme shall bee no more*, what A *Minute* is
the life of the Durablest *Creature*, compared to that? And what a Minute
is Mans life in respect of the *Sunnes*, or of a tree? and yet how little of
our *life* is *Occasion*, *opportunity* to receyve good in; and how litle of that
occasion, doe wee apprehend, and lay hold of? How busie, and perplexed
a *Cobweb*, is the *Happinesse* of Man here, that must bee made up with a
Watchfulnesse, to lay hold upon *Occasion*, which is but a little peece of
that, which is *Nothing*, *Tyme*? And yet the best things are *Nothing*
without that. *Honors*, *Pleasures*, *Possessions*, presented to us, out of time,
in our decrepit, and distasted, and unapprehensive *Age*, loose their *office*,
and loose their *Name*; They are not *Honors* to us, that shall never appeare,
nor come abroad into the Eyes of the people, to receive *Honor*, from
them who give it: Nor *pleasures* to us, who have lost our sense to taste
them; nor *possessions* to us, who are departing from the possession of
them. Youth is their *Criticall Day*; that *Judges* them, that *Denominates*
them, that *inanimates*, and *informes* them, and makes them *Honors*, and
pleasures, and *Possessions*; and when they come in an unapprehensive
Age, they come as a *Cordiall* when the bell rings out,[56] as a *Pardon*, when
the Head is off. We rejoyce in the Comfort of *fire*, but does any man
cleave to it at *Midsomer*; Wee are glad of the freshnesse, and coolenes of
a *Vault*, but does any man keepe his *Christmas* there; or are the pleasures
of the *Spring* acceptable in *Autumne*? If happinesse be in the *season*, or in
the *Clymate*, how much happier then are *Birdes* than *Men*, who can
change the *Climate*, and accompanie, and enjoy the same season ever.

15. INTEREÀ INSOMNES   *I sleepe not day nor night.*
NOCTES EGO DUCO, DIESQUE.

15. MEDITATION

Naturall *Men*[57] have conceived a twofold use of *sleepe*; That it is a
refreshing of the body in this life; That it is a *preparing* of the *soule* for the
next; That it is a *feast*, and it is the *Grace* at that feast; That it is our
recreation, and cheeres us, and it is our *Catechisme* and instructs us; wee lie
downe in a hope, that wee shall rise the stronger; and we lie downe in a
knowledge, that wee may rise no more. *Sleepe* is an *Opiate* which gives
us *rest*, but such an *Opiate*, as perchance, being under it, we shall wake
no more. But though naturall men, who have induced secondary and

figurative considerations, have found out this second, this *emblematicall* use of *sleepe*, that it should be a *representation of death*, *God*, who wrought and perfected his worke, before *Nature* began, (for *Nature* was but his *apprentice*, to learne in the first *seven daies*, and now is his *foreman*, and works next under him) *God*, I say, intended *sleepe* onely for the *refreshing* of man by bodily rest, and not for a *figure of death*, for he intended not *death* it selfe then. But *Man* having induced *death* upon himselfe, *God* hath taken *Mans Creature*, *death*, into his hand, and mended it; and whereas it hath in it selfe a fearefull forme and aspect, so that Man is afraid of his own *Creature*, *God* presents it to him, in a *familiar*, in an *assiduous*, in an *agreeable*, and *acceptable* forme, in *sleepe*, that so when hee awakes from *sleepe*, and saies to himselfe, shall I bee no otherwise when I am dead, than I was even now, when I was asleep, hee may bee ashamed of his waking *dreames*, and of his *Melancholique* fancying out a horrid and an affrightfull figure of that *death* which is so like sleepe. As then wee need *sleepe* to live out our *threescore and ten yeeres*, so we need *death*, to live that *life* which we cannot *out-live*. And as *death* being our *enemie*, *God* allowes us to defend our selves against it (for wee *victuall* our selves against *death*, *twice* every day, as often as we *eat*) so *God* having so sweetned *death* unto us, as hee hath in *sleepe*, wee put our selves into our *Enemies* hands *once* every day; so farre, as *sleepe* is *death*; and *sleepe* is as much *death*, as *meat* is *life*. This then is the *misery* of my *sicknesse*, That death as it is produced from mee, and is mine owne *Creature*, is now before mine *Eyes*, but in that forme, in which *God* hath mollified it to us, and made it acceptable, in *sleepe*, I cannot see it: how many *prisoners*, who have even hollowed themselves their *graves* upon that *Earth*, on which they have lien long under heavie fetters, yet at this *houre* are *asleepe*, though they bee yet working upon their owne *graves* by their owne *waight*? hee that hath seene his *friend* die to *day*, or knowes hee shall see it to *morrow*, yet will sinke into a sleepe betweene. I cannot; and oh, if I be entring now into *Eternitie*, where there shall bee no more distinction of *houres*, why is it al my businesse now *to tell Clocks*? why is none of the *heavinesse* of my *heart*, dispensed into mine *Eie-lids*, that they might fall as my heart doth? And why, since I have lost my delight in all *objects*, cannot I discontinue the facultie of seeing them, by closing mine *eies* in *sleepe*? But why rather being entring into that presence, where I shall wake continually and never sleepe more, doe I not interpret my continuall waking here, to bee a *parasceve*,[58] and a *preparation* to that?

16. ET PROPERARE MEUM   *From the bels of the Church*
CLAMANT, È TURRE PROPINQUA,   *adjoyning, I am daily*
OBSTREPERAE CAMPANAE ALIORUM   *remembred of my buriall in the*
IN FUNERE, FUNUS.   *funeralls of others.*[59]

16. MEDITATION

We have a *Convenient Author*, who writ a *Discourse of Bells* when hee
was Prisoner in *Turky*.[60] How would hee have enlarged[61] himselfe if
he had beene my *fellow Prisoner* in this *sicke bed*, so neere to that *steeple*,
which never ceases, no more than the *harmony of the spheres*, but is more
heard. When the *Turkes* took *Constantinople*, they melted the *Bells* into
Ordnance; I have heard both *Bells* and *Ordnance*, but never been so much
affected with those, as with these *Bells*. I have *lien* near a *steeple*, in which
there are said to be more than *thirty Bels*; And neere another, where
there is one so bigge, as that the *Clapper* is said to weigh more than *six
hundred pound*,[62] yet never so affected as here. Here the *Bells* can scarse
solemnise the funerall of any person, but that I knew him, or knew that
hee was my *Neighbour*: we dwelt in houses neere to one another before,
but now hee is gone into that house, into which I must follow him.
There is a way of correcting the *Children* of great persons, that other
Children are corrected in their *behalfe*, and in their *names*, and this workes
upon them, who indeed had more deserved it. And when these *Bells* tell
me, that now one, and now another is buried, must not I acknowledge,
that they have the *correction* due to me, and paid the *debt* that I owe?
There is a story[63] of a *Bell* in a *Monastery*, which, when any of the house
was sicke to death, rung alwaies *voluntarily*, and they knew the inevitablenesse of the danger by that. It rung once, when no man was sick;
but the next day one of the house, fell from the *steeple*, and died, and the
Bell held the reputation of a *Prophet* still. If these *Bells* that warne to a
Funerall now, were appropriated to none, may not I, by the houre of
the *funerall*, supply? How many men that stand at an *execution*, if they
would aske, for what dies that *Man*, should heare their owne faults
condemned, and see themselves executed, by *Atturney*? We scarce heare
of any man *preferred*, but wee thinke of our selves, that wee might very
well have beene that *Man*; Why might not I have beene that *Man*, that
is carried to his *grave* now? Could I fit my selfe, to *stand*, or *sit* in any
Mans *place*, and not to lie in any mans *grave*? I may lacke much of the

good parts of the meanest, but I lacke nothing of the *mortality* of the weakest; They may have acquired better *abilities* than I, but I was borne to as many *infirmities* as they. To be an *incumbent* by lying down in a *grave*, to be a *Doctor* by teaching *Mortification*[64] by *Example*, by *dying*, though I may have *seniors*, others may be *elder* than I, yet I have proceeded apace in a good *University*, and gone a great way in a little time, by the furtherance of a vehement *fever*; and whomsoever these *Bells* bring to the ground to day, if hee and I had beene compared yesterday, perchance I should have been thought likelier to come to this preferment, then, than he. *God* hath kept the power of *death* in his owne hands, lest any Man should *bribe death*. If man knew the *gaine of death*, the *ease of death*, he would solicite, he would provoke *death* to assist him, by any hand, which he might use.[65] But as when men see many of their owne professions preferd, it ministers a hope that they may light upon them; so when these hourley *Bells* tell me of so many *funerals* of men like me, it presents, if not a *desire* that it may, yet a *comfort* whensoever mine shall come.

17. NUNC LENTO SONITU   *Now, this Bell tolling softly for*
DICUNT, MORIERIS.   *another, saies to me, Thou must die.*

17. MEDITATION

Perchance hee for whom this *Bell* tolls, may bee so ill, as that he knowes not it *tolls* for him; And perchance I may thinke my selfe so much better than I am, as that they who are about mee, and see my state, may have caused it to toll for mee, and I know not that. The *Church* is *Catholike*, *universall*, so are all her *Actions*; *All* that she does, belongs to *all*. When she *baptizes a child*, that action concernes mee; for that child is thereby connected to that *Head* which is my *Head* too, and engraffed into that *body*, whereof I am a *member*. And when she *buries a Man*, that action concernes me: All *mankinde* is of one *Author*, and is one *volume*; when one Man dies, one *Chapter* is not *torne* out of the *booke*, but *translated* into a better *language*; and every *Chapter* must be so *translated*; *God* emploies several *translators*; some peeces are translated by *Age*, some by *sicknesse*, some by *warre*, some by *justice*; but *Gods* hand is in every *translation*; and his hand shall binde up all our scattered leaves againe, for that *Librarie* where every *booke* shall lie open to one another:[66] As therefore the *Bell* that rings to a *Sermon*, calls not upon the *Preacher* onely, but upon the *Congregation* to come; so this *Bell* calls us all: but how much more *mee*, who am brought so neere the *doore* by this *sicknesse*. There was a *contention* as farre as a *suite*,[67] (in which both *pietie* and *dignitie*, *religion*, and *estimation*, were mingled) which of the religious *Orders* should ring to *praiers* first in the *Morning*; and it was *determined*, that *they should ring first that rose earliest*. If we understand aright the *dignitie* of this *Bell*, that tolls for our *evening prayer*, wee would bee glad to make it ours, by rising early, in that *application*, that it might bee ours, as wel as his, whose indeed it is. The *Bell* doth toll for him that *thinkes* it doth; and though it *intermit* againe, yet from that *minute*, that that occasion wrought upon him, hee is united to *God*. Who casts not up his *Eie* to the *Sunne* when it rises? but who takes off his *Eie* from a *Comet* when that breakes out? who bends not his *eare* to any *bell*, which upon any occasion rings? but who can remove it from that *bell*, which is passing a *peece of himselfe* out of this *world*? No man is an *Iland*, intire of itselfe; every man is a peece of the *Continent*, a part of the *maine*; if a *Clod* bee washed away by the *Sea*, *Europe* is the lesse, as well as if a *Promontorie* were, as well as if a *Mannor* of thy *friends*, or of *thine owne* were; Any Mans *death* diminishes *me*, because I am involved in *Mankinde*; And therefore never send to know for whom the *bell* tolls; It tolls for *thee*. Neither can we call this a *begging* of *Miserie* or a *borrowing* of *Miserie*, as though we were not miserable enough of our selves, but must fetch in more from the next house, in taking upon us the *Miserie* of our *Neighbours*. Truly it were an excusable *covetousnesse* if wee did; for *affliction* is a *treasure;* and scarce any Man hath *enough* of it. No Man hath *affliction* enough, that is not matured, and ripened by it, and made fit for *God* by that *affliction*. If a man carry *treasure* in *bullion*, or in a *wedge* of *gold*, and have none coined into *currant Monies*, his *treasure* will not defray him as he travells. *Tribulation* is *Treasure* in the *nature* of it, but it is not *currant money* in the *use* of it, except wee get nearer and nearer our *home*, *heaven*, by it. Another Man may be *sicke* too, and sick to *death*, and this *affliction* may lie in his *bowels*, as *gold* in a *Mine*, and be of no use to him; but this *bell*, that tells me of his *affliction*, digs out, and applies that *gold* to *mee*: if by this consideration of anothers danger, I take mine owne into contemplation, and so secure my selfe, by making my recourse to my *God*, who is our onely *securitie*.

18. AT INDE MORTUUS
ES, SONITU CELERI,
PULSUQUE AGITATO.

The bell rings out,
and tells me in him,
that I am dead.

18. MEDITATION

The *Bell* rings out; the *pulse* thereof is changed; the *tolling* was a *faint*, and *intermitting pulse*, upon one side; this *stronger*, and argues *more* and *better life*. His *soule* is gone out; and as a Man who had a lease of 1000. *yeeres* after the expiration of a short one, or an inheritance after the *life* of a Man in a *Consumption*, he is now entred into the possession of his *better estate*. His *soule* is gone; *whither*? Who saw it *come in*, or who saw it *goe out*? *No body*; yet every body is sure, he *had one*, and *hath none*. If I will aske meere *Philosophers*, what the *soule* is, I shall finde amongst them, that will tell me, it is nothing, but the *temperament* and *harmony*, and *just and equall composition of the Elements in the body*, which produces all those *faculties* which we ascribe to the *soule*; and so, in it selfe is *nothing*, no *separable substance*, that overlives the *body*.[68] They see the *soule* is nothing else in other *Creatures*, and they affect an *impious humilitie*, to think *as low* of Man. But if my *soule* were no more than the soul of a *beast*, I could not thinke so; that *soule* that can *reflect* upon it selfe, *consider* it selfe, is *more* than so. If I will aske, not meere *Philosophers*, but *mixt* Men, *Philosophicall Divines*, how the *soule*, being a *separate substance*, enters into *Man*, I shall finde some that will tell me, that it is by *generation*, and *procreation* from *parents*,[69] because they thinke it hard, to charge the *soule* with the guiltinesse of *Originall* sinne, if the *soule* were infused into a *body*, in which it must necessarily grow *foule*, and contract *originall sinne*, whether it *will* or *no*; and I shall finde some that will tell mee, that it is by *immediate infusion from God*, because they think it hard, to maintaine an *immortality* in such a *soule*, as should be begotten, and derived with the *body* from *Mortall parents*. If I will aske, not *a few men*, but almost *whole bodies*, *whole Churches*, what becomes of the *soules* of the *righteous*, at the *departing* thereof from the *body*, I shall bee told by some, *That they attend an expiation, a purification in a place of torment*; By some, that *they attend the fruition of the sight of God, in a place of rest; but yet, but of expectation*; By some, that *they passe to an immediate possession of the presence of God*.[70] S. *Augustine* studied the *Nature* of the *soule*, as much as any thing, but the *salvation of the soule*; and he sent an expresse

Messenger to Saint *Hierome*, to consult of some things concerning the *soule*: But he satisfies himselfe with this: *Let the departure of my soule to salvation be evident to my faith, and I care the lesse, how darke the entrance of my soule, into my body, bee to my reason.* It is the *going out*, more than the *comming in*, that concernes us. This *soule*, this *Bell* tells me is *gone out*; *Whither*? Who shall tell mee that? I know not *who* it is; much lesse *what he was*; The condition of the Man, and the course of his life, which should tell mee *whither* hee is gone, I know not. I was not there, in his *sicknesse*, nor at his *death*; I saw not his *way*, nor his *end*, nor can aske them, who did, thereby to *conclude*, or *argue*, whither he is gone. But yet I have one neerer mee than all these; mine owne *Charity*; I aske that; and that tels me, *He is gone to everlasting rest,* and *joy*, and *glory*: I owe him a good *opinion*; it is but *thankfull charity* in mee, because I received *benefit* and *instruction* from him when his *Bell* told: and I, being made the fitter to *pray*, by that disposition, wherein I was assisted by his occasion, did *pray* for him; and I *pray* not without *faith*; so I doe *charitably*, so I do *faithfully* beleeve, that that *soule* is gone to everlasting *rest*, and *joy*, and *glory*. But for the *body*, How poore a wretched thing is *that*? wee cannot expresse it *so fast*, as it growes *worse* and *worse*. That *body* which scarce *three minutes* since was such a *house*, as that that *soule*, which made but one step from thence to *Heaven*, was scarse thorowly content, to leave that for *Heaven*: that *body* hath lost the *name* of a *dwelling house*, because none dwels in it, and is making haste to lose the name of a *body*, and dissolve to *putrefaction*. Who would not bee affected, to see a cleere and sweet *River* in the *Morning*, grow a *kennell*[71] of muddy land water by *noone*, and condemned to the saltnesse of the *Sea* by *night*? And how lame a *Picture*, how faint a *representation*, is that, of the precipitation of mans body to *dissolution*? *Now* all the parts built up, and knit by a lovely *soule*, *now* but a *statue* of *clay*, and *now*, these limbs melted off, as if that *clay* were but *snow*; and now, the whole *house* is but a *handfull of sand*, so much *dust*, and but a *pecke* of *Rubbidge*, so much *bone*. If *he*, who, as this *Bell* tells mee, is gone now, were some *excellent Artificer*, who comes to him for a *cloke*, or for a *garment* now? or for *counsaile*, if hee were a *Lawyer*? If a *Magistrate*, for *justice*? Man before hee hath his *immortall soule*, hath a *soule of sense*, and a *soule of vegitation* before that:[72] This *immortall soule* did not forbid other *soules*, to be in us before, but when this *soule* departs, it carries all with it; no more *vegetation*, no more *sense*: such a *Mother in law* is the *Earth*, in respect of our *naturall Mother*; in her *wombe* we *grew*; and when she was delivered of us, wee were planted in some *place*, in some *calling* in the *world*; In the wombe of the Earth, wee *diminish*, and when shee is *delivered* of us, our *grave* opened for another, wee are not *transplanted*, but *transported*, our *dust* blowne away with *prophane dust*, with every wind.

| 19. OCEANO TANDEM EMENSO, ASPICIENDA RESURGIT TERRA; VIDENT, JUSTIS, MEDICI, JAM COCTA MEDERI SE POSSE, INDICIIS. | *At last, the Physitians, after a long and stormie voyage, see land; They have so good signes of the concoction* [73] *of the disease, as that they may safely proceed to purge.* |

19. MEDITATION

All this while the *Physitians* themselves have been *patients*, patiently attending when they should see any land in this *Sea*, any *earth*, any *cloud*, any *indication* of *concoction* in these *waters*. Any *disorder* of mine, any *pretermission* of theirs, exalts the disease, accelerates the rages of it; no *diligence* accelerates the *concoction*, the *maturitie* of the *disease*; they must stay till the *season* of the sicknesse come, and till it be ripened of it selfe, and then they may put to their hand, to *gather* it, before it *fall* off, but they cannot hasten the *ripening*. Why should wee looke for it in a *disease*, which is the *disorder*, the *discord*, the *irregularitie*, the *commotion*, and *rebellion* of the *body*? It were scarce a *disease*, if it could bee *ordered*, and made obedient to our *times*. Why should wee looke for that in *disorder*, in a *disease*, when we cannot have it in *Nature*, who is so *regular*, and so *pregnant*, so forward to bring her *worke* to perfection, and to light? yet we cannot awake the *July-flowers* in *January*, nor retard the *flowers* of the *spring* to *Autumne*. We cannot bid the *fruits* come in *May*, nor the *leaves* to *sticke* on in *December*. A *woman* that is weake, cannot put off her *ninth moneth* to a *tenth*, for her *deliverie*, and say shee will stay till shee bee *stronger*; nor a *Queene* cannot hasten it to a *seventh*, that shee may bee ready for some other pleasure. *Nature* (if we looke for *durable* and *vigorous* effects) will not admit *preventions*, nor *anticipations*, nor *obligations* [74] upon her; for they are *precontracts*, and she will bee left to her *libertie*. *Nature* would not be spurred, nor forced to mend her pace; nor *power*, the *power of man*; *greatnesse* loves not that kinde of *violence* neither. There are of *them* that will *give*, that will doe *justice*, that will *pardon*, but they have their owne *seasons* for al these, and he that knowes not *them*, shall *starve* before that gift come, and *ruine*, before the Justice, and *dye* before the pardon save him: some *tree* beares no fruit, except much *dung* be laid about it; and *Justice* comes not from some, till they bee richly manured: some *trees* require much *visiting*, much *watring*, much *labour*; and some men give not their *fruits* but upon *importunitie*; some *trees* require *incision*, and *pruning*, and *lopping*; some men must bee *intimidated* and *syndicated* with *Commissions*,[75] before they will deliver the fruits of *Justice*; some *trees* require the *early* and the *often* accesse of the *Sunne*; some men *open* not, but upon the *favours* and *letters* of *Court mediation*; some trees must bee *housd* and kept within doores; some men locke up, not onely their liberalitie, but their *Justice*, and their *compassion*, till the sollicitation of a *wife*, or a *sonne*, or a *friend*, or a *servant* turne the *key*. *Reward* is the *season* of one man, and *importunitie* of another; *feare* the *season* of one man, and *favour* of another; *friendship* the *season* of one man, and *naturall affection* of another; and hee that knowes not their *seasons*, nor cannot *stay* them, must lose the *fruits*; As *Nature* will not, so *power* and *greatnesse* will not bee put to change their *seasons*; and shall wee looke for this *Indulgence* in a *disease*, or thinke to shake it off before it bee *ripe*? All this while, therefore, we are but upon a *defensive warre*, and that is but a *doubtfull state*; Especially where they who are *besieged* doe know the *best* of their *defences*, and doe not know the *worst* of their *enemies power*; when they cannot mend their *works within*, and the *enemie* can increase his *numbers without*. O how many farre more miserable, and farre more worthy to be lesse miserable than I, are besieged with this *sicknesse*, and lacke their *Sentinels*, their *Physitians* to *watch*. and lacke *munition*, their *cordials* to *defend*, and perish before the *enemies* weaknesse might invite them to *sally*, before the *disease* shew any *declination*, or admit any way of *working* upon it selfe? In me the *siege* is so farre slackned, as that we may come to *fight*, and so die in the *field*, if I *die*, and not in a *prison*.

20. ID AGUNT.   *Upon these Indications of digested*
                                 matter, they proceed to purge.

20. MEDITATION

Though *counsel* seeme rather to consist of *spirituall parts*, than *action*, yet *action* is the *spirit* and the *soule* of *counsell*. *Counsels* are not alwaies determined in *Resolutions*; wee cannot alwaies say, *this was concluded*; *actions* are alwaies determined in *effects*; wee can say *this was done*. Then have *Lawes* their *reverence*, and their *majestie*, when wee see the *Judge* upon the *Bench* executing them. Then have *counsels of warre* their *impressions*, and their *operations*, when we see the *seale* of an *Armie* set to them. It was an ancient way of celebrating the *memorie* of such as deserved well of the *State*, to afford them that kinde of *statuarie representation*, which was then called *Hermes*;[76] which was, *the head and shoulders of a man, standing upon a Cube*, but those *shoulders* without *armes* and *hands*. All together it figured a *constant supporter of the state*, by his *counsell*: But in this *Hierogliphique*, which they made without *hands*, they passe their consideration no farther, but that the *Counsellor* should bee without *hands*, so farre as *not to reach out his hand to forraigne tentations of bribes, in matters of Counsell*, and, that it was not necessary, that the *head* should employ *his owne hand*; that *the same men* should serve in the *execution*, which assisted in the *Counsell*; but that there should not belong *hands* to every *head*, *action* to every *counsell*, was never intended, so much as in *figure*, and *representation*. For, as *matrimonie* is scarce to bee called *matrimonie*, where there is a *resolution* against the *fruits of matrimonie*, against the having of *Children*, so *counsels* are not *counsels*, but *illusions*, where there is from the beginning no purpose to execute the determinations of those *counsels*. The *arts* and *sciences* are most properly referred to the *head*; that is their proper *Element* and *Spheare*; But yet the *art of proving*, *Logique*, and the *art of perswading*, *Rhetorique*, are deduced to the *hand*, and *that* expressed by a *hand* contracted into a *fist*, and *this* by a *hand* enlarged, and expanded;[77] and evermore the *power of man*, and the *power of God* himselfe is expressed so, *All things are in his hand*;[78] neither is *God* so often presented to us, by names that carry our consideration upon *counsell*, as upon *execution* of *counsell*; he is oftner called the *Lord of Hosts*, than by all other *names*, that may be referred to the other signification. Hereby therefore wee take into our *meditation*, the slipperie condition of *man*, whose *happinesse*, in any kinde, the defect of *any one thing*, conducing to that *happinesse*, may *ruine*; but it must have *all the peeces* to make it up. Without *counsell*, I had not got thus farre; without *action* and *practise*, I should goe no farther towards *health*. But what is the present necessary *action*? purging: A *withdrawing*, a violating of *Nature*, a *farther weakening*: O *deare price*, and O *strange* way of *addition*, to doe it by *substraction*; of *restoring* Nature, to *violate Nature*; of *providing strength*, by *increasing weaknesse*. Was I not *sicke* before? And is it a *question* of *comfort* to be asked now, Did *your Physicke make you sicke*? Was that it that my *Physicke* promised, to make me *sicke*? This is another *step*, upon which we may stand, and see farther into the *miserie of man*, the *time*, the *season* of his *Miserie*; It must bee done *now*: O *over-cunning, over-watchfull, over-diligent*, and *over-sociable misery of man*, that seldome comes alone, but then when it may accompanie other *miseries*, and so put one another into the higher *exaltation*, and better *heart*. I am ground even to an *attentuation*, and must proceed to *evacuation*, all waies to exinanition and annihilation.[79]

21. ATQUE ANNUIT ILLE, QUI,   *God prospers their practise, and*
PER EOS, CLAMAT, LINQUAS   *he, by them, calls* Lazarus *out*
JAM, LAZARE, LECTUM.   *of his tombe, mee out of my bed.*

21. MEDITATION

If man had beene left *alone* in this *world*, at first, shall I thinke, that he would not have *fallen*? If there had beene no *Woman*, would not *Man* have served, to have beene his own *Tempter*? When I see him now, subject to infinite weakenesses, fall into *infinite sinne*, without any *forraine tentations*, shall I thinke, hee would have had *none*, if hee had beene *alone*? GOD saw that Man needed a *Helper*, if hee should bee well; but to make *Woman* ill, the *Devill* saw, that there needed no *third*. When *God*, and *wee* were *alone*, in *Adam*, that was not enough; when the *Devill* and wee were *alone*, in *Eve*, it was enough. O what a *Giant* is *Man*, when hee fights against himselfe, and what a *dwarfe* when hee *needs*, or *exercises* his owne assistance for himselfe? I cannot *rise* out of my bed, till the *Physitian enable* mee, nay I cannot tel, that I am able to rise, till *hee tell* me so. I doe nothing, I *know* nothing of my selfe: how little, and how impotent a peece of the *world*, is any *Man* alone? and how much lesse a peece of *himselfe* is *that Man*? So little, as that when it falls out, (as it falls out in some cases) that more *misery*, and more *oppression*, would bee an *ease* to a *man*, he cannot give himselfe that *miserable addition*, of *more misery*; A man that is *pressed to death*,[80] and might be eased by more *weights*, cannot lay those more *weights* upon himselfe: Hee can sinne *alone*, and suffer *alone*, but not *repent*, not bee *absolved*, without *another*. Another tels mee, *I may rise*; and *I doe* so. But is every *raising* a *preferment*?

or is every present *preferment* a *station*? I am readier to fall to the *Earth* now I am up, than I was when I *lay* in the bed: O *perverse way, irregular motion* of *Man*; even *rising* it selfe is the way to *Ruine*. How many *men* are raised, and then doe not *fill* the place they are raised to? No *corner* of any place can bee *empty*; there can be no *vacuity*; If that *Man* doe not fill the place, *other men* will; complaints of his *insufficiency* will *fill* it; Nay, such an abhorring is there in *Nature*, of *vacuity*, that if there be but an *imagination* of not *filling*, in any *man*, that which is but *imagination* neither, will *fill* it, that is, *rumor* and *voice*, and it will be *given out*, (upon no ground, but *Imagination*, and no man knowes, *whose imagination*) that hee is *corrupt* in his place, or *insufficient* in his place, and another prepared to *succeed* him in his place. A man *rises*, sometimes, and *stands* not, because hee doth not, or is not beleeved to *fill* his place; and sometimes he *stands* not, because hee *over-fills* his place: Hee may bring so much *vertue*, so much *Justice*, so much *integrity* to the place, as shall *spoile* the place, *burthen* the place; his *integrity* may bee a *Libell* upon his *Predecessor*, and cast an *infamy* upon him, and a *burden* upon his *successor*, to proceede by *example*, and to bring the place it-selfe to an *under-value*, and the *market* to an *uncertainty*. I am *up*, and I seeme to *stand*, and I goe *round*; and I am a *new Argument* of the *new Philosophie*, That the *Earth* moves round;[81] why may I not beleeve, that the *whole earth* moves in a *round motion*, though that seeme to mee to *stand*, when as I seeme to *stand* to my *Company*, and yet am carried in a giddy, and *circular motion*, as I *stand*? Man hath no *center*, but *misery*; *there* and onely *there*, hee is *fixt*, and sure to finde himselfe. How little soever he bee *raised*, he *moves*, and moves in a *circle*, giddily; and as in the *Heavens*, there are but a few *Circles*, that goe about the whole world,[82] but many *Epicircles*, and other lesser *Circles*, but yet *Circles*, so of those men, which are *raised*, and put into *Circles*, few of them move from *place* to *place*, and passe through many and beneficiall places, but fall into little *Circles*, and within a step or two, are at their *end*, and not so well, as they were in the *Center*, from which they were *raised*. Every thing serves to *exemplifie*, to *illustrate* mans *misery*; But I need goe no farther, than *my selfe*; for a long time, I was not able to *rise*; At last, I must bee *raised* by others; and now I am up, I am ready to sinke *lower* than before.

22. SIT MORBI FOMES
TIBI CURA;

The Physitians consider the root and
occasion, the embers, and coales, and
fuell of the disease, and seeke to purge
or correct that.

22. MEDITATION

How *ruinous* a *farme* hath *man* taken, in taking *himselfe*? how ready is the *house* every day to fall downe, and how is all the *ground* over-spread with *weeds*, all the *body* with *diseases*? where not onely every *turfe*, but every *stone*, beares *weeds*; not onely every *muscle* of the *flesh*, but every *bone* of the *body*, hath some *infirmitie*; every little *flint* upon the *face* of this *soile*, hath some *infectious weede*, every *tooth* in our *head*, such a *paine*, as a *constant man* is afraid of, and yet *ashamed* of that *feare*, of that sense of the paine. How *deare*, and how *often* a *rent* doth Man pay for this *farme*? hee paies *twice a day*, in double *meales*, and how little time he hath to *raise his rent*? How many *holy daies* to call him from his *labour*? Every day is *halfe-holy day*, halfe spent in *sleepe*. What *reparations*, and *subsidies*, and *contributions* he is put to, besides his *rent*? What *medicines*, besides his *diet*? and what *Inmates* he is faine to take in, besides his owne *familie*, what infectious diseases, *from other* men. *Adam* might have had *Paradise* for *dressing* and *keeping* it; and *then* his *rent* was not *improved* to such a *labour*, as would have made his *brow sweat*; and yet he gave it over; how farre greater a *rent* doe wee pay for this *farme*, this *body*, who pay *our selves*, who pay the *farme it selfe*, and cannot *live* upon it? Neither is our *labour* at an end, when wee have cut downe some *weed*, as soon as it sprung up, corrected some *violent* and dangerous *accident* of a *disease*, which would have destroied *speedily*; nor when wee have pulled up that *weed*, from the very *root*, recovered *entirely* and *soundly*, from that *particular disease*; but the whole *ground* is of an *ill nature*, the whole soile *ill disposed*; there are inclinations, there is a *propensnesse* to *diseases* in the *body*, out of which without any other *disorder*, *diseases* will grow, and so wee are put to a continuall labour upon this *farme*, to a continuall studie of the whole *complexion* and *constitution* of our *body*. In the *distempers* and *diseases* of *soiles*, *sourenesse*, *drinesse*, *weeping*, any kinde of *barrennesse*, the *remedy* and the *physicke*, is, for a great part, sometimes in *themselves*; sometimes the very *situation* releeves them, the *hanger*[83] of a *hill*, will purge and vent his owne *malignant moisture*; and the burning of the upper *turfe* of some ground (as *health* from *cauterizing*) puts a *new* and a *vigorous youth* into that *soile*, and there rises a kinde of *Phoenix* out of the *ashes*, a *fruitfulnesse* out of that which was *barren* before, and *by that*, which is the barrennest of all, *ashes*. And where the *ground* cannot give it selfe *physicke*, yet it receives *Physicke* from other grounds, from other soiles, which are not the worse, for having contributed that helpe to them, from *Marle*[84] in other *hils*, or from *slimie sand* in other *shoares*: grounds helpe *themselves*, or hurt not other *grounds*, from whence they receive *helpe*. But I have taken a *farme* at this *hard rent*, and upon those *heavie covenants*, that it can afford it selfe no *helpe*; (no part of my *body*, if it were cut off, would *cure* another part; in some cases it might *preserve* a sound part, but in no case *recover* an infected) and, if my *body* may have any *Physicke*, any *Medicine* from another *body*, one *Man* from the flesh of another *Man* (as by Mummy,[85] or any such *composition*,) it must bee from a man that is dead, and not, as in other *soiles*, which are never the worse for contributing their *Marle*, or their fat slime to my *ground*. There is nothing in the same *man*, to helpe *man*, nothing in *mankind* to helpe *one another* (in this sort, by way of *Physicke*) but that hee who *ministers* the *helpe*, is in as ill case, as he that *receives* it would have beene, if he had not had it; for hee, from whose *body* the *Physicke* comes, is *dead*. When therefore I took this *farme*, undertooke this body, I undertooke to *draine*, not a *marish*, but a *moat*, where there was, not water *mingled* to offend, but all was *water*; I undertooke to *perfume dung*, where no one part, but all was equally *unsavory*; I undertooke to make such a thing *wholsome*, as was not *poison* by any manifest quality, *intense heat*, or *cold*, but *poison* in the *whole substance*, and in the *specifique forme* of it. To cure the *sharpe accidents* of *diseases*, is a great *worke*; to cure the *disease it selfe* is a greater; but to cure the *body*, the *root*, the *occasion* of *diseases*, is a worke reserved for the great *Phisitian*, which he doth never any other way, but by *glorifying* these *bodies* in the next world.[86]

23. METUSQUE, RELABI.   *They warne mee of the fearefull danger of relapsing.*[87]

23. MEDITATION

It is not in *mans body*, as it is in the *Citie*, that when *the Bell* hath rung, to cover your *fire*,[88] and rake up the *embers*, you may lie downe, and sleepe without feare. Though you have by *physicke* and *diet*, raked up the *embers* of your *disease*, stil there is a feare of a *relapse*; and the greater *danger* is in that. Even in *pleasures*, and in *paines*, there is a *propriety*, a *Meum & Tuum*; and a man is most affected with that *pleasure* which is *his*, *his* by former enjoying and experience, and most intimidated with those *paines* which are *his*, *his* by a wofull sense of them, in former afflictions. A *covetous* person, who hath preoccupated all his senses, filled all his capacities, with the *delight* of *gathering*, wonders how any man can have *any taste* of *any pleasure* in *any opennesse*, or *liberalitie*; So also in *bodily paines*, in a fit of the *stone*, the patient wonders why any man should call the *Gout* a *paine*: And hee that hath felt neither, but the *tooth-ach*, is as much afraid of a fit of that, as either of the other, of either of the other. *Diseases*, which we never *felt* in our selves, come but to a *compassion* of others that have endured them; Nay, *compassion* it selfe, comes to no great *degree*, if wee have not *felt*, in some *proportion*, in *our selves*, that which wee lament and condole in another. But when wee have had those torments in their *exaltation*, *our selves*, wee tremble at a relapse. When wee must *pant* through all those *fierie heats*, and *saile* thorow all those *overflowing sweats*, when wee must *watch* through all those long *nights*, and *mourne* through all those long *daies*, (*daies* and *nights*, so *long*, as that *Nature* her selfe shall seeme to be *perverted*, and to have put the *longest day*, and the *longest night*, which should bee *six moneths* asunder, into one *naturall, unnaturall day*) [89] when wee must stand at the same *barre*, expect the returne of *Physitians* from their *consultations*, and not bee sure of the same *verdict*, in any good *Indications*, when we must goe the same *way* over againe, and not see the same *issue*, this is a *state*, a *condition*, a *calamitie*, in respect of which, any other *sicknesse*, were a *convalescence*, and any *greater*, *lesse*. It adds to the *affliction*, that *relapses* are, (and for the most part justly) imputed to *our selves*, as occasioned by some *disorder* in us; and so we are not onely *passive*, but *active*, in our owne *ruine*; we doe not onely stand under a *falling house*, but *pull* it downe upon us; and wee are not onely *executed*, (that implies *guiltinesse*) but wee are *executioners*, (that implies *dishonor*) and *executioners* of *our selves*, (and that implies *impietie*.) And wee fall from that *comfort* which wee might have in our first *sicknesse*, from that *meditation*, *Alas, how generally miserable is Man, and how subject to diseases*, (for in that it is some degree of *comfort*, that wee are but in the state *common* to all) we fall, I say, to this *discomfort*, and *selfe accusing*, and *selfe condemning*; *Alas, how unprovident, and in that, how unthankfull to God and his instruments am I, in making so ill use of so great benefits, in destroying so soone, so long a worke, in relapsing, by my disorder, to that from which they had delivered mee;* and so my *meditation* is fearefully transferred from the *body* to the *minde*, and from the consideration of the *sicknesse* to *that sinne*, that sinful *carelessnes*, by which I have occasioned my *relapse*. And amongst the many *weights* that aggravate a *relapse*, this also is one, that a *relapse* proceeds with a more violent dispatch, and more *irremediably*, because it finds the *Countrie weakned*, and *depopulated* before. Upon a *sicknesse*, which as yet appeares not, wee can scarce fix a *feare*, because wee know not what to feare; but as *feare* is the *busiest* and *irksomest affection*, so is a *relapse* (which is still *ready to come*) into that, which is but newly gone, the *nearest object*, the *most immediate* exercise of that *affection* of *feare*.

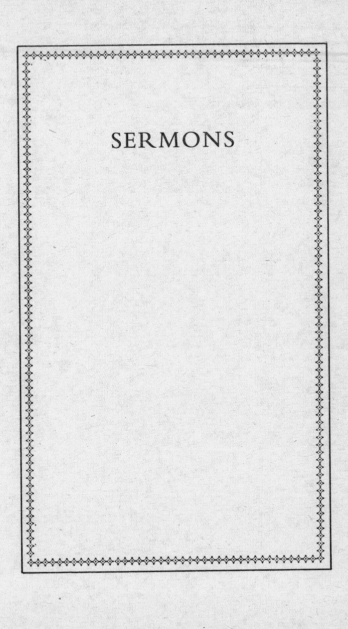

SERMONS

1. FROM A SERMON PREACHED AT WHITE-HALL, 21 APRIL 1616[1]

How desperate a state art thou in, if nothing will convert thee, but a speedie execution, after which, there is no possibility, no room left for a Conversion? God is *the Lord of hosts,* and he can proceed by Martial Law: he can hang thee upon the next tree; he can choak thee with a crum, with a drop, at a voluptuous feast; he can sink down the Stage and the Player, The bed of wantonness, and the wanton actor, into the jaws of the earth, into the mouth of hell: he can surprise thee, even in the act of sin; and dost thou long for such a speedy execution, for such an expedition? Thou canst not lack Examples, that he hath done so upon others, and will no proof serve thee, but a speedy judgement upon thy self? Scatter thy thoughts no farther then, contract them in thy self, and consider Gods speedy execution upon thy soul, and upon thy body, and upon thy soul and body together. Was not Gods judgement executed speedily enough upon thy soul, when in the same instant that it was created, and conceiv'd, and infus'd, it was put to a necessity of contracting Original sin, and so submitted to the penalty of *Adam's* disobedience, the first minute? Was not Gods judgement speedily enough executed upon thy body, if before it had any temporal life, it had a spiritual death; a sinful conception, before any inanimation? If hereditary diseases from thy parents, Gouts and Epilepsies, were in thee, before the diseases of thine own purchase, the effects of thy licentiousness and thy riot; and that from the first minute that thou beganst to live, thou beganst to die too? Are not the judgements of God speedily enough executed upon thy soul and body together, every day, when as soon as thou commitst a sin, thou art presently left to thine Impenitence, to thine Insensibleness, and Obduration?[2] Nay, the judgement is more speedy than so: for, that very sin it self, was a punishment of thy former sins.

2. FROM A SERMON PREACHED AT PAULS
CROSS, 24 MARCH 1617[3]

Love, in Divinity, is such an attribute, or such a notion, as designs to us one person in the Trinity; and that person who communicates, and applies to us, the other two persons, that is, *The Holy Ghost:* So that, as there is no *power,* but with relation to the *Father,* nor *wisdom* but with relation to the *Son,* so there should be no *love* but in the *Holy Ghost,* from whom comes this pureness of heart, and consequently the love of it necessarily: For, the love of this pureness is part of this pureness it self, and no man hath it, except he love it. All love which is placed upon lower things, admits satiety; but this love of this pureness, always grows, always proceeds: It does not onely file off the rust of our hearts,[4] in purging us of old habits, but proceeds to a daily polishing of the heart, in an exact watchfulness, and brings us to that brightness, *Ut ipse videas faciem in corde, & alii videant cor in facie,* That thou maist see thy face in thy heart, and the world may see thy heart in thy face; indeed, that to both, both heart and face may be all one: Thou shalt be a Looking-glass to thy self, and to others too.

The highest degree of other love, is the love of woman: Which love, when it is rightly placed upon one woman, it is dignified by the Apostle with the highest comparison, *Husbands love your wives, as Christ loved his Church:* And God himself forbad not that this love should be great enough to change natural affection, *Relinquet patrem,* (for this, a man shall leave his Father) yea, to change nature it self, *caro una,* two shall be one. Accordingly *David* expresses himself so, in commemoration of *Jonathan, Thy love to me was wonderful, passing the love of women:* A love above that love, is wonderful. Now, this love between man and woman, doth so much confess a satiety, as that if a woman think to hold a man long, she provides herself some other capacity, some other title, than meerly as she is a woman: Her wit, and her conversation, must continue this love; and she must be a *wife,* a *helper;* else, meerly as a woman, this love must necessarily have intermissions. And therefore St *Jerome* notes a custom of his time, (perchance prophetically enough of our times too) that to uphold an unlawful love, and make it continue, they used to call one another *Friend,* and *Sister,* and *Cousen, Ut etiam peccatis induant nomina caritatis,* that they might apparel ill affections in good names; and those names of natural and civil love might carry on, and continue a work, which otherwise would sooner have withered. In Parables, and in Mythology, and in the application of Fables, this affection of love, for the often change of subjects, is described to have *wings;* whereas the true nature of a good love (such as the love of this Text) is a constant union. But our love of earthly things is not so good as to be *volatilis,* apt to fly; for it is always groveling upon the earth, and earthly objects: As in spiritual fornications, the Idols are said to have ears and hear not, and eyes and see not; so in this idolatrous love of the Creature, love hath wings, and flies not; it flies not upward, it never ascends to the contemplation of the Creator, in the Creature. The *Poets* afford us but one Man, that in his love flew so high as the Moon; *Endymion* loved the Moon. The sphear of our loves is sublunary, upon things naturally inferior to our selves.[5]

Let none of this be so mistaken, as though women were thought improper for divine, or for civil conversation: For, they have the same soul; and of their good using the faculties of that soul, the Ecclesiastick story, and the Martyrologies, give us abundant examples of great things done, and suffered by women for the advancement of Gods glory: But yet, as when the woman was taken out of man, God caused a heavy sleep to fall upon man, and he slept; so doth the Devil cast a heavy sleep upon him too, when the woman is so received into man again, as that she possesses him, fills him, transports him.[6] I know the Fathers are frequent in comparing and paralleling *Eve,* the Mother of Man, and *Mary* the Mother of God. But, God forbid any should say, That the Virgin *Mary* concurred to our good, so, as *Eve* did to our ruine. It is said truly, *That as by one man sin entred, and death,* so by one man entred life. It may be said, *That by one woman sin entred, and death,* (and that rather than by the man; for, *Adam was not deceived, but the woman being deceived, was in the transgression.*) But it cannot be said, in that sense, or that manner, that by one woman innocence entred, and life: The Virgin *Mary* had not the same interest in our salvation, as *Eve* had in our destruction; nothing that she did entred into that treasure, that ransom that redeemed us.

3. FROM A SERMON PREACHED TO QUEEN ANNE, AT DENMARK-HOUSE, 14 DECEMBER 1617[7]

I

As the Prophets, and the other Secretaries of the holy Ghost in penning the books of Scriptures, do for the most part retain, and express in their writings some impressions, and some air of their former professions; those that had been bred in Courts and Cities, those that had been Shepheards and Heardsmen, those that had been Fishers, and so of the rest; ever inserting into their writings some phrases, some metaphors, some allusions, taken from that profession which they had exercised before; so that soul, that hath been transported upon any particular worldly pleasure, when it is intirely turn'd upon God, and the contemplation of his all-sufficiency and abundance, doth find in God fit subject, and just occasion to exercise the same affection piously, and religiously, which had before so sinfully transported, and possest it.

A covetous person, who is now truly converted to God, he will exercise a spiritual covetousness still, he will desire to have him all,[8] he will have good security, the seal and assurance of the holy Ghost; and he will have his security often renewed by new testimonies, and increases of those graces in him; he will have witnesses enough; he will have the testimonie of all the world, by his good life and conversation; he will gain every way at Gods hand, he will have wages of God, for he will be his servant; he will have a portion from God, for he will be his Son; he will have a reversion, he will be sure that his name is in the book of life; he will have pawns, the seals of the Sacraments, nay, he will have a present possession; all that God hath promised, all that Christ hath purchased, all that the holy Ghost hath the stewardship and dispensation of, he will have all in present, by the appropriation and investiture of an actual and applying faith; a covetous person converted will be spiritually covetous still.

So will a voluptuous man, who is turned to God, find plenty and deliciousnes enough in him, to feed his soul, as with marrow, and with fatness, as *David* expresses it; and so an angry and passionate man, will find zeal enough in the house of God to eat him up.

All affections which are common to all men, and those too, which in particular, particular men have been addicted unto, shall not only be justly employed upon God, but also securely employed, because we cannot exceed, nor go too far in imploying them upon him. According to this Rule, St *Paul,* who had been so vehement a persecutor, had ever his thoughts exercised upon that; and thereupon after his conversion, he fulfils the rest of the sufferings of Christ in his flesh, he suffers most, he makes most mention of his suffering of any of the Apostles.

And according to this Rule too, *Salomon,* whose disposition was amorous, and excessive in the love of women, when he turn'd to God, he departed not utterly from his old phrase and language, but having put a new, and a spiritual tincture, and form and habit into all his thoughts, and words, he conveyes all his loving approaches and applications to God, and all Gods gracious answers to his amorous soul, into songs, and Epithalamions, and meditations upon contracts, and marriages between God and his Church, and between God and his soul; as we see so evidently in all his other writings, and particularly in this text, *I love them, &c.*

In which words is expressed all that belongs to love, all which, is to desire, and to enjoy; for to desire without fruition, is a rage,[9] and to enjoy without desire is a stupidity: In the first alone we think of nothing, but that which we then would have; and in the second alone, we are not for that, when we have it; in the first, we are without it; in the second, we are as good as if we were without it, for we have no pleasure in it; nothing then can give us satisfaction, but where those two concurr, *amare* and *frui,* to love and to enjoy.

In sensual love it is so; *Quid erat quod me delectabat nisi amare et amari?* I took no joy in this world, but in loving, and in being beloved;[10] in sensual love it is so, but in sensual love, when we are come so far, there is no satisfaction in that; the same Father confesseth more of himself, than any Commission, any oath would have put him to, *Amatus sum, et perveni occulte ad fruendum,* I had all I desir'd, and I had it with that advantage of having it secretly; but what got I by all that, *Ut cæderer virgis ardentibus ferreis, zeli suspicionis et rixarum;* nothing but to be scourg'd with burning iron rods, rods of jealousie, of suspition, and of quarrels; but in the love and enjoying of this text, there is no room for Jealousie, nor suspition, nor quarrelsome complaining.

2

But can we love God when we will? do we not find, that in the love of some other things, or some courses of life, of some waies in our actions, and of some particular persons, that we would fain love them, and cannot? when we can object nothing against it, when we can multiply arguments, why we should love them, yet we cannot: but it is not so towards God; every man may love him, that will; but can every man have this will, this desire? certainly we cannot begin this love; except God love us first, we cannot love him; but God doth love us all so well, from the beginning, as that every man may see the fault was in the perversness of his own will, that he did not love God better. If we look for the root of this love, it is in the Father; for, though the death of Christ be towards us, as a root, as a cause of our love, and of the acceptableness of it, yet, *Meritum Christi est effectus amoris Dei erga nos,* the death of Christ was but an effect of the love of God towards us, *So God loved the world that he gave his Son:* if he had not lov'd us first, we had never had his Son; here is the root then, the love of the Father, and the tree, the merit of the Son; except there be fruit too, love in us, to them again, both root and tree will wither in us, howsoever they grew in God. *I have loved thee with an everlasting love,* (saies God) *therfore with mercy I have drawn thee,* if therefore we do not perceive, that we are drawn to love again by this love, 'tis not an everlasting love, that shines upon us.

All the sunshine, all the glory of this life, though all these be testimonies of Gods love to us, yet all these bring but a winters day, a short day, and a cold day, and a dark day,[11] for except we love too, God doth not love with an everlasting love: God will not suffer his love to be idle, and since it profits him nothing, if it profits us nothing neither, he will withdraw it; *Amor Dei ut lumen ignis, ut splendor solis, ut odor lucis, non praebenti proficit, sed utenti,* The sun hath no benefit by his own light, nor the fire by his own heat, nor a perfume by the sweetness thereof, but only they who make their use, and enjoy this heat and fragrancy.

4. FROM A SERMON PREACHED AT
LINCOLNS INNE [SPRING OR SUMMER 1618][12]

And then, these arrows *stick in us;* the raine fals, but that cold sweat hangs not upon us; Hail beats us, but it leaves no pock-holes in our skin. These arrows doe not so fall about us, as that they misse us; nor so hit us, as they rebound back without hurting us; But we complain with *Jeremy, The sons of his quiver are entred into our reins.* The Roman Translation reads that *filias, The daughters of his quiver;* If it were but so, *daughters,* we might limit these arrows in the signification of *tentations,* by the many occasions of tentation, arising from *that sex.* But the Originall hath it *filios,* the sons of his quiver, and therefore we consider these arrows in a stronger signification, *tribulations,* as well as *tentations; They stick in us.* Consider it but in one kinde, *diseases,* sicknesses. They stick to us so, as that we are not sure, that any old diseases mentioned in Physicians books are worn out, but that every year produces *new,* of which they have no mention, we are sure. We can scarce expresse the number, scarce sound the names of the diseases of mans body; 6000 year hath scarce taught us what they are, how they affect us, how they shall be cur'd in us, nothing, on this side the *Resurrection,* can teach us. They stick to us so, as that they passe by *inheritance,* and last more generations in families, than the inheritance it self does; and when no land, no Manor, when no title, no honour descends upon the heir, the stone, or the gout descends upon him. And as though our bodies had not *naturally diseases,* and infirmities enow, we contract more, inflict more, (and that, out of necessity too) in *mortifications,* and *macerations,* and *Disciplines* of this rebellious flesh. I must have this body with me to heaven, or else salvation it self is not perfect; And yet I cannot have this body thither, except as S. *Paul* did his, *I beat down this body,* attenuate this body by mortification; *Wretched man that I am, who shall deliver me from this body of death?* I have not body enough for my body, and I have too much body for my soul; not body enough, not bloud enough, not strength enough, to sustain my self in *health,* and yet body enough to destroy my soul, and frustrate the grace of God in that miserable, perplexed, riddling condition of man; sin makes the body of man miserable, and the remedy of sin, *mortification,* makes it miserable too; If we enjoy the good things of this world, *Duriorem carcerem praeparamus,* wee doe but carry an other wall about our prison, an other story of unwieldy flesh about our souls; and if wee give our selves as much *mortification* as our body needs, we live a life of *Fridays,* and see no *Sabbath,* we make up our years of *Lents,* and see no other *Easters,* and whereas God meant us *Paradise,* we make all the world a *wildernesse.* Sin hath cast a curse upon all the creatures of the world, they are all worse than they were at first, and yet we dare not receive so much blessing, as is left in the creature, we dare not eat or drink, and enjoy them. The *daughters* of Gods quiver, and the *sons* of his quiver, the arrows of *tentation,* and the arrows of *tribulation,* doe so stick in us, that as he lives miserably, that lives in *sicknes,* and he as miserably, that lives in *physick:* so *plenty* is a misery, and *mortification* is a misery too; plenty, if we consider it in the *effects,* is a *disease,* a continuall sicknes, for it breeds diseases; And *mortification,* if we should consider it without the *effects,* is a disease too, a continuall hunger, and fasting; and if we consider it at best, and in the effects, mortification is but a *continuall physick,* which is misery enough.

5. FROM A SERMON PREACHED TO THE LORDS UPON EASTER-DAY, AT THE COMMUNION, THE KING BEING THEN DANGEROUSLY SICK AT NEW-MARKET [28 MARCH 1619][13]

I

Wee are all conceived in close Prison; in our Mothers wombes, we are close Prisoners all; when we are borne, we are borne but to the liberty of the house; Prisoners still, though within larger walls; and then all our life is but a going out to the place of Execution, to death. Now was there ever any man seen to sleep in the Cart, between New-gate, and Tyborne? between the Prison, and the place of Execution, does any man sleep? And we sleep all the way; from the womb to the grave we are never throughly awake; but passe on with such dreames, and imaginations as these, I may live as well, as another, and why should I dye, rather than another? but awake, and tell me, sayes this Text, *Quis homo?* who is that other that thou talkest of? *What man is he that liveth, and shall not see death?*

2

Take a flat Map, a Globe *in plano,* and here is East, and there is West, as
far asunder as two points can be put: but reduce this flat Map to
roundnesse, which is the true form, and then East and West touch one
another, and are all one:[14] So consider mans life aright, to be a Circle,
*Pulvis es, & in pulverem reverteris, Dust thou art, and to dust thou must
return; Nudus egressus, Nudus revertar, Naked I came, and naked I must go;*
In this, the circle, the two points meet, the womb and the grave are but
one point, they make but one station, there is but a step from that to
this. This brought in that custome amongst the Greek Emperours, that
ever at the day of their Coronation, they were presented with severall
sorts of Marble, that they might then bespeak their Tombe. And this
brought in that Custome into the Primitive Church, that they called the
Martyrs dayes, wherein they suffered, *Natalitia Martyrum,* their birth
dayes; birth, and death is all one.

Their death was a birth to them into another life, into the glory of
God; It ended one Circle, and created another; for immortality, and
eternity is a Circle too; not a Circle where two points meet, but a Circle
made at once; This life is a Circle, made with a Compasse, that passes
from point to point; That life is a Circle stamped with a print, an
endlesse, and perfect Circle, as soone as it begins. Of this Circle, the
Mathematician is our great and good God; The other Circle we make
up our selves; we bring the Cradle, and Grave together by a course of
nature.[15]

3

If I can say, (and my conscience doe not tell me, that I belye mine owne
state) if I can say, That the blood of my Saviour runs in my veines, That
the breath of his Spirit quickens all my purposes, that all my deaths have
their Resurrection, all my sins their remorses, all my rebellions their
reconciliations, I will harken no more after this question, as it is intended
de morte naturali, of a naturall death, I know I must die that death, what
care I? nor *de morte spirituali,* the death of sin, I know I doe, and shall die
so; why despaire I? but I will finde out another death, *mortem raptus,* a
death of rapture, and of extasie, that death which S. *Paul* died more than
once, The death which S. *Gregory* speaks of, *Divina contemplatio quoddam
sepulchrum animae,* The contemplation of God, and heaven, is a kinde of
buriall, and Sepulchre, and rest of the soule; and in this death of rapture,

and extasie, in this death of the Contemplation of my interest in my Saviour, I shall finde my self, and all my sins enterred, and entombed in his wounds, and like a Lily in Paradise, out of red earth, I shall see my soule rise out of his blade, in a candor, and in an innocence, contracted there, acceptable in the sight of his Father.

6. A SERMON OF VALEDICTION AT MY GOING INTO GERMANY, AT LINCOLNS-INNE, 18 APRIL 1619[16]

Wee may consider two great virtues, one for the society of this life, Thankfulness, and the other for attaining the next life, Repentance; as the two pretious Mettles, Silver and Gold: Of Silver (of the virtue of thankfulness) there are whole Mines, books written by Philosophers, and a man may grow rich in that mettle, in that virtue, by digging in that Mine, in the Precepts of moral men; of this Gold (this virtue of Repentance) there is no Mine in the Earth; in the books of Philosophers, no doctrine of Repentance; this Gold is for the most part in the washes;[17] this Repentance in matters of tribulation; but God directs thee to it in this Text, before thou come to those waters of Tribulation, remember now thy Creator before those evill dayes come, and then thou wilt repent the not remembring him till now. Here then the holy-Ghost takes the neerest way to bring a man to God, by awaking his memory; for, for the understanding, that requires long and cleer instruction; and the will requires an instructed understanding before, and is in it self the blindest and boldest faculty; but if the memory doe but fasten upon any of those things which God hath done for us, it is the neerest way to him. Remember therefore, and remember now, though the Memory be placed in the hindermost part of the brain, defer not thou thy re-membring to the hindermost part of thy life, but doe that now *in die,* in the day, whil'st thou hast light, now *in diebus*, in the days, whilst God presents thee many lights, many means; and *in diebus juventutis,* in the days of thy youth, of strength, whilst thou art able to doe that which thou purposest to thy self; And as the word imports, *Bechurotheica*,[18] *in diebus Electionum tuarum,* in the dayes of thy choice, whilst thou art able to make thy choyce, whilst the Grace of God shines so brightly upon thee, as that thou maist choose the way, and so powerfully upon thee, as that thou maist walke in that way. Now, *in this day,* and *in these dayes* Remember first the Creator, That all these things which thou laborest for, and delightest in, were created, made of nothing; and therfore thy memory looks not far enough back, if it stick only upon the Creature, and reach not to the Creator, Remember the Creator, and remember thy Creator; and in that, first that he made thee, and then what he made thee; He made thee of nothing, but of that nothing he hath made thee such a thing as cannot return to nothing, but must remain for ever; whether happy or miserable, that depends upon thy *Remembring thy Creator now in the dayes of thy youth.*

First *remember;* which word is often used in the Scripture for considering and taking care: for, God remembred *Noah* and every beast with him in the Ark; as the word which is contrary to that, forgetting, is also for the affection contrary to it, it is neglecting, *Can a woman forget her child, and not have compassion on the son of her womb?* But here we take not remembring so largly, but restrain it to the exercise of that one faculty, the memory; for it is *Stomachus animae.* The memory, sayes St *Bernard,* is the stomach of the soul, it receives and digests, and turns into good blood, all the benefits formerly exhibited to us in particular, and exhibited to the whole Church of God: present that which belongs to the understanding, to that faculty, and the understanding is not presently setled in it; present any of the prophecies made in the captivity, and a Jews understanding takes them for deliverances from *Babylon,* and a Christians understanding takes them for deliverances from sin and death, by the Messias Christ Jesus; present any of the prophecies of the Revelation concerning Antichrist, and a Papist will understand it of a single, and momentane, and transitory man, that must last but three yeer and a half; and a Protestant may understand it of a succession of men, that have lasted so 1000. yeers already: present but the name of Bishop or of elder, out of the Acts of the Apostle[s], or their Epistles, and other men will take it for a name of equality, and parity, and we for a name and office of distinction in the Hierarchy of Gods Church. Thus it is in the understanding that's often perplexed; consider the other faculty, the will of man, by those bitternesses which have passed between the Jesuits and the Dominicans, (amongst other things belonging to the will) whether the same proportion of grace, offered to men alike disposed, must necessarily work alike upon both their wills? And amongst persons neerer to us, whether that proportion of grace, which doth convert a man, might not have been resisted by perversness of his will? By all these difficulties we may see, how untractable, and untameable a faculty the wil of man is. But come not with matter of law, but matter of fact, *Let God make his wonderful works to be had in remembrance:* present the history of Gods protection of his children, from the beginning, in the ark, in both captivities, in infinite dangers; present this to the memory, and howsoever the understanding be beclouded, or the will perverted, yet both Jew and Christian, Papist and Protestant, Puritan and Protestant, are affected with a thankfull acknowledgment of his former mercies and benefits, this issue of that faculty of their memory is alike in them all: And therefore God in giving the law, works upon no other faculty but this, *I am the Lord thy God which brought thee out of the land of Egypt;* He only presents to their memory what he had done for them. And so in delivering the Gospel in one principal seal thereof, the sacrament of his body, he recommended it only to their memory, *Do this in remembrance of me.* This is the faculty that God desires to work upon; And therefore if thine understanding cannot reconcile differences in all Churches, if thy will cannot submit it self to the ordinances of thine own Church, go to thine own memory; for as St *Bernard* calls that the stomach of the soul, we may be bold to call it the Gallery of the soul, hang'd with so many, and so lively pictures of the goodness and mercies of thy God to thee, as that every one of them shall be a catachism to thee, to instruct thee in all thy duties to him for those mercies: And as a well made, and well plac'd picture, looks always upon him that looks upon it; so shall thy God look upon thee, whose memory is thus contemplating him, and shine upon thine understanding, and rectifie thy will too. If thy memory cannot comprehend his mercy at large shewed to his whole Church, (as it is almost an incomprehensible thing, that in so few yeers he made us of the Reformation, equall even in number to our adversaries of the Roman Church,) If thy memory have not held that picture of our general deliverance from the Navy,[19] (if that mercy be written in the water and in the sands, where it was perform'd, and not in thy heart) if thou remember not our deliverance from that artificiall Hell, the Vault, (in which, though his instruments failed of their plot, they did not blow us up; yet the Devil goes forward with his plot, if ever he can blow out; if he can get that deliverance to be forgotten.) If these be too large pictures for thy gallery, for thy memory, yet every man hath a pocket picture about him, a manuall, a bosome book, and if he will turn over but one leaf, and remember what God hath done for him even since yesterday, he shall find even by that little branch a navigable river, to sail into that great and endless Sea of Gods mercies towards him, from the beginning of his being.

Do but remember, but remember now: Of his own wil begat he us with the word of truth, that we should be as the first fruits of his creatures: That as we consecrate all his creatures to him, in a sober, and religious use of them, so as the first fruits of all, we should principally consecrate our selves to his service betimes. Now there were three payments of first fruits appointed by God to the Jews: The first was, *Primitiae Spicarum,* of their Ears of Corn, and this was early about *Easter;* The second was *Primitiae panum,* of Loaves of Bread, after their corn was converted to that use; and this, though it were not so soon, yet it was early too, about *Whitsontide;* The third was *Primitiae frugum,* of all their Fruits and Revenues; but this was very late in *Autumn,* at the fall of the leaf, in the end of the yeer. The two first of these, which were offered early, were offered partly to God, and partly to Man, to the Priest; but in the last, which came late, God had no part: He had his part in the corn, and in the loaves, but none in the latter fruits. Offer thy self to God; first, as *Primitias spicarum,* (whether thou glean in the world, or bind up whole sheaves, whether thy increase be by little and little, or apace;) And offer thy self, as *primitias panum,* (when thou hast kneaded up riches, and honor, and favour in a setled and established fortune) offer at thy *Easter,* whensoever thou hast any resurrection, any sense of raising thy soul from the shadow of death; offer at thy Pentecost, when the holy Ghost visits thee, and descends upon thee in a fiery tongue, and melts thy bowels by the power of his word; for if thou defer thy offering til thy fal, til thy winter, til thy death, howsoever they may be thy first fruits, because they be the first that ever thou gavest, yet they are such, as are not acceptable to God; God hath no portion in them, if they be not offered til then; offer thy self now; for that's an easie request; yea offer to thy self now, that's more easie; *Viximus mundo; vivamus reliquum nobis ipsis;* Thus long we have served the world; let us serve our selves the rest of our time, that is, the best part of our selves, our souls. *Expectas ut febris te vocet ad paenitentiam?* Hadst thou rather a sickness should bring thee to God, than a sermon? hadst thou rather be beholden to a Physitian for thy salvation, than to a Preacher? thy business is to remember; stay not for thy last sickness, which may be a Lethargy in which thou mayest forget thine own name, and his that gave thee the name of a Christian, Christ Jesus himself: thy business is to remember, and thy time is now; stay not till that Angel come which shall say and swear, that time shall be no more.

Remember then, and remember now; *In Die,* in the day; The Lord will hear us *In die qua invocaverimus,* in the day that we shall call upon him; and *in quacunque die,* in what day soever we call, and *in quacunque die velociter exaudiet,* as soon as we call in any day. But all this is *Opus diei,* a work for the day; for in the night, in our last night, those thoughts that fall upon us, they are rather dreams, than true re-membrings; we do rather dream that we repent, than repent indeed, upon our death-bed. To him that travails by night a bush seems a tree, and a tree seems a man, and a man a spirit; nothing hath the true shape to him; to him that repents by night, on his death-bed, neither his own sins, nor the mercies of God have their true proportion. Fool, saies Christ, this night they will fetch away thy soul; but he neither tels him, who they be that shall fetch it, nor whether they shall carry it; he hath no light but lightnings;[20] a sodain flash of horror first, and then he goes into fire without light. *Numquid Deus nobis ignem paravit? non, sed Diabolo, et Angelis:* did God ordain hell fire for us? no, but for the Devil, and his Angels. And yet we that are vessels so broken, as that there is not a sheard left, to fetch water at the pit, that is, no means in our selves, to derive one drop of Christs blood upon us, nor to wring out one tear of true repentance from us, have plung'd our selves into this everlasting, and this dark fire, which was not prepared for us: A wretched covet-ousness, to be intruders upon the Devil; a wretched ambition, to be usurpers upon damnation. God did not make the fire for us; but much less did he make us for that fire; that is, make us to damn us.[21] But now the Judgment is given, *Ite maledicti,* go ye accursed; but yet this is the way of Gods justice, and his proceeding, that his Judgments are not alwaies executed, though they be given. The Judgments and Sentences of Medes and Persians are irrevocable, but the Judgments and Sentences of God, if they be given, if they be published, they are not executed. The Ninevites had perished, if the sentence of their destruction had not been given; and the sentence preserv'd them; so even in this cloud of *Ite maledicti,* go ye accursed, we may see the day break, and discern beams of saving light, even in this Judgment of eternal darkness; if the contemplation of his Judgment brings us to remember him in that day, in the light and apprehension of his anger and correction.

For this circumstance is enlarged; it is not *in die,* but *in diebus,* not in one, but in many dayes; for God affords us many dayes, many lights to see and remember him by. This remembrance of God is our regeneration, by which we are new creatures; and therefore we may consider as many dayes in it, as in the first creation. The first day was the making of light; and our first day is the knowledg of him, who saies of himself, *ego sum lux mundi,* I am the light of the world, and of whom St *John* testifies, *Erat lux vera,* he was the true light, that lighteth every man into the world. This is then our first day the true profession of Christ Jesus. God made light first, that the other creatures might be seen; *Frustra essent si non viderentur,* It had been to no purpose to have made creatures, if there had been no light to manifest them. Our first day is the light and love of the Gospel; for the noblest creatures of Princes, (that is, the noblest actions of Princes, war, and peace, and treaties) *frustra sunt,* they are good for nothing, they are nothing, if they be not shew'd and tried by this light, by the love and preservation of the Gospel of Christ Jesus: God made light first, that his other works might appear, and he made light first, that himself (for our example) might do all his other works in the light: that we also, as we had that light shed upon us in our baptism, so we might make all our future actions justifiable by that light, and not *Erubescere Evangelium,* not be ashamed of being too jealous in this profession of his truth. Then God saw that the light was good: the seeing implies a consideration; that so a religion be not accepted blindly, nor implicitly; and the seeing it to be good implies an election of that religion, which is simply good in it self, and not good by reason of advantage, or conveniency, or other collateral and by-respects. And when God had seen the light, and seen that it was good, then he severed light from darkness; and he severed them, *non tanquam duo positiva,* not as two essential, and positive, and equal things; not so, as that a brighter and a darker religion, (a good and a bad) should both have a beeing together, but *tanquam positivuum et primitivum,* light and darkness are primitive, and positive, and figure this rather, that a true religion should be established, and continue, and darkness utterly removed; and then, and not till then, (till this was done, light severed from darkness) there was a day; And since God hath given us this day, the brightness of his Gospel, that this light is first presented, that is, all great actions begun with this consideration of the Gospel; since all other things are made by this light, that is, all have relation to the continuance of the Gospel, since God hath given us such a head, as is sharp-sighted in seeing the several lights, wise in discerning the true light, powerful in resisting forraign darkness; since God hath given us this day, *qui non humiliabit animam suam in die hac,* as *Moses* speaks of the dayes of God's institution, he that will not remember God now in this day, is impious to him, and unthankful to that great instrument of his, by whom this day spring from on high hath visited us.

To make shorter dayes of the rest, (for we must pass through all the six dayes in a few minuts) God in the second day made the firmament to divide between the waters above, and the waters below; and this firmament in us, is *terminus cognoscibilium,* the limits of those things which God hath given man means and faculties to conceive, and understand: he hath limited our eyes with a firmament beset with stars, our eyes can see no farther: he hath limited our understanding in matters of religion with a starry firmament too; that is, with the knowledg of those things, *quae ubique, quae semper,* which those stars which he hath kindled in his Church, the Fathers and Doctors, have ever from the beginning proposed as things necessary to be explicitely believ'd, for the salvation of our souls; for the eternal decrees of God, and his unreveal'd mysteries, and the inextricable perplexities of the School,[22] they are waters above the firmament: here *Paul* plants, and here *Apollo* waters; here God raises up men to convey to us the dew of his grace, by waters under the firmament; by visible sacraments, and by the word so preach'd, and so interpreted, as it hath been constantly, and unanimously from the beginning of the Church. And therefore this second day is perfited in the third, in the *congregentur aquae,* let the waters be gathered together; God hath gathered all the waters, all the waters of life in one place; that is, all the doctrine necessary for the life to come, into his Church: And then *producet terra,* here in this world are produced to us all herbs and fruits, all that is necessary for the soul to feed upon. And in this third daies work God repeats here that testimony, *vidit quod bonum,* he saw that it was good; good, that here should be a gathering of waters in one place, that is, no doctrine receiv'd that had not been taught in the Church; and *vidit quod bonum,* he saw it was good, that all herbs and trees should be produced that bore seed; all doctrines that were to be proseminated and propagated, and to be continued to the end, should be taught in the Church: but for doctrines which were but to vent the passion of vehement men, or to serve the turns of great men for a time, which were not seminal doctrines, doctrines that bore seed, and were to last from the beginning to the end; for these interlineary doctrines, and marginal, which were no part of the first text, here's no testimony that God sees that they are good. And, *In diebus istis,* if in these two daies, the day when God makes thee a firmament, shewes thee what thou art, to limit thine understanding and thy faith upon, and the day where God makes thee a sea, a collection of the waters, (showes thee where these necessary things must be taught in the Church) if in those daies thou wilt not remember thy Creator, it is an irrecoverable Lethargy.

In the fourth daies work, let the making of the Sun to rule the day be the testimony of Gods love to thee, in the sunshine of temporal prosperity, and the making of the Moon to shine by night, be the refreshing of his comfortable promises in the darkness of adversity; and then remember that he can make thy sun to set at noon, he can blow out thy taper of prosperity when it burns brightest, and he can turn the Moon into blood, he can make all the promises of the Gospel, which should comfort thee in adversity, turn into despair and obduration. Let the fift daies work, which was the creation *Omnium reptibilium,* and *omnium volatilium,* of all creeping things, and of all flying things, produc'd out of water, signifie and denote to thee, either thy humble devotion, in which thou saist of thy self to God, *vermis ego et non homo,* I am a worm and no man; or let it be the raising of thy soul in that, *pennas columbae dedisti,* that God hath given thee the wings of a dove to fly to the wilderness, in a retiring from, or a resisting of tentations of this world; remember still that God can suffer even thy humility to stray, and degenerate into an uncomly dejection and stupidity, and senselessness of the true dignity and true liberty of a Christian: and he can suffer this retiring thy self from the world, to degenerate into a contempt and despising of others, and an overvaluing of thine own perfections. Let the last day in which both man and beasts were made out of the earth, but yet a living soul breath'd into man, remember thee that this earth which treads upon thee, must return to that earth which thou treadst upon; thy body, that loads thee, and oppresses thee to the grave, and thy spirit to him that gave it. And when the Sabbath day hath also remembered thee, that God hath given thee a temporal Sabbath, plac'd thee in a land of peace, and an ecclesiastical Sabbath, plac'd thee in a Church of peace, perfect all in a spirituall Sabbath, a conscience of peace, by remembring now thy Creator, at least in one of these daies of the week of thy regeneration, either as thou hast light created in thee, in the first day, that is, thy knowledg of Christ; or as thou hast a firmament created in thee the second day, that is, thy knowledg what to seek concerning Christ, things appertaining to faith and salvation; or as thou hast a sea created in thee the third day, that is, a Church where all the knowledg is reserv'd and presented to thee; or as thou hast a sun and moon in the fourth day, thankfulness in prosperity, comfort in adversity, or as thou hast *reptilem humilitatem,* or *volatilem fiduciam,* a humiliation in thy self, or an exaltation in Christ in thy fift day, or as thou hast a contemplation of thy mortality and immortality in the sixth day, or a desire of a spiritual Sabbath in the seaventh, In those daies remember thou thy Creator.

Now all these daies are contracted into less room in this text, *In diebus Bechurotheica,* is either, *in the daies of thy youth,* or *electionum tuarum,* in the daies of thy hearts desire, when thou enjoyest all that thou couldest wish. First, therefore if thou wouldest be heard in *Davids* prayer; *Delicta juventutis;* O Lord remember not the sins of my youth; remember to come to this prayer, *In diebus juventutis,* in the dayes of thy youth. *Job* remembers with much sorrow, how he was in the dayes of his youth, when Gods providence was upon his Tabernacle: and it is a late, but a sad consideration, to remember with what tenderness of conscience, what scruples, what remorces we entred into sins in our youth, how much we were afraid of all degrees and circumstances of sin for a little while, and how indifferent things they are grown to us, and how obdurate we are grown in them now. This was *Jobs* sorrow, and this was *Tobias* comfort, when I was but young, all my Tribes fell away; but I alone went after to *Jerusalem.* Though he lacked the counsail, and the example of his Elders, yet he served God; for it is good for a man, that he bear his yoke in his youth: For even when God had delivered over his people purposely to be afflicted, yet himself complains in their behalf, *That the persecutor laid the very heaviest yoke upon the ancient:* It is a lamentable thing to fall under a necessity of suffering in our age. *Labore fracta instrumenta, ad Deum ducis, quorum nullus usus?* wouldest thou consecrate a Chalice to God that is broken? no man would present a lame horse, a disordered clock, a torn book to the King. *Caro jumentum,* thy body is thy beast; and wilt thou present that to God, when it is lam'd and tir'd with excesse of wantonness? when thy clock, (the whole course of thy time) is disordered with passions, and perturbations; when thy book (the history of thy life,) is torn, 1000. sins of thine own torn out of thy memory, wilt thou then present thy self thus defac'd and mangled to almighty God? *Temperantia non est temperantia in senectute, sed impotentia incontinentiae,* chastity is not chastity in an old man, but a disability to be unchast; and therefore thou dost not give God that which thou pretendest to give, for thou hast no chastity to give him. *Senex bis puer,* but it is not *bis juvenis;* an old man comes to the infirmities of childhood again; but he comes not to the strength of youth again.

Do this then *In diebus juventutis,* in thy best strength, and when thy natural faculties are best able to concur with grace; but do it *In diebus electionum,* in the dayes when thou hast thy hearts desire; for if thou have worn out this word, in one sense, that it be too late now, *to remember him in the dayes of youth,* (that's spent forgetfully) yet as long as thou art able to make a new choise, to chuse a new sin, that when thy heats of youth are not overcome, but burnt out, then thy middle age chooses ambition, and thy old age chooses covetousness; as long as thou art able to make thy choice thou art able to make a better than this; God testifies that power, that he hath given thee; *I call heaven and earth to record this day, that I have set before you life and death; choose life:* If this choice like you not, *If it seem evil unto you to serve the Lord,* saith *Josuah* then, *choose ye this day whom ye will serve.* Here's the election day; bring that which ye would have, into comparison with that which ye should have; that is, all that this world keeps from you, with that which God offers to you; and what will ye choose to prefer before him? for honor, and favor, and health, and riches, perchance you cannot have them though you choose them; but can you have more of them than they have had, to whom those very things have been occasions of ruin? The Market is open till the bell ring; till thy last bell ring the Church is open, grace is to be had there: but trust not upon that rule, that men buy cheapest at the end of the market, that heaven may be had for a breath at last, when they that hear it cannot tel whether it be a sigh or a gasp, a religious breathing and anhelation [23] after the next life, or natural breathing out, and exhalation of this; but find a spiritual good husbandry in that other rule, that the prime of the market is to be had at first: for howsoever, in thine age, there may be by Gods strong working, *Dies juventutis,* A day of youth, in making thee then a new creature; (for as God is *antiquissimus dierum,* so in his school no man is super-annated,) yet when age hath made a man impotent to sin, this is not *Dies electionum,* it is not a day of choice; but remember God now, when thou hast a choice, that is, a power to advance thy self, or to oppress others by evil means; now *in die electionum,* in those thy happy and sun-shine dayes, *remember him.*

This is then the faculty that is excited, the memory; and this is the time, now, now whilest ye have power of election: The object is, the Creator, *Remember the Creator:* First, because the memory can go no farther than the creation; and therefore we have no means to conceive, or apprehend any thing of God before that. When men therefore speak of decrees of reprobation, decrees of condemnation, before decrees of creation; this is beyond the counsail of the holy Ghost here, *Memento creatoris,* Remember the Creator, for this is to remember God a condemner before he was a creator: This is to put a preface to *Moses* his *Genesis,* not to be content with his *in principio,* to know that *in the beginning God created heaven and earth,* but we must remember what he did *ante principium,* before any such beginning was. *Moses* his *in principio,* that beginning, the creation we can remember; but St *Johns in principio,* that beginning, eternity, we cannot; we can remember Gods *fiat* in *Moses,* but not Gods *erat* in St *John:* what God hath done for us, is the object of our memory, not what he did before we were: and thou hast a good and perfect memory, if it remember all that the holy Ghost proposes in the Bible; and it determines in the *memento Creatoris:* There begins the Bible, and there begins the Creed, *I believe in God the Father, maker of Heaven and Earth;* for when it is said, *The holy Ghost was not given, because Jesus was not glorified,* it is not truly *Non erat datus,* but *non erat;* for, *non erat nobis antequam operaretur;* It is not said there, the holy Ghost was not given, but it is the holy Ghost was not: for he is not, that is, he hath no being to us ward, till he works in us, which was first in the creation: *Remember the Creator then,* because thou canst remember nothing backward beyond him, and remember him so too, that thou maist stick upon nothing on this side of him, That so neither *height, nor depth, nor any other creature may separate thee from God;* not only not separate thee finally, but not separate so, as to stop upon the creature, but to make the best of them, thy way to the Creator; We see ships in the river; but all their use is gone, if they go not to sea; we see men fraighted with honour, and riches, but all their use is gone, if their respect be not upon the honor and glory of the Creator; and therefore sayes the Apostle, *Let them that suffer, commit their souls to God, as to a faithful Creator;* that is, He made them, and therefore will have care of them. This is the true contracting, and the true extending of the memory, to *Remember the Creator*, and stay there, because there is no prospect farther, and to *Remember the Creator*, and get thither, because there is no safe footing upon the creature, til we come so far.

Remember then the Creator, and *remember thy Creator*, for, *Quis magis fidelis Deo?* who is so faithful a Counsailor as God? *Quis prudentior Sapiente?* who can be wiser than wisdome? *Quis utilior bono?* or better than goodness? *Quis conjunctior Creatore?* or neerer than our Maker? and therefore remember him. What purposes soever thy parents or thy Prince have to make thee great, how had all those purposes been frustrated, and evacuated if God had not made thee before? this very being is thy greatest degree; as in Arithmatick how great a number soever a man expresse in many figures, yet when we come to number all, the very first figure is the greatest and most of all; so what degrees or titles soever a man have in this world, the greatest and the foundation of all, is, that he had a being by creation: For the distance from nothing to a little, is ten thousand times more, than from it to the highest degree in this life: and therefore *remember thy Creator*, as by being so, he hath done more for thee than all the world besides; and remember him also, with this consideration, that whatsoever thou art now, yet once thou wast nothing.

He created thee, *ex nihilo,* he gave thee a being, there's matter of exaltation, and yet all this from nothing; thou wast worse than a worm, there's matter of humiliation; but he did not create thee *ad nihilum,* to return to nothing again, and there's matter for thy consideration, and study, how to make thine immortality profitable unto thee; for it is a deadly immortality, if thy immortality must serve thee for nothing but to hold thee in immortal torment. To end all, that being which we have from God shall not return to nothing, nor the being which we have from men neither. As St *Bernard* sayes of the Image of God in mans soul, *uri potest in gehenna, non exuri,* That soul that descends to hell, carries the Image [of] God in the faculties of that soul thither, but there that Image can never be burnt out, so those Images and those impressions, which

we have received from men, from nature, from the world, the image of
a Lord, the image of a Counsailor, the image of a Bishop, shall all burn
in Hell, and never burn out; not only these men, but these offices are
not to return to nothing; but as their being from God, so their being
from man, shal have an everlasting being, to the aggravating of their
condemnation. And therefore *remember thy Creator,* who, as he is so, by
making thee of nothing, so he will ever be so, by holding thee to his
glory, though to thy confusion, from returning to nothing; for the
Court of Heaven is not like other Courts, that after a surfet of pleasure
or greatness, a man may retire; after a surfet of sin there's no such
retiring, as a dissolving of the soul into nothing; but God is from the
beginning the Creator, he gave all things their being, and he is still thy
Creator, thou shalt evermore have that being, to be capable of his
Judgments.

Now to make up a circle, by returning to our first word, remember:
As we remember God, so for his sake, let us remember one another. In
my long absence, and far distance from hence, remember me, as I shall
do you in the ears of that God, to whom the farthest East, and the
farthest West are but as the right and left ear in one of us; we hear with
both at once, and he hears in both at once; remember me, not my
abilities; for when I consider my Apostleship that I was sent to you, I am
in St *Pauls quorum, quorum ego sum minimus,* the least of them that have
been sent; and when I consider my infirmities, I am in his *quorum,* in
another commission, another way, *Quorum ego maximus;* the greatest of
them; but remember my labors, and endeavors, at least my desire, to
make sure your salvation. And I shall remember your religious cheer-
fulness in hearing the word, and your christianly respect towards all
them that bring that word unto you, and towards myself in particular
far [a]bove my merit. And so as your eyes that stay here, and mine that
must be far of, for all that distance shall meet every morning, in
looking upon that same Sun, and meet every night, in looking upon
that same Moon; so our hearts may meet morning and evening in that
God, which sees and hears every where; that you may come thither to
him with your prayers, that I, (if I may be of use for his glory, and your
edification in this place) may be restored to you again; and may come to
him with my prayer that what *Paul* soever plant amongst you, or what
Apollos soever water, God himself will give the increase: That if I never
meet you again till we have all passed the gate of death, yet in the gates

of heaven, I may meet you all, and there say to my Saviour and your Saviour, that which he said to his Father and our Father, *Of those whom thou hast given me, have I not lost one.* Remember me thus, you that stay in this Kingdome of peace, where no sword is drawn, but the sword of Justice, as I shal remember you in those Kingdomes, where ambition on one side, and a necessary defence from unjust persecution on the other side hath drawn many swords; and Christ Jesus remember us all in his Kingdome, to which, though we must sail through a sea, it is the sea of his blood, where no soul suffers shipwrack;[24] though we must be blown with strange winds, with sighs and groans for our sins, yet it is the Spirit of God that blows all this wind, and shall blow away all contrary winds of diffidence or distrust in Gods mercy; where we shall be all Souldiers of one Army, the Lord of Hostes, and Children of one Quire, the God of Harmony and consent: where all Clients shall retain but one Coun-sellor, our Advocate Christ Jesus, nor present him any other fee but his own blood, and yet every Client have a Judgment on his side, not only in a not guilty, in the remission of his sins, but in a *Venite benedicti*, in being called to the participation of an immortal Crown of glory: where there shall be no difference in affection, nor in mind, but we shall agree as fully and perfectly in our *Allelujah,* and *gloria in excelsis,* as God the Father, Son, and Holy Ghost agreed in the *faciamus hominem* at first; where we shall end, and yet begin but then; where we shall have continuall rest, and yet never grow lazie; where we shall be stronger to resist, and yet have no enemy; where we shall live and never die, where we shall meet and never part.

7. FROM TWO SERMONS, TO THE PRINCE AND PRINCESS PALATINE, 16 JUNE 1619[25]

And this is brought neerer and neerer unto us, as we come neerer and neerer to our end. As he that travails weary, and late towards a great City, is glad when he comes to a place of execution, becaus he knows that is neer the town; so when thou comest to the gate of death, be glad of that, for it is but one step from that to thy *Jerusalem.* Christ hath brought us in some neerness to Salvation, as he is *vere Salvator mundi,* in that we *know, that this is indeed the Christ, the Saviour of the world:* and he hath brought it neerer than that, as he is *Salvator corporis sui,* in that we know, *That Christ is the head of the Church, and the Saviour of that body:* And neerer than that, as he is *Salvator tuus sanctus,* In that we know, *He is the Lord our God, the holy One of Israel, our Saviour:* But neerest of all, in the *Ecce Salvator tuus venit,* Behold thy Salvation commeth. It is not only promised in the Prophets, nor only writ in the Gospel, nor only seal'd in the Sacraments, nor only prepared in the visitations of the holy Ghost, but *Ecce,* behold it, now, when thou canst behold nothing else: The sun is setting to thee, and that for ever; thy houses and furnitures, thy gardens and orchards, thy titles and offices, thy wife and children are departing from thee, and that for ever; a cloud of faintnesse is come over thine eyes, and a cloud of sorrow over all theirs; when his hand that loves thee best hangs tremblingly over thee to close thine eyes, *Ecce Salvator tuus venit,* behold then a new light, thy Saviours hand shall open thine eyes, and in his light thou shalt see light; and thus shalt see, that though in the eyes of men thou lye upon that bed, as a Statue on a Tomb, yet in the eyes of God, thou standest as a *Colossus,* one foot in one, another in another land; one foot in the grave, but the other in heaven; one hand in the womb of the earth, and the other in *Abrahams* bosome: And then *vere prope,* Salvation is truly neer thee, and neerer than when thou believedst, which is our last word.

8. FROM A SERMON PREACHED AT LINCOLNS INNE [? EASTER TERM, 1620][26]

I

Corruption in the skin, says *Job;* In the outward beauty, These be the Records of velim, these be the parchmins, the endictments, and the evidences that shall condemn many of us, at the last day, our *own skins;* we have the book of God, the Law, written in our own hearts; we have the image of God imprinted in our own souls; wee have the character, and seal of God stamped in us, in our baptism;[27] and all this is bound up in this velim, in this parchmin, in this skin of ours, and we neglect book, and image, and character, and seal, and all for the covering. It is not a clear case, if we consider the originall words properly, That *Jesabel did paint;* and yet all translators, and expositors have taken a just occasion, out of the ambiguity of those words, to cry down that abomination of painting. It is not a clear case, if we consider the propriety of the words, That *Absolon was hanged by the hair of the head;* and yet the Fathers and others have made use of that indifferency, and verisimilitude, to explode that abomination, of cherishing and curling haire, to the enveagling, and ensnaring, and entangling of others; *Judicium patietur aeternum,* says *Saint Hierome,* Thou art guilty of a murder, though no body die; *Quia vinum attulisti, si fuisset qui bibisset;* Thou has poyson'd a cup, if any would drink, thou hast prepar'd a tentation, if any would swallow it. *Tertullian* thought he had done enough, when he had writ his book *De Habitu muliebri,* against the excesse of women in clothes, but he was fain to adde another with more vehemence, *De cultu foeminarum,* that went beyond their clothes to their skin. And he concludes, *Illud ambitionis crimen,* there's vain-glory in their excesse of clothes, but, *Hoc prostitutionis,* there's prostitution in drawing the eye to the skin. *Pliny* says, that when their thin silke stuffes were first invented at Rome, *Excogitatum ad foeminas denudandas;* It was but an invention that women might go naked in clothes, for their skins might bee seen through those clothes, those thinne stuffes: Our women are not so carefull, but they expose their nakednesse professedly, and paint it, to cast bird-lime for the passengers eye. Beloved, good dyet makes the best Complexion, and a good Conscience is a continuall feast; A cheerfull heart makes the best blood, and peace with God is the true cheerfulnesse of heart. Thy Saviour neglected his skin so much, as that at last, hee scarse had any; all was torn with the whips, and scourges; and thy skin shall come to that absolute corruption, as that, though a hundred years after thou art buryed, one may find thy bones, and say, this was a *tall* man, this was a *strong* man, yet we shall soon be past saying, upon any relique of thy skinne, This was a *fair* man; Corruption seises the skinne, all outward beauty quickly, and so it does the body, the whole frame and constitution, which is another consideration; *After my skinne, my Body.*

If the whole body were an eye, or an ear, where were the body, says Saint Paul; but, when of the whole body there is neither eye nor ear, nor any member left, where is the body? And what should an eye do there, where there is nothing to be seen but loathsomnesse; or a nose there, where there is nothing to be smelt, but putrefaction; or an ear, where in the grave they doe not praise God? Doth not that body that boasted but yesterday of that priviledge above all creatures, that it onely could goe upright, lie to day as flat upon the earth as the body of a horse, or of a dogge? And doth it not to morrow lose his other priviledge, of looking up to heaven? Is it not farther remov'd from the eye of heaven, the Sunne, than any dogge, or horse, by being cover'd with the earth, which they are not? Painters have presented to us with some horrour, the *sceleton,* the frame of the bones of a mans body; but the state of a body, in the dissolution of the grave, no pencil can present to us. Between that excrementall jelly that thy body is made of at first, and that jelly which thy body dissolves to at last; there is not so noysome, so putrid a thing in nature.

2

We passe on. As in *Massa damnata,* the whole lump of mankind is under the condemnation of *Adams* sinne, and yet the good purpose of God severs some men from that condemnation, so, at the resurrection, all shall rise; but not all to glory. But, amongst them, that doe, *Ego,* say *Job,* I shall. I, as I am the same man, made up of the same body, and the same soule. Shall I imagine a difficulty in my body, because I have lost an Arme in the East, and a leg in the West? because I have left some bloud in the North, and some bones in the South? Doe but remember, with what ease you have sate in the chaire, casting an account, and made a shilling on one hand, a pound on the other, or five shillings below, ten above, because all these lay easily within your reach. Consider how much lesse, all this earth is to him, that sits in heaven, and spans all this world, and reunites in an instant armes, and legs, bloud, and bones, in what corners so ever they be scattered. The greater work may seem to be in reducing the soul; That that soule which sped so ill in that body, last time it came to it, as that it contracted *Originall sinne* then, and was put to the slavery to serve that body, and to serve it in the ways of sinne, not for an Apprentiship of seven, but seventy years after, that that soul after it hath once got loose by death, and liv'd God knows how many thousands of years, free from that body, that abus'd it so before, and in the sight and fruition of that God, where it was in no danger, should willingly, nay desirously, ambitiously seek this scattered body, this Eastern, and Western, and Northern, and Southern body, this is the most inconsiderable consideration; and yet, *Ego*, I, I the same body, and the same soul, shall be recompact again, and be identically, numerically, individually the same man. The same integrity of body, and soul, and the same integrity in the Organs of my body, and in the faculties of my soul too; I shall be all there, my body, and my soul, and all my body, and all my soul. I am not all here, I am here now preaching upon this text, and I am at home in my Library considering whether *S. Gregory*, or *S. Hierome*, have said best of this text, before. I am here speaking to you, and yet I consider by the way, in the same instant, what it is likely you will say to one another, when I have done. You are not all here neither; you are here now, hearing me, and yet you are thinking that you have heard a better Sermon somewhere else, of this text before; you are here, and yet you think you could have heard some other doctrine of downright *Predestination*, and *Reprobation* roundly delivered somewhere else with more edification to you; you are here, and you remember your selves that now yee think of it, this had been the fittest time, now, when every body else is at Church, to have made such and such a private visit; and because you would bee there, you are there. I cannot say, you cannot say so perfectly, so entirely now, as at the Resurrection, *Ego*, I am here; I, body and soul; I, soul and faculties; as Christ sayd to *Peter*, *Noli timere*, *Ego sum*, *Fear nothing, it is I;* so I say to my selfe, *Noli timere;* My soul, why art thou so sad, my body, why dost thou languish? *Ego*, I, body and and soul, soul and faculties, shall say to Christ Jesus, *Ego sum*, Lord, it is I, and hee shall not say, *Nescio te, I know thee not*, but avow me, and place me at his right hand. *Ego sum, I am the man that hath seen affliction, by the rod of his wrath; Ego sum,* and I the same man, shall receive the crown of glory which shall not fade.

Ego, I, the same person; *Ego videbo*, I shall see; I have had no lookingglasse in my grave, to see how my body looks in the dissolution; I know not how. I have had no houre-glasse in my grave to see how my time passes; I know not when: for, when my eylids are closed in my deathbed, *the Angel hath said to me, That time shall be no more;* Till I see eternity, the ancient of days, I shall see no more; but then I shall. Now, why is *Job* gladder of the use of this sense of seeing, than of any of the other? He is not; He is glad of seeing, but not of the sense, but of the Object. It is true that is said in the School, *Viciniùs se habent potentiae sensitivae ad animam quam corpus;* Our sensitive faculties have more relation to the soul, than to the body; but yet to some purpose, and in some measure, *all* the senses shall be in our glorifyed bodies, *In actu,* or *in potentia,* say they; so as that wee shall use them, or so as that we might. But this sight that *Job* speaks of, is onely the fruition of the presence of God, in which consists eternall blessednesse. Here, in this world, we see God *per speculum,* says the Apostle, by reflection, upon a glasse; we see a creature; and from that there arises an assurance that there is a Creator; we see him *in aenigmate,* says he; which is not ill rendred in the margin, in a *Riddle;* we see him in the Church, but men have made it a riddle, which is the Church; we see him in the Sacrament, but men have made it a riddle, by what light, and at what window: Doe I see him at the window of bread and wine; Is he in that; or doe I see him by the window of faith; and is he onely in that? still it is in a riddle. Doe I see him *a Priore,* (I see that I am elected, and therefore I cannot sinne to death?) Or doe I see him *a Posteriore,* (because I see my selfe carefull not to sin to death, therefore I am elected?) I shall see all problematicall things come to be dogmaticall, I shall see all these rocks in Divinity, come to bee smooth alleys; I shall see Prophesies untyed, Riddles dissolved, controversies reconciled; but I shall never see that, till I come to this sight which follows in our text, *Videbo Deum, I shall see God.*

No man ever saw God and liv'd; and yet, I shall not live till I see God; and when I have seen him I shall never dye. What have I ever seen in this world, that hath been truly the same thing that it seemed to me? I have seen marble buildings, and a chip, a crust, a plaster, a face of marble hath pilld off, and I see brick-bowels within. I have seen beauty, and a strong breath from another, tels me, that that complexion is from without, not from a sound constitution within. I have seen the state of Princes, and all that is but ceremony; and, I would be loath to put a *Master of ceremonies* to define *ceremony,* and tell me what it is, and to include so various a thing as ceremony, in so constant a thing, as a Definition. I see a great Officer, and I see a man of mine own profession, of great revenues, and I see not the interest of the money, that was paid for it, I see not the pensions, nor the Annuities, that are charged upon that Office, or that Church. As he that fears God, fears nothing else, so, he that sees God, sees every thing else: when we shall see God, *Sicuti est,* as he is, we shall see all things *Sicuti sunt,* as they are; for that's their Essence, as they conduce to his glory. We shall be no more deluded with outward appearances: for, when this sight, which we intend here comes, there will be no delusory thing to be seen. All that we have

made as though we saw, in this world, will be vanished, and I shall see
nothing but God, and what is in him; and him I shall see *In carne, in the
flesh,* which is another degree of Exaltation in mine Exinanition.[28]

9. FROM A SERMON PREACHED AT WHITE-HALL,
8 APRIL 1621[29]

We know the receipt, the capacity of the ventricle, the stomach of man,
how much it can hold; and wee know the receipt of all the receptacles
of blood, how much blood the body can have; so wee doe of all the
other conduits and cisterns of the body; But this infinite Hive of honey,
this insatiable whirlpoole of the covetous mind, no Anatomy, no dis-
section hath discovered to us. When I looke into the larders, and cellars,
and vaults, into the vessels of our body for drink, for blood, for urine,
they are pottles, and gallons; when I looke into the furnaces of our
spirits, the ventricles of the heart and of the braine, they are not thimbles;
for spirituall things, the things of the next world, we have no roome;
for temporall things, the things of this world, we have no bounds. How
then shall this over-eater bee filled with his honey? So filled, as that he
can receive nothing else. More of the same honey hee can; Another
Mannor, and another Church, is but another bit of meat, with another
sauce to him; Another Office, and another way of Extortion, is but
another garment, and another lace to him. But he is too full to receive
any thing else; Christ comes to this Bethlem, (Bethlem which is *Domus
panis*) this house of abundance, and there is no roome for Christ in this
Inne; there are no crums for Christ under this table; There comes *Boanerges,* (*Boanerges,* that is, *filius Tonitrui,* the sonne of Thunder) and he
thunders out the *Vae's,* the Comminations, the Judgements of God
upon such as hee; but if the Thunder spoile not his drink, he sees no
harme in Thunder; As long as a Sermon is not a Sentence in the Starre-
chamber, that a Sermon cannot fine and imprison him, hee hath no
roome for any good effect of a Sermon. The Holy Ghost, the Spirit of
Comfort comes to him, and offers him the consolation of the Gospel;
but hee will die in his old religion, which is to sacrifice to his owne
Nets, by which his portion is plenteous; he had rather have the God of

the Old Testament, that payes in this world with milke and honey, than the God of the New Testament, that cals him into his Vineyard in this World, and payes him no wages till the next: one *Jupiter* is worth all the three *Elohims,* or the three *Jehovahs* (if we may speake so) to him. *Jupiter* that can come in a showre of gold,[30] outwaighs *Jehova,* that comes but in a showre of water, but in a sprinkling of water in Baptisme, and sels that water so deare, as that he will have showres of teares for it, nay showres of blood for it, when any Persecutor hath a mind to call for it. The voyce of God whom he hath contemned, and wounded, The voyce of the Preacher whom he hath derided, and impoverished, The voyce of the poore, of the Widow, of the Orphans, of the prisoner, whom he hath oppressed, knocke at his doore, and would enter, but there is no roome for them, he is so full. This is the great danger indeed that accompanies this fulnesse, but the danger that affects him more is that which is more literally in the text, *Evomet,* he shall be so filled as that he shall *vomit;* even that fulnesse, those temporall things which he had, he shall cast up.

10. FROM A SERMON PREACHED AT A MARIAGE, 30 MAY 1621[31]

I

In this spirituall mariage we consider first Christ and his Church, for the Persons, but more particularly Christ and my soul. And can these persons meet? in such a distance, and in such a disparagement can these persons meet? the Son of God and the son of man? When I consider Christ to be *Germen Jehovae,* the bud and blossome, the fruit and off-spring of Jehovah, Jehovah himself, and my self before he took me in hand, to be, not a Potters vessell of earth, but that earth of which the Potter might make a vessel if he would, and break it if he would when he had made it: When I consider Christ to have been from before all beginnings, and to be still the Image of the Father, the same stamp upon the same metall, and my self a peece of rusty copper, in which those lines of the Image of God which were imprinted in me in my Creation are defaced and worn, and washed and burnt, and ground away, by my many, and many, and many sins:[32] When I consider Christ in his Circle, in glory with his Father, before he came into this world, establishing a glorious Church when he was in this world, and glorifying that Church with that glory which himself had before, when he went out of this world; and then consider my self in my circle, I came into this world washed in mine own tears, and either out of compunction for my self or compassion for others, I passe through this world as through a valley of tears, where tears settle and swell, and when I passe out of this world I leave their eyes whose hands close mine, full of tears too, can these persons, this Image of God, this God himself, this glorious God, and this vessell of earth, this earth it self, this inglorious worm of the earth, meet without disparagement?

They doe meet and make a mariage; because I am not a body onely, but a body and soul, there is a mariage, and Christ maries me.

2

Consider then how poore and needy a thing, all the riches of this world, how flat and tastlesse a thing, all the pleasures of this world, how pallid, and faint and dilute a thing, all the honours of this world are, when the very Treasure, and Joy, and glory of heaven it self were unperfect, if it were not eternall, and my mariage shall be soe, *In aeternum,* for ever.

The Angels were not maried so; they incurr'd an irreparable Divorce from God, and are separated for ever, and I shall be maried to him, *in aeternum,* for ever. The Angels fell in love, when there was no object presented, before any thing was created; when there was nothing but God and themselves, they fell in love with themselves, and neglected God, and so fell *in aeternum,* for ever. I shall see all the beauty, and all the glory of all the Saints of God, and love them all, and know that the Lamb loves them too, without jealousie, on his part, or theirs, or mine, and so be maried *in aeternum,* for ever, without interruption, or diminution, or change of affections. I shall see the Sunne black as sackcloth of hair, and the Moon become as blood, and the Starres fall as a Figgetree casts her untimely Figges, and the heavens roll'd up together as a Scroll. I shall see a divorce between Princes and their Prerogatives, between nature and all her elements, between the spheres, and all their intelligences,[33] between matter it self, and all her forms, and my mariage shall be, *in aeternum,* for ever. I shall see an end of faith, nothing to be beleeved that I doe not know; and an end of hope, nothing to be

wisht that I doe not enjoy, but no end of that love in which I am maried
to the Lamb for ever.

11. FROM A SERMON PREACHED UPON
TRINITY-SUNDAY [? TRINITY TERM, 1621][34]

The Lord then, the Son of God, had a *Sitio* in heaven, as well as upon
the Crosse; He thirsted our salvation there; and in the midst of the
fellowship of the Father from whom he came, and of the Holy Ghost,
who came from him and the Father, and all the Angels, who came (by a
lower way) from them all, he desired the conversation of Man, for
Mans sake; He that was God *The Lord,* became *Christ,* a man, and he
that was *Christ,* became *Jesus,* no man, a dead man, to save man: To
save man, all wayes, in all his parts, And to save all men, in all parts of
the world: To save his soule from hell, where we should have felt pains,
and yet been dead, then when we felt them; and seen horrid spectacles,
and yet been in darknes and blindnes, then when we saw them; And
suffered unsufferable torments, and yet have told over innumerable ages
in suffering them: To save this soule from that hell, and to fill that
capacity which it hath, and give it a capacity which it hath not, to
comprehend the joyes and glory of Heaven, this *Christ* became *Jesus.* To
save this body from the condemnation of everlasting corruption, where
the wormes that we breed are our betters, because they have a life,
where the dust of dead Kings is blowne into the street, and the dust of
the street blowne into the River, and the muddy River tumbled into
the Sea, and the Sea remaunded[35] into all the veynes and channels of
the earth; to save this body from everlasting dissolution, dispersion,
dissipation, and to make it in a glorious Resurrection, not onely a
Temple of the holy Ghost, but a Companion of the holy Ghost in the
kingdome of heaven, This *Christ* became this *Jesus.* To save this man,
body and soule together, from the punishments due to his former sinnes,
and to save him from falling into future sinnes by the assistance of his
Word preached, and his Sacraments administred in the Church, which
he purchased by his bloud, is this person, The *Lord,* the *Christ,* become
this *Jesus,* this Saviour. To save so, All wayes, In soule, in body, in both;

And also to save all men. For, to exclude others from that Kingdome, is a tyrannie, an usurpation; and to exclude thy selfe, is a sinfull, and a rebellious melancholy. But as melancholy in the body is the hardest humour to be purged, so is the melancholy in the soule, the distrust of thy salvation too. Flashes of presumption a calamity will quench, but clouds of desperation calamities thicken upon us; But even in this inordinate dejection thou exaltest thy self above God, and makest thy worst better than his best, thy sins larger than his mercy. Christ hath a Greek name, and an Hebrew name; *Christ* is Greeke, *Jesus* is Hebrew; He had commission to save all nations, and he hath saved all; Thou givest him another Hebrew name, and another Greek, when thou makest his name *Abaddon,* and *Apollyon,* a Destroyer; when thou wilt not apprehend him as a Saviour, and love him so.

12. FROM A SERMON PREACHED AT SAINT PAULS UPON CHRISTMASSE DAY, 1621 [36]

I

They had a precious composition for *lamps,* amongst the *ancients,* reserved especially for *Tombes,* which kept light for many hundreds of yeares; we have had *in our age* experience, in some casuall openings of ancient vaults, of finding such lights, as were kindled, (as appeared by their inscriptions) *fifteen* or *sixteen hundred* yeares before; [37] but, as soon as that light comes to our light, it vanishes. So this *eternall,* and this *supernaturall light, Christ* and *faith,* enlightens, warmes, purges, and does all the profitable offices of *fire,* and *light,* if we keep it in the right spheare, in the proper place, (that is, if wee consist in *points necessary* to salvation, and *revealed* in the Scripture) but when wee bring this light to the common light of *reason,* to our inferences, and consequencies, it may be in danger to vanish it selfe, and perchance extinguish our reason too; we may search so far, and reason so long of *faith* and *grace,* as that we may lose not onely *them,* but even our reason too, and sooner become *mad* then *good.* Not that we are bound to believe any thing *against reason,* that is, to believe, we know not why. It is but a slacke opinion, it is not *Beliefe,* that is not grounded upon reason. He that should come to a *Heathen man,* a meere naturall man, uncatechized, uninstructed in the rudiments of the Christian Religion, and should at first, without any preparation, present him first with this necessitie; Thou shalt burn in fire and brimstone eternally, except thou believe *a Trinitie of Persons, in an unitie of one God,* Except thou believe the *Incarnation* of the second Person of the Trinitie, the Sonne of God, Except thou believe that *a Virgine had a Sonne,* and the same Sonne that God had, and that God was Man too, and being the immortall God, yet died, he should be so farre from working any spirituall cure upon this poore soule, as that he should rather bring Christian Mysteries into scorne, than *him* to a beliefe. For, that man, if you proceed so, Believe all, or you burne in Hell, would finde an easie, an obvious way to escape all; that is, first not to believe *Hell* it selfe, and then nothing could binde him to believe the rest.

The *reason* therefore of Man, must first be satisfied; but the way of such satisfaction must be *this,* to make him see, That this World, a frame of so much harmony, so much concinnitie and conveniencie, and such a correspondence, and subordination in the parts thereof, must necessarily have had a workeman, for nothing can make it selfe: That no such workeman would deliver over a frame, and worke, of so much Majestie, to be governed by *Fortune,* casually, but would still retain the Administration thereof in his owne hands: That if he doe so, if he made the World, and *sustaine* it still by his watchfull Providence, there belongeth a worship and service to him, for doing so: That therefore he hath certainly revealed to man, what kinde of worship, and service, shall be acceptable to him: That this manifestation of his Will, must be permanent, it must be *written,* there must be a *Scripture,* which is his *Word* and his *Will:* And that therefore, from that Scripture, from that Word of God, all Articles of our Beliefe are to bee drawne.

If then his *Reason* confessing all this, aske farther proofe, how he shall know that *these Scriptures* accepted by the Christian Church, are the true Scriptures, let him bring any other Booke which pretendeth to be the Word of God, into comparison with these; It is true, we have not a *Demonstration;* not such an Evidence as that one and two, are three, to prove these to be Scriptures of God; God hath not proceeded in that manner, to drive our Reason into a pound, and to force it by a peremptory necessitie to accept these for Scriptures, for then, here had been no exercise of our *Will,* and our assent, if we could not have resisted. But yet these Scriptures have so orderly, so sweet, and so powerfull a working upon the reason, and the understanding, as if any third man, who were utterly discharged of all preconceptions and anticipations in matter of Religion, one who were altogether *neutrall,* disinteressed, unconcerned in either party, nothing towards a *Turke,* and as little toward a *Christian,* should heare a *Christian* pleade for his Bible, and a *Turke* for his Alcoran,[38] and should weigh the evidence of both; the Majesty of the *Style,* the punctuall accomplishment of the *Prophecies,* the harmony and concurrence of the *foure Evangelists,* the consent and unanimity of the *Christian Church* ever since, and many other such reasons, he would be drawne to such an Historicall, such a Grammaticall, such a Logicall beliefe of our Bible, as to preferre it before any other, that could be pretended to be the Word of God. He would believe it, and he would know *why* he did so. For let no man thinke that *God* hath given him so much ease here, as to save him by believing he knoweth not what, or why. *Knowledge* cannot save us, but we cannot be saved without Knowledge; Faith is not on this side Knowledge, but beyond it; we must necessarily come to *Knowledge* first, though we must not stay at it, when we are come thither.[39] For, a regenerate Christian, being now a *new Creature,* hath also *a new facultie of Reason:* and so believeth the Mysteries of Religion, out of another Reason, than as a meere naturall Man, he believed naturall and morall things. He believeth them for their own sake, by *Faith,* though he take *Knowledge* of them before, by that common Reason, and by those humane Arguments, which worke upon other men, in naturall or morall things. Divers men may walke by the Sea side, and the same beames of the Sunne giving light to them all, one gathereth by the benefit of that light pebles, or speckled shells, for curious vanitie, and another gathers precious Pearle, or medicinall Ambar, by the same light. So the common light of reason illumins us all; but one imployes this light upon the searching of impertinent vanities, another by a better use of the same light, finds out the Mysteries of Religion; and when he hath found them, loves them, not for the lights sake, but for the naturall and true worth of the thing it self. Some men by the benefit of this light of Reason, have found out things profitable and usefull to the whole world; As in particular, *Printing,* by which the learning of the whole world is communicable to one another, and our minds and our inventions, our wits and compositions may trade and have commerce together, and we may participate of one anothers understandings, as

well as of our Clothes, and Wines, and Oyles, and other Merchandize:
So by the benefit of this light of reason, they have found out *Artillery,*
by which warres come to quicker ends than heretofore, and the great
expence of bloud is avoyded: for the numbers of men slain now, since
the invention of Artillery, are much lesse than before, when the sword
was the executioner. Others, by the benefit of this light have searched
and found the secret corners of gaine, and profit, wheresoever they lie.
They have found wherein the weakenesse of another man consisteth,
and made their profit of that, by circumventing him in a bargain: They
have found his riotous, and wastefull inclination, and they have fed and
fomented that disorder, and kept open that leake, to their advantage, and
the others ruine. They have found where was the easiest, and most acces-
sible way, to sollicite the Chastitie of a woman, whether *Discourse,*
Musicke, or *Presents,* and according to that discovery, they have pursued
hers, and *their* own eternall destruction. By the benefit of this light, men
see through the darkest, and most impervious places, that are, that is,
Courts of Princes, and the greatest *Officers* in Courts; and can submit
themselves to second, and to advance the humours of men in great
place, and so make their profit of the weaknesses which they have
discovered in these great men. All the wayes, both of *Wisdome,* and of
Craft lie open to this light, this light of naturall reason: But when they
have gone all these wayes by the benefit of this light, they have got no
further, than to have walked by a tempestuous Sea, and to have gathered
pebles, and speckled cockle shells. Their light seems to be great out of
the same reason, that a Torch in a misty night, seemeth greater than in a
clear, because it hath kindled and inflamed much thicke and grosse Ayre
round about it. So the light and wisedome of worldly men, seemeth
great, because he hath kindled an admiration, or an applause in Aiery
flatterers, not because it is so in deed.

2

Doe thou therefore prevent the Preacher; Accuse thyselfe before he
accuse thee; offer up thy sinne thy selfe; Bring it to the top of thy
memory, and thy conscience, that he finding it there, may sacrifice it for
thee; Tune the instrument, and it is the fitter for his hand. Remember
thou thine own sins, first, and then every word that fals from the
preachers lips shall be a drop of the *dew of heaven,* a dram of the *balme of*
Gilead, a portion of the bloud of thy Saviour, to wash away that sinne,

so presented by thee to be so sacrified by him; for, if thou onely of all the congregation finde that the preacher hath not touched *thee,* nor hit *thy sinnes,* know then, that thou wast not in his Commission for the *Remission* of sinnes, and be afraid, that thy conscience is either *gangrend,* and unsensible of all incisions, and *cauterizations,* that can be made by denouncing the *Judgements* of God, (which is as far as the preacher can goe) or that thy whole constitution, thy complexion, thy composition is sinne; the preacher cannot hit thy particular sinne, because thy whole life, and the whole body of thy actions is one continuall sin. As long as a man is alive, if there appeare any offence in his breath, the physician will assigne it to some *one* corrupt *place,* his *lungs,* or *teeth,* or *stomach,* and thereupon apply convenient remedy thereunto. But if he be dead, and putrefied, no man askes *from whence that ill aire and offence comes,* because it proceeds from thy whole carcasse. So, as long as there is in you a *sense* of your sinnes, as long as we can touch the offended and wounded part, and be felt by you, you are not desperate, though you be froward, and impatient of our increpations. But when you *feele nothing,* whatsoever wee say, your soule is in an *Hectique fever,* where the distemper is not in any one humor, but in the whole substance; nay, your soule it selfe is become a carcasse.

13. FROM A SERMON PREACHED AT WHITE-HALL, 8 MARCH 1622[40]

I

We have other Enemies; Satan about us, sin within us; but the power of both those, this enemie shall destroy; but when they are destroyed, he shall retaine a hostile, and triumphant dominion over us. But *Vsque quo Domine?* How long O Lord? for ever? No, *Abolebitur:* wee see this Enemy all the way, and all the way we feele him; but we shall see him destroyed; *Abolebitur.* But how? or when? At, and by the resurrection of our bodies: for as upon my expiration, my transmigration from hence, as soone as my soule enters into Heaven, I shall be able to say to the Angels, I am of the same stuffe as you, spirit, and spirit, and therefore let me stand with you, and looke upon the face of your God, and my God; so at the Resurrection of this body, I shall be able to say to the Angel of the great Councell, the Son of God, Christ Jesus himselfe, I am of the same stuffe as you, Body and body, Flesh and flesh, and therefore let me sit downe with you, at the right hand of the Father in an everlasting security from this last enemie, who is now destroyed, death. And in these seven steps we shall passe apace, and yet cleerely through this paraphrase.

We begin with this; That the Kingdome of Heaven hath not all that it must have to a consummate perfection, till it have bodies too. In those infinite millions of millions of generations, in which the holy, blessed, and glorious Trinity enjoyed themselves one another, and no more, they thought not their glory so perfect, but that it might receive an addition from creatures; and therefore they made a world, a materiall world, a corporeall world, they would have bodies. In that noble part of that world which *Moses* cals the Firmament, that great expansion from Gods chaire to his footstoole, from Heaven to earth, there was a defect, which God did not supply that day, nor the next, but the fourth day, he did; for that day he made those bodies, those great, and lightsome bodies, the Sunne, and Moone, and Starres, and placed them in the Firmament. So also the Heaven of Heavens, the Presence Chamber of God himselfe, expects the presence of our bodies.

No State upon earth, can subsist without those bodies, Men of their owne. For men that are supplied from others, may either in necessity, or in indignation, be withdrawne, and so that State which stood upon forraine legs, sinks. Let the head be gold, and the armes silver, and the belly brasse, if the feete be clay, Men that may slip, and molder away, all is but an Image, all is but a dreame of an Image: for forraine helps are rather crutches than legs. There must be bodies, Men, and able bodies, able men; Men that eate the good things of the land, their owne figges and olives; Men not macerated with extortions: They are glorified bodies that make up the kingdome of Heaven; bodies that partake of the good of the State, that make up the State. Bodies, able bodies, and lastly, bodies inanimated with one soule: one vegetative soule, head and members must grow together, one sensitive soule, all must be sensible and compassionate of one anothers miserie; and especially one Immortall soule, one supreame soule, one Religion.

2

Doth not man die even in his birth? The breaking of prison is death, and what is our birth, but a breaking of prison? As soon as we were clothed by God, our very apparell was an Embleme of death. In the skins of dead beasts, he covered the skins of dying men. As soon as God set us on work, our very occupation was an Embleme of death; It was to digge the earth; not to digge pitfals for other men, but graves for our selves. Hath any man here forgot to day, that yesterday is dead? And the Bell tolls for to day, and will ring out anon; and for as much of every one of us, as appertaines to this day. *Quotidie morimur, & tamen nos esse aeternos putamus,* sayes S. *Hierome;* We die every day, and we die all the day long; and because we are not absolutely dead, we call that an eternity, an eternity of dying: And is there comfort in that state? why, that is the state of hell it self, Eternall dying, and not dead.

But for this there is enough said, by the Morall man; (that we may respite divine proofes, for divine points anon, for our severall Resurrections) for this death is meerly naturall, and it is enough that the morall man sayes, *Mors lex, tributum, officium mortalium.*[41] First it is *lex,* you were born under that law, upon that condition to die: so it is a rebellious thing not to be content to die, it opposes the Law. Then it is *Tributum,* an imposition which nature the Queen of this world layes upon us, and which she will take, when and where she list; here a yong man, there an old man, here a happy, there a miserable man; And so it is a seditious thing not to be content to die, it opposes the prerogative. And lastly, it is *Officium,* men are to have their turnes, to take their time, and then to give way by death to successors; and so it is *Incivile, inofficiosum,* not to be content to die, it opposes the frame and form of government. It comes equally to us all, and makes us all equall when it comes. The ashes of an Oak in the Chimney, are no Epitaph of that Oak, to tell me how high or how large that was; It tels me not what flocks it sheltered while it stood, nor what men it hurt when it fell. The dust of great persons graves is speechlesse too, it sayes nothing, it distinguishes nothing: As soon the dust of a wretch whom thou wouldest not, as of a Prince whom thou couldest not look upon, will trouble thine eyes, if the winde blow it thither; and when a whirle-winde hath blowne the dust of the Church-yard into the Church, and the man sweeps out the dust of the Church into the Church-yard, who will undertake to sift those dusts again, and to pronounce, This is the Patrician, this is the noble flowre, and this the yeomanly, this the Plebeian bran?

*

3

Death is the last, and in that respect the worst enemy. In an enemy, that appeares at first, when we are or may be provided against him, there is some of that, which we call Honour: but in the enemie that reserves himselfe unto the last, and attends our weake estate, there is more danger. Keepe it, where I intend it, in that which is my spheare, the Conscience: If mine enemie meet me betimes in my youth, in an object of tentation, (so *Josephs* enemie meet him in *Putifars* Wife) yet if I doe not adhere to this enemy, dwell upon a delightfull meditation of that sin, if I doe not fuell, and foment that sin, assist and encourage that sin, by high diet, wanton discourse, other provocation, I shall have reason on my side, and I shall have grace on my side, and I shall have the History of a thousand that have perished by that sin, on my side; Even Spittles[42] will give me souldiers to fight for me, by their miserable example against that sin; nay perchance sometimes the vertue of that woman, whom I sollicite, will assist me. But when I lye under the hands of that enemie, that hath reserved himselfe to the last, to my last bed, then when I shall be able to stir no limbe in any other measure than a Feaver or a Palsie shall shake them, when everlasting darknesse shall have an inchoation in the present dimnesse of mine eyes, and the everlasting gnashing in the present chattering of my teeth, and the everlasting worme in the present gnawing of the Agonies of my body, and anguishes of my minde, when the last enemie shall watch my remedilesse body, and my disconsolate soule there, there, where not the Physitian, in his way, perchance not the Priest in his, shall be able to give any assistance, And when he hath sported himselfe with my misery upon that stage, my death-bed, shall shift the Scene, and throw me from that bed, into the grave, and there triumph over me, God knowes, how many generations, till the Redeemer, my Redeemer, the Redeemer of all me, body, as well as soule, come againe; As death is *Novissimus hostis,* the enemy which watches me, at my last weaknesse, and shall hold me, when I shall be no more, till that Angel come, *Who shall say, and sweare that time shall be no more,* in that consideration, in that apprehension, he is the powerfullest, the fearefulest enemy; and yet even there this enemy *Abolebitur,* he shall be destroyed.

14. FROM A SERMON PREACHED UPON
EASTER-DAY [? 21 APRIL 1622][43]

I

The dead heare not Thunder, nor feele they an Earth-quake. If the
Canon batter that Church walls, in which they lye buryed, it wakes
not them, nor does it shake or affect them, if that dust, which they are,
be thrown out, but yet there is a voyce, which the dead shall heare; *The
dead shall heare the voyce of the Son of God,* (sayes the Son of God himself)
and they that heare shall live; And that is the voyce of our Text. It is here
called a clamour, a vociferation, a shout, and varied by our Translators,
and Expositors, according to the origination of the word, to be *clamor
hortatorius,* and *suasorius,* and *jussorius,* A voyce that carries with it a
penetration, (all shall heare it) and a perswasion, (all shall beleeve it, and
be glad of it) and a power, a command, (all shall obey it.) Since that
voyce at the Creation, *Fiat,* Let there be a world, was never heard such a
voyce as this, *Surgite mortui,* Arise ye dead. That was spoken to that that
was meerely nothing, and this to them, who in themselves shall have no
cooperation, no concurrence to the hearing or answering this voyce.

The power of this voyce is exalted in that it is said to be the *voyce of
the Archangel.* Though legions of Angels, millions of Angels shall be
employed about the Resurrection, to recollect their scattered dust, and
recompact their ruined bodies, yet those bodies so recompact, shall not
be able to heare a voyce. They shall be then but such bodies, as they
were when they were laid downe in the grave, when, though they were
intire bodies, they could not heare the voice of the mourner. But this
voyce of the Archangel shall enable them to heare; The Archangel shall
re-infuse the severall soules into their bodies, and so they shall heare that
voyce, *Surgite mortui,* Arise ye that were dead, and they shall arise.

2

First *Erimus, We shall Bee,* we shall have a Beeing. There is nothing
more contrary to God, and his proceedings, than annihilation, to Bee
nothing, Do nothing, Think nothing. It is not so high a step, to raise the
poore out of the dust, and to lift the needy from the dunghill, and set
him with Princes, To make a King of a Beggar is not so much, as to
make a Worm of nothing. Whatsoever God hath made thee since, yet

his greatest work upon thee, was, that he made thee; and howsoever he extend his bounty in preferring thee, yet his greatest largenesse, is, in preserving thee in thy Beeing. And therefore his own name of Majesty, is Jehovah, which denotes his Essence, his Beeing. And it is usefully moved, and safely resolved in the School, that the devill himself cannot deliberately wish himselfe nothing. Suddenly a man may wish himself nothing, because that seemes to deliver him from the sense of his present misery; but deliberately he cannot; because whatsoever a man wishes, must be something better than he hath yet; and whatsoever is better, is not nothing. *Nihil contrarium Deo,* There is nothing truly contrary to God; To do nothing, is contrary to his working; but contrary to his nature, contrary to his Essence there is nothing. For whatsoever is any thing, even in that Beeing, and therefore because it is, hath a conformity to God, and an affinity with God, who is Beeing, Essence it self.[44] *In him we have our Beeing,* sayes the Apostle. But here it is more than so; not only *In illo,* but *Cum illo,* not only *In him,* but *With him,* not only in his Providence, but in his Presence.

15. FROM A SERMON PREACHED AT THE SPITTLE, UPON EASTER-MONDAY, 1622[45]

I

Our God is not out of breath, because he hath blown one tempest, and swallowed a Navy: Our God hath not burnt out his eyes, because he hath looked upon a Train of Powder: In the light of Heaven, and in the darkness of hell, he sees alike; he sees not onely all Machinations of hands, when things come to action; but all Imaginations of hearts, when they are in their first Consultations: past, and present, and future, distinguish not his *Quando;* all is one time to him: Mountains and Vallies, Sea and Land, distinguish not his *Ubi;* all is one place to him: *When I begin,* says God to *Eli, I will make an end;* not onely that all Gods purposes shall have their certain end, but that even then, when he begins, he makes an end: from the very beginning, imprints an infallible assurance, that whom he loves, he loves to the end: as a Circle is printed all at once, so his beginning and ending is all one.

2

The drowning of the first world, and the repairing that again; the burning of this world, and establishing another in heaven, do not so much strain a mans Reason, as the Creation, a Creation of all out of nothing. For, for the repairing of the world after the Flood, compared to the Creation, it was eight to nothing; eight persons to begin a world upon, then; but in the Creation, none. And for the glory which we receive in the next world, it is (in some sort) as the stamping of a print upon a Coyn; the metal is there already, a body and a soul to receive glory: but at the Creation, there was no soul to receive glory, no body to receive a soul, no stuff, no matter, to make a body of. The less any thing is, the less we know it: how invisible, how inintelligible a thing then, is this *Nothing!* We say in the School, *Deus cognoscibilior Angelis,* We have better means to know the nature of God, than of Angels, because God hath appeared and manifested himself more in actions, than Angels have done: we know what they are, by knowing what they have done; and it is very little that is related to us what Angels have done: what then is there that can bring this Nothing to our understanding? what hath that done? A Leviathan, a Whale, from a grain of Spawn; an Oke from a buried Akehorn, is a great; but a great world from nothing, is a strange improvement.

3

And for the knowledge of Angels,[46] that is not in them *per essentiam,* for whosoever knows so, as the Essence of the thing flows from him, knows all things, and that's a knowledge proper to God only: Neither doe the Angels know *per species,* by those resultances and species, which rise from the Object, and pass through the Sense to the Understanding, for that's a deceiveable way, both by the indisposition of the Organ, sometimes, and sometimes by the depravation of the Judgment; and therefore, as the first is too high, this is too low a way for the Angels. Some things the Angels do know by the dignity of their Nature, by their Creation, which we know not; as we know many things which inferior Creatures do not; and such things all the Angels, good and bad know. Some things they know by the Grace of their confirmation, by which they have more given them, than they had by Nature in their Creation; and those things only the Angels that stood, but all they, do know. Some things they know by Revelation, when God is pleased to manifest them unto them; and so some of the Angels know that, which the rest, though confirm'd, doe not know. By Creation, they know as his Subjects; by Confirmation, they know as his servants; by Revelation, they know as his Councel. Now, *Erismus sicut Angeli,* says Christ, *There we shall be as the Angels:* The knowledge which I have by Nature, shall have no Clouds; here it hath: that which I have by Grace, shall have no reluctation, no resistance; here it hath: That which I have by Revelation, shall have no suspition, no jealousie; here it hath: sometimes it is hard to distinguish between a respiration from God, and a suggestion from the Devil. There our curiosity shall have this noble satisfaction, we shall know how the Angels know, by knowing as they know. We shall not pass from Author, to Author, as in a Grammar School, nor from Art to Art, as in an University; but, as that General which Knighted his whole Army, God shall Create us all Doctors in a minute. That great Library, those infinite Volumes of the Books of Creatures,[47] shall be taken away, quite away, no more Nature; those reverend Manuscripts, written with Gods own hand, the Scriptures themselves, shall be taken away, quite away; no more preaching, no more reading of Scriptures, and that great School-Mistress, Experience, and Observation shall be remov'd, no new thing to be done, and in an instant, I shall know more, than they all could reveal unto me. I shall know, not only as I know already, that a Bee-hive, that an Ant-hill is the same Book in *Decimo sexto,* as a Kingdom is in *Folio,* That a Flower that lives but a day, is an abridgment of that King, that lives out his threescore and ten yeers; but I shall know too, that all these Ants, and Bees, and Flowers, and Kings, and Kingdoms, howsoever they may be Examples, and Comparisons to one another, yet they are all as nothing, altogether nothing, less than nothing, infinitely less than nothing, to that which shall then be the subject of my knowledge, for, *it is the knowledge of the glory of God.*

16. FROM A SERMON PREACHED AT HANWORTH, TO MY LORD OF CARLILE, 25 AUGUST 1622[48]

The power of *oratory,* in the force of perswasion, the strength of conclusions, in the pressing of *Philosophy,* the harmony of *Poetry,* in the sweetnesse of composition, never met in any man, so fully as in the Prophet *Esay*, nor in the Prophet *Esay* more, than where he says, *Levate Oculos, Lift up your eyes, on high, and behold who hath created these things;* behold them, *therefore,* to know that they are created, and to know who is their creator. All other authors we distinguish by *tomes,* by *parts,* by *volumes;* but who knowes the volumes of this Author; how many volumes of Spheares involve one another, how many tomes of Gods Creatures there are? Hast thou not room, hast thou not money, hast thou not understanding, hast thou not leasure, for great volumes, for the *bookes of heaven,* (for the *Mathematiques*) nor for the books of *Courts,* (the *Politiques*) take but the *Georgiques,*⁴⁹ the consideration of the *Earth,* a farme, a garden, nay seven foot of earth, a grave, and that will be book enough. Goe lower; every *worme* in the grave, lower, every *weed* upon the grave, is an abridgement of all; nay lock up all doores and windowes, see nothing but *thy selfe;* nay let thy selfe be locked up in a close prison, that thou canst not see thy selfe, and doe but feel thy *pulse;* let thy pulse be intermitted, or stupefied, that thou feel not that, and doe but thinke, and a *worme, a weed,* thy *selfe,* thy *pulse,* thy *thought,* are all testimonies, that *All,* this *All,* and all the parts thereof, are *Opus,* a *work made,* and *opos ejus, his work,* made by *God.* He that made a Clock or an Organ, will be sure to ingrave his *Me fecit,* such a man made me; he that builds a faire house, takes it ill, if a passenger will not aske, *whose house is it?* he that bred up his Sonne to a capacity of noble employments, looks that the world should say, *he had a wise and an honourable Father;* Can any man look upon the frame of this world, and not say, there is a *powerfull,* upon the administration of this world, and not say, there is a *wise* and a *just* hand over it? Thus is the object, 'tis but *Illud,* the world; but such a world, as may well justifie *Saint Hieromes* translation, who renders it *Illum;* not onely that *every man may see it,* the *work,* the *world;* but may see *him; God* in that work.

17. FROM A SERMON PREACHED UPON
WHITSUNDAY [? 1622][50]

In the great Ant-hill of the whole world, I am an Ant; I have my part in
the Creation, I am a Creature; But there are ignoble Creatures. God
comes nearer; In the great field of clay, of red earth, that man was made
of, and mankind, I am a clod; I am a man, I have my part in the
Humanity; But Man was worse than annihilated again. When Satan in
that serpent was come, as *Hercules* with his club into a potters shop, and
had broke all the vessels, destroyed all mankind, And the gracious
promise of a Messias to redeeme all mankind, was shed and spread upon
all, I had my drop of that dew of Heaven, my sparke of that fire of
heaven, in the universall promise, in which I was involved; But this
promise was appropriated after, in a particular Covenant, to one people,
to the Jewes, to the seed of *Abraham*. But for all that I have my portion
there; for all that professe Christ Jesus are by a spirituall engrafting, and
transmigration, and transplantation, in and of that stock, and that seed
of *Abraham;* and I am one of those. But then, of those who doe professe
Christ Jesus, some grovell still in the superstitions they were fallen into,
and some are raised, by Gods good grace, out of them; and I am one of
those; God hath afforded me my station, in that Church, which is
departed from Babylon.

Now, all this while, my soule is in a cheerefull progresse; when I
consider what God did for Goshen in Egypt, for a little parke in the
midst of a forest; what he did for Jury,[51] in the midst of enemies, as a
shire that should stand out against a Kingdome round about it: How
many Sancerraes he hath delivered from famins, how many Genevaes
from plots, and machinations against her; all this while my soule is in a
progresse: But I am at home, when I consider Buls of excommunications,
and solicitations of Rebellions, and pistols, and poysons, and the discoveries of those; There is our *Nos, We,* testimonies that we are in the
favour, and care of God; We, our Nation, we, our Church; There I am
at home; but I am in my Cabinet at home, when I consider, what God
hath done for me, and my soule; There is the *Ego,* the particular, the
individuall, I.

18. FROM A SERMON PREACHED TO THE EARLE OF CARLILE, AND HIS COMPANY, AT SION [? AUTUMN 1622][52]

I

That *Christ is conceived,* and *borne,* and *crucified,* and *dead,* and *buried,* and *risen,* and *ascended,* there is some savour in this; But yet, if when we shall come to *Judgement,* I must carry into his presence, a menstruous[53] conscience, and an ugly face, in which his Image, by which he should know me, is utterly defaced, all this *Myrrhe* of his Merits, and his Mercies, is but a savour of death unto death unto me, since I, that knew the horror of my owne guiltinesse, must know too, that whatsoever he be to others, he is a just Judge, and therefore a condemning Judge to me; If I get farther than this in the Creed, to the *Credo in Spiritum Sanctum, I beleeve in the Holy Ghost,* where shall I finde the Holy Ghost? I lock my doore to my selfe, and I throw my selfe downe in the presence of my God, I devest my selfe of all worldly thoughts, and I bend all my powers, and faculties upon God, as I think, and suddenly I finde my selfe scattered, melted, fallen into vaine thoughts, into no thoughts; I am upon my knees, and I talke, and think nothing; I deprehend my selfe in it, and I goe about to mend it, I gather new forces, new purposes to try againe, and doe better, and I doe the same thing againe. *I beleeve in the Holy Ghost,* but doe not finde him, if I seeke him onely in private prayer; But *in Ecclesia,* when I goe to meet him in the *Church,* when I seeke him where hee hath promised to bee found, when I seeke him in the execution of that Commission, which is proposed to our faith in this Text, in his Ordinances, and meanes of salvation in his Church, instantly the savour of this *Myrrhe* is exalted, and multiplied to me; not a dew, but a shower is powred out upon me.

2

That God should let my soule fall out of his hand, into a bottomlesse pit, and roll an unremoveable stone upon it, and leave it to that which it finds there, (and it shall finde that there, which it never imagined, till it came thither) and never thinke more of that soule, never have more to doe with it. That of that providence of God, that studies the life and preservation of every weed, and worme, and ant, and spider, and toad, and viper, there should never, never any beame flow out upon me; that that God, who looked upon me, when I was nothing, and called me when I was not, as though I had been, out of the womb and depth of darknesse, will not looke upon me now, when, though a miserable, and a banished, and a damned creature, yet I am his creature still, and contribute something to his glory, even in my damnation; that that God, who hath often looked upon me in my foulest uncleannesse, and when I had shut out the eye of the day, the Sunne, and the eye of the night, the Taper, and the eyes of all the world, with curtaines and windows and doores, did yet see me,[54] and see me in mercy, by making me see that he saw me, and sometimes brought me to a present remorse, and (for that time) to a forbearing of that sinne, should so turne himselfe from me, to his glorious Saints and Angels, as that no Saint nor Angel, nor Christ Jesus himselfe, should ever pray him to looke towards me, never remember him, that such a soule there is; that that God, who hath so often said to my soule, *Quare morieris?* Why wilt thou die? and so often sworne to my soule, *Vivit Dominus,* As the Lord liveth, I would not have thee dye, but live, will neither let me dye, nor let me live, but dye an everlasting life, and live an everlasting death; that that God, who, when he could not get into me, by standing, and knocking, by his ordinary meanes of entring, by his Word, his mercies, hath applied his judgements, and hath shaked the house, this body, with agues and palsies, and set this house on fire, with fevers and calentures, and frighted the Master of the house, my soule, with horrors, and heavy apprehensions, and so made an entrance into me; That that God should loose and frustrate all his owne purposes and practises upon me, and leave me, and cast me away, as though I had cost him nothing, that this God at last, should let this soule goe away, as a smoake, as a vapour, as a bubble, and that then this soule cannot be a smoake, nor a vapour, nor a bubble, but must lie in darknesse, as long as the Lord of light is light it selfe, and never a sparke of that light reach to my soule; What Tophet is not Paradise, what Brimstone is not Amber, what gnashing is not a comfort, what gnawing of the worme is not a tickling, what torment is not a marriage bed to this damnation, to be secluded eternally, eternally, eternally from the sight of God? Especially to us, for as the perpetuall losse of that is most heavy, with which we have been best acquainted, and to which wee have been most accustomed; so shall this damnation, which consists in the losse of the sight and presence of God, be heavier to us than others, because God hath so graciously, and so evidently, and so diversly appeared to us, in his pillar of fire, in the light of prosperity, and in the pillar of the Cloud, in hiding himselfe for a while from us; we that have seene him in the Execution of all the parts of this Commission, in his Word, in his Sacraments, and in good example, and not beleeved, shall be further removed from his sight, in the next world, than they to whom he never appeared in this. But *Vincenti & credenti,* to him that beleeves aright, and overcomes all tentations to a wrong beliefe, God shall give the accomplishment of fulnesse, and fulnesse of joy, and joy rooted in glory, and glory established in eternity, and this eternity is God; To him that beleeves and overcomes, God shall give himselfe in an everlasting presence and fruition, *Amen.*

19. FROM A SERMON PREACHED UPON THE PENITENTIALL PSALMES [DATE UNKNOWN][55]

Though your sins be as Scarlet, they shall be as white as snow. Esay was an Euangelicall Prophet, a propheticall Euangelist, and speaks still of the state of the Christian Church. There, by the ordinary meanes exhibited there, our Scarlet sins are made as white as Snow; And the whitenesse of Snow, is a whitenesse that no art of man can reach to; So Christs garments in his Transfiguration are expressed to have beene *as white as Snow, so, as no Fuller on earth could white them.* Nothing in this world can send me home in such a whitenesse, no morall counsaile, no morall comfort, no morall constancy; as Gods Absolution by his Minister, as the profitable hearing of a Sermon, the worthy receiving of the Sacrament do. This is to be as white as snow; In a good state for the present. But *David* begs a whitenesse above Snow; for Snow melts, and then it is not white; our present Sanctification withers, and we lose that cheerful verdure, the testimony of an upright conscience; And Snow melted, Snow water, is the coldest water of all; Devout men departed from their former fervor are the coldest and the most irreducible to true zeale, true holinesse. Therefore *David* who was metall tried seven times in the fire, and desired to be such gold as might be laid up in Gods Treasury, might consider, that in transmutation of metals,[56] it is not enough to come to a calcination, or a liquefaction of the metall, (that must be done) nor to an Ablution, to sever drosse from pure, nor to a Transmutation, to make it a better metall, but there must be a Fixion, a settling thereof, so that it shall not evaporate into nothing, nor returne to his former nature. Therefore he saw that he needed not only a liquefaction, a melting into teares, nor only an Ablution, and a Transmutation, those he had by this purging and this washing, this station in the Church of God, and this present Sanctification there, but he needed *Fixionem,* an establishment, which the comparison of Snow afforded not; That as he had purged him with Hyssop, and so cleansed him, that is, enwrapped him in the Covenant, and made him a member of the true Church; and there washed him so, as that he was restored to a whitenesse, that is, made his Ordinances so effectuall upon him, as that then he durst deliver his soule into his hands at that time: So he would exalt that whitenesse, above the whitenesse of Snow, so as nothing might melt it, nothing discolour it, but that under the seale of his blessed Spirit, he might ever dwell in that calme, in that assurance, in that acquiescence, that as he is in a good state this minute, he shall be in no worse, whensoever God shall be pleased to translate him.

20. A SERMON PREACHED TO THE HONOURABLE COMPANY OF THE VIRGINIAN PLANTATION, 13 NOVEMBER 1622[57]

[DEDICATORY EPISTLE]

To the Honorable Company of the Virginian Plantation

By your favours, I had some place amongst you, before: but now I am an Adventurer; *if not to* VIRGINIA, *yet for* VIRGINIA; *for, every man, that* Prints, Adventures. *For the* Preaching *of this Sermon, I was but under your* Invitation; *my Time was mine owne, and my* Meditations *mine owne: and I had beene excusable towards you, if I had turnd that* Time, *and those* Meditations, *to* GODS *service, in any other place. But for the* Printing *of this Sermon, I am not onely under your* Invitation, *but under your* Commandement; *for, after it was preach'd, it was not mine, but yours: And*

therefore, if I gave it at first, I doe but restore it now. The first was an act of Love; *this,
of* Justice; *both which* Vertues, Almighty God *evermore promove, and exalt in all
your proceedings. Amen.*

Your humble Servant
in *Christ Jesus*
JOHN DONNE

There are reckoned in this booke, 22. *Sermons* of the *Apostles;* and yet
the booke is not called the *Preaching*, but the *Practise*, not the *Words*, but
the *Acts* of the *Apostles:* and the *Acts* of the *Apostles* were to convay that
name of *Christ Jesus*, and to propagate his *Gospell*, over all the world:
Beloved, you are *Actors* upon the same Stage too: the uttermost parts of
the Earth are your *Scene:* act over the *Acts* of the *Apostles;* bee you a
light to the *Gentiles*, that sit in darkenesse; be you content to carry him
over these *Seas*, who dryed up one *Red Sea* for his first people, and hath
powred out another *red Sea*, his owne bloud, for them and us. When
man was fallen, *God* clothed him; made him a Leather Garment; there
God descended to one occupation; when the time of mans redemption
was come, then *God*, as it were, to house him, became a *Carpenters
Sonne;* there *God* descended to another occupation. Naturally, without
doubt, man would have beene his own Taylor, and his owne Carpenter;
something in these two kinds man would have done of himselfe, though
hee had no patterne from *God*: but in preserving man who was fallen, to
this redemption, by which he was to be raisd, in preserving man from
perishing, in the Flood, *God* descended to a third occupation, to be his
Shipwright, to give him the modell of a Ship, an *Arke*, and so to be the
author of that, which man himselfe in likelihood, would never have
thought of, a means to passe from *Nation* to *Nation*. Now, as G O D
taught us to make cloathes, not onely to cloath our selves, but to cloath
him in his poore and naked members heere; as *God* taught us to build
houses, not to house our selves, but to house him, in erecting *Churches*,
to his glory: So *God* taught us to make Ships, not to transport our
selves, but to transport him, *That when wee have received power, after that
the Holy Ghost is come upon us, we might be witnesses unto him, both in*
Jerusalem, *and in all* Judaea, *and in* Samaria, *and unto the uttermost parts of
the Earth.*

As I speake now principally to them who are concernd in this
Plantation of *Virginia*, yet there may be divers in this Congregation, who,

though they have no interest in this *Plantation,* yet they may have benefit and edification, by that which they heare me say, so *Christ* spoke the words of this *Text,* principally to the *Apostles,* who were present and questioned him at his *Ascension,* but they are in their just extention, and due accomodation, appliable to our present occation of meeting heere: As *Christ* himselfe is *Alpha,* and *Omega,* so first, as that hee is last too, so these words which he spoke in the *East,* belong to us, who are to glorifie him in the *West; That we having received power, after that the* Holy Ghost *is come upon us, might be witnesses unto him, both in* Jerusalem, *and in all* Judea, *and in* Samaria, *and unto the uttermost parts of the Earth.*

The first word of the Text is the *Cardinall* word, the word, the *hinge* upon which the whole *Text* turnes; The first word, *But,* is the *But,* that all the rest shoots at. First it is an *exclusive* word; something the *Apostles* had required, which might not bee had; not that; And it is an *inclusive* word; something *Christ* was pleasd to affoord to the *Apostles,* which they thought not of; not that, not that which you beat upon, *But,* but yet, something else, something better than that, you shall have. That which this but, *excludes,* is that which the *Apostles* expresse in the *Verse* immediatly before the *Text, a Temporall Kingdome; Wilt thou restore againe the kingdome of Israel?* No; not a temporall Kingdome; let not the riches and commodities of this World, be in your contemplation in your adventures. Or, because they aske more, *Wilt thou now restore that?* not yet: If I will give you riches, and commodities of this world, yet if I doe it not at first, if I doe it not yet, be not you discouraged; you shall not have *that,* that is not *Gods* first intention; and though that be in Gods intention, to give it you hereafter, you shall not have it yet; thats the *exclusive* part; *But;* there enters the *inclusive, You shall receive power, after that the Holy Ghost is come upon you, and you shall bee witnesses unto mee, both in* Jerusalem, *and in all* Judaea, *and in* Samaria, *and unto the uttermost parts of the Earth.* In which second part, we shall passe by these steps; *Superveniet Spiritus,* The *holy Ghost* shall come upon you, *The Spirit* shall witnesse to *your Spirit,* and rectifie your Conscience; And then, by that, you shall receive *power;* A new power besides the power you have from the *State,* and that power shall enable you, to be witnesses of *Christ,* that is, to make his doctrine the more credible, by your testimony, when you conforme your selves to him, and doe as hee did; and this witnesse you shall beare, this conformity you shall declare, first in *Jerusalem,* in this *Citie;* And in *Judaea,* in all the parts of the *Kingdome;*

and in *Samaria,* even amongst them who are departed from the true worship of *God,* the *Papists;* and to the uttermost part of the Earth, to those poore *Soules,* to whom you are continually sending. Summarily, If from the *Holy Ghost* you have a good testimony in your owne Conscience, you shall be witnesses for *Christ,* that is, as he did, you shall give satisfaction to all, to the *Citie,* to the *Countrey,* to the *Calumniating Adversary,* and the *Naturals* of the place, to whom you shall present both *Spirituall* and *Temporall* benefit to. And so you have the *Modell* of the whole frame, and of the partitions; we proceede now to the furnishing of the particular roomes.

I. PART

First then, this first word, *But,* excludes a temporall Kingdome; the *Apostles* had fill'd themselves with an expectation, with an ambition of it; but that was not intended them. It was no wonder, that a woman could conceive such an expectation, and such an ambition, as to have her two sonnes sit at *Christs* right hand, and at his left, in his Kingdome, when the *Apostles* expected such a Kingdome, as might affoord them honours and preferment upon Earth. More than once they were in that disputation, in which *Christ* deprehended them, *Which of them should bee the greatest in his Kingdome.* Neither hath the *Bishop of Rome,* any thing, wherein he may so properly call himselfe *Apostolicall,* as this error of the *Apostles,* this their infirmitie, that he is evermore too conversant upon the contemplation of temporal Kingdomes. They did it all the way, when *Christ* was with them, and now at his last step, *Cum actu ascendisset,* when *Christ* was not *Ascending,* but in part *ascended,* when one foot was upon the Earth, and the other in the cloud that tooke him up, they aske him now, wilt thou at this time, restore the Kingdome? So women put their husbands, and men their fathers, and friends, upon their torture, at their last gaspe, and make their death-bed a racke to make them stretch and encrease joyntures, and portions, and legacies, and signe Scedules and Codicils, with their hand, when his hand that presents them, is ready to close his eyes, that should signe them: And when they are upon the wing for heaven, men tye lead to their feet, and when they are laying hand-fast upon *Abrahams* bosome, they must pull their hand out of his bosome againe, to obey importunities of men, and signe their papers: so undeterminable is the love of this World, which determines every minute. GOD, as hee is three persons, hath three Kingdomes; There is *Regnum potentiae,* The Kingdome of power; and this wee attribute to the *Father;* it is power and providence: There is *Regnum gloriae,* the Kingdome of glorie; this we attribute to the *Sonn* and to his purchase; for he is *the King* that shall say, *Come ye blessed of my Father, inherit the Kingdome prepared for you, from the foundation of the World.* And then betweene these there is *Regnum gratiae,* The kingdome of Grace, and this we attribute to the *Holy Ghost;* he takes them, whom the king of power, Almighty *God* hath rescued from the *Gentiles,* and as the king of grace, *Hee gives them the knowledge of the misterie of the kingdome of* GOD, that is, of *future glory,* by sanctifying them with his grace, in his *Church.* The two first kingdomes are in this world, but yet neither of them, are of this world; because both they referre to the kingdome of glory. The kingdome of the *Father,* which is the providence of *God,* does but preserve us; The kingdome of the *Holy Ghost* which is the grace of *God,* does but prepare us to the kingdome of the *Sonne,* which is the glory of GOD; and thats in heaven. And therefore, though to good men, this world be the way to that kingdome, yet this kingdome is not of this world, sayes Christ himselfe: Though the *Apostles* themselves, as good a *Schoole* as they were bred in, could never take out that lesson, yet that lesson *Christ* gives, and repeates to all, you seeke a Temporall kingdome, *But,* sayes the Text, stop there, A kingdome you must not have.

Beloved in him, whose kingdome, and Ghospell you seeke to advance, in this Plantation, our *Lord* and *Saviour Christ Jesus,* if you seeke to establish a temporall kingdome there, you are not rectified, if you seeke to bee *Kings* in either acceptation of the word; To be a *King* signifies *Libertie* and *independency,* and *Supremacie,* to bee under no man, and to be a *King* signifies *Abundance,* and *Omnisufficiencie,* to neede no man. If those that governe there, would establish such a government, as should not depend upon this, or if those that goe thither, propose to themselves an exemption from Lawes, to live at their libertie, this is to be *Kings,* to devest *Allegeance,* to bee under no man: and if those that adventure thither, propose to themselves present benefit, and profit, a sodaine way to bee rich, and an aboundance of all desirable commodities from thence, this is to bee sufficient of themselves, and to need no man: and to be under no man and to need no man, are the two acceptations of being *Kings.* Whom liberty drawes to goe, or present profit drawes to adventure, are not yet in the right way. O, if you could once bring a *Catechisme* to bee as good ware amongst them as a bugle, as a knife, as a hatchet: O, if you would be as ready to hearken at the returne of a *Ship*, how many *Indians* were converted to *Christ Jesus*, as what Trees, or druggs, or Dyes that Ship had brought, then you were in your right way, and not till then; *Libertie* and *Abundance*, are Characters of kingdomes, and a kingdome is excluded in the *Text;* The *Apostles* were not to looke for it, in their employment, nor you in this your Plantation.

At least CHRIST expresses himselfe thus farre, in this answer, that if he would give them a kingdome, hee would not give it them yet. They aske him, *Wilt thou at this time, restore the kingdome?* and hee answers, *It is not for you to know the times:* whatsoever *God* will doe, Man must not appoint him his time. The *Apostles* thought of a *kingdome* presently after *Christs* departure; the comming of the *Holy Ghost*, who ledd them into all truthes, soone deliver'd them of that error. Other men in favour of the *Jewes*, interpreting all the prophesies, which are of a *Spirituall kingdome*, the kingdome of the *Gospell*, (into which, the *Jewes* shall be admitted) in a literall sense, have thought that the *Jewes* shall have, not onely a temporall kingdome in the same place, in *Jerusalem* againe, but because they find that kingdome which is promised, (that is the kingdome of the *Gospell*) to bee expressed in large phrases, and in an abundant manner, applying all that largenesse to a temporall kingdome, they thinke, that the *Jewes* shall have such a kingdome, as shall swallowe and annihilate all other kingdomes, and bee the sole *Empire* and *Monarchy* of the world. After this, very great men in the *Church* upon these words, of One thousand yeares after the Resurrection, have imagin'd a *Temporall Kingdome* of the *Saints* of *God* heere upon Earth, before they entred the joyes of Heaven: and Saint *Augustine*[58] himselfe, had at first some declinations towards that opinion, though he dispute powerfully against it, after: That there should bee *Sabbatismus in terris;* that as the world was to last Sixe thousand yeares in troubles, there should be a Seventh thousand, in such joyes as this world could give.

And some others, who have avoided both the *Temporall kingdome* imagin'd by the *Apostles*, presently after the *Ascension*, And the *Emperiall kingdome* of the *Jewes*, before the *Resurrection*, And the *Carnall kingdome* of the *Chiliasts*,[59] the *Millenarians*, after the *Resurrection*, though they speake of no kingdome, but the true kingdome, the kingdome of glory, yet they erre as much in assigning a certaine time when that kingdome shall beginne, when the ende of this world, when the Resurrection, when the Judgement shall be. *Non est vestrum nosse tempora,* sayes *Christ* to his *Apostles* then; and lest it might be thought, that they might know these things, when the *Holy Ghost* came upon them, *Christ* denies that he himselfe knew that, as *Man;* and as *Man, Christ* knew more, than ever the *Apostles* knew. Whatsoever therefore *Christ* intended to his *Apostles* heere, hee would not give it presently, *non adhuc,* hee would not binde himselfe to a certaine time, *Non est vestrum nosse tempora,* It belongs not to us to know *Gods* times.

Beloved, use godly meanes, and give *God* his leisure. You cannot beget a Sonne, and tell the Mother, I will have this Sonne born within five Moneths; nor, when he is borne, say, you will have him past daunger of *Wardship* [60] within five yeares. You cannot sow your Corne to day, and say it shall bee above ground to morrow, and in my Barne next weeke. Howe soone the best Husbandman, sow'd the best Seede, in the best ground? GOD cast the promise of a *Messias,* as the seede of all, in Paradise; *In Semine Mulieris; The Seed of the Woman shall bruise the Serpents head;* and yet this *Plant* was Foure thousand yeares after before it appeared; this *Messias* Foure thousand yeares before he came. GOD shew'd the ground where that should growe, Two thousand yeares after the Promise; in *Abrahams* Family; *In semine tuo, In thy Seed all Nations shall be blessed.* God hedg'd in this Ground almost One thousand yeares after that; In *Micheas* time, *Et tu Bethlem, Thou Bethlem shalt bee the place;* and God watered that, and weeded that, refreshed that dry expectation, with a Succession of *Prophets;* and yet it was so long before this *expectation of Nations,* this *Messias* came. So GOD promised the *Jewes* a Kingdome, in *Jacobs* Prophecie to *Juda, That the Scepter should not depart from his Tribe.* In Two hundred yeares more, he saies no more of it; then he ordaines some institutions for their *King,* when they should have one. And then it was Foure hundred yeares after that, before they had a *King.* GOD meant from the first howre, to people the whole earth; and *God* could have made men of clay, as fast as they made Brickes of Clay in *Egypt;* but he began upon two, and when they had beene multiplying and replenishing the Earth One thousand sixe hundred yeares, the *Flood* washed all that away, and GOD was almost to begin againe upon eight persons; and they have serv'd to people *Earth* and *Heaven* too; Bee not you discouraged, if the Promises which you have made to your selves, or to others, be not so soone discharg'd; though you see not your money, though you see not your men, though a *Flood*, a *Flood* of *bloud* have broken in upon them,[61] be not discouraged. Great Creatures ly long in the wombe; *Lyons* are litterd perfit, but *Beare-whelpes* lick'd unto their shape; actions which Kings undertake, are cast in a mould; they have their perfection quickly; actions of private men, and private purses, require more hammering, and more filing to their perfection. Onely let your principall ende, bee the propagation of the *glorious Gospell*, and though there bee an *Exclusive* in the *Text*, GOD does not promise you a *Kingdome, ease,* and *abundance* in all things, and that which he does intend to you, he does not promise presently, yet there is an *Inclusive* too; not that, *But*, but something equivalent at least, *But yee shall receive power, after that the Holy Ghost is come upon you, and yee shall be witnesses unto me, both in* Jerusalem, *and in all* Judaea, *and in* Samaria, *and unto the uttermost parts of the Earth.*

2. PART

Now our *Saviour Christ* does not say to these men, since you are so importunate you shall have no *Kingdome; now* nor *never;* tis, *not yet; But,* he does not say, you shall have *no kingdome, nor any thing else;* tis *not that; But:* the importunitie of beggers, sometimes drawes us to such a froward answer, for this importunitie, I will never give you any thing. Our patterne was not so froward; hee gave them not that, but as good as that. *Samuel* was sent to superinduct a *King* upon *Saul,* to annoint a new King. Hee thought his *Commission* had bene determined in *Eliab, Surely this is the Lords Annointed.* But the *Lord* said, not he; nor the next, *Aminadab;* nor the next, *Shammah;* nor none of the next seven; *But;* but yet there is one in the field, keeping sheepe, annoint him; *David* is he. Saint *Paul* prayed earnestly, and frequently, to be discharged of that *Stimulus Carnis:*[62] *God* saies no; *not that;* but *Gratia mea sufficit,* Thou shalt have grace to overcome the tentation, though the tentation remaine. *God* sayes to you, *No Kingdome,* not *ease,* not *abundance;* nay *nothing at all yet;* the Plantation shall not discharge the Charges, not defray it selfe yet; but yet already, now at first, it shall conduce to great uses; It shall redeeme many a wretch from the Jawes of death, from the hands of the Executioner, upon whom, perchaunce a small fault, or perchance a first fault, or perchance a fault heartily and sincerely repented, perchance no fault, but malice, had otherwise cast a present, and ignominious death. It shall sweep your streets, and wash your dores, from idle persons, and the children of idle persons, and imploy them: and truely, if the whole Countrey were but such a *Bridewell*,[63] to force idle persons to work, it had a good use. But it is already, not onely a *Spleene*, to draine the ill humors of the body, but a *Liver*, to breed good bloud; already the imployment breeds Marriners; already the place gives essayes, nay Fraytes of Marchantable commodities; already it is a marke for the Envy, and for the ambition of our Enemies; I speake but of our *Doctrinall*, not *Nationall* Enemies;[64] as they are *Papists*, they are sory we have this Countrey; and surely, twenty Lectures in matter of Controversie, doe not so much vexe them, as one Ship that goes, and strengthens that Plantation. Neither can I recommend it to you, by any better *Rhetorique* than their malice. They would gladly have it, and therefore let us bee glad to hold it.

Thus then this *Text* proceedes, and gathers upon you. All that you would have by this Plantation, you shall not have; GOD bindes not himselfe to measures; All that you shall have, you have not yet; GOD bindes not himselfe to times, but something you shall have; nay, you have already, some great things; and of those that in the *Text* is, *The Holy Ghost shall come upon you.* Wee find the *Holy Ghost* to have come upon men, foure times in this Booke. First, upon the *Apostles* at *Pentecost*. Then, when the whole Congregation was in prayer for the imprisonment of *Peter* and *John*. Againe, when *Peter* preached in *Cornelius* his house, the *Holy Ghost fell upon all them that heard him*. And fourthly, when Saint *Paul* laid his hands upon them, who had beene formerly baptized at *Ephesus*. At the three latter times, it is evident that the *Holy Ghost* fell upon whole and promiscuous Congregations, and not upon the *Apostles* onely: and in the first, at *Pentecost*, the contrary is not evident; nay, the Fathers, for the most part, that handle that, concurre in that, that the *Holy Ghost* fell then upon the whole Congregation, men and women. The *Holy Ghost* fell upon *Peter* before hee preach'd, and it fell upon the hearers when he preach'd, and it hath fallen upon every one of them, who have found motions in themselves, to propagate the *Gospell* of *Christ Jesus* by this meanes. The *Sonne of* GOD did not abhorre the *Virgins* wombe, when hee would be made man; when he was man, he did not disdaine to ride upon an *Asse* into *Jerusalem:* the third person of the *Trinity*, the *Holy Ghost* is as humble as the second, hee refuses *Nullum vehiculum,* no conveyance, no doore of entrance into you; whether the example and precedent of other good men, or a probable imagination of future profit, or a willingnes to concurre to the vexation of the Enemie, what collaterall respect soever drew thee in, if now thou art in, thy principall respect be the glory of God, that occasion, whatsoever it was, was *vehiculum Spiritus Sancti,* that was the Petard,[65] that broke open thy Iron gate, that was the Chariot, by which he entred into thee, and now hee is fallen upon thee, if thou do not *Depose,* (lay aside all consideration of profit for ever, never to looke for returne) No not *Sepose,* (leave out the consideration of profit for a time) (for that, and Religion may well consist together,) but if thou doe but *Post-pose* the consideration of temporall gaine, and study first the advancement of the *Gospell* of *Christ Jesus,* the *Holy Ghost* is fallen upon you, for by that, *you receive power,* sayes the *Text.*

There is a *Power* rooted in *Nature,* and a *Power* rooted in *Grace;* a power yssuing from the Law of *Nations,* and a power growing out of the *Gospell.* In the Law of *Nature* and *Nations,* A Land never inhabited, by any, or utterly derelicted and immemorially abandoned by the former Inhabitants, becomes theirs that wil posesse it. So also is it, if the inhabitants doe not in some measure fill the Land, so as the Land may bring foorth her increase for the use of men: for as a man does not become proprietary of the Sea, because he hath two or three Boats, fishing in it, so neither does a man become Lord of a maine Continent, because hee hath two or three Cottages in the Skirts thereof. That rule which passes through all *Municipal Lawes* in particular States, *Interest reipublicae ut quis re sua bene utatur, The State must take order, that every man improove that which he hath, for the best advantage of that State,* passes also through the Law of *Nations,* which is to all the world, as the *Municipall* Law is to a particular State, *Interest mundo, The whole world, all Mankinde must take care, that all places be emprov'd, as farre as may be, to the best advantage of Mankinde in generall.* Againe if the Land be peopled, and cultivated by the people, and that Land produce in abundance such things, for want whereof their neghbours, or others (being not enemies) perish, the Law of *Nations* may justifie some force, in seeking, by permutation of other commodities which they neede, to come to some of theirs. Many cases may be put, when not onely *Commerce,* and *Trade,* but *Plantations* in lands, not formerly our owne, may be lawfull. And for that, *Accepistis potestatem,* you have your *Commission,* your *Patents,* your *Charters,* your *Seales* from *him,* upon whose acts, any private Subject, in Civill matters, may safely rely. But then, *Accipietis potestatem, You shall receive power,* sayes the *text;* you shall, when the *Holy Ghost* is come upon you; that is, when the instinct, the influence, the motions of the *Holy Ghost* enables your Conscience to say, that your principall ende is not gaine, nor glory, but to gaine Soules to the glory of GOD, this Seales the great Seale, this justifies Justice it selfe, this authorises Authoritie, and gives power to strength it selfe. Let the Conscience bee upright, and then *Seales,* and *Patents,* and *Commissions* are wings; they assist him to flye the faster; let the Conscience be lame, and distorted, and he that goes upon *Seales,* and *Patents,* and *Commissions,* goes upon weake and feeble crouches. When the *Holy Ghost* is come upon you, your Conscience rectified, you shall have *Power,* a new power out of that; what to doe? that followes, to bee *witnesses unto Christ.*

Infamy is one of the highest punishments that the Law inflicts upon man; for it lyes upon him even after death: *Infamy* is the worst punishment, and *Intestabilitie,* (to be made *intestable*) is one of the deepest wounds of *infamy;* and then the worst degree of *intestabilitie,* is not to bee beleeved, not to bee admitted to be a witnesse of any other: he is *Intestable* that cannot make a *Testament,* not give his owne goods; and hee *Intestable* that can receive nothing by the *Testament* of another; hee is *Intestable,* in whose behalfe no testimony may be accepted; but he is the most miserably *Intestable* of all, the most detestably intestable, that discredits another man by speaking well of him, and makes him the more suspitious, by his commendations. A *Christian* in profession, that is not a *Christian* in life, is so intestable, hee discredits *Christ,* and hardens others against him. *John Baptist* was more than a *Prophet,* because he was a *Witnesse* of *Christ;* and he was a *Witnesse,* because hee was like him, he did as hee did, he lead a holy and a religious life; so he was a *Witnesse.* That great and glorious name of *Martyr,* is but a *Witnesse.* Saint *Stephen* was *Proto-martyr, Christs* first *Witnesse,* because hee was the first that did as he did, that put on his colours, that drunke of his *Cup,* that was baptised with his *Baptisme,* with his owne bloud: so hee was a *Witnesse.* To be *Witnesses* for *Christ,* is to be like *Christ;* to conforme your selves to *Christ;* and they in the Text, and you, are to be *witnesses of Christ in* Jerusalem, *and in all* Judaea, *and in* Samaria, *and unto the uttermost parts of the Earth.*

Saint *Hierome* notes that *John Baptist* was not bid to beare witnesse in

Jerusalem, in the *Citie,* but in the *Wildernesse;* he, and none but he: there were but few men to witnes to there; and those few that were, came thither with a good disposition to be wrought upon there; and there there were fewe witnesses to oppose *Johns* Testimony, few tentations, few worldly allurements, few worldly businesses. One was enough for the *Wildernesse;* but for *Jerusalem,* for the *Citie,* where all the excuses in the *Gospell* doe alwaies meete, they have bought commodities, and they must utter them, they have purchased Lands, and they must state them, they have maried Wives, and they must study them, to the *Citie,* to *Jerusalem, Christ* sends all his *Apostles,* and all little inough. Hee hath sent a great many *Apostles, Preachers,* to this *Citie;* more than to any other, that I know. *Religious persons* as they call them, *Cloistered Friars* are not sent to the *Citie;* by their first *Canons,* they should not preach abroad: but for those who are to doe that service, there are more in this *Citie,* than in others, for there are more *Parish Churches* heere than in others. Now, beloved, if in this *Citie,* you have taken away a great part of the revenue of the *Preacher,* to your selves, take thus much of his labour upon your selves to, as to preach to one another by a holy and exemplar life, and a religious conversation. Let those of the *Citie,* who have interest in the Government of this *Plantation,* be *Witnesses* of *Christ* who is *Truth it selfe,* to all other *Governours* of *Companies,* in all true and just proceedings: that as CHRIST said to them who thought themselves greatest, *Except you become as this little Childe,* so we may say to the *Governours* of the greatest Companies, Except you proceed with the integrity, with the justice, with the clearnesse, of your *little Sister,* this *Plantation,* you doe not take, you doe not follow a good example. This is to beare witnesse of *Christ* in *Jerusalem,* in the *Citie,* to bee examples of *Truth,* and *Justice,* and *Clearenesse,* to others, in, and of this *Citie.*

The *Apostles* were to do this in *Judaea* too, their service lay in the *Countrey* as well as in the *Citie.* Birds that are kept in cages may learne some Notes, which they should never have sung in the Woods or Fields; but yet they may forget their naturall Notes too. *Preachers* that binde themselves alwaies to *Cities* and *Courts,* and *great Auditories,* may learne new Notes; they may become *occasionall* Preachers, and make the emergent affaires of the time, their *Text,* and the humors of the hearers their *Bible;* but they may loose their Naturall Notes, both the *simplicitie,* and the *boldnesse* that belongs to the Preaching of the *Gospell:* both their power upon lowe understandings to raise them, and upon high affections

to humble them. They may thinke that their errand is but to knocke at
the doore, to delight the eare, and not to search the House, to ransacke
the conscience. *Christ* left the *Ninetie and nine* for one Sheepe; populous
Cities are for the most part best provided; remoter parts need our labour
more, and we should not make such differences. *Yeoman*, and *Labourer*,
and *Spinster*, are distinctions upon Earth; in the Earth, in the grave there
is no distinction. The *Angell* that shall call us out of that dust, will not
stand to survay, who lyes naked, who in a Coffin, who in Wood, who
in Lead, who in a fine, who in a courser Sheet; In that one day of the
Resurrection, there is not a forenoone for Lords to rise first, and an
afternoone for meaner persons to rise after. *Christ* was not whip'd to
save Beggars, and crown'd with Thornes to save Kings: he dyed, he
suffered all, for all; and we whose bearing witnesse of him, is to doe, as
hee did, must conferre our labours upon all, upon *Jerusalem*, and upon
Judaea too, upon the *Citie*, and upon the *Country* too. You, who are his
witnesses too, must doe so too; preach in your just actions, as to the
Citie, to the *Countrey* too. Not to seale up the secrets, and the misteries
of your businesse within the bosome of *Merchants*, and exclude all
others: to nourish an incompatibility betweene *Merchants* and *Gentlemen*;
that *Merchants* shall say to them in reproach, you have plaid the *Gentlemen*, and they in equall reproach, you have playd the *Merchant*; but as
Merchants growe up into worshipfull Families, and worshipfull Families
let fall branches amongst *Merchants* againe, so for this particular Plantation, you may consider *Citie* and *Countrey* to bee one body, and as
you give example of a just government to other companies in the *Citie*,
(thats your bearing witnesse in *Jerusalem*,) so you may be content to
give reasons of your proceedings, and account of moneyes levied, over
the *Countrey*, for thats your bearing witnes in *Judaea*.

But the *Apostles Dioces* is enlarged, farther than *Jerusalem*, farther than
Judaea, they are carried into *Samaria; you must beare witnesse of me in*
Samaria. Beloved, when I have remembred you, who the *Samaritans*
were, Men that had not renounced GOD, but mingled other *Gods* with
him, Men that had not burnt the Law of GOD, but made Traditions of
Men equall to it, you will easily guesse to whom I apply the name of
Samaritans now. A *Jesuit* hath told us (an ill Intelligencer I confesse, but
even his Intelligencer, the *Devill* himselfe, sayes true sometimes) *Mal-
donate*[66] sayes, the *Samaritans* were odious to the *Jewes*, upon the same
grounds as *Heretiques* and *Scismatiques* to us; and they, we know were

odious to them for mingling false *Gods*, and false worships with the true. And if that be the Caracter of a *Samaritan*, wee knowe who are the *Samaritans*, who the *Heretiques*, who the *Scismatiques* of our times. In the highest reproach to *Christ*, the Jewes said, *Samaritanus es & Daemonium habes*, *Thou art a Samaritan & hast a Devill*. In our just detestation of these *Men*, we justly fasten both those upon them. For as they delight in lyes, and fill the world with weekely rumors, *Daemonium habent*, they have a *Devill, quia mendax est & pater eius*. As they multiply assassinats upon Princes, and Massacres upon people, *Daemonium habent*, they have a *Devill, quia homicida ab initio:* as they tosse, and tumble, and dispose kingdomes, *Daemonium habent*, they have a *Devill, Omnia haec dabo* was the Devils complement: but as they mingle truthes and falshoods to-gether in Religion, as they carry the word of G O D, and the Traditions of Men, in an even balance, *Samaritani sunt*, they are *Samaritanes*. At first *Christ* forbad his *Apostles*, to goe into any Citie of the *Samaritans:* after, they did preach in many of them. Beare witnesse first in *Jerusalem*, and in *Judaea;* give good satisfaction especially to those of the houshold of the faithfull, in the *Citie* and *Countrey*, but yet satisfie even those *Samaritans* too.

They would be satisfied, what Miracles you work in *Virginia;* and what people you have converted to the *Christian Faith*, there. If we could as easily cal naturall effects Miracles, or casuall accidents miracles, or Magical illusions, miracles, as they do, to make a miraculous drawing of a tooth, a miraculous cutting of a corn, or, as *Justus Baronius* saies, when he was converted to them, that he was miraculously cur'd of the *Cholique*, by stooping to kisse the *Popes* foot, If we would pile up Miracles so fast, as *Pope John* 22. did in the Canonization of *Aquinas, Tot Miracula confecit, quot determinavit quaestiones,* he wrought as many miracles, as he resolv'd questions, we might find Miracles too. In truth, their greatest Miracle to me, is, that they find men to beleeve their miracles. If they rely upon miracles, they imply a confession that they induce new doctrines; that that is old and receiv'd, needs no miracles; If they require miracles, because, though that be ancient Doctrine, it is newly broght into those parts, we have the confession of their *Jesuit*, *Acosta*,[67] that they doe no miracle in those *Indies*, and he assignes very good reasons, why they are not necessary, nor to bee expected there. But yet beare witnesse to these *Samaritans*, in the other point; labour to give them satisfaction in the other point of their chardge, What Heathens you have converted to the Faith, which is that which is intended in the next, which is the last branch, *You are to be witnesses unto me both in* Jerusalem, *& in all* Judaea, *& in* Samaria, *and unto the uttermost parts of the Earth.*

Literally, the *Apostles* were to bee such witnesses for *Christ:* were they so? did the *Apostles* in person, preach the *Gospell,* over all the World? I know that it is not hard to multiply places of the *Fathers,* in confirmation of that opinion, that the *Apostles* did actually, and personally preach the *Gospell* in all Nations, in their life. *Christ* saies, *the Gospell of the Kingdome shall be preach'd in all the World;* and there hee tels the *Apostles,* that they shall see something done, after that; Therefore they shall live to it. So he saies to them, *You shal be brought before Rulers and Kings for my sake;* but the *Gospell* must first be published among all Nations: In one *Evangelist* there is the *Commission; Preach in my name to all Nations.* And in another, the *Execution* of this *Commission, And they went and preach'd every where.* And after the *Apostle* certifies, and returnes the execution of this Commission, *The Gospell is come and bringeth forth fruit to all the world:* and upon those, and such places, have some of the *Fathers* beene pleasd, to ground their literall exposition, of an actuall and personall preaching of the Apostles over all the world. But had they dream'd of this world which hath been discover'd since, into which, wee dispute with perplexitie, and intricacy enough, how any men came at first, or how any beastes, especially such beastes as men were not likely to carry, they would never have doubted to have admitted a *Figure,* in that, *The Gospell was preached to all the world;* for when *Augustus* his Decree went out, *That all the world should bee taxed,* the Decree and the Taxe went not certainly into the *West Indies;* when Saint *Paul* says, *That their Faith was spoken of throughout the whole world,* and that *their obedience was come abroad unto all men,* surely the *West Indies* had not heard of the *faith* and the *obedience* of the *Romanes.* But as in *Moses* time, they call'd the *Mediterranean Sea,* the *great Sea,* because it was the greatest that those men had then seene, so in the *Apostles* time, they call'd that all the world, which was knowne and traded in then; and in all that, they preach'd the *Gospell.* So that as *Christ* when he said to the *Apostles; I am with you, unto the end of the World,* could not intend that of them in person, because they did not last to the ende of the world, but in a succession of Apostolike men, so when he sayes, the *Apostles* should preach him to all the world, it is of the *Succession* too.

Those of our profession that goe, you, that send them who goe, doe all an *Apostolicall* function. What action soever, hath in the first intention thereof, a purpose to propagate the Gospell of *Christ Jesus,* that is an *Apostolicall* action; Before the ende of the world come, before this mortality shall put on immortalitie, before the Creature shall be delivered of the bondage of corruption under which it groanes, before the Martyrs under the Altar shalbe silenc'd, before al things shal be subdued to *Christ,* his kingdome perfited, and the last Enemy Death destroied, the Gospell must be preached to those men to whom ye send; to all men. Further and hasten you this blessed, this joyfull, this glorious consummation of all, and happie reunion of all bodies to their Soules, by preaching the *Gospell* to those men. Preach to them Doctrinally, preach to them Practically; Enamore them with your *Justice,* and, (as farre as may consist with your security) your *Civilitie;* but inflame them with your *godlinesse,* and your *Religion.* Bring them to *love* and *Reverence* the name of that *King,* that sends men to teach them the wayes of *Civilitie* in this world, but to *feare* and *adore* the Name of that *King of Kings,* that sends men to teach them the waies of Religion, for the next world. Those amongst you, that are old now, shall passe out of this world with this great comfort, that you contributed to the beginning of that Common Wealth, and of that Church, though they live not to see the groath thereof to perfection: *Apollos* watred, but *Paul* planted; hee that begun the worke, was the greater man. And you that are young, now, may live to see the Enemy as much empeach'd by that place, and your friends, yea Children, as well accommodated in that place, as any other. You shall have made this *Iland,* which is but as the *Suburbs* of the old world, a Bridge, a Gallery to the new; to joyne all to that world that shall never grow old, the Kingdome of heaven, You shall add persons to this Kingdome, and to the Kingdome of heaven, and adde names to the Bookes of our Chronicles, and to the Booke of Life.

To end all, as the *Orators* which declaimd in the presence of the *Roman Emperors,* in their *Panegyriques,* tooke that way to make those *Emperours* see, what they were bound to doe, to say in those publique Orations, that those *Emperors* had done so, (for that increased the love of the Subject to the Prince, to bee so tolde, that hee had done those great things, and then it convayd a Counsell into the Prince to doe them after) As their way was to procure things to bee done, by saying they were done, so beloved I have taken a contrary way: for when I, by way of exhortation, all this while have seem'd to tell you what should be done by you, I have, indeed, but told the Congregation, what hath beene done already: neither do I speake to move a wheele that stood still, but to keepe the wheele in due motion; nor perswade you to begin, but to continue a good worke, nor propose forreigne, but your own Examples, to do still, as you have done hitherto. For, for that, that which is especially in my contemplation, the conversion of the people, as I have receiv'd, so I can give this Testimony, that of those persons, who have sent in moneys, and conceal'd their names, the greatest part, almost all, have limited their devotion, and contribution upon that point, the propagation of Religion, and the conversion of the people; for the building and beautifying of the house of GOD, and for the instruction and education of their young Children. *Christ Jesus* himselfe *is yesterday, and to day, and the same for ever.* In the advancing of his glory, be you so to, yesterday, and to day, and the same for ever, here; and hereafter, when time shall be no more, no more yesterday, no more to day, yet for ever and ever, you shall enjoy that joy, and that glorie, which no ill accident can attaine to diminish, or Eclipse it.

PRAYER

We returne to thee againe, O GOD, with *praise* and *prayer;* as for all thy mercies from before minutes began, to this minute, from our Election to this present beame of Sanctification which thou hast shed upon us now. And more particularly, that thou hast afforded us that great dignity, to be, this way, witnesses of thy Sonne *Christ Jesus*, and instruments of his glory. Looke gratiously, and looke powerfully upon this body, which thou hast bene now some yeares in building and compacting together, this Plantation. Looke gratiously upon the Head of this Body, our *Soveraigne* and blesse him with a good disposition to this work, and blesse him for that disposition: Looke gratiously upon them, who are as the *braine* of this body, those who by his power, counsell and advise, and assist in the Government thereof; blesse them with [a] disposition to unity and concord, and blesse them for that disposition: Looke gratiously upon them who are as *Eyes* of this Body, those of the *Clergy,* who have any interest therein: blesse them with a disposition to preach there, to pray heere, to exhort every where for the advancement thereof, and bless them for that disposition. Blesse them who are the *Feete* of this body, who goe thither, and the *Hands* of this body, who labour there, and them who are the *Heart* of this bodie, all that are heartily affected, and declare actually that heartinesse to this action, blesse them all with a cheerefull disposition to that, and bless them for that disposition. Bless it so in this calme, that when the tempest comes, it may ride it out safely; blesse it so with friends now, that it may stand against Enemies hereafter; prepare thy selfe a glorious harvest there, and give us leave to be thy Labourers, That so the number of thy *Saints* being fulfilled, wee may with better assurance joyne in that prayer, *Come Lord Jesus come quickly,* and so meet all in that kingdome which the Sonne of GOD hath purchased for us with the inestimable price of his incorruptible bloud. To which glorious Sonne of GOD, &c. *Amen.*

21. FROM A SERMON PREACHED AT ST PAULS, UPON CHRISTMAS DAY, 1622[68]

And these reconcilings are reconcilings enow; for these are all that are in heaven and earth. If you will reconcile things in heaven, and earth, with things in hell, that is a reconciling out of this Text. If you will mingle the service of God, and the service of this world, there is no reconciling of God and Mammon in this Text. If you will mingle a true religion, and a false religion, there is no reconciling of God and Belial in this Text. For the adhering of persons born within the Church of Rome, to the Church of Rome, our law sayes nothing to them if they come; But for reconciling to the Church of Rome, by persons born within the Allegeance of the King, or for perswading of men to be so reconciled, our law hath called by an infamous and Capitall name of Treason, and yet every Tavern, and Ordinary is full of such Traitors.[69] Every place from jest to earnest is filled with them; from the very stage to the death-bed; At a Comedy they will perswade you, as you sit, as you laugh, And in your sicknesse they will perswade you, as you lye, as you dye. And not only in the bed of sicknesse, but in the bed of wantonnesse they perswade too; and there may be examples of women, that have thought it a fit way to gain a soul, by prostituting themselves, and by entertaining unlawfull love, with a purpose to convert a servant, which is somewhat a strange Topique, to draw arguments of religion from. Let me see a Dominican and a Jesuit reconciled, in doctrinall papistry, for freewill and predestination, Let me see a French papist and an Italian papist reconciled in State-papistry, for the Popes jurisdiction, Let me see the Jesuits, and the secular priests reconciled in England, and when they are reconciled to one another, let them presse reconciliation to their Church. To end all, Those men have their bodies from the earth, and they have their soules from heaven; and so all things in earth and heaven are reconciled: but they have their Doctrine from the Devill; and for things in hell, there is no peace made, and with things in hell, there is no reconciliation to be had by the blood of his Crosse, except we will tread that blood under our feet, and make a mock of Christ Jesus, and crucifie the Lord of Life againe.

22. FROM A SERMON PREACHED UPON CANDLEMAS DAY [2 FEBRUARY ?1623][70]

I

That soule, that is accustomed to direct her selfe to God, upon every occasion, that, as a flowre at Sun-rising, conceives a sense of God, in every beame of his, and spreads and dilates it selfe towards him, in a thankfulnesse, in every small blessing that he sheds upon her; that soule, that as a flowre at the Suns declining, contracts and gathers in, and shuts up her selfe, as though she had received a blow, when soever she heares her Saviour wounded by an oath, or blasphemy, or execration; that soule, who, whatsoever string be strucken in her, base or treble, her high or her low estate, is ever tun'd toward God, that soule prayes sometimes when it does not know that it prayes. I heare that man name God, and aske him what said you, and perchance he cannot tell; but I remember, that he casts forth some of those *ejaculationes animae,* (as S. *Augustine* calls them) some of those darts of a devout soule, which, though they have not particular deliberations, and be not formall prayers, yet they are the *indicia,* pregnant evidences and blessed fruits of a religious custome; much more is it true, which S. *Bernard* saies there, of them, *Deus audit,*

God heares that voice of the heart, which the heart it selfe heares not, that is, at first considers not. Those occasionall and transitory prayers, and those fixed and stationary prayers, for which, many times, we binde our selves to private prayer at such a time, are payments of this debt, in such peeces, and in such summes, as God, no doubt, accepts at our hands. But yet the solemne dayes of payment, are the Sabbaths of the Lord, and the place of this payment, is the house of the Lord, where, as *Tertullian*[71] expresses it, *Agmine facto,* we muster our forces together, and besiege God; that is, not taking up every tatter'd fellow, every sudden ragge or fragment of speech, that rises from our tongue, or our affections, but mustering up those words, which the Church hath levied for that service, in the Confessions, and Absolutions, and Collects, and Litanies of the Church, we pay this debt, and we receive our acquittance.

2

Begin therefore to pay these debts to thy selfe betimes; for, as we told you at beginning, some you are to tender at noone, some at evening. Even at your noon and warmest Sun-shine of prosperity, you owe your selves a true information, how you came by that prosperity, who gave it you, and why he gave it. Let not the Olive boast of her own fatnesse, nor the Fig-tree of her own sweetnesse, nor the Vine of her own fruitfulnesse, for we were all but Brambles. Let no man say, I could not misse a fortune, for I have studied all my youth; How many men have studied more nights, than he hath done hours, and studied themselves blinde, and mad in the Mathematiques, and yet wither in beggery in a corner? Let him never adde, But I studied in a usefull and gainfull profession; How many have done so too, and yet never compassed the favour of a Judge? And how many that have had all that, have struck upon a Rock, even at full Sea, and perished there? In their Grandfathers and great Grandfathers, in a few generations, whosoever is greatest now, must say, With this staffe came I over Jordan; nay, without any staffe came I over Jordan, for he had in them at first, a beginning of nothing. As for spiritual happinesse, *Non volentis, nec currentis, sed miserentis Dei,* It is not in him that would run, nor in him that doth, but only in God that prospers his course; so for the things of this world, it is in vain to rise early, and to lie down late, and to eat the bread of sorrow, for, *nisi Dominus aedificaverit, nisi Dominus custodierit,* except the Lord build the house, they labour in vaine; except the Lord keep the City, the watchman waketh but in vain. Come not therefore to say, I studied more than my fellows, and therefore am richer than my fellows, but say, God that gave me my contemplations at first, gave me my practice after, and hath given me his blessing now. How many men have worn their braines upon other studies, and spent their time and themselves therein? how many men have studied more in thine own profession, and yet, for diffidence in themselves, or some disfavour from others, have not had thy practice? How many men have been equall to thee, in study, in practice, and in getting too, and yet upon a wanton confidence, that that world would alwayes last, or upon the burden of many children, and an expensive breeding of them, or for other reasons, which God hath found in his wayes, are left upon the sand at last, in a low fortune? whilest the Sun shines upon thee in all these, pay thy self the debt, of knowing whence, and why all this came, for else thou canst not know how much, or how little is thine, nor thou canst not come to restore that which is none of thine, but unjustly wrung from others. Pay therefore this debt of surveying thine estate, and then pay thy selfe thine owne too, by a chearfull enjoying and using that which is truly thine, and doe not deny nor defraud thy selfe of those things which are thine, and so become a wretched debtor, to thy back, or to thy belly, as though the world had not enough, or God knew not what were enough for thee.

Pay this debt to thy selfe of looking into thy debts, of surveying, of severing, of serving thy selfe with that which is truly thine, at thy noone, in the best of thy fortune, and in the strength of thine understanding; that when thou commest to pay thy other, thy last debt to thy self, which is, to open a doore out of this world, by the dissolution of body and soule, thou have not all thy money to tell over when the Sun is ready to set, all the account to make of every bag of money, and of every quillet [72] of land, whose it is, and whether it be his that looks for it from thee, or his from whom it was taken by thee; whether it belong to thine heire, that weepes joyfull tears behinde the curtain, or belong to him that weeps true, and bloody teares, in the hole in a prison. There will come a time, when that land that thou leavest shall not be his land, when it shall be no bodies land, when it shall be no land, for the earth must perish; there will be a time when there shall be no Mannors, no Acres in the world, and yet there shall lie Mannors and Acres upon thy soul, when land shall be no more, when time shall be no more, and thou passe away, not into the land of the living, but of eternall death. Then the Accuser will be ready to interline the schedules of thy debts, thy sins, and insert false debts, by abusing an over-tendernesse, which may be in thy conscience then, in thy last sicknesse, in thy death-bed: Then he will be ready to adde a cyphar[73] more to thy debts, and make hundreds thousands, and abuse the faintnesse which may be in thy conscience then, in thy last sicknesse, in thy death-bed. Then he will be ready to abuse even thy confidence in God, and bring thee to think, that as a Pirate ventures boldly home, though all that he hath be stoln, if he be rich enough to bribe for a pardon; so, howsoever those families perish whom thou hast ruined, and those whole parishes whom thou hast depopulated, thy soule may goe confidently home too, if thou bribe God then, with an Hospitall or a Fellowship in a Colledge, or a Legacy to any pious use in apparance, and in the eye of the world.

23. FROM A SERMON PREACHED AT WHITE-HALL, THE FIRST FRIDAY IN LENT, 1623[74]

First then, Jesus wept *Humanitus,* he tooke a necessary occasion to shew that he was true Man. He was now in hand with the greatest Miracle that ever he did, the raising of *Lazarus,* so long dead. Could we but do so in our spirituall raising, what a blessed harvest were that? What a comfort to finde one man here to day, raised from his spirituall death, this day twelve-month? Christ did it every yeare, and every yeare he improved his Miracle. In the first yeare, he raised the Governours Daughter: she was newly dead, and as yet in the house. In the beginning of sin, and whilst in the house, in the house of God, in the Church, in a glad obedience to Gods Ordinances and Institutions there, for the reparation and resuscitation of dead soules, the worke is not so hard. In his second yeare, Christ raised the Widows Son; and him he found without, ready to be buried. In a man growne cold and stiffe in sin, impenetrable, inflexible by denouncing the Judgements of God, almost buried in a stupidity, and insensiblenesse of his being dead, there is more difficultie. But in his third yeare, Christ raised this *Lazarus;* he had been long dead, and buried, and in probability, putrified after foure daies.

This Miracle Christ meant to make a pregnant proofe of the Resurrection, which was his principall intention therein. For, the greatest arguments against the Resurrection, being for the most part of this kinde, when a Fish eates a man, and another man eates that fish, or when one man eates another, how shall both these men rise again? When a body is resolv'd in the grave to the first principles, or is passed into other substances, the case is somewhat neere the same; and therefore Christ would worke upon a body neare that state, a body putrified. And truly, in our spirituall raising of the dead, to raise a sinner putrified in his owne earth, resolv'd in his owne dung, especially that hath passed many transformations, from shape to shape, from sin to sin, (he hath beene a Salamander and lived in the fire, in the fire successively, in the fire of lust in his youth, and in his age in the fire of Ambition; and then he hath beene a Serpent, a Fish, and lived in the waters, in the water successively, in the troubled water of sedition in his youth, and in his age in the cold waters of indevotion) how shall we raise this Salamander and this Serpent, when this Serpent and this Salamander is all one person, and must have contrary musique to charme him, contrary physick to cure him?[75] To raise a man resolv'd into diverse substances, scattered into diverse formes of severall sinnes, is the greatest worke. And therefore this Miracle (which implied that) S. *Basil* calls *Miraculum in Miraculo,* a pregnant, a double Miracle. For here is *Mortuus redivivus,* A dead man lives; that had been done before; but *Alligatus ambulat,* saies *Basil;* he that is fettered, and manacled, and tyed with many difficulties, he walks.

And therfore as this Miracle raised him most estimation, so (for they ever accompany one another) it raised him most envy: Envy that extended beyond him, to *Lazarus* himselfe, who had done nothing; and yet, *The chiefe Priests consulted how they might put Lazarus to death, because by reason of him, many beleeved in Jesus.* A disease, a distemper, a danger which no time shall ever be free from, that wheresoever there is a coldnesse, a dis-affection to Gods Cause, those who are any way occasionally instruments of Gods glory, shall finde cold affections. If they killed *Lazarus,* had not Christ done enough to let them see that he could raise him againe? for *Caeca saevitia, si aliud videtur mortuus, aliud occisus;* It was a blinde malice, if they thought, that Christ could raise a man naturally dead, and could not if he were violently killed. This then being his greatest Miracle, preparing the hardest Article of the Creed, the Resurrection of the body, as the Miracle it selfe declared sufficiently his Divinity, that nature, so in this declaration that he was God, he would declare that he was man too, and therefore *Jesus wept*.

24. FROM A SERMON PREACHED UPON THE PENITENTIALL PSALMES [APRIL, MAY OR JUNE, 1623][76]

I

Not that the duty of thanksgiving is lesse than that of prayer; for if we could compare them, it is rather greater; because it contributes more to Gods glory, to acknowledge by thanks, that God hath given, than to acknowledge by prayer, that God can give. But therefore might *David* be later and shorter here, in expressing that duty of thanks, first, because being reserved to the end, and close of the Psalme, it leaves the best impression in the memory. And therefore it is easie to observe, that in all Metricall compositions, of which kinde the booke of Psalmes is, the force of the whole piece, is for the most part left to the shutting up; the whole frame of the Poem is a beating out of a piece of gold, but the last clause is as the impression of the stamp, and that is it that makes it currant.

2

The Holy Ghost in penning the Scriptures delights himself, not only with a propriety, but with a delicacy, and harmony, and melody of language; with height of Metaphors, and other figures, which may work greater impressions upon the Readers, and not with barbarous, or triviall, or market, or homely language: It is true, that when the Grecians, and the Romanes, and S. *Augustine* himselfe,[77] undervalued and despised the Scriptures, because of the poore and beggerly phrase, that they seemed to be written in, the Christians could say little against it, but turned still upon the other safer way, Wee consider the matter, and not the phrase, because for the most part, they had read the Scriptures only in Translations, which could not maintaine the Majesty, nor preserve the elegancies of the Originall.

Their case was somewhat like ours, at the beginning of the Reformation; when, because most of those men who laboured in that Reformation, came out of the Romane Church, and there had never read the body of the Fathers at large; but only such ragges and fragments of those Fathers, as were patcht together in their Decretat's, and Decretals,[78] and other such Common placers, for their purpose, and to serve their turne, therefore they were loath at first to come to that issue, to try controversies by the Fathers. But as soone as our men that imbraced the Reformation, had had time to reade the Fathers, they were ready enough to joyne with the Adversary in that issue: and still we protest, that we accept that evidence, the testimony of the Fathers, and refuse nothing, which the Fathers unanimly delivered, for matter of faith; and howsoever at the beginning some men were a little ombrageous,[79] and startling at the name of the Fathers, yet since the Fathers have been well studied, for more than threescore yeares, we have behaved our selves with more reverence towards the Fathers, and more confidence in the Fathers, than they of the Romane perswasion have done, and been lesse apt to suspect or quarrell their Books, or to reprove their Doctrines, than our Adversaries have been. So, howsoever the Christians at first were fain to sink a little under that imputation, that their Scriptures have no Majesty, no eloquence, because these embellishments could not appeare in Translations, nor they then read Originalls, yet now, that a perfect knowledge of those languages hath brought us to see the beauty and the glory of those Books, we are able to reply to them, that there are not in all the world so eloquent Books as the Scriptures; and that nothing is more demonstrable, than that if we would take all those Figures, and Tropes, which are collected out of secular Poets, and Orators, we may give higher, and livelier examples, of every one of those Figures, out of the Scriptures, than out of all the Greek and Latine Poets, and Orators; and they mistake it much, that thinke, that the Holy Ghost hath rather chosen a low, and barbarous, and homely style, than an eloquent, and powerfull manner of expressing himselfe.

3

As soone as *Adam* came to be ashamed of his nakednesse, he presently thought of some remedy; if one should come and tell thee, that he looked through the doore, that he stood in a window over against thine, and saw thee doe such or such a sin, this would put thee to a shame, and thou wouldest not doe that sin, till thou wert sure he could not see thee. O, if thou wouldest not sin, till thou couldst think that God saw thee not, this shame had wrought well upon thee. There are complexions that cannot blush; there growes a blacknesse, a sootinesse upon the soule, by custome in sin, which overcomes all blushing, all tendernesse.[80] While alone is palenesse, and God loves not a pale soule, a soule possest with a horror, affrighted with a diffidence, and distrusting his mercy. Rednesse alone is anger, and vehemency, and distemper, and God loves not such a red soule, a soule that sweats in sin, that quarrels for sin, that revenges in sin. But that whitenesse that preserves it selfe, not onely from being died all over in any foule colour, from contracting the name of any habituall sin, and so to be called such or such a sinner, but from taking any spot, from comming within distance of a tentation, or of a suspition, is that whitenesse, which God meanes, when he sayes, *Thou art all faire my Love, and there is no spot in thee.* Indifferent looking, equall and easie conversation, appliablenesse to wanton discourses, and notions, and motions, are the Devils single money, and many pieces of these make up an Adultery. As light a thing as a Spangle[81] is, a Spangle is silver; and Leafe-gold, that is blowne away, is gold; and sand that hath no strength, no coherence, yet knits the building; so doe approaches to sin, become sin, and fixe sin. To avoid these spots, is that whitenesse that God loves in the soule. But there is a rednesse that God loves too; which is this Erubescence that we speak of; an aptnesse in the soule to blush, when any of these spots doe fall upon it.

25. FROM A SERMON PREACHED AT S. PAULS, UPON EASTER-DAY, 1624[82]

I

In the first book of the Scriptures, that of Genesis, there is danger in departing from the letter; In this last book, this of the Revelation, there is as much danger in adhering too close to the letter.[83] The literall sense is alwayes to be preserved; but the literall sense is not alwayes to be discerned: for the literall sense is not alwayes that, which the very Letter and Grammer of the place presents, as where it is literally said, *That Christ is a Vine,* and literally, *That his flesh is bread,* and literally, *That the new Jerusalem is thus situated, thus built, thus furnished:* But the literall sense of every place, is the principall intention of the Holy Ghost, in that place: And his principall intention in many places, is to expresse things by allegories, by figures; so that in many places of Scripture, a figurative sense is the literall sense, and more in this book than in any other. As then to depart from the literall sense, that sense which the very letter presents, in the book of Genesis, is dangerous, because if we do so there, we have no history of the Creation of the world in any other place to stick to; so to binde our selves to such a literall sense in this book, will take from us the consolation of many spirituall happinesses, and bury us in the carnall things of this world.

2

That soule, which being borne free, is made a slave to this body, by comming to it; It must act, but what this body will give it leave to act, according to the Organs, which this body affords it; and if the body be lame in any limme, the soule must be lame in her operation, in that limme too; It must doe, but what the body will have it doe, and then it must suffer, whatsoever that body puts it to, or whatsoever any others will put that body to: If the body oppresse it selfe with Melancholy, the soule must be sad; and if other men oppresse the body with injury, the soule must be sad too; Consider, (it is too immense a thing to consider it) reflect but one thought, but upon this one thing in the soule, here, and hereafter, In her grave, the body, and in her Resurrection in Heaven; That is the knowledge of the soule.

Here saies S. *Augustine,* when the soule considers the things of this world, *Non veritate certior, sed consuetudine securior;* She rests upon such things as she is not sure are true, but such as she sees, are ordinarily received and accepted for truths: so that the end of her knowledge is not Truth, but opinion, and the way, not Inquisition, but ease: But saies he, when she proceeds in this life, to search into heavenly things, *Verberatur luce veritatis,* The beames of that light are too strong for her, and they sink her, and cast her downe, *Et ad familiaritatem tenebrarum suarum, non electione sed fatigatione convertitur;* and so she returnes to her owne darknesse, because she is most familiar, and best acquainted with it; *Non electione,* not because she loves ignorance, but because she is weary of the trouble of seeking out the truth, and so swallowes even any Religion to escape the paine of debating, and disputing; and in this lazinesse she sleeps out her lease, her terme of life, in this death, in this grave, in this body.

But then in her Resurrection, her measure is enlarged, and filled at once; There she reads without spelling, and knowes without thinking, and concludes without arguing; she is at the end of her race, without running; In her triumph, without fighting; In her Haven, without sayling: A free-man, without any prentiship; at full yeares, without any wardship; and a Doctor, without any proceeding: She knowes truly, and easily, and immediately, and entirely, and everlastingly; Nothing left out at first, nothing worne out at last, that conduces to her happinesse. What a death is this life? what a resurrection is this death? For though this world be a sea, yet (which is most strange) our Harbour is larger than the sea; Heaven infinitely larger than this world. For, though that be not true, which *Origen* [84] is said to say, That at last all shall be saved, nor that evident, which *Cyril* of Alexandria saies, That without doubt the number of them that are saved, is far greater than of them that perish, yet surely the number of them, with whom we shall have communion in Heaven, is greater than ever lived at once upon the face of the earth: And of those who lived in our time, how few did we know? and of those whom we did know, how few did we care much for? In Heaven we shall have Communion of Joy and Glory with all, alwaies; *Ubi non intrat inimicus, nec amicus exit,* Where never any man shall come in that loves us not, nor go from us that does.

26. FROM A SERMON PREACHED TO THE EARL OF EXETER, 13 JUNE 1624 [85]

Our first step then in this first part, is, the *sociablenesse,* the *communicablenesse* of God; [86] He loves holy meetings, he loves the *communion of Saints,* the *houshold of the faithfull: Deliciae ejus,* says *Solomon, his delight is to be with the Sons of men,* and that the Sons of men should be with him: Religion is not a *melancholy;* the spirit of God is not a *dampe;* the Church is not a *grave:* it is a *fold,* it is an *Arke,* it is a *net,* it is a *city,* it is a *kingdome,* not onely a house, but a house that hath *many mansions* in it: still it is a *plurall* thing, consisting of *many:* and very good *grammarians* amongst the *Hebrews,* have thought, and said, that that *name,* by which God notifies himself to the world, in the very beginning of *Genesis,* which is *Elohim,* as it is a *plurall word* there, so it hath no *singular:* they say we cannot name God, but *plurally:* so sociable, so communicable, so extensive, so derivative of himself, is God, and so manifold are the beames, and the emanations that flow out from him.

It is a garden worthy of your walking in it: Come into it, but by the gate of *nature:* The naturall man had much to do, to conceive God: a God that should be but *one God:* and therefore scattered his thoughts upon a multiplicity of Gods: and he found it, (as he thought) reasonable to think, that there should be a God of *Justice,* a God of *Wisedome,* a God of *Power,* and so made the severall *Attributes* of God, severall *Gods,* and thought that one God might have enough to do, with the matters of *Justice,* another with the causes that belonged to *power,* and so also, with the courts of *Wisedome:* the naturall man, as he cannot conceive a *vacuity,* that any thing should be empty, so he cannot conceive that any one thing, though that be a *God,* should fill all things: and therefore strays upon a *pluralty* of Gods, upon many Gods, though, in truth, (as *Athanasius* expresses it) *ex multitudine numinum, nullitas numinum,* he that constitutes many Gods destroys all God; for no God can be God, if he be not *all-sufficient;* yet naturally, (I mean in such nature, as our nature is) a man does not easily conceive God to be *alone,* to be but *one;* he thinks there should be company in the Godhead.

27. FROM A SERMON PREACHED AT PAULS, UPON CHRISTMAS DAY, 1624[87]

I

We begin with that which is elder than our beginning, and shall over-live our end, The mercy of God. *I will sing of thy mercy and judgement,* says *David;* when we fixe our selves upon the meditation and modulation of the mercy of God, even his judgements cannot put us out of tune, but we shall sing, and be chearefull, even in them. As God made grasse for beasts, before he made beasts, and beasts for man, before he made man: As in that first generation, the Creation, so in the regeneration, our re-creating, he begins with that which was necessary for that which followes, Mercy before Judgement. Nay, to say that mercy was first, is but to post-date mercy; to preferre mercy but so, is to diminish mercy; The names of first or last derogate from it, for first and last are but ragges of time,[88] and his mercy hath no relation to time, no limitation in time, it is not first, nor last, but eternall, everlasting; Let the Devill make me so far desperate as to conceive a time when there was no mercy, and he hath made me so far an Atheist, as to conceive a time when there was no God; if I despoile him of his mercy, any one minute, and say, now God hath no mercy, for that minute I discontinue his very Godhead, and his beeing. Later Grammarians have wrung the name of mercy out of misery; *Misericordia praesumit miseriam,* say these, there could be no subsequent mercy, if there were no precedent misery; But the true roote of the word mercy, through all the Prophets, is *Racham,* and *Racham* is *diligere,* to love; as long as there hath been love (and *God is love*) there hath been mercy: And mercy considered externally, and in the practise and in the effect, began not at the helping of man, when man was fallen and become miserable, but at the making of man, when man was nothing. So then, here we consider not mercy as it is radically in God, and an essentiall attribute of his, but productively in us, as it is an action, a working upon us, and that more especially, as God takes all occasions to exercise that action, and to shed that mercy upon us: for particular mercies are feathers of his wings, and that prayer, *Lord let thy mercy lighten upon us, as our trust is in thee,* is our birdlime; particular mercies are that cloud of Quailes which hovered over the host of Israel, and that prayer, *Lord let thy mercy lighten upon us,* is our net to catch, our Gomer to fill of those Quailes. The aire is not so full of Moats, of Atomes, as the Church is of Mercies; and as we can suck in no part of aire, but we take in those Moats, those Atomes; so here in the Congregation we cannot suck in a word from the preacher, we cannot speak, we cannot sigh a prayer to God, but that that whole breath and aire is made of mercy. But we call not upon you from this Text, to consider Gods ordinary mercy, that which he exhibites to all in the ministery of his Church; nor his miraculous mercy, his extraordinary deliverances of States and Churches; but we call upon particular Consciences, by occasion of this Text, to call to minde Gods occasionall mercies to them; such mercies as a regenerate man will call mercies, though a naturall man would call them accidents, or occurrences, or contingencies; A man wakes at midnight full of unclean thoughts, and he heares a passing Bell; this is an occasionall mercy, if he call that his own knell, and consider how unfit he was to be called out of the world then, how unready to receive that voice, *Foole, this night they shall fetch away thy soule.* The adulterer, whose eye waites for the twy-light, goes forth, and casts his eyes upon forbidden houses, and would enter, and sees a *Lord have mercy upon us* upon the doore; this is an occasionall mercy, if this bring him to know that they who lie sick of the plague within, passe through a furnace, but by Gods grace, to heaven; and hee without, carries his own furnace to hell, his lustfull loines to everlasting perdition. What an occasionall mercy had *Balaam,* when his Asse Catechized him? What an occasionall mercy had one Theefe, when the other catechized him so, *Art thou not afraid being under the same condemnation?* What an occasionall mercy had all they that saw that, when the Devil himself fought for the name of Jesus, and wounded the sons of *Sceva* [89] for exorcising in the name of Jesus, with that indignation, with that increpation, *Jesus we know, and Paul we know, but who are ye?* If I should declare what God hath done (done occasionally) for my soule, where he instructed me for feare of falling, where he raised me when I was fallen, perchance you would rather fixe your thoughts upon my illnesse, and wonder at that, than at Gods goodnesse, and glorifie him in that; rather wonder at my sins, than at his mercies, rather consider how ill a man I was, than how good a God he is. If I should inquire upon what occasion God elected me, and writ my name in the book of Life, I should sooner be afraid that it were not so, than finde a reason why it should be so. God made Sun and Moon to distinguish seasons, and day, and night, and we cannot have the fruits of the earth but in their seasons: But God hath made no decree to distinguish the seasons of his mercies; In paradise, the fruits were ripe, the first minute, and in heaven it is alwaies Autumne, his mercies are ever in their maturity. We ask *panem quotidianum,* our daily bread, and God never sayes you should have come yesterday, he never sayes you must againe to morrow, but *to day if you will heare his voice*, to day he will heare you. If some King of the earth have so large an extent of Dominion, in North, and South, as that he hath Winter and Summer together in his Dominions, so large an extent East and West, as that he hath day and night together in his Dominions, much more hath God mercy and judgement together: He brought light out of darknesse, not out of a lesser light; he can bring thy Summer out of Winter, though thou have no Spring; though in the wayes of fortune, or understanding, or conscience, thou have been benighted till now, wintred and frozen, clouded and eclypsed, damped and benummed, smothered and stupified till now, now God comes to thee, not as in the dawning of the day, not as in the bud of the spring, but as the Sun at noon to illustrate all shadowes,[90] as the sheaves in harvest, to fill all penuries, all occasions invite his mercies, and all times are his seasons.

2

One of the most convenient Hieroglyphicks[91] of God, is a Circle; and a Circle is endlesse; whom God loves, hee loves to the end: and not onely to their own end, to their death, but to his end, and his end is, that he might love them still. His hailestones, and his thunderbolts, and his showres of bloud (emblemes and instruments of his Judgements) fall downe in a direct line, and affect and strike some one person, or place: His Sun, and Moone, and Starres, (Emblemes and Instruments of his Blessings) move circularly, and communicate themselves to all. His Church is his chariot; in that, he moves more gloriously, than in the Sun; as much more, as his begotten Son exceeds his created Sun, and his Son of glory, and of his right hand, the Sun of the firmament; and this Church, his chariot, moves in that communicable motion, circularly; It began in the East, it came to us, and is passing now, shining out now, in the farthest West. As the Sun does not set to any Nation, but withdraw it selfe, and returne againe; God, in the exercise of his mercy, does not set to thy soule, though he benight it with an affliction.

28. FROM A SERMON PREACHED AT S. PAULS, THE SUNDAY AFTER THE CONVERSION OF S. PAUL, 30 JANUARY 1625[92]

The Lord knowes how to strike us so, as that we shall lay hold upon that hand that strikes us, and kisse that hand that wounds us. *Ad vitam interficit, ad exaltationem prosternit,* sayes the same Father; [93] No man kills his enemy therefore, that his enemy might have a better life in heaven; that is not his end in killing him: It is Gods end; Therefore he brings us to death, that by that gate he might lead us into life everlasting; And he hath not discovered, but made that Northerne passage, to passe by the frozen Sea of calamity, and tribulation, to Paradise, to the heavenly Jerusalem. There are fruits that ripen not, but by frost; There are natures, (there are scarce any other) that dispose not themselves to God, but by affliction. And as Nature lookes for the season for ripening, and does not all before, so Grace lookes for the assent of the soule, and does not perfect the whole worke, till that come. It is Nature that brings the season, and it is Grace that brings the assent; but till the season for the fruit, till the assent of the soule come, all is not done.

Therefore God begun in this way with *Saul,* and in this way he led him all his life. *Tot pertulit mortes, quot vixit dies,* He dyed as many deaths, as he lived dayes; for so himselfe sayes, *Quotidie morior, I die daily;* God gave him sucke in blood, and his owne blood was his daily drink; He catechized him with calamities at first, and calamities were his daily Sermons, and meditations after; and to authorize the hands of others upon him, and to accustome him to submit himself to the hands of others without murmuring, Christ himself strikes the first blow, and with that, *Cecidit, he fell* (which was our first consideration, in his humiliation) and then, *Cecidit in terram, He fell to the ground,* which is our next.

I take no farther occasion from this Circumstance, but to arme you with consolation, how low soever God be pleased to cast you, Though it be to the earth, yet he does not so much cast you downe, in doing that, as bring you home. Death is not a banishing of you out of this world; but it is a visitation of your kindred that lie in the earth; neither are any nearer of kin to you, than the earth it selfe, and the wormes of the earth. You heap earth upon your soules, and encumber them with more and more flesh, by a superfluous and luxuriant diet; You adde earth to earth in new purchases, and measure not by Acres, but by Manors, nor by Manors, but by Shires; And there is a little Quillet, a little Close, worth all these, A quiet Grave. And therefore, when thou readest, That God makes thy bed in thy sicknesse, rejoyce in this, not onely that he makes that bed, where thou dost lie, but that bed where thou shalt lie; That that God, that made the whole earth, is now making thy bed in the earth, a quiet grave, where thou shalt sleep in peace, till the Angels Trumpet wake thee at the Resurrection, to that Judgement where thy peace shall be made before thou commest, and writ, and sealed, in the blood of the Lamb.

29. FROM A SERMON PREACHED AT S. PAULS, IN THE EVENING, UPON EASTER-DAY, 1625[94]

And therefore be content to wonder at this, That God would have such a care to dignifie, and to crown, and to associate to his own everlasting presence, the body of man. God himself is a Spirit, and heaven is his place; my soul is a spirit, and so proportioned to that place; That God, or Angels, or our Soules, which are all Spirits, should be in heaven, *Ne miremini,* never wonder at that. But since we wonder, and justly, that some late Philosophers have removed the whole earth from the Center, and carried it up, and placed it in one of the Spheares of heaven,[95] That this clod of earth, this body of ours should be carried up to the highest heaven, placed in the eye of God, set down at the right hand of God, *Miramini hoc,* wonder at this; That God, all Spirit, served with Spirits, associated to Spirits, should have such an affection, such a love to this body, this earthly body, this deserves this wonder. The Father was pleased to breathe into this body, at first, in the Creation; The Son was pleased to assume this body himself, after, in the Redemption; The Holy Ghost is pleased to consecrate this body, and make it his Temple, by his sanctification; In that *Faciamus hominem, Let us,* all us, *make man,* that consultation of the whole Trinity in making man, is exercised even upon this lower part of man, the dignifying of his body. So far, as that amongst the ancient Fathers, very many of them, are very various, and irresolved, which way to pronounce, and very many of them cleare in the negative, in that point, That the soule of man comes not to the presence of God, but remaines in some out-places till the Resurrection of the body: That observation, that consideration of the love of God, to the body of man, withdrew them into that error, That the soul it self should lack the glory of heaven, till the body were become capable of that glory too.[96]

They therefore oppose God in his purpose of dignifying the body of man, first, who violate, and mangle this body, which is the Organ in which God breathes; And they also which pollute and defile this body, in which Christ Jesus is apparelled; and they likewise who prophane this body, which the Holy Ghost, as the high Priest, inhabites, and consecrates.

Transgressors in the first kinde, that put Gods Organ out of tune, that discompose, and teare the body of man with violence, are those inhumane persecutors, who with racks, and tortures, and prisons, and fires, and exquisite inquisitions, throw downe the bodies of the true Gods true servants, to the Idolatrous worship of their imaginary Gods; that torture men into hell, and carry them through the inquisition into damnation. S. *Augustine* moves a question, and institutes a disputation, and carries it somewhat problematically, whether torture be to be admitted at all, or no.[97] That presents a faire probability, which he sayes against it: we presume, sayes he, that an innocent man should be able to hold his tongue in torture; That is no part of our purpose in torture, sayes he, that hee that is innocent, should accuse himselfe, by confession, in torture. And, if an innocent man be able to doe so, why should we not thinke, that a guilty man, who shall save his life, by holding his tongue in torture, should be able to doe so? And then, where is the use of torture? *Res fragilis, & periculosa quaestio,* sayes that Lawyer, who is esteemed the law, alone, *Ulpian:*[98] It is a slippery triall, and uncertaine, to convince by torture: For, many times, sayes S. *Augustine* againe, *Innocens luit pro incerto scelere certissimas poenas;* He that is yet but questioned, whether he be guilty or no, before that be knowne, is, without all question, miserably tortured. And whereas, many times, the passion of the Judge, and the covetousnesse of the Judge, and the ambition of the Judge, are calamities heavy enough, upon a man, that is accused, in this case of torture, *Ignorantia Judicis est calamitas plerumque innocentis,* sayes that Father, for the most part, even the ignorance of the Judge, is the greatest calamity of him that is accused: If the Judge knew that he were innocent, he should suffer nothing; If he knew he were guilty, he should not suffer torture; but because the Judge is ignorant, and knowes nothing, therefore the Prisoner must bee racked, and tortured, and mangled, sayes that Father.

30. FROM A SERMON PREACHED AT DENMARK HOUSE, SOME FEW DAYS BEFORE THE BODY OF KING JAMES, WAS REMOVED FROM THENCE, TO HIS BURIALL, 26 APRIL 1625 [99]

But then the hand of God, hath *not set up,* but *laid down another Glasse,* wherein thou maist see thy self; a glasse that reflects thy self, and nothing but thy selfe. Christ, who was the other glasse, *is like thee in every thing,* but not absolutely, for *sinne* is *excepted;* but in this glasse presented now (*The Body of our Royall,* but *dead Master and Soveraigne*) we cannot, we doe not except sinne. Not onely the greatest man is subject to *naturall infirmities,* (Christ himself was so) but the holiest man is subject to *Originall and Actuall sinne,* as thou art, and so a fit glasse for thee, to see thyself in. *Jeat* [100] showes a man his face, as well as *Crystall;* nay, a Crystall glasse will not show a man his face, except it be steeled, except it be darkned on the backside: Christ as he was a pure *Crystall* glasse, as he was *God,* had not been a glasse for us, to have seen ourselves in, except he had been *steeled, darkened with our humane nature;* Neither was he ever so throughly darkened, as that he could present us wholly to our selves, because he had no *sinne,* without seeing of which we do not see our selves. Those therefore that are like thee in all things, subject to humane *infirmities,* subject to *sinnes,* and yet are translated, and *translated by Death,* to everlasting *Joy,* and *Glory,* are nearest and clearest glasses for thee, to seé thy self in; and such is this glasse, which God hath proposed to thee, in this house. And therefore, change the word of the Text, in a letter or two, from *Egredimini,* to *Ingredimini;* never go forth to see, but *Go in and see a Solomon crowned with his mothers crown, &c.* And when you shall find that hand that had signed to one of you a *Patent* for *Title,* to another for *Pension*, to another for *Pardon*, to another for *Dispensation*, *Dead:* That hand that settled Possessions by his *Seale*, in the *Keeper*, and rectified *Honours* by the *sword*, in his *Marshall*, and distributed relief to the *Poore*, in his *Almoner*, and *Health* to the *Diseased*, by his *immediate Touch*,[101] Dead: That Hand that ballanced his *own three Kingdomes* so equally, as that none of them complained of one another, nor of him, and carried the *Keyes* of all the Christian world, and locked up, and let out *Armies* in their due season, Dead; how poore, how faint, how pale, how momentany, how transitory, how empty, how frivolous, how Dead things, must you necessarily thinke *Titles*, and *Possessions*, and *Favours*, and all, when you see that Hand, which was the *hand of Destinie*, of *Christian Destinie*, of the *Almighty God*, lie dead? It was not so *hard* a hand when we touched it last, not so *cold* a hand when we kissed it last: That hand which was wont *to wipe all teares from all our eyes*, doth now but presse and squeaze us as so many spunges, filled one with one, another with another cause of teares. Teares that can have no other banke to bound them, but the declared and manifested *will of God:* For, till our teares flow to that heighth, that they might be called a *murmuring* against the declared will of God, it is against our Allegiance, it is *Disloyaltie*, to give our teares any stop, any termination, any measure. It was a great part of *Annaes prayse, That she departed not from the Temple, day nor night;* visit Gods Temple often in the day, meet him in his owne House, and depart not from his *Temples*, (The *dead bodies* of his Saints are his Temples till) even at *midnight;* at midnight remember them, who resolve into dust, and make them thy glasses to see thy self in. Looke now especially upon him whom God hath presented to thee now, and with as much cheerfulnesse as ever thou heardst him say, *Remember my Favours, or remember my Commandements;* heare him say now with the wise man, *Remember my Judgement, for thine also shall be so; yesterday for me, and to day for thee;* He doth not say *to morrow*, but *to Day*, for thee. Looke upon him as a beame of that Sunne, as an abridgement of that *Solomon* in the Text; for every Christian truely reconciled to God, and *signed* with his hand in the *Absolution*, and *sealed* with his bloud in the *Sacrament*, (and this was his case) is a beame, and an abridgement of *Christ* himselfe. *Behold him* therefore *Crowned with the Crown that his Mother gives him: His Mother, The Earth.* In antient times, when they used to reward Souldiers with particular kinds of *Crowns*, there was a great dignity *in Corona graminea*, in a Crown of Grasse: That denoted a

Conquest, or a Defence of that land. He that hath but *Coronam Gram-ineam,* a turfe of grasse in *a Church yard,* hath a Crown from his *Mother,* and even in that buriall taketh *seisure* of the *Resurrection,* as by a turfe of grasse men give seisure of land. *He is crowned in the day of his Marriage;* for though it be a day of *Divorce* of us from him, and of *Divorce* of his body from his soul, yet neither of these Divorces breake the Marriage: His *soule* is married to him that made it, and his body and soul shall meet again, and all we, both then in that Glory where we shall acknowledge, that there is no way to this *Marriage,* but this *Divorce,* nor to *Life,* but by *Death.* And lastly, he is *Crowned in the day of the gladnesse of his heart:* He leaveth that heart, which was accustomed to the halfe joyes of the earth, in the earth; and he hath enlarged his heart to a greater capacity of Joy, and Glory, and God hath filled it according to that new capacity. And therefore, to end all with the Apostles words, *I would not have you to be ignorant, Brethren, concerning them, which are asleepe, that ye sorrow not, as others that have no hope; for if ye beleeve that Jesus died, and rose again, even so, them also, which sleepe in him, will God bring with him.* But when you have performed this *Ingredimini,* that you have gone in, and mourned upon him, and performed the *Egredimini,* you have gone forth, and laid his Sacred body, in Consecrated Dust, and come then to another *Egredimini,* to a going forth in many severall wayes: some to the service of their *new Master,* and some to the enjoying of their Fortunes conferred by their old; some to the raising of new *Hopes,* some to the burying of old, and all; some to new, and busie endeavours in Court, some to contented retirings in the Countrey; let none of us, goe so farre from him, or from one another, in any of our wayes, but that all we that have served him, may meet once a day, the first time we see the Sunne, in the eares of almighty God, with humble and hearty prayer, that he will be pleased to hasten that day, in which it shall be *an addition,* even to the joy of that place, as perfect as it is, and as infinite as it is, to see that face againe, and to see those eyes open there, which we have seen closed here. Amen.

31. FROM A SERMON PREACHED AT S. PAULS, 8 MAY 1625[102]

God hath not onely given man such an immortall soule, but a body that shall put on Incorruption and Immortality too, which he hath given to none of the Angels. In so much, that howsoever it be, whether an Angel may wish it selfe an Archangel, or an Archangel wish it selfe a Cherubin; yet man cannot deliberately wish himselfe an Angel, because he should lose by that wish, and lacke that glory, which he shall have in his body. *We shall be like the Angels,* sayes Christ; In that wherein we can be like them, we shall be like them, in the exalting and refining of the faculties of our soules; But they shall never attaine to be like us in our glorified bodies.[103] Neither hath God onely reserved this treasure and dignity of man to the next world, but even here he hath made him *filium Dei,* The Sonne of God, and *Semen Dei,* The seed of God, and *Consortem divinae naturae,* Partaker of the divine Nature, and *Deos ipsos,* Gods themselves, for *Ille dixit Dii estis,* he hath said we are Gods. So that, as though the glory of heaven were too much for God alone, God hath called up man thither, in the ascension of his Sonne, to partake thereof; and as though one God were not enough for the administration of this world, God hath multiplied gods here upon Earth, and imparted, communicated, not onely his power to every Magistrate, but the Divine nature to every sanctified man. *David* asks that question with a holy wonder, *Quid est homo? What is man that God is so mindfull of him?* But I may have his leave, and the holy Ghosts, to say, since God is so mindfull of him, since God hath set his minde upon him, What is not man? Man is all.

Since we consider men in the place that they hold, and value them according to those places, and aske not how they got thither, when we see Man made The Love of the Father, The Price of the Sonne, The Temple of the Holy Ghost, the Signet upon Gods hand, The Apple of Gods eye, Absolutely, unconditionally we cannot annihilate man, not evacuate, not evaporate, not extenuate man to the levity, to the vanity, to the nullity of this Text (*Surely men altogether, high and low, are lighter than vanity.*) For, man is not onely a contributary Creature, but a totall Creature; He does not onely make one, but he is all; He is not a piece of the world, but the world it selfe; and next to the glory of God, the reason why there is a world.

32. FROM A SERMON PREACHED AT ST DUNSTANS, 15 JANUARY 1626[104]

Lastly, in this fourth House, the House where we stand now, the House of God, and of his Saints, God affords us a fair beam of this consolation, in the phrase of this Text also, *They were dead.* How appliable to you, in this place, is that which God said to *Moses, Put off thy shoes, for thou treadest on holy ground;* put off all confidence, all standing, all relying upon worldly assurances, and consider upon what ground you tread; upon ground so holy, as that all the ground is made of the bodies of Christians, and therein hath received a second consecration. Every puff of wind within these walls, may blow the father into the sons eys, or the wife into her husbands, or his into hers, or both into their childrens, or their childrens into both. Every grain of dust that flies here, is a piece of a Christian; you need not distinguish your Pews by figures; you need not say, I sit within so many of such a neighbour, but I sit within so many inches of my husbands, or wives, or childes, or friends grave. Ambitious men never made more shift for places in Court, than dead men for graves in Churches; and as in our later times, we have seen two and two almost in every Place and Office, so almost every Grave is oppressed with twins;[105] and as at Christs resurrection some of the dead arose out of their graves, that were buried again; so in this lamentable calamity, the dead were buried, and thrown up again before they were resolved to dust, to make room for more. But are all these dead? *They were,* says the Text; they were in your eyes, and therefore we forbid not that office of the eye, that holy tenderness, to weep for them that are so dead. But there was a part in every one of them, that could not die; which the God of life, who breathed it into them, from his own mouth, hath suck'd into his own bosome. And in that part which could die, *They were dead,* but they are not. The soul of man is not safer wrapt up in the bosome of God, than the body of man is wrapt up in the Contract, and in the eternal Decree of the Resurrection. As soon shall God tear a leaf out of the Book of Life, and cast so many of the Elect into Hell fire, as leave the body of any of his Saints in corruption for ever. To what body shall Christ Jesus be loth to put to his hand, to raise it from the grave, then, that put to his very God-head, the Divinity it self, to assume all our bodies, when in one person, he put on all mankinde in his Incarnation? As when my true repentance hath re-ingraffed me in my God, and re-incorporated me in my Savior, no man may reproach me, and say, Thou wast a sinner: So, since all these dead bodies shall be restored by the power, and are kept alive in the purpose of Almighty God, we cannot say, *They are,* scarce that they were dead. When time shall be no more, when death shall be no more, they shall renew, or rather continue their being. But yet, beloved, for this state of their grave, (for it becomes us to call it a state; it is not an annihilation, no part of Gods Saints can come to nothing) as this state of theirs is not to be lamented, as though they had lost any thing which might have conduced to their good, by departing out of this world; so neither is it a state to be joyed in so, as that we should expose ourselves to dangers unnecessarily, in thinking that we want any thing conducing to our good, which the dead enjoy. As between two men of equal age, if one sleep, and the other wake all night, yet they rise both of an equal age in the morning; so they who shall have slept out a long night of many ages in the grave, and they who shall be caught up in the clouds, to meet the Lord Jesus in the aire, at the last day, shall enter all at once in their bodies into Heaven. No antiquity, no seniority for their bodies; neither can their souls who went before, be said to have been there a minute before ours, because we shall all be in a place that reckons not by minutes. Clocks and Sun-dials were but a late invention upon earth; but the Sun it self, and the earth it self, was but a late invention in heaven. God had been an infinite, a super-infinite, an unimaginable space, millions of millions of unimaginable spaces in heaven, before the Creation. And our afternoon shall be as long as Gods forenoon; for, as God never saw beginning, so we shall never see end; but they whom we tread upon now, and we whom others shall tread upon hereafter, shall meet at once, where, though we were dead, dead in our several houses, dead in a sinful *Egypt,* dead in our family, dead in our selves, dead in the Grave, yet we shall be received, with that consolation, and glorious consolation, you were dead, but are alive. *Enter ye blessed into the Kingdom, prepared for you, from the beginning. Amen.*

33. THE SECOND OF MY PREBEND SERMONS UPON MY FIVE PSALMES. PREACHED AT S. PAULS, 29 JANUARY 1626[106]

The Psalmes are the Manna of the Church. As Manna tasted to every man like that that he liked best, so doe the Psalmes minister Instruction, and satisfaction, to every man, in every emergency and occasion. *David* was not onely a cleare Prophet of Christ himselfe, but a Prophet of every particular Christian; He foretels what I, what any shall doe, and suffer, and say. And as the whole booke of Psalmes is *Oleum effusum,* (as the Spouse speaks of the name of Christ) an Oyntment powred out upon all sorts of sores, A Searcloth[107] that souples all bruises, A Balme that searches all wounds; so are there some certaine Psalmes, that are Imperiall Psalmes, that command over all affections, and spread themselves over all occasions, Catholique, universall Psalmes, that apply themselves to all necessities. This is one of those; for, of those Constitutions which are called Apostolicall, one is, That the Church should meet every day, to sing this Psalme. And accordingly, S. *Chrysostome* testifies, That it was decreed, and ordained by the Primitive Fathers, that no day should passe without the publique singing of this Psalme. Under both these obligations, (those ancient Constitutions, called the Apostles,[108] and those ancient Decrees made by the primitive Fathers) belongs to me, who have my part in the service of Gods Church, the especiall meditation, and recommendation of this Psalme. And under a third obligation too, That it is one of those five psalmes, the daily rehearsing whereof, is injoyned to me, by the Constitutions of this Church, as five other are to every other person of our body. As the whole booke is Manna, so these five Psalmes are my Gomer,[109] which I am to fill and empty every day of this Manna.

Now as the spirit and soule of the whole booke of Psalmes is contracted into this psalme, so is the spirit and soule of this whole psalme contracted into this verse. The key of the psalme, (as S. *Hierome* calls the Titles of the psalms) tells us, that *David* uttered this psalme, *when he was in the wildernesse of Judah;* There we see the present occasion that moved him; And we see what was passed between God and him before, in the first clause of our Text; (*Because thou hast been my helpe*) And then we see what was to come, by the rest, (*Therefore in the shadow of thy wings will I rejoyce.*) So that we have here the whole compasse of Time, Past, Present, and Future; and these three parts of Time, shall be at this time, the three parts of this Exercise; first, what *Davids* distresse put him upon for the present; and that lyes in the Context; secondly, how *David* built his assurance upon that which was past; (*Because thou hast been my help*) And thirdly, what he established to himselfe for the future, (*Therefore in the shadow of thy wings will I rejoyce.*) First, His distresse in the Wildernesse, his present estate carried him upon the memory of that which God had done for him before, And the Remembrance of that carried him upon that, of which he assured himselfe after. Fixe upon God any where, and you shall finde him a Circle; He is with you now, when you fix upon him; He was with you before, for he brought you to this fixation; and he will be with you hereafter, for *He is yesterday, and to day, and the same for ever.*

For *Davids* present condition, who was now in a banishment, in a persecution in the Wildernesse of Judah, (which is our first part) we shall onely insist upon that, (which is indeed spread over all the psalme to the Text, and ratified in the Text) That in all those temporall calamities *David* was onely sensible of his spirituall losse; It grieved him not that he was kept from *Sauls* Court, but that he was kept from Gods Church. For when he sayes, by way of lamentation, *That he was in a dry and thirsty land, where no water was,* he expresses what penury, what barrennesse, what drought and what thirst he meant; *To see thy power, and thy glory, so as I have seene thee in the Sanctuary.* For there, *my soule shall be satisfied as with marrow, and with fatnesse,* and there, *my mouth shall praise thee with joyfull lips.* And in some few considerations conducing to this, That spirituall losses are incomparably heavier than temporall, and that therefore, The Restitution to our spirituall happinesse, or the continuation of it, is rather to be made the subject of our prayers to God, in all pressures and distresses, than of temporall, we shall determine that first part. And for the particular branches of both the other parts, (The Remembring of Gods benefits past, And the building of an assurance for the future, upon that Remembrance) it may be fitter to open them to you, anon when we come to handle them, than now. Proceed we now to our first part, The comparing of temporall and spirituall afflictions.

In the way of this Comparison, falls first the Consideration of the universality of afflictions in generall, and the inevitablenesse thereof. It is a blessed Metaphore, that the Holy Ghost hath put into the mouth of the Apostle, *Pondus Gloriae,* That our *afflictions* are but *light,* because there is an *exceeding,* and an *eternall waight of glory* attending them. If it were not for that exceeding waight of glory, no other waight in this world could turne the scale, or waigh downe those infinite waights of afflictions that oppresse us here. There is not onely *Pestis valde gravis,* (*the pestilence grows heavy upon the Land*) but there is *Musca valde gravis,* God calls in but the fly, to vexe Egypt, and even the fly is a heavy burden unto them. It is not onely *Job* that complains, *That he was a burden to himselfe,* but even *Absaloms* haire was a burden to him, till it was polled. It is not onely *Jeremy* that complains, *Aggravavit compedes,* That God had made their fetters and their chains heavy to them, but the workmen in harvest complaine, That God had made a faire day heavy unto them, (*We have borne the heat, and the burden of the day.*) *Sand is heavy,* sayes *Solomon;* And how many suffer so? under a sand-hill of crosses, daily, hourely afflictions, that are heavy by their number, if not by their single waight? And *a stone is heavy;* (sayes he in the same place) And how many suffer so? How many, without any former preparatory crosse, or comminatory, or commonitory[110] crosse, even in the midst of prosperity, and security, fall under some one stone, some grindstone, some mil-stone, some one insupportable crosse that ruines them? But then, (sayes *Solomon* there) *A fooles anger is heavier than both;* And how many children, and servants, and wives suffer under the anger, and morosity, and peevishnesse, and jealousie of foolish Masters, and Parents, and Husbands, though they must not say so? *David* and *Solomon* have cryed out, That all this world is *vanity,* and *levity;* And (God knowes) all is waight, and burden, and heavinesse, and oppression; And if there were not a waight of future glory to counterpoyse it, we should all sinke into nothing.

I aske not *Mary Magdalen,* whether lightnesse were not a burden; (for sin is certainly, sensibly a burden) But I aske *Susanna* whether even chast beauty were not a burden to her; And I aske *Joseph* whether personall comelinesse were not a burden to him. I aske not *Dives,* who perished in the next world, the question; but I aske them who are made examples of *Solomons* Rule, of that *sore evill,* (as he calls it) *Riches kept to the owners thereof for their hurt,* whether Riches be not a burden.

All our life is a continuall burden, yet we must not groane; A continuall squeasing, yet we must not pant; And as in the tendernesse of our childhood, we suffer, and yet are whipt if we cry, so we are complained of, if we complaine, and made delinquents if we call the times ill. And that which addes waight to waight, and multiplies the sadnesse of this consideration, is this, That still the best men have had most laid upon them. As soone as I heare God say, that he hath found *an upright man, that feares God, and eschews evill,* in the next lines I finde a Commission to Satan, to bring in Sabeans and Chaldeans upon his cattell, and servants, and fire and tempest upon his children, and loathsome diseases upon himselfe. As soone as I heare God say, That he hath found *a man according to his own heart,* I see his sonnes ravish his daughters, and then murder one another, and then rebell against the Father, and put him into straites for his life. As soone as I heare God testifie of Christ at his Baptisme, *This is my beloved Sonne in whom I am well pleased,* I finde that Sonne of his *led up by the Spirit, to be tempted of the Devill.* And after I heare God ratifie the same testimony againe, at his Transfiguration, (*This is my beloved Sonne, in whom I am well pleased*) I finde that beloved Sonne of his, deserted, abandoned, and given over to Scribes, and Pharisees, and Publicans, and Herodians, and Priests, and Souldiers, and people, and Judges, and witnesses, and executioners, and he that was called the beloved Sonne of God, and made partaker of the glory of heaven, in this world, in his Transfiguration, is made now the Sewer of all the corruption, of all the sinnes of this world, as no Sonne of God, but a meere man, as no man, but a contemptible worme. As though the greatest weaknesse in this world, were man, and the greatest fault in man were to be good, man is more miserable than other creatures, and good men more miserable than any other men.

But then there is *Pondus Gloriae, An exceeding waight of eternall glory,* and that turnes the scale; for as it makes all worldly prosperity as dung, so it makes all worldly adversity as feathers. And so it had need; for in the scale against it, there are not onely put temporall afflictions, but spirituall too; And to these two kinds, we may accommodate those words, *He that fals upon this stone,* (upon temporall afflictions) may be bruised, broken, *But he upon whom that stone falls,* (spirituall afflictions) *is in danger to be ground to powder.* And then, the great, and yet ordinary danger is, That these spirituall afflictions grow out of temporall; Murmuring, and diffidence in God, and obduration, out of worldly calamities; And so against nature, the fruit is greater and heavier than the Tree, spirituall heavier than temporall afflictions.

They who write of Naturall story,[111] propose that Plant for the greatest wonder in nature, which being no firmer than a bull-rush, or a reed, produces and beares for the fruit thereof no other but an intire, and very hard stone. That temporall affliction should produce spirituall stoninesse, and obduration, is unnaturall, yet ordinary. Therefore doth God propose it, as one of those greatest blessings, which he multiplies upon his people, *I will take away your stony hearts, and give you hearts of flesh;* And, Lord let mee have a fleshly heart in any sense, rather than a stony heart. Wee finde mention amongst the observers of rarities in Nature, of hairy hearts, hearts of men, that have beene overgrowne with haire; but of petrified hearts, hearts of men growne into stone, we read not; for this petrefaction of the heart, this stupefaction of a man, is the last blow of Gods hand upon the heart of man in this world. Those great afflictions which are powred out of the Vials of the seven Angels upon the world, are still accompanied with that heavy effect, that that affliction hardned them. *They were scorched with heats and plagues,* by the fourth Angel, and it followes, *They blasphemed the name of God, and repented not, to give him glory.* Darknesse was induced upon them by the fift Angel, and it followes, *They blasphemed the God of heaven, and repented not of their deeds.* And from the seventh Angel there fell haile-stones of the waight of talents, (perchance foure pound waight) upon men; And yet these men had so much life left, as to *blaspheme God,* out of that respect, which alone should have brought them to glorifie God, *Because the plague thereof was exceeding great.* And when a great plague brings them to blaspheme, how great shall that second plague be, that comes upon them for blaspheming?

Let me wither and weare out mine age in a discomfortable, in an unwholesome, in a penurious prison, and so pay my debts with my bones, and recompence the wastfulnesse of my youth, with the beggery of mine age; Let me wither in a spittle under sharpe, and foule, and infamous diseases, and so recompence the wantonnesse of my youth, with that loathsomenesse in mine age; yet, if God with-draw not his spirituall blessings, his Grace, his Patience, If I can call my suffering his Doing, my passion his Action, All this that is temporall, is but a cater-piller got into one corner of my garden, but a mill-dew fallen upon one acre of my Corne; The body of all, the substance of all is safe, as long as the soule is safe. But when I shall trust to that, which wee call a good spirit, and God shall deject, and empoverish, and evacuate that spirit,

when I shall rely upon a morall constancy, and God shall shake, and
enfeeble, and enervate, destroy and demolish that constancy; when I
shall think to refresh my selfe in the serenity and sweet ayre of a good
conscience, and God shall call up the damps and vapours of hell it selfe,
and spread a cloud of diffidence,[112] and an impenetrable crust of desperation upon my conscience; when health shall flie from me, and I shall lay
hold upon riches to succour me, and comfort me in my sicknesse, and
riches shall flie from me, and I shall snatch after favour, and good
opinion, to comfort me in my poverty; when even this good opinion
shall leave me, and calumnies and misinformations shall prevaile against
me; when I shall need peace, because there is none but thou, O Lord,
that should stand for me, and then shall finde, that all the wounds that I
have, come from thy hand, all the arrowes that stick in me, from thy
quiver; when I shall see, that because I have given my selfe to my
corrupt nature, thou hast changed thine; and because I am all evill
towards thee, therefore thou hast given over being good towards me;
When it comes to this height, that the fever is not in the humors, but in
the spirits, that mine enemy is not an imaginary enemy, fortune, nor a
transitory enemy, malice in great persons, but a reall, and an irresistible,
and an inexorable, and an everlasting enemy, The Lord of Hosts himselfe, The Almighty God himselfe, the Almighty God himselfe onely
knowes the waight of this affliction, and except hee put in that *pondus
gloriae,* that exceeding waight of an eternall glory, with his owne hand,
into the other scale, we are waighed downe, we are swallowed up,
irreparably, irrevocably, irrecoverably, irremediably.

This is the fearefull depth, this is spirituall misery, to be thus fallen
from God. But was this *Davids* case? was he fallen thus farre, into a
diffidence in God? No. But the danger, the precipice, the slippery
sliding into that bottomlesse depth, is, to be excluded from the meanes
of comming to God, or staying with God; And this is that that *David*
laments here, That by being banished, and driven into the wildernesse
of Judah, hee had not accesse to the Sanctuary of the Lord, to sacrifice
his part in the praise, and to receive his part in the prayers of the
Congregation; for Angels passe not to ends, but by wayes and
meanes,[113] nor men to the glory of the triumphant Church, but by
participation of the Communion of the Militant. To this note *David* sets
his Harpe, in many, many Psalms: Sometimes, that God had suffered his
enemies to possesse his Tabernacle, (*Hee forsooke the Tabernacle of Shiloh,*

Hee delivered his strength into captivity, and his glory into the enemies hands)
But most commonly he complaines, that God disabled him from
comming to the Sanctuary. In which one thing he had summed up all
his desires, all his prayers, (*One thing have I desired of the Lord, that will I
looke after; That I may dwell in the house of the Lord, all the dayes of my life,
to behold the beauty of the Lord, and to enquire in his Temple*) His vehement
desire of this, he expresses againe, (*My soule thirsteth for God, for the living
God; when shall I come and appeare before God?*) He expresses a holy
jealousie, a religious envy, even to the sparrows and swallows, (yea, *the
sparrow hath found a house, and the swallow a nest for her selfe, and where she
may lay her yong, Even thine Altars, O Lord of Hosts, my King and my
God.*) Thou art my King, and my God, and yet excludest me from that,
which thou affordest to sparrows, *And are not we of more value than many
sparrows?*

And as though *David* felt some false ease, some half-tentation, some
whispering that way, That God is *in the wildernesse of Judah*, in every
place, as well as in his *Sanctuary*, there is in the Originall in that place, a
patheticall, a vehement, a broken expressing expressed, *O thine Altars;* It
is true, (sayes *David*) thou art here in the wildernesse, and I may see thee
here, and serve thee here, but, *O thine Altars, O Lord of hosts, my King
and my God.* When *David* could not come in person to that place, yet he
bent towards the Temple, (*In thy feare will I worship towards thy holy
Temple.*) Which was also *Daniels* devotion; when he prayed, *his Chamber
windowes were open towards Jerusalem;* And so is *Hezekias* turning to the
wall to weepe, and to pray in his sick bed, understood to be to that
purpose, to conforme, and compose himselfe towards the Temple. In
the place consecrated for that use, God by *Moses* fixes the service, and
fixes the Reward; And towards that place, (when they could not come
to it) doth *Solomon* direct their devotion in the Consecration of the
Temple, (*when they are in the warres, when they are in Captivity, and pray
towards this house, doe thou heare them.*) For, as in private prayer, when
(according to Christs command) we are shut in our chamber, there is
exercised *Modestia fidei*, The modesty and bashfulnesse of our faith, not
pressing upon God in his house: so in the publique prayers of the
Congregation, there is exercised the fervor, and holy courage of our
faith, for *Agmine facto obsidemus Deum*, It is a Mustering of our forces,
and a besieging of God. Therefore does *David* so much magnifie their
blessednesse, that are in this house of God; (*Blessed are they that dwell in*

thy house, for they will be still praising thee) Those that looke towards it, may praise thee sometimes, but those men who dwell in the Church, and whose whole service lyes in the Church, have certainly an advantage of all other men (who are necessarily withdrawne by worldly businesses) in making themselves acceptable to almighty God, if they doe their duties, and observe their Church-services aright.

Man being therefore thus subject naturally to manifold calamities, and spirituall calamities being incomparably heavier than temporall, and the greatest danger of falling into such spirituall calamities being in our absence from Gods Church, where onely the outward meanes of happinesse are ministred unto us, certainely there is much tendernesse and deliberation to be used, before the Church doores be shut against any man. If I would not direct a prayer to God, to excommunicate any man from the Triumphant Church, (which were to damne him) I would not oyle the key, I would not make the way too slippery for excommunications in the Militant Church; For, that is to endanger him. I know how distastfull a sin to God, contumacy, and contempt, and disobedience to Order and Authority is; And I know, (and all men, that choose not ignorance, may know) that our Excommunications (though calumniators impute them to small things, because, many times, the first complaint is of some small matter) never issue but upon contumacies, contempts, disobediences to the Church. But they are reall contumacies, not interpretative, apparant contumacies, not presumptive, that excommunicate a man in Heaven; And much circumspection is required, and (I am far from doubting it) exercised in those cases upon earth; for, though every Excommunication upon earth be not sealed in Heaven, though it damne not the man, yet it dammes up that mans way, by shutting him out of that Church, through which he must goe to the other; which being so great a danger, let every man take heed of Excommunicating himselfe. The imperswasible Recusant [114] does so; The negligent Libertin does so; The fantastique Separatist does so; The halfe-present man, he, whose body is here, and minde away, does so; And he, whose body is but halfe here, his limbes are here upon a cushion, but his eyes, his eares are not here, does so: All these are selfe-Excommunicators, and keepe themselves from hence. Onely he enjoyes that blessing, the want whereof *David* deplores, that is here intirely, and is glad he is here, and glad to finde this kinde of service here, that he does, and wishes no other.

And so we have done with our first Part, *Davids* aspect, his present condition, and his danger of falling into spirituall miseries, because his persecution, and banishment amounted to an Excommunication, to an excluding of him from the service of God, in the Church. And we passe, in our Order proposed at first, to the second, his retrospect, the Consideration, what God had done for him before, *Because thou hast beene my helpe.*

Through this second part, we shall passe by these three steps. First, That it behoves us, in all our purposes, and actions, to propose to our selves a copy to write by, a patterne to worke by, a rule, or an example to proceed by, Because it hath beene thus heretofore, sayes *David*, I will resolve upon this course for the future. And secondly, That the copy, the patterne, the precedent which we are to propose to our selves, is, The observation of Gods former wayes and proceedings upon us, Because God hath already gone this way, this way I will awaite his going still. And then, thirdly and lastly, in this second part, The way that God had formerly gone with *David,* which was, That he had been his helpe, (*Because thou hast beene my helpe.*)

First then, from the meanest artificer, through the wisest Philosopher, to God himselfe, all that is well done, or wisely undertaken, is undertaken and done according to our pre-conceptions, fore-imaginations, designes, and patterns proposed to our selves beforehand. A Carpenter builds not a house, but that he first sets up a frame in his owne minde, what kinde of house he will build. The little great Philosopher *Epictetus,*[115] would undertake no action, but he would first propose to himselfe, what *Socrates,* or *Plato,* what a wise man would do in that case, and according to that, he would proceed. Of God himselfe, it is safely resolved in the Schoole, that he never did any thing in any part of time, of which he had not an eternall pre-conception, an eternall Idea, in himselfe before.[116] Of which Ideaes, that is, pre-conceptions, pre-determinations in God, S. *Augustine* pronounces, *Tanta vis in Ideis constituitur,* There is so much truth, and so much power in these Ideaes, as that without acknowledging them, no man can acknowledge God, for he does not allow God Counsaile, and Wisdome, and deliberation in his Actions, but sets God on worke, before he have thought what he will doe. And therefore he, and others of the Fathers read that place, (which we read otherwise) *Quod factum est, in ipso vita erat;* that is, in all their Expositions, whatsoever is made, in time, was alive in God, before it

was made, that is, in that eternall Idea, and patterne which was in him.
So also doe divers of those Fathers read those words to the Hebrews,
(which we read, *The things that are seene, are not made of things that doe*
appeare) *Ex invisibilibus visibilia facta sunt, Things formerly invisible, were*
made visible; that is, we see them not till now, till they are made, but
they had an invisible being, in that Idea, in that pre-notion, in that
purpose of God before, for ever before. Of all things in Heaven, and
earth, but of himselfe, God had an Idea, a patterne in himselfe, before he
made it.

And therefore let him be our patterne for that, to worke after pat-
ternes; To propose to our selves Rules and Examples for all our actions;
and the more, the more immediately, the more directly our actions
concerne the service of God. If I aske God, by what Idea he made me,
God produces his *Faciamus hominem ad Imaginem nostram,* That there was
a concurrence of the whole Trinity, to make me in *Adam,* according to
that Image which they were, and according to that Idea, which they had
pre-determined. If I pretend to serve God, and he aske me for my Idea,
How I meane to serve him, shall I bee able to produce none? If he aske
me an Idea of my Religion, and my opinions, shall I not be able to say,
It is that which thy word, and thy Catholique Church hath imprinted
in me? If he aske me an Idea of my prayers, shall I not be able to say, It is
that which my particular necessities, that which the forme prescribed by
thy Son, that which the care, and piety of the Church, in conceiving fit
prayers, hath imprinted in me? If he aske me an Idea of my Sermons,
shall I not be able to say, It is that which the Analogy of Faith, the
edification of the Congregation, the zeale of thy worke, the meditations
of my heart have imprinted in me? But if I come to pray or to preach
without this kind of Idea, if I come to extemporall prayer, and extemporall preaching, I shall come to an extemporall faith, and extemporall religion; and then I must looke for an extemporall Heaven, a
Heaven to be made for me; for to that Heaven which belongs to the
Catholique Church, I shall never come, except I go by the way of the
Catholique Church, by former Idea's, former examples, former patterns,
To beleeve according to ancient beliefes, to pray according to ancient
formes, to preach according to former meditations. God does nothing,
man does nothing well, without these Idea's, these retrospects, this
recourse to pre-conceptions, pre-deliberations.

Something then I must propose to my selfe, to be the rule, and the reason of my present and future actions; which was our first branch in this second Part; And then the second is, That I can propose nothing more availably, than the contemplation of the history of Gods former proceeding with me; which is *Davids* way here, Because this was Gods way before, I will looke for God in this way still. That language in which God spake to man, the Hebrew, hath no present tense; They forme not their verbs as our Westerne Languages do, in the present, *I heare,* or *I see,* or *I reade,* But they begin at that which is past, *I have seene* and *heard,* and *read.* God carries us in his Language, in his speaking, upon that which is past, upon that which he hath done already; I cannot have better security for present, nor future, than Gods former mercies exhibited to me. *Quis non gaudeat,* sayes S. *Augustine,* Who does not triumph with joy, when hee considers what God hath done? *Quis non & ea, quae nondum venerunt, ventura sperat, propter illa, quae jam tanta impleta sunt?* Who can doubt of the performance of all, that sees the greatest part of a Prophesie performed? If I have found that true that God hath said, of the person of Antichrist, why should I doubt of that which he sayes of the ruine of Antichrist? *Credamus modicum quod restat,* sayes the same Father, It is much that wee have seene done, and it is but little that God hath reserved to our faith, to beleeve that it shall be done.

There is no State, no Church, no Man, that hath not this tie upon God, that hath not God in these bands, That God by having done much for them already, hath bound himselfe to doe more. Men proceed in their former wayes, sometimes, lest they should confesse an error, and acknowledge that they had beene in a wrong way. God is obnoxious to no error, and therefore he does still, as he did before. Every one of you can say now to God, Lord, Thou broughtest me hither, therefore enable me to heare; Lord, Thou doest that, therefore make me understand; And that, therefore let me beleeve; And that too, therefore strengthen me to the practise; And all that, therefore continue me to a perseverance. Carry it up to the first sense and apprehension that ever thou hadst of Gods working upon thee, either in thy selfe, when thou camest first to the use of reason, or in others in thy behalfe, in thy baptisme, yet when thou thinkest thou art at the first, God had done something for thee before all that; before that, hee had elected thee, in that election which S. *Augustine* speaks of, *Habet electos, quos creaturus est eligendos,* God hath elected certaine men, whom he intends to create, that he may elect them; that is, that he may declare his Election upon them. God had thee, before he made thee; He loved thee first, and then created thee, that thou loving him, he might continue his love to thee. The surest way, and the nearest way to lay hold upon God, is the consideration of that which he had done already. So *David* does; And that which he takes knowledge of, in particular, in Gods former proceedings towards him, is, Because God had been his helpe, which is our last branch in this part, *Because thou hast beene my helpe*.

From this one word, That God hath been my *Helpe*, I make account that we have both these notions; first, That God hath not left me to my selfe, He hath come to my succour, He hath helped me; And then, That God hath not left out my selfe; He hath been my Helpe, but he hath left some thing for me to doe with him, and by his helpe. My security for the future, in this consideration of that which is past, lyes not onely in this, That God hath delivered me, but in this also, that he hath delivered me by way of a Helpe, and Helpe alwayes presumes an endevour and co-operation in him that is helped. God did not elect me as a helper, nor create me, nor redeeme me, nor convert me, by way of helping me; for he alone did all, and he had no use at all of me. God infuses his first grace, the first way, meerly as a Giver; intirely, all himselfe; but his subsequent graces, as a helper; therefore we call them Auxiliant graces, Helping graces; and we alwayes receive them, when we endevour to make use of his former grace. *Lord, I beleeve*, (sayes the Man in the Gospel to Christ) *Helpe mine unbeliefe*. If there had not been unbeliefe, weaknesse, unperfectnesse in that faith, there had needed no helpe; but if there had not been a Beliefe, a faith, it had not been capable of helpe and assistance, but it must have been an intire act, without any concurrence on the mans part.

So that if I have truly the testimony of a rectified Conscience, That God hath helped me, it is in both respects; first, That he hath never forsaken me, and then, That he hath never suffered me to forsake my selfe; He hath blessed me with that grace, that I trust in no helpe but his, and with this grace too, That I cannot looke for his helpe, except I helpe my selfe also. God did not helpe heaven and earth to proceed out of nothing in the Creation, for they had no possibility of any disposition towards it; for they had no beeing: But God did helpe the earth to produce grasse, and herbes; for, for that, God had infused a seminall disposition into the earth, which, for all that, it could not have perfected without his farther helpe. As in the making of Woman, there is the very word of our Text, *Gnazar*, God made him a *Helper*, one that was to doe

much for him, but not without him. So that then, if I will make Gods
former working upon me, an argument of his future gracious purposes,
as I must acknowledge that God hath done much for me, so I must
finde, that I have done what I could, by the benefit of that grace with
him; for God promises to be but a helper. *Lord open thou my lips,* sayes
David; that is Gods worke intirely; And then, *My mouth, My mouth shall
shew forth thy praise;* there enters *David* into the worke with God. And
then, sayes God to him, *Dilata os tuum, Open thy mouth,* (It is now made
Thy mouth, and therefore doe thou open it) *and I will fill it;* All in-
choations [117] and consummations, beginnings and perfectings are of
God, of God alone; but in the way there is a concurrence on our part,
(by a successive continuation of Gods grace) in which God proceeds as a
Helper; and I put him to more than that, if I doe nothing. But if I pray
for his helpe, and apprehend and husband his graces well, when they
come, then he is truly, properly my helper; and upon that security, that
testimony of a rectified Conscience, I can proceed to *Davids* confidence
for the future, *Because thou hast been my Helpe, therefore in the shadow of
thy wings will I rejoyce;* which is our third, and last generall part.

In this last part, which is, (after *Davids* aspect, and consideration of his
present condition, which was, in the effect, an Exclusion from Gods
Temple, And his retrospect, his consideration of Gods former mercies
to him, That he had been his Helpe) his prospect, his confidence for the
future, we shall stay a little upon these two steps; first, That that which
he promises himselfe, is not an immunity from all powerfull enemies,
nor a sword of revenge upon those enemies; It is not that he shall have
no adversary, nor that that adversary shall be able to doe him no harme,
but that he should have a refreshing, a respiration, *In velamento alarum,*
under the shadow of Gods wings. And then, (in the second place) That
this way which God shall be pleased to take, this manner, this measure
of refreshing, which God shall vouchsafe to afford, (though it amount
not to a full deliverance) must produce a joy, a rejoycing in us; we must
not onely not decline to a murmuring, that we have no more, no nor
rest upon a patience for that which remains, but we must ascend to a
holy joy, as if all were done and accomplished, *In the shadow of thy wings
will I rejoyce.*

First then, lest any man in his dejection of spirit, or of fortune, should
stray into a jealousie or suspition of Gods power to deliver him, As
God hath spangled the firmament with starres, so hath he his Scriptures

with names, and Metaphors, and denotations of power. Sometimes he shines out in the name of a *Sword,* and of a *Target,*[118] and of a *Wall,* and of a *Tower,* and of a *Rocke,* and of a *Hill;* And sometimes in that glorious and manifold constellation of all together, *Dominus exercituum, The Lord of Hosts.* God, as God, is never represented to us, with Defensive Armes; He needs them not. When the Poets present their great Heroes, and their Worthies, they alwayes insist upon their Armes, they spend much of their invention upon the description of their Armes; both because the greatest valour and strength needs Armes, (*Goliah* himselfe was armed) and because to expose ones selfe to danger unarmed, is not valour, but rashnesse. But God is invulnerable in himself, and is never represented armed; you finde no shirts of mayle, no Helmets, no Cuirasses in Gods Armory. In that one place of *Esay,* where it may seeme to be otherwise, where God is said *to have put on righteousnesse as a breastplate, and a Helmet of Salvation upon his head;* in that prophecy God is Christ, and is therefore in that place, called *the Redeemer.* Christ needed defensive armes, God does not. Gods word does; His Scriptures doe; And therefore S. *Hierome* hath armed them, and set before every booke his *Prologum galeatum,* that prologue that armes and defends every booke from calumny. But though God need not, nor receive not defensive armes for himselfe, yet God is to us a Helmet, a Breastplate, a strong tower, a rocke, every thing that may give us assurance and defence; and as often as he will, he can refresh that Proclamation, *Nolite tangere Christos meos,* Our enemies shall not so much as touch us.

But here, by occasion of his Metaphore in this Text, (*Sub umbra alarum, In the shadow of thy wings*) we doe not so much consider an absolute immunity, That we shall not be touched, as a refreshing and consolation, when we are touched, though we be pinched and wounded. The Names of God, which are most frequent in the Scriptures, are these three, *Elohim,* and *Adonai,* and *Jehovah;* and to assure us of his Power to deliver us, two of these three are Names of Power. *Elohim* is *Deus fortis,* The mighty, The powerfull God: And (which deserves a particular consideration) *Elohim* is a plurall Name; It is not *Deus fortis,* but *Dii fortes,* powerfull Gods. God is all kinde of Gods; All kinds, which either Idolaters and Gentils can imagine, (as Riches, or Justice, or Wisdome, or Valour, or such) and all kinds which God himself hath called gods, (as Princes, and Magistrates, and Prelates, and all that assist and helpe one another) God is *Elohim,* All these Gods, and all these in their height and best of their power; for *Elohim*, is *Dii fortes*, Gods in the plurall, and those plurall gods in their exaltation.

The second Name of God, is a Name of power too, *Adonai*. For, *Adonai* is *Dominus*, The Lord, such a Lord, as is Lord and Proprietary of all his creatures, and all creatures are his creatures; And then, *Dominium est potestas tum utendi, tum abutendi*, sayes the law; To be absolute Lord of any thing, gives that Lord a power to doe what he will with that thing. God, as he is *Adonai, The Lord,* may give and take, quicken and kill, build and throw downe, where and whom he will. So then two of Gods three Names are Names of absolute power, to imprint, and re-imprint an assurance in us, that hee can absolutely deliver us, and fully revenge us, if he will. But then, his third Name, and that Name which hee chooses to himselfe, and in the signification of which Name, hee employes *Moses,* for the reliefe of his people under Pharaoh, that Name *Jehovah,* is not a Name of Power, but onely of Essence, of Being, of Subsistence, and yet in the vertue of that Name, God relieved his people. And if, in my afflictions, God vouchsafe to visit mee in that Name, to preserve me in my being, in my subsistence in him, that I be not shaked out of him, disinherited in him, excommunicate from him, devested of him, annihilated towards him, let him, at his good pleasure, reserve his *Elohim,* and his *Adonai,* the exercises and declarations of his mighty Power, to those great publike causes, that more concerne his Glory, than any thing that can befall me; But if he impart his *Jehovah,* enlarge himselfe so far towards me, as that I may live, and move, and have my beeing in him, though I be not instantly delivered, nor mine enemies absolutely destroyed, yet this is as much as I should promise my selfe, this is as much as the Holy Ghost intends in this Metaphor, *Sub umbra alarum, Under the shadow of thy wings,* that is a Refreshing, a Respiration, a Conservation, a Consolation in all afflictions that are inflicted upon me.

Yet, is not this Metaphor of *Wings* without a denotation of Power. As no Act of Gods, though it seeme to imply but spirituall comfort, is without a denotation of power, (for it is the power of God that comforts me; To overcome that sadnesse of soule, and that dejection of spirit, which the Adversary by temporall afflictions would induce upon me, is an act of his Power) So this Metaphor, *The shadow of his wings,* (which in this place expresses no more, than consolation and refreshing in misery, and not a powerfull deliverance out of it) is so often in the Scriptures made a denotation of Power too, as that we can doubt of no act of power, if we have this shadow of his wings. For, in this Metaphor of *Wings*, doth the Holy Ghost expresse the *Maritime* power, the power of some Nations at Sea, in Navies, (*Woe to the land shadowing with wings;*) that is, that hovers over the world, and intimidates it with her sailes and ships. In this Metaphor doth God remember his people, of his powerfull deliverance of them, (*You have seene what I did unto the Egyptians, and how I bare you on Eagles wings, and brought you to my selfe.*) In this Metaphor doth God threaten his and their enemies, what hee can doe, (*The noise of the wings of his Cherubims, are as the noise of great waters, and of an Army.*) So also, what hee will doe, (*Hee shall spread his wings over Bozrah, and at that day shall the hearts of the mighty men of Edom, be as the heart of a woman in her pangs.*) So that, if I have the shadow of his wings, I have the earnest of the power of them too; If I have refreshing, and respiration from them, I am able to say, (as those three Confessors did to *Nebuchadnezzar*) *My God is able to deliver me,* I am sure he hath power; *And my God will deliver me,* when it conduces to his glory, I know he will; *But, if he doe not, bee it knowne unto thee, O King, we will not serve thy Gods;* Be it knowne unto thee, O Satan, how long soever God deferre my deliverance, I will not seeke false comforts, the miserable comforts of this world. I will not, for I need not; for I can subsist under this shadow of these Wings, though I have no more.

The Mercy-seat it selfe was covered with the Cherubims Wings; and who would have more than Mercy? and a Mercy-seat; that is, established, resident Mercy, permanent and perpetuall Mercy; present and familiar Mercy; a Mercy-seat. Our Saviour Christ intends as much as would have served their turne, if they had laid hold upon it, when hee sayes, *That hee would have gathered Jerusalem, as a henne gathers her chickens under her wings.* And though the other Prophets doe (as ye have heard) mingle the signification of Power, and actuall deliverance, in this Metaphor of Wings, yet our Prophet, whom wee have now in especiall consideration, *David,* never doth so; but in every place where hee uses this Metaphor of Wings (which are in five or sixe severall Psalmes) still hee rests and determines in that sense, which is his meaning here; That though God doe not actually deliver us, nor actually destroy our enemies, yet if hee refresh us in the shadow of his Wings, if he maintaine our subsistence (which is a religious Constancy) in him, this should not onely establish our patience, (for that is but halfe the worke) but it should also produce a joy, and rise to an exultation, which is our last circumstance, *Therefore in the shadow of thy wings, I will rejoice.*

I would always raise your hearts, and dilate your hearts, to a holy Joy, to a joy in the Holy Ghost. There may be a just feare, that men doe not grieve enough for their sinnes; but there may bee a just jealousie, and suspition too, that they may fall into inordinate griefe, and diffidence of Gods mercy; And God hath reserved us to such times, as being the later times, give us even the dregs and lees of misery to drinke. For, God hath not onely let loose into the world a new spirituall disease; which is, an equality, and an indifferency, which religion our children, or our servants, or our companions professe; (I would not keepe company with a man that thought me a knave, or a traitor; with him that thought I loved not my Prince, or were a faithlesse man, not to be beleeved, I would not associate my selfe; And yet I will make him my bosome companion, that thinks I doe not love God, that thinks I cannot be saved) but God hath accompanied, and complicated almost all our bodily diseases of these times, with an extraordinary sadnesse, a predominant melancholy, a faintnesse of heart, a chearlesnesse, a joylesnesse of spirit, and therefore I returne often to this endeavor of raising your hearts, dilating your hearts with a holy Joy, Joy in the holy Ghost, for *Under the shadow of his wings,* you may, you should, *rejoyce.*

If you looke upon this world in a Map, you find two Hemisphears, two half worlds. If you crush heaven into a Map, you may find two Hemisphears too, two half heavens; Halfe will be Joy, and halfe will be Glory; for in these two, the joy of heaven, and the glory of heaven, is all heaven often represented unto us. And as of those two Hemisphears of the world, the first hath been knowne long before, but the other, (that of America, which is the richer in treasure) God reserved for later Discoveries; So though he reserve that Hemisphear of heaven, which is the Glory thereof, to the Resurrection, yet the other Hemisphear, the Joy of heaven, God opens to our Discovery, and delivers for our habitation even whilst we dwell in this world. As God hath cast upon the unrepentant sinner two deaths, a temporall, and a spirituall death, so hath he breathed into us two lives; for so, as the word for death is doubled, *Morte morieris, Thou shalt die the death,* so is the word for life expressed in the plurall, *Chaiim, vitarum, God breathed into his nostrils the breath of lives,* of divers lives. Though our naturall life were no life, but rather a continuall dying, yet we have two lives besides that, an eternall

life reserved for heaven, but yet a heavenly life too, a spirituall life, even
in this world; And as God doth thus inflict two deaths, and infuse two
lives, so doth he also passe two Judgements upon man, or rather repeats
the same Judgement twice. For, that which Christ shall say to thy soule
then at the last Judgement, *Enter into thy Masters joy,* Hee sayes to thy
conscience now, *Enter into thy Masters joy.* The everlastingnesse of the
joy is the blessednesse of the next life, but the entring, the inchoation is
afforded here. For that which Christ shall say then to us, *Venite benedicti,
Come ye blessed,* are words intended to persons that are comming, that
are upon the way, though not at home; Here in this world he bids us
Come, there in the next, he shall bid us *Welcome.* The Angels of heaven
have joy in thy conversion, and canst thou bee without that joy in thy
selfe? If thou desire revenge upon thine enemies, as they are Gods
enemies, That God would bee pleased to remove, and root out all such
as oppose him, that Affection appertaines to Glory; Let that alone till
thou come to the Hemisphear of Glory; There joyne with those Martyrs
under the Altar, *Usquequo Domine,* How long O Lord, dost thou deferre
Judgement? and thou shalt have thine answere there for that. Whilst
thou art here, here joyne with *David,* and the other Saints of God, in
that holy increpation [119] of a dangerous sadnesse, *Why art thou cast downe
O my soule? why art thou disquieted in mee?* That soule that is dissected and
anatomized to God, in a sincere confession, washed in the teares of true
contrition, embalmed in the blood of reconciliation, the blood of Christ
Jesus, can assigne no reason, can give no just answer to that Inter-
rogatory, *Why art thou cast downe O my soule? why art thou disquieted in
me?* No man is so little, as that he can be lost under these wings, no man
so great, as that they cannot reach to him; *Semper ille major est, quan-
tumcumque creverimus,* To what temporall, to what spirituall greatnesse
soever wee grow, still pray wee him to shadow us under his Wings; for
the poore need those wings against oppression, and the rich against
envy. The Holy Ghost, who is a Dove, shadowed the whole world
under his wings; *Incubabat aquis,* He hovered over the waters, he sate
upon the waters, and he hatched all that was produced, and all that was
produced so, was good. Be thou a Mother where the Holy Ghost would
be a Father; Conceive by him; and be content that he produce joy in
thy heart here. First thinke, that as a man must have some land, or els he
cannot be in wardship, so a man must have some of the love of God, or
els he could not fall under Gods correction; God would not give him his

physick, God would not study his cure, if he cared not for him. And then thinke also, that if God afford thee the shadow of his wings, that is, Consolation, respiration, refreshing, though not a present, and plenary deliverance, in thy afflictions, not to thanke God, is a murmuring, and not to rejoyce in Gods wayes, is an unthankfulnesse. Howling is the noyse of hell, singing the voyce of heaven; Sadnesse the damp of Hell, Rejoycing the serenity of Heaven. And he that hath not this joy here, lacks one of the best pieces of his evidence for the joyes of heaven; and hath neglected or refused that Earnest, by which God uses to binde his bargaine, that true joy in this world shall flow into the joy of Heaven, as a River flowes into the Sea; This joy shall not be put out in death, and a new joy kindled in me in Heaven; But as my soule, as soone as it is out of my body, is in Heaven,[120] and does not stay for the possession of Heaven, nor for the fruition of the sight of God, till it be ascended through ayre, and fire, and Moone, and Sun, and Planets, and Firmament, to that place which we conceive to be Heaven, but without the thousandth part of a minutes stop, as soone as it issues, is in a glorious light, which is Heaven, (for all the way to Heaven is Heaven; And as those Angels, which came from Heaven hither, bring Heaven with them, and are in Heaven here, So that soule that goes to Heaven, meets Heaven here; and as those Angels doe not devest Heaven by comming, so these soules invest Heaven, in their going.) As my soule shall not goe towards Heaven, but goe by Heaven to Heaven, to the Heaven of Heavens, So the true joy of a good soule in this world is the very joy of Heaven; and we goe thither, not that being without joy, we might have joy infused into us, but that as Christ sayes, *Our joy might be full,* perfected, sealed with an everlastingnesse; for, as he promises, *That no man shall take our joy from us,* so neither shall Death it selfe take it away, nor so much as interrupt it, or discontinue, it, But as in the face of Death, when he layes hold upon me, and in the face of the Devill, when he attempts me, I shall see the face of God, (for, every thing shall be a glasse, to reflect God upon me) so in the agonies of Death, in the anguish of that dissolution, in the sorrowes of that valediction, in the irreversiblenesse of that transmigration, I shall have a joy, which shall no more evaporate, than my soule shall evaporate, A joy, that shall passe up, and put on a more glorious garment above, and be joy super-invested in glory. *Amen.*

34. FROM A SERMON PREACHED AT S. PAULS, IN THE EVENING, UPON EASTER-DAY, 1626[121]

I

This then is our first Resurrection, for the duty that belongs to the soule, That the soule doe at all times think upon God, and at some times think upon nothing but him; And for that, which in this respect belongs to the body, That we neither enlarge, and pamper it so, nor so adorne and paint it, as though the soule required a spacious, and specious palace to dwell in. Of that excesse, *Porphyrie,*[122] who loved not Christ nor Christians, said well, out of meer Morality, That this enormous fatning and enlarging our bodies by excessive diet, was but a shoveling of more and more fat earth upon our soules to bury them deeper: *Dum corpus augemus, mortaliores efficimur,* sayes he, The more we grow, the more mortall we make our selves, and the greater sacrifice we provide for death, when we gather so much flesh: with that elegancy speaks he, speaking out of Nature, and with this simplicity and homelinesse speaks S. *Hierom,* speaking out of Grace, *Qui Christum desiderat, & illo pane vescitur, de quam preciosis cibis stercus conficiat, non quaerit,* He that can rellish Christ, and feed upon that Bread of life, will not be so diligent to make precious dung, and curious excrements, to spend his purse, or his wit, in that, which being taken into him, must passe by so ignoble a way from him.

The flesh that God hath given us, is affliction enough; but the flesh that the devill gives us, is affliction upon affliction; and to that, there belongs a woe. *Per tenuitatem assimilamur Deo,* saies the same Author; The attenuation, the slendernesse, the deliverance of the body from the encumbrance of much flesh, gives us some assimilation, some conformity to God, and his Angels; The lesse flesh we carry, the liker we are to them, who have none: That is still, the lesse flesh of our owne making: for, for that flesh, which God, and his instrument, Nature, hath given us, in what measure, or proportion soever, that does not oppresse us, to this purpose, neither shall that be laid to our charge; but the flesh that we have built up by curious diet, by meats of provocation, and witty sawces, or by a slothfull and drowsie negligence of the works of our calling. All flesh is sinfull flesh; sinfull so, as that it is the mother of sin, it occasions sin, naturall flesh is so; But this artificiall flesh of our owne making, is sinfull so, as that it is also the daughter of sin; It is, indeed, the punishment of former sins, and the occasion of future.

The soule then requires not so large, so vast a house of sinfull flesh, to dwell in: But yet on the other side, ye may not by inordinate abstinencies, by indiscreet fastings, by inhumane flagellations, by unnaturall macerations, and such Disciplines, as God doth not command, nor authorize, so wither, and shrinke, and contract the body, as though the soule were sent into it, as into a prison, or into fetters, and manacles, to wring, and pinch, and torture it. *Nihil interest,* saies S. *Hierome,* It is all one whether thou kill thy selfe at one blow, or be long in doing it, if thou do it. All one, whether thou fall upon thine own sword, or sterve thy selfe with such a fasting, as thou discernest to induce that effect: for, saies he, *Descendit a dignitate viri & notas insaniae incurrit,* He departs from that dignity, which God hath imprinted in man, in giving him the use, and the dominion over his creatures, and he gives the world just occasion to thinke him mad.

2

Thus it is, when a soule is scattered upon the daily practise of any one predominant, and habituall sin, but when it is indifferently scattered upon all, how much more is it so? In him, that swallowes sins in the world, as he would doe meats at a feast; passes through every dish, and never askes Physitian the nature, the quality, the danger, the offence of any dish: That baits at every sin that rises, and poures himselfe into every sinfull mold he meets: That knowes not when he began to spend his soule, nor where, nor upon what sin he laid it out; no, nor whether he have, whether ever he had any soule, or no; but hath lost his soule so long agoe, in rusty, and in incoherent sins, (not sins that produced one another, as in *Davids* case (and yet that is a fearfull state, that concatenation of sins, that pedegree of sins) but in sins which he embraces, meerely out of an easinesse to sin, and not out of a love, no, nor out of a tentation to that sin in particular) that in these incoherent sins hath so scattered his soule, as that he hath not soule enough left, to seek out the rest. And therefore *David* makes it the Title of the whole Psalme, *Domine ne disperdas, O Lord doe not scatter us:* And he begins to expresse his sense of Gods Judgements, in the next Psalme, so, *O Lord thou hast cast us out, thou hast scattered us, turn again unto us;* for even from this aversion, there may be conversion, and from this last and lowest fall, a resurrection. But how?

In the generall resurrection upon naturall death, God shall work upon this dispersion of our scattered dust, as in the first fall, which is the Divorce, by way of Re-union, and in the second, which is Putrifaction, by way of Re-efformation; so in this third, which is Dispersion, by way of Re-collection; where mans buried flesh hath brought forth grasse, and that grasse fed beasts, and those beasts fed men, and those men fed other men, God that knowes in which Boxe of his Cabinet all this seed Pearle lies, in what corner of the world every atome, every graine of every mans dust sleeps, shall recollect that dust, and then recompact that body, and then re-inanimate that man, and that is the accomplishment of all.

35. FROM A SERMON PREACHED TO THE KING IN MY ORDINARY WAYTING AT WHITE-HALL, 18 APRIL 1626[123]

God hath a progresse house,[124] a removing house here upon earth, His house of prayer; At this houre, God enters into as many of these houses, as are opened for his service at this houre: But his standing house, his house of glory, is that in Heaven, and that he promises them. God himselfe dwelt in Tents in this world, and he gives them a House in Heaven. A House, in the designe and survay whereof, the Holy Ghost himselfe is figurative, the Fathers wanton, and the School-men wilde. The Holy Ghost, in describing this House, fills our contemplation with foundations, and walls, and gates, of gold, of precious stones, and all materialls, that we can call precious. The Holy Ghost is figurative; And the Fathers are wanton in their spirituall elegancies, such as that of S. *Augustins,* (if that booke be his) *Hiems horrens, Aestas torrens,* And, *Virent prata, vernant sata,*[125] and such other harmonious, and melodious, and mellifluous cadences of these waters of life. But the School-men are wild;[126] for as one Author, who is afraid of admitting too great a hollownesse in the Earth, lest then the Earth might not be said to be solid, pronounces that Hell cannot possibly be above three thousand miles in compasse, (and then one of the torments of Hell will be the throng, for their bodies must be there, in their dimensions, as well as their soules) so when the School-men come to measure this house in heaven, (as they will measure it, and the Master, God, and all his Attributes, and tell us how Allmighty, and how Infinite he is) they pronounce, that every soule in that house shall have more roome to it selfe, than all this world is. We know not that; nor see we that the consolation lyes in that; we rest in this, that it is a House, It hath a foundation, no Earth-quake shall shake it, It hath walls, no Artillery shall batter it, It hath a roofe, no tempest shall pierce it. It is a house that affords security, and that is one beame; And it is *Domus patris,* His Fathers house, a house in which he hath interest, and that is another beame of his Consolation.

It was his Fathers, and so his; And his, and so ours; for we are not joynt purchasers of Heaven with the Saints, but we are co-heires with Christ Jesus. We have not a place there, because they have done more than enough for themselves, but because he hath done enough for them and us too. By death we are gathered to our Fathers in nature; and by death, through his mercy, gathered to his Father also. Where we shall have a full satisfaction, in that wherein S. *Philip* placed all satisfaction, *Ostende nobis patrem, Lord, shew us thy Father, and it is enough.* We shall see his Father, and see him made ours in him.

And then a third beame of this Consolation is, That in this house of his Fathers, thus by him made ours, there are *Mansions;* In which word, the Consolation is not placed, (I doe not say, that there is not truth in it) but the Consolation is not placed in this, That some of these Mansions are below, some above staires, some better seated, better lighted, better vaulted, better fretted, better furnished than others; but onely in this, That they are *Mansions;* which word, in the Originall, and Latin, and our Language, signifies a *Remaining,* and denotes the perpetuity, the everlastingnesse of that state. A state but of one Day, because no Night shall over-take, or determine it, but such a Day, as is not of a thousand yeares, which is the longest measure in the Scriptures, but of a thousand millions of millions of generations: *Qui nec praeceditur hesterno, nec excluditur crastino,* A day that hath no *pridie,* nor *postridie,* yesterday doth not usher it in, nor to morrow shall not drive it out. *Methusalem,* with all his hundreds of yeares, was but a Mushrome of a nights growth, to this day, And all the foure Monarchies,[127] with all their thousands of yeares, And all the powerfull Kings, and all the beautifull Queenes of this world, were but as a bed of flowers, some gathered at six, some at seaven, some at eight, All in one Morning, in respect of this Day. In all the two thousand yeares of Nature, before the Law given by *Moses*, And the two thousand yeares of Law, before the Gospel given by Christ, And the two thousand of Grace, which are running now, (of which last houre we have heard three quarters strike, more than fifteen hundred of this last two thousand spent) In all this six thousand, and in all those, which God may be pleased to adde, *In domo patris,* In this House of his Fathers, there was never heard quarter clock to strike, never seen minute glasse to turne. No time lesse than it selfe would serve to expresse this time, which is intended in this word *Mansions;* which is also exalted with another beame, that they are *Multa, In my Fathers House there are many Mansions.*

In this Circumstance, an Essentiall, a Substantiall Circumstance, we would consider the joy of our society, and conversation in heaven, since society and conversation is one great element and ingredient into the joy, which we have in this world. We shall have an association with Christ himselfe; for *where he is,* it is his promise, *that we also shall be.* We shall have an association with the Angels, and such a one, as we shall be such as they. We shall have an association with the Saints, and not onely so, to be such as they, but to be they: And with all *who come from the East, and from the West, and from the North, and from the South, and sit down with Abraham, and Isaac, and Jacob in the kingdome of heaven.* Where we shall be so far from being enemies to one another, as that we shall not be strangers to one another: And so far from envying one another, as that all that every one hath, shall be every others possession: where all soules shall be so intirely knit together, as if all were but one soule, and God so intirely knit to every soule, as if there were as many Gods as soules.

36. FROM A SERMON PREACHED UPON WHITSUNDAY[1626][128]

I

When the Holy Ghost hath brought us into the Ark from whence we may see all the world without, sprawling and gasping in the flood, (the flood of sinfull courses in the world, and of the anger of God) when we can see this violent flood, (the anger of God) break in at windowes, and there devoure the licentious man in his sinfull embracements, and make his bed of wantonnesse his death-bed; when we can see this flood (the anger of God) swell as fast as the ambitious man swels, and pursue him through all his titles, and at last suddenly, and violently wash him away in his owne blood, not alwayes in a vulgar, but sometimes in an ignominious death; when we shall see this flood (the flood of the anger of God) over-flow the valley of the voluptuous mans gardens, and orchards, and follow him into his Arbours, and Mounts, and Terasses, and carry him from thence into a bottomless Sea, which no Plummet can sound, (no heavy sadnesse relieve him) no anchor take hold of, (no repentance stay his tempested and weather-beaten conscience) when wee finde ourselves in this Ark, where we have first taken in the fresh water of Baptisme, and then the Bread, and Wine, and Flesh, of the Body and Blood of Christ Jesus, Then are we reproved, forbidden all scruple, then are we convinced, That as *the twelve Apostles shall sit upon twelve seats, and judge the twelve Tribes at the last day;* So doth the Holy Ghost make us Judges of all the world now, and inables us to pronounce that sentence, That all but they, who have sincerely accepted the Christian Religion, are still *sub peccato*, under sin, and without remedy. For we must not waigh God with leaden, or iron, or stone waights, how much land, or metall, or riches he gives one man more than another, but how much grace in the use of these, or how much patience in the want, or in the losse of these, we have above others.

2

Now, in respect of the time after this judgement, (which is Eternity) the time between this and it cannot be a minute; and therefore think thy self at that Tribunall, that judgement now: Where thou shalt not onely heare all thy sinfull workes, and words, and thoughts repeated, which thou thy selfe hadst utterly forgot, but thou shalt heare thy good works, thine almes, thy comming to Church, thy hearing of Sermons given in evidence against thee, because they had hypocrisie mingled in them; yea thou shalt finde even thy repentance to condemne thee, because thou madest that but a doore to a relapse. There thou shalt see, to thine inexpressible terror, some others cast downe into hell, for thy sins; for those sins which they would not have done, but upon thy provocation. There thou shalt see some that occasioned thy sins, and accompanied thee in them, and sinned them in a greater measure than thou didst, taken up into heaven, because in the way, they remembred the end, and thou shalt sink under a lesse waight, because thou never lookedst towards him that would have eased thee of it. *Quis non cogitans haec in desperationis rotetur abyssum?* Who can once thinke of this and not be tumbled into desperation? But who can think of it twice, maturely, and by the Holy Ghost, and not finde comfort in it, when the same light that shewes mee the judgement, shewes me the Judge too?

37. FROM THE THIRD OF MY PREBEND SERMONS UPON MY FIVE PSALMES, 5 NOVEMBER 1626[129]

Upon this earth, a man cannot possibly make one step in a straight, and a direct line. The earth it selfe being round, every step wee make upon it, must necessarily bee a segment, an arch of a circle. But yet though no piece of a circle be a straight line, yet if we take any piece, nay if wee take the whole circle, there is no corner, no angle in any piece, in any intire circle. A perfect rectitude we cannot have in any wayes in this world; In every Calling there are some inevitable tentations. But, though wee cannot make up our circle of a straight line, (that is impossible to humane frailty) yet wee may passe on, without angles, and corners,[130] that is, without disguises in our Religion, and without the love of craft, and falsehood, and circumvention in our civill actions. A Compasse is a necessary thing in a Ship, and the helpe of that Compasse brings the Ship home safe, and yet that Compasse hath some variations, it doth not looke directly North; Neither is that starre which we call the North-pole, or by which we know the North-pole, the very Pole it selfe; but we call it so, and we make our uses of it, and our conclusions by it, as if it were so, because it is the neerest starre to that Pole. He that comes as neere uprightnesse, as infirmities admit, is an upright man, though he have some obliquities. To God himselfe we may alwayes go in a direct line, a straight, a perpendicular line; For God is verticall to me, over my head now, and verticall now to them, that are in the East, and West-Indies; To our Antipodes, to them that are under our feet, God is verticall, over their heads, then when he is over ours.[131]

38. FROM A SERMON PREACHED AT THE FUNERALS OF SIR WILLIAM COCKAYNE, KNIGHT, ALDERMAN OF LONDON, 12 DECEMBER 1626[132]

I

God made the first Marriage, and man made the first Divorce; God married the Body and Soule in the Creation, and man divorced the Body and Soule by death through sinne, in his fall. God doth not admit, not justifie, not authorize such Superinductions upon such Divorces, as some have imagined; That the soule departing from one body, should become the soule of another body, in a perpetuall revolution and transmigration of soules[133] through bodies, which hath been the giddinesse of some Philosophers to think; Or that the body of the dead should become the body of an evill spirit, that that spirit might at his will, and to his purposes informe, and inanimate that dead body; God allowes no such Super-inductions, no such second Marriages upon such divorces by death, no such disposition of soule or body, after their dissolution by death. But because God hath made the band of Marriage indissoluble but by death, farther than man can die, this divorce cannot fall upon man; As farre as man is immortall, man is a married man still, still in possession of a soule, and a body too; And man is for ever immortall in both; Immortall in his soule by Preservation, and immortall in his body by Reparation in the Resurrection. For, though they be separated *a Thoro & Mensa*, from Bed and Board, they are not divorced;

Though the soule be at the *Table of the Lambe,* in Glory, and the body but at the table of *the Serpent, in dust;* Though the soule be *in lecto florido,* in that bed which is alwayes green, in an everlasting spring, in *Abrahams bosome;* And the body but in that green-bed, whose covering is but a yard and a halfe of Turfe, and a Rugge of grasse, and the sheet but a winding sheet, yet they are not divorced; they shall returne to one another againe, in an inseparable re-union in the Resurrection.[134]

2

And how imperfect is all our knowledge? What one thing doe we know perfectly? Whether wee consider Arts, or Sciences, the servant knows but according to the proportion of his Masters knowledge in that Art, and the Scholar knows but according to the proportion of his Masters knowledge in that Science; Young men mend not their sight by using old mens Spectacles; and yet we looke upon Nature, but with *Aristotles* Spectacles, and upon the body of man, but with *Galens,*[135] and upon the frame of the world, but with *Ptolomies* Spectacles. Almost all knowledge is rather like a child that is embalmed to make Mummy,[136] than that is nursed to make a Man; rather conserved in the stature of the first age, than growne to be greater; And if there be any addition to knowledge, it is rather a new knowledge, than a greater knowledge; rather a singularity in a desire of proposing something that was not knowne at all before, than an emproving, an advancing, a multiplying of former inceptions; and by that means, no knowledge comes to be perfect. One Philosopher thinks he is dived to the bottome, when he sayes, he knows nothing but this, That he knows nothing; and yet another thinks, that he hath expressed more knowledge than he, in saying, That he knows not so much as that, That he knows nothing. S. *Paul* found that to be all knowledge, To know Christ; And Mahomet thinks himselfe wise therefore, because he knows not, acknowledges not Christ, as S. *Paul* does. Though a man knew not, that every sin casts another shovell of Brimstone upon him in Hell, yet if he knew that every riotous feast cuts off a year, and every wanton night seaven years of his seventy in this world, it were some degree towards perfection in knowledge. He that purchases a Mannor, will thinke to have an exact Survey of the Land: But who thinks of taking so exact a survey of his Conscience, how that money was got, that purchased that Mannor? We call that a mans meanes, which he hath; But that is truly his meanes, what way he came by it. And yet how few are there, (when a state comes to any great proportion) that know that; that know what they have, what they are worth? We have seen great Wills, dilated into glorious uses, and into pious uses, and then too narrow an estate to reach to it; And we have seen Wills, where the Testator thinks he hath bequeathed all, and he hath not knowne halfe his own worth. When thou knowest a wife, a sonne, a servant, a friend no better, but that that wife betrayes thy bed, and that sonne thine estate, and that servant thy credit, and that friend thy secret, what canst thou say thou knowest? But we must not insist upon this Consideration of knowledge; for, though knowledge be of a spirituall nature, yet it is but as a terrestriall Spirit, conversant upon Earth; Spirituall things, of a more rarified nature than knowledge, even faith it selfe, and all that grows from that in us, falls within this Rule, which we have in hand, That even in spirituall things, nothing is perfect.

3

When we consider with a religious seriousnesse the manifold weaknesses of the strongest devotions in time of Prayer, it is a sad consideration. I throw my selfe downe in my Chamber, and I call in, and invite God, and his Angels thither, and when they are there, I neglect God and his Angels, for the noise of a Flie, for the ratling of a Coach, for the whining of a doore; I talke on, in the same posture of praying; Eyes lifted up; knees bowed downe; as though I prayed to God; and, if God, or his Angels should aske me, when I thought last of God in that prayer, I cannot tell: Sometimes I finde that I had forgot what I was about, but when I began to forget it, I cannot tell. A memory of yesterdays pleasures, a feare of to morrows dangers, a straw under my knee, a noise in mine eare, a light in mine eye, an any thing, a nothing, a fancy, a Chimera in my braine, troubles me in my prayer. So certainely is there nothing, nothing in spirituall things, perfect in this world.

4

I need not call in new Philosophy, that denies a settlednesse, an ac-quiescence in the very body of the Earth, but makes the Earth to move in that place, where we thought the Sunne had moved; I need not that helpe, that the Earth it selfe is in Motion, to prove this, That nothing upon Earth is permanent; The Assertion will stand of it selfe, till some man assigne me some instance, something that a man may relie upon, and find permanent. Consider the greatest Bodies upon Earth, The Monarchies; Objects, which one would thinke, Destiny might stand and stare at, but not shake; Consider the smallest bodies upon Earth, The haires of our head, Objects, which one would thinke, Destiny would not observe, or could not discerne; And yet Destiny, (to speak to a naturall man) And God, (to speake to a Christian) is no more troubled to make a Monarchy ruinous, than to make a haire gray. Nay, nothing needs be done to either, by God, or Destiny; A Monarchy will ruine, as a haire will grow gray, of it selfe. In the Elements themselves, of which all sub-elementary things are composed, there is no acquiescence, but a vicissitudinary transmutation into one another; Ayre condensed becomes water, a more solid body, And Ayre rarified becomes fire, a body more disputable, and in-apparant. It is so in the Conditions of men too; A Merchant condensed, kneaded and packed up in a great estate, becomes a Lord; And a Merchant rarified, blown up by a perfidious Factor, or by a riotous Sonne, evaporates into ayre, into nothing, and is not seen. And if there were any thing permanent and durable in this world, yet we got nothing by it, because howsoever that might last in it selfe, yet we could not last to enjoy it; If our goods were not amongst Moveables, yet we our selves are; if they could stay with us, yet we cannot stay with them; which is another Consideration in this part.

The world is a great Volume, and man the Index of that Booke; Even in the body of man, you may turne to the whole world; This body is an Illustration of all Nature;[137] Gods recapitulation of all that he had said before, in his *Fiat lux*, and *Fiat firmamentum*, and in all the rest, said or done, in all the six dayes. Propose this body to thy consideration in the highest exaltation thereof; as it is the *Temple of the Holy Ghost:* Nay, not in a Metaphor, or comparison of a Temple, or any other similitudinary thing, but as it was really and truly the very body of God, in the person of Christ, and yet this body must wither, must decay, must languish, must perish. When *Goliah* had armed and fortified this body, And *Jezabel* had painted and perfumed this body, And *Dives* had pampered and larded this body, As God said to *Ezekiel*, when he brought him to the *dry bones, Fili hominis, Sonne of Man, doest thou thinke these bones can live?* They said in their hearts to all the world, Can these bodies die? And they are dead. *Jezabels* dust is not Ambar, nor *Goliahs* dust *Terra sigillata*,[138] Medicinall; nor does the Serpent, whose meat they are both, finde any better relish in *Dives* dust, than in *Lazarus*. But as in our former part, where our foundation was, That in nothing, no spirituall thing, there was any perfectnesse, which we illustrated in the weaknesses of Knowledge, and Faith, and Hope, and Charity, yet we concluded, that for all those defects, God accepted those their religious services; So in this part, where our foundation is, That nothing in temporall things is permanent, as we have illustrated that, by the decay of that which is Gods noblest piece in Nature, The body of man; so we shall also conclude that, with this goodnesse of God, that for all this dissolution, and putre-faction, he affords this Body a Resurrection.

The Gentils, and their Poets, describe the sad state of Death so, *Nox una obeunda,*[139] That it is one everlasting Night; To them, a Night; But to a Christian, it is *Dies Mortis,* and *Dies Resurrectionis,* The day of Death, and The day of Resurrection; We die in the light, in the sight of Gods presence, and we rise in the light, in the sight of his very Essence. Nay, Gods corrections, and judgements upon us in this life, are still expressed so, *Dies visitationis,* still it is a Day, though a *Day of visitation;* and still we may discerne God to be in the action. The *Lord of Life* was the first that named *Death; Morte morieris,* sayes God, Thou shalt die the Death. I doe the lesse feare, or abhorre Death, because I finde it in his mouth; Even a malediction hath a sweetnesse in his mouth; for there is a blessing wrapped up in it; a mercy in every correction, a Resurrection upon every Death. When *Jezabels* beauty, exalted to that height which it had by art, or higher than that, to that height which it had in her own opinion, shall be infinitely multiplied upon every Body; And as God shall know no man from his own Sonne, so as not to see the very righteousnesse of his own Sonne upon that man; So the Angels shall know no man from Christ, so as not to desire to looke upon that mans face, because the most deformed wretch that is there, shall have the very beauty of Christ himselfe; So shall *Goliahs* armour, and *Dives* fulnesse, be doubled, and redoubled upon us. And every thing that we can call good, shall first be infinitely exalted in the goodnesse, and then infinitely multiplied in the proportion, and againe infinitely extended in the duration. And since we are in an action of preparing this dead Brother of ours to that state, (for the Funerall is the Easter-eve, The Buriall is the depositing of that man for the Resurrection) As we have held you, with Doctrine of Mortification, by extending the Text, from *Martha* to this occasion; so shall we dismisse you with Consolation, by a like occasionall inverting the Text, from passion in *Martha's* mouth, *Lord, if thou hadst been here, my Brother had not dyed,* to joy in ours, *Lord, because thou wast here, our Brother is not dead.*

The Lord was with him in all these steps; with him in his life; with him in his death; He is with him in his funerals, and he shall be with him in his Resurrection; and therefore, because the Lord was with him, our Brother is not dead. He was with him in the beginning of his life, in this manifestation, That though he were of Parents of a good, of a great Estate, yet his possibility and his expectation from them, did not slacken his own industry; which is a Canker that eats into, nay that hath eat up many a family in this City, that relying wholly upon what the Father hath done, the Sonne does nothing for himselfe. And truly, it falls out too often, that he that labours not for more, does not keepe his own. God imprinted in him an industrious disposition, though such hopes from such parents might have excused some slacknesse, and God prospered his industry so, as that when his Fathers estate came to a distribution by death, he needed it not. God was with him, as with *David* in a Dilatation, and then in a Repletion; God enlarged him, and then he filled him; He gave him a large and a comprehensive understanding, and with it, A publique heart; And such as perchance in his way of education, and in our narrow and contracted times, in which every man determines himselfe in himselfe, and scarce looks farther, it would be hard to finde many Examples of such largenesse. You have, I thinke, a phrase of Driving a Trade; And you have, I know, a practise of Driving away Trade, by other use of money; And you have lost a man, that drove a great Trade, the right way in making the best use of our home-commodity. To fetch in Wine, and Spice, and Silke, is but a drawing of Trade; The right driving of trade, is, to vent our owne outward; And yet, for the drawing in of that, which might justly seeme most behoofefull, that is, of Arts, and Manufactures, to be imployed upon our owne Commodity within the Kingdome, he did his part, diligently, at least, if not vehemently, if not passionately. This City is a great Theater, and he Acted great and various parts in it; And all well; And when he went higher, (as he was often heard in Parliaments, at Councell tables, and in more private accesses to the late King of ever blessed memory) as, for that comprehension of those businesses, which he pretended to understand, no man doubts, for no man lacks arguments and evidences of his ability therein, So for his manner of expressing his intentions, and digesting and uttering his purposes, I have sometimes heard the greatest

Master of Language and Judgement, which these times, or any other did, or doe, or shall give, (that good and great King of ours) say of him, That he never heard any man of his breeding, handle businesses more rationally, more pertinently, more elegantly, more perswasively; And when his purpose was, to do a grace to a Preacher, of very good abilities, and good note in his owne Chappell, I have heard him say, that his language, and accent, and manner of delivering himselfe, was like this man. This man hath God accompanied all his life; and by performance thereof seemes to have made that Covenant with him, which he made to *Abraham, Multiplicabo te vehementer, I will multiply thee exceedingly.* He multiplied his estate so, as was fit to endow many and great Children; and he multiplied his Children so, both in their number, and in their quality, as they were fit to receive a great Estate. God was with him all the way, In *a Pillar of Fire,* in the brightnesse of prosperity, and in the *Pillar of Clouds* too, in many darke, and sad, and heavy crosses: So great a Ship, required a great Ballast, So many blessings, many crosses; And he had them, and sailed on his course the steadier for them; The *Cloud* as well as the *Fire,* was a *Pillar* to him; His crosses, as well as his blessings established his assurance in God; And so, in all the course of his life, *The Lord was here,* and therefore *our Brother is not dead;* not dead in the evidences and testimonies of life; for he, whom the world hath just cause to celebrate, for things done, when he was alive, is alive still in their celebration.

The Lord was here, that is, with him at his death too. He was served with the Processe [140] here in the City, but his cause was heard in the Country; Here he sickned, There he languished, and dyed there. In his sicknesse there, those that assisted him, are witnesses, of his many expressings, of a religious and a constant heart towards God, and of his pious joyning with them, even in the holy declaration of kneeling, then, when they, in favour of his weakenesse, would disswade him from kneeling. I must not defraud him of this testimony from my selfe, that into this place where we are now met, I have observed him to enter with much reverence, and compose himselfe in this place with much declaration of devotion. And truly it is that reverence, which those persons who are of the same ranke that he was in the City, that reverence that they use in this place, when they come hither, is that that makes us, who have now the administration of this Quire, glad, that our Predecessors, but a very few yeares before our time, (and not before all our times neither) admitted these Honourable and worshipfull Persons of this City, to sit in this Quire, so, as they do upon Sundayes; The Church receives an honour in it; But the honour is more in their reverence, than in their presence; though in that too: And they receive an honour, and an ease in it; and therefore they do piously towards God, and prudently for themselves, and gratefully towards us, in giving us, by their reverent comportment here, so just occasion of continuing that honour, and that ease to them here, which to lesse reverend, and unrespective persons, we should be lesse willing to doe. To returne to him in his sicknesse; He had but one dayes labour, and all the rest were Sabbaths, one day in his sicknesse he converted to businesse; Thus; He called his family, and friends together; Thankfully he acknowledged Gods manifold blessings, and his owne sins as penitently: And then, to those who were to have the disposing of his estate, joyntly with his Children, he recommended his servants, and the poore, and the Hospitals, and the Prisons, which, according to his purpose, have beene all taken into consideration; And after this (which was his Valediction to the world) he seemed alwaies loath to returne to any worldly businesse, His last Commandement to Wife and Children was Christs last commandement to his Spouse the Church, in the Apostles, *To love one another*. He blest them, and the Estate devolved upon them, unto them: And by Gods grace shall prove as true a Prophet to them in that blessing, as he was to himselfe, when in entring his last bed, two dayes before his Death, he said, *Help me off with my earthly habit, and let me go to my last bed*. Where, in the second night after, he said, *Little know ye what paine I feele this night, yet I know, I shall have joy in the morning;* And in that morning he dyed. The forme in which he implored his Saviour, was evermore, towards his end, this, *Christ Jesus, which dyed on the Crosse, forgive me my sins; He have mercy upon me:* And his last and dying words were the repetition of the name of Jesus; And when he had not strength to utter that name distinctly and perfectly, they might heare it from within him, as from a man a far off; even then, when his hollow and remote naming of Jesus, was rather a certifying of them, that he was with his Jesus, than a prayer that he might come to him. And so *The Lord was here,* here with him in his Death; and because *the Lord was here, our Brother is not dead;* not dead in the eyes and eares of God; for as the blood of *Abel* speaks yet, so doth the zeale of Gods Saints; and their last prayers (though we heare them not) God continues still; and they pray in Heaven, as the Martyrs under the Altar, even till the Resurrection.

He is with him now too; Here in his Funerals. Buriall, and Christian Buriall, and Solemne Buriall are all evidences, and testimonies of Gods presence. God forbid we should conclude, or argue an absence of God, from the want of Solemne Buriall, or Christian Buriall, or any Buriall; But neither must we deny it, to be an evidence of his favour and presence, where he is pleased to afford these. So God makes that the seale of all his blessings to *Abraham, That he should be buried in a good age;* God established *Jacob* with that promise, *That his Son Joseph should have care of his Funerals:* And *Joseph* does cause his servants, *The Physitians, to embalme him, when he was dead.* Of Christ it was Prophecied, *That he should have a glorious Buriall;* And therefore Christ interprets well that profuse, and prodigall piety of the Woman that poured out the Oyntment upon him, *That she did it to Bury him;* And so shall *Joseph* of Arimathea be ever celebrated, for his care in celebrating Christs Funerals. If we were to send a Son, or a friend, to take possession of any place in Court, or forraine parts, we would send him out in the best equipage: Let us not grudge to set downe our friends, in the Anti-chamber of Heaven, the Grave, in as good manner, as without vaine-gloriousnesse, and wastfulnesse we may; And, in inclining them, to whom that care belongs, to expresse that care as they doe this day, *The Lord is with him,* even in this Funerall; And because *The Lord is here, our brother is not dead;* Not dead in the memories and estimation of men.

And lastly, that we may have God present in all his Manifestations, *Hee that was, and is, and is to come,* was with him, in his life and death, and is with him in this holy Solemnity, and shall bee with him againe in the Resurrection. God sayes to *Jacob, I will goe downe with thee into Egypt, and I will also surely bring thee up againe.* God goes downe with a good man into the Grave, and will surely bring him up againe. When? The Angel promised to returne to *Abraham* and *Sarah,* for the assurance of the birth of *Isaac, according to the time of life;* that is, in such time, as by nature a woman may have a childe. God will returne to us in the Grave, *according to the time of life;* that is, in such time, as he, by his gracious Decree, hath fixed for the Resurrection. And in the meane time, no more than the God-head departed from the dead body of our Saviour, in the grave, doth his power, and his presence depart from our dead bodies in that darknesse; But that which *Moses* said to the whole Congregation, I say to you all, both to you that heare me, and to him that does not, *All ye that did cleave unto the Lord your God, are alive, every one of you, this day;* Even hee, whom we call dead, is alive this day. In the presence of God, we lay him downe; In the power of God, he shall rise; In the person of Christ, he is risen already. And so into the same hands that have received his soule, we commend his body; beseeching his blessed Spirit, that as our charity enclines us to hope confidently of his good estate, our faith may assure us of the same happinesse, in our owne behalfe; And that for all our sakes, but especially for his own glory, he will be pleased to hasten the consummation of all, in that kingdome which that Son of God hath purchased for us, with the inestimable price of his incorruptible blood. *Amen.*

39. FROM A SERMON PREACHED AT S. PAULS UPON CHRISTMAS DAY, 1626[141]

This then is truly to depart in peace, by the Gospell of peace, to the God of peace. My body is my prison; and I would be so obedient to the Law, as not to break prison; I would not hasten my death by starving, or macerating this body: But if this prison be burnt down by continuall feavers, or blowen down with continuall vapours, would any man be so in love with that ground upon which that prison stood, as to desire rather to stay there, than to go home? Our prisons are fallen, our bodies are dead to many former uses; Our palate dead in a tastlesnesse; Our stomach dead in an indigestiblenesse; our feete dead in a lamenesse, and our invention in a dulnesse, and our memory in a forgetfulnesse; and yet, as a man that should love the ground, where his prison stood, we love this clay, that was a body in the dayes of our youth, and but our prison then, when it was at best; wee abhorre the graves of our bodies; and the body, which, in the best vigour thereof, was but the grave of the soule, we over-love, *Pharaohs* Butler, and his Baker went both out of prison in a day; and in both cases, *Joseph*, in the interpretation of their dreames, calls that, (their very discharge out of prison) a lifting up of their heads, a kinde of preferment: Death raises every man alike, so far, as that it delivers every man from his prison, from the incumbrances of this body: both Baker and Butler were delivered of their prison; but they passed into divers states after, one to the restitution of his place, the other to an ignominious execution. Of thy prison thou shalt be delivered whether thou wilt or no; thou must die; Foole, this night thy soule may be taken from thee; and then, what thou shalt be to morrow, prophecy upon thy selfe, by that which thou hast done to day; If thou didst depart from that Table in peace, thou canst depart from this world in peace. And the peace of that Table is, to come to it *in pace desiderii,* with a contented minde, and with an enjoying of those temporall blessings which thou hast, without macerating thy self, without usurping upon others, without murmuring at God; And to be at that Table, *in pace cogitationum,* in the peace of the Church, without the spirit of contradiction, or inquisition, without uncharitablenesse towards others, without curiosity in thy selfe: And then to come from that Table *in pace domestica,* with a bosome peace, in thine own Conscience, in that seale of thy reconciliation, in that Sacrament; that so, riding at that Anchor, and in that calme, whether God enlarge thy voyage, by enlarging thy life, or put thee into the harbour, by the breath, by the breathlesnesse of Death, either way, East or West, thou maist depart in peace, according to his word, that is, as he shall be pleased to manifest his pleasure upon thee.

40. FROM A SERMON PREACHED TO THE KING, AT WHITEHALL, THE FIRST SUNDAY IN LENT [PROBABLY 11 FEBRUARY 1627][142]

I

Peace is in *Sion;* Gods whole Quire is in tune; Nay, here is the musick of the Sphears; all the Sphears (all Churches) all the Stars in those Sphears (all Expositours in all Churches) agree in the sense of these words; and agree the words to be a Prophesie, of the Distillation, nay Inundation, of the largenesse, nay the infinitenesse of the blessings, and benefits of Almighty God, prepared and meditated before, and presented, and accomplisht now in the Christian Church. The Sun was up betimes, in the *light of nature,* but then the Sun moved but in the *winter Tropick,* short and cold, dark and cloudy dayes; A *Diluculum* and a *Crepusculum, a Dawning* and *a Twilight,* a little *Traditionall* knowledge for the past, and a little *Conjecturall* knowledge for the future, made up their day. The Sunne was advanced higher to the *Jewes* in the *Law;* But then the Sunne was but in *Libra;* as much day as night: There was as much *Baptisme,* as *Circumcision* in that Sacrament; and as much *Lamb* as *Christ,* in that Sacrifice; The Law was their *Equinoctiall,* in which, they might see both the Type, and that which was figured in the Type: But in the Christian Church the Sun is in a *perpetuall Summer Solstice;* which are high degrees, and yet there is a higher, the Sun is in a perpetuall *Meridian* and *Noon,* in that Summer solstice. There is not onely a *Surge Sol,* but a *Siste sol:* God hath brought the Sunne to the height, and fixt the Sun in that height in the Christian Church; where he in his own *Sonne* by his Spirit hath promised to dwell, *usque ad consummationem,* till the end of the world.

2

What can be certain in this world, if even the mercy of God admit a variation? what can be endlesse here, if even the mercy of God receive a determination? and *sin* doth vary the nature, *sin* doth determine even the infinitenesse of the mercy of God himself, for though *The childe shall die a hundred yeares old,* yet *the sinner being a hundred years old shall be accursed.* Disconsolate soul, dejected spirit, bruised and broken, ground and trodden, attenuated, evaporated, annihilated heart come back; heare thy *reprieve,* and sue for thy *pardon;* God will not take thee away in thy sins, thou shalt have time to repent, *The childe shall die a hundred years old.* But then lame and decrepit soul, gray and inveterate sinner, behold the full ears of corn blasted with a mildew, behold this long day shutting up in such a night, as shall never see light more, the night of death; in which, the deadliest pang of thy *Death* will be thine *Immortality:* In this especially shalt thou die, that thou canst not die, when thou art dead; but must live dead for ever: for *The sinner being a hundred yeers old, shall be accursed,* he shall be so for ever.

3

So then we have brought our Sunne to his *Meridianall height,* to a full Noon, in which all shadows are removed: for even the *shadow of death,* death it self is a blessing, and in the number of his Mercies. But the *Afternoon shadows* break out upon us, in our second part of the Text. And as afternoon shadowes do, these in our Text do also; they grow greater and greater upon us, till they end in night, in everlasting night, *The sinner being a hundred yeares old shall be accursed.* Now of shadowes it is appliably said, *Umbrae non sunt tenebrae sed densior lux,* shadowes are not utter darknesse, but a thicker light;[143] shadowes are thus much nearer to the nature of light than darknesse is, that shadowes presume light, which darknesse doth not; shadowes could not be, except there were light. The first shadowes in this dark part of our Text, have thus much light in them, that it is but the *sinner,* onely the sinner that is accursed. The Object of Gods malediction, is not *man,* but *sinfull man.* If God make a man sinne, God curses the man; but if sinne make God curse, God curses but the sinne. *Non talem Deum tuum putes, qualis nec tu debes esse,* Never propose to thy self such a God, as thou wert not bound to imitate: Thou mistakest God, if thou make him to be any such thing, or make him do any such thing, as thou in thy proportion shouldst not be, or shouldst not do. And shouldst thou curse any man that had never offended, never transgrest, never trespast thee? Can God have done so? Imagine God, as the Poet saith, *Ludere in humanis,* to play but a *game at Chesse* with this world;[144] to sport himself with making little things great, and great things nothing: Imagine God to be but at play with us, but a gamester; yet will a gamester *curse,* before he be in danger of losing any thing? Will God curse man, before man have sinned?

4

The *Hieroglyphique* of silence, is the hand upon the mouth; If the hand of God be gone from the mouth, it is gone to strike. If it be come to an *Os Domini locutum,* that the mouth of the Lord have spoken it, it will come presently to an *Immittam manum,* That God will lay his hand upon us, in which one Phrase, all the plagues of Egypt are denounced. *Solomon* puts both *hand* and *tongue* together; *In manibus linguae,* saith he, *Death and Life are in the hand of the tongue:* Gods *Tongue* hath a *hand;* where his Sentence goeth before, the execution followeth. Nay, in the execution of the last sentence, we shall feel the Hand, before we heare the Tongue, the execution is before the sentence; It is, *Ite maledicti,* go ye accursed: First, you must *Go, go out of the presence of God;* and by that being gone, you shall know, that you are accursed; Whereas in other proceedings, the sentence denounces the execution, here the execution denounces the sentence. But be all this allowed to be thus; There is a malediction deposited in the Scriptures, denounced by the Church, ratified by God, brought into execution, yet it may be born, men doe bear it. How men do bear it, we know not; what passes between God and those men, upon whom the curse of God lieth, in their dark *horrours at midnight*,[145] they would not have us know, because it is part of their curse, to envy God that glory. But we may consider in some part the insupportablenesse of that weight, if we proceed but so farre, as to accomodate to God, that which is ordinarily said of naturall things, *Corruptio optimi pessima;* when the best things change their nature, they become worst. When God, who is all sweetnesse, shall have learned frowardnesse from us, as *David* speaks; and being all rectitude, shall have learned perversenesse and crookednesse from us, as *Moses* speaks; and being all providence, shall have learned negligence from us: when God who is all Blessing, hath learned to curse of us, and being of himself spread as an universall Hony-combe over All, takes in an impression, a tincture, an infusion of gall from us, what extraction of Wormwood can be so bitter, what exaltation of fire can be so raging, what multiplying of talents can be so heavy, what stiffnesse of destiny can be so inevitable, what confection of gnawing worms, of gnashing teeth, of howling cries, of scalding brimstone, of palpable darknesse, can be so, so insupportable, so inexpressible, so in-imaginable, as the curse and malediction of God? *And therefore* let not us by our works provoke, nor by our words teach God to curse. Lest if *with the same tongue that we blesse God, we curse Men;* that is, seem to be in Charity in our Prayers here, and carry a ranckerous heart, and venemous tongue home with us God come to say (and Gods *saying* is *doing*) *As he loved cursing, so let it come unto him; as he clothed himself with cursing, as with a garment, so let it be as a girdle, wherewith he is girded continually:* When a man curses out of *Levity,* and makes a loose habit of that sinne, God shall so gird it to him, as he shall never devest it. The Devils grammar is *Applicare Activa Passivis,* to apply Actives to Passives; where he sees an inclination, to subminister a temptation; where he seeth a froward choler, to blow in a curse. And Gods grammar is to *change* Actives into Passives: where a man delights in cursing, to make that man accursed. And if God do this to them who do but curse men, will he do lesse to them, who blaspheme himself? where man wears out *Aeternum suum,* (as Saint *Gregory* speaketh) his own eternity, his own hundred yeares; that is, his whole life, in cursing and blaspheming, God shall also extend his curse, *In aeterno suo,* in his eternity, that is, for *ever.* Which is that, that falls to the bottome, as the heaviest of all, and is our last consideration; that all the rest, that there is a curse deposited in the Scriptures, denounced by the Church, avowed by God, reduced to execution, and that insupportable in this life, is infinitely aggravated by this, that he shall be *accursed for ever*.

This is the *Anathema Maran-atha,* accursed *till the Lord come;* and when the Lord cometh, he cometh not to reverse, nor to alleviate, but to ratifie and aggravate that curse. As soon as Christ curst the *fig-tree,* it withered, and it never recovered: for saith that Gospell, he curst it *In aeternum,* for ever. In the course of our sinne, the *Holy Ghost* hath put here a number of yeares, a hundred yeares: We sinne long, as long as we can, but yet sinne hath an end. But in this curse of God in the Text, there is no number; it is an *indefinite* future; *He shall be accursed:* A mile of cyphers or figures, added to the former hundred, would not make up a minute of this eternity. Men have calculated how many particular graines of sand, would fill up all the vast space between the Earth and the Firmament: and we find, that a few lines of cyphers will designe and expresse that number.[146] But if every grain of sand were that number, and multiplied again by that number, yet all that, all that inexpressible, inconsiderable number, made not up one minute of this eternity; neither would this curse, be a minute the shorter for having been indured so many Generations, as there were grains of sand in that number. Our *Esse,* our *Being,* is from Gods saying, *Dixit & facti,* God spoke, and we were made: our *Bene esse,* our *Well-being,* is from Gods saying too; *Bene-dicit* God blesses us, in speaking gratiously to us. Even our *Ill-being,* our condemnation is from Gods saying also: for *Malediction* is *Damnation.* So far God hath gone with us that way, as that our Being, our well-being, our ill-being is from his saying: But God shall never come to a *Non esse,* God shall never say to us, *Be nothing,* God shall never succour us with an *annihilation,* nor give us the ease of resolving into nothing, for this curse flowes on into an *everlasting* future, *He shall be accurst,* he shall be so for *ever.* In a true sense we may say, that Gods *fore-knowledge* growes lesse and lesse every day; for his fore-knowledge is of *future* things, and many things which were future heretofore are past, or present now; and therefore cannot fall under his fore-knowledge: His fore-knowledge in that sense, growes lesse, and decaieth. But his eternity decayeth in no sense; and as long as his eternity lasts, as long as God is God, God shall never see that soul, whom he hath accurst, delivered from that curse, or eased in it.

But we are now in the work of an houre, and no more. If there be a minute of sand left, (There is not) If there be a minute of patience left, heare me say, This minute that is left, is that eternitie which we speake of; upon this minute dependeth that eternity: And this minute, God is in this Congregation, and puts his eare to every one of your hearts, and hearkens what you will bid him say to your selves: whether he shall blesse you for your acceptation, or curse you for your refusall of him this minute: for this minute makes up your *Century,* your hundred yeares, your eternity, because it may be your last minute. We need not call that a *Fable,* but a *Parable,* where we heare, That a Mother to still her froward childe told him, she would cast him to the Wolf, the Wolf should have him; and the Wolf which was at the doore, and within hearing, waited, and hoped he should have the childe indeed: but the childe being still'd, and the Mother pleased, then she saith, so shall we kill the Wolf, the Wolf shall have none of my childe, and then the Wolf stole away. No metaphor, no comparison is too high, none too low, too triviall, to imprint in you a sense of Gods everlasting goodnesse towards you. God bids your Mother the Church, and us her Servants for your Souls, to denounce his judgements upon your sinnes, and we do it; and the executioner *Satan,* beleeves us, before you beleeve us, and is ready on his part. Be you also ready on your part, to lay hold upon those conditions, which are annext to all Gods maledictions, Repentance of former, *preclusion* against *future sinnes,* and we shall be alwayes ready, on our part to assist you with the *Power* of our *Intercession,* to deliver you with the *Keies* of our *Absolution,* and to establish you with the *seales* of *Reconciliation,* and so disappoint that *Wolf,* that roaring *Lion,* that seeks whom he may devour: Go in Peace, and be this your Peace, to know this, *Maledictus qui pendet in Cruce,* God hath laid the whole curse belonging to us upon him, that hangs upon the Crosse; But *Benedictus qui pendet in pendentem;* To all them that hang upon him, that hangeth there, God offereth now, all those blessings, which he that hangeth there hath purchased with the inestimable price of his Incorruptible blood; And to this glorious *Sonne* of God, who hath suffered all this, and to the most Almighty *Father,* who hath *done* all this, and to the *blessed Spirit of God,* who offereth now to *apply* all this, be ascribed by us, and by the whole Church, All power, praise, might, majesty, glory, and dominion, now and for evermore *Amen.*

41. FROM A SERMON PREACHED AT S. PAULS,
UPON EASTER-DAY, 1627[147]

I

Our virility, our holy manhood, our true and religious strength, consists in the assurance, that though death have divided us, and though we never receive our dead raised to life again in this world, yet we do live together already, in a holy Communion of Saints, and shal live together for ever, hereafter, in a glorious Resurrection of bodies. Little know we, how little a way a soule hath to goe to heaven, when it departs from the body; Whether it must passe locally, through Moone, and Sun, and Firmament,[148] (and if all that must be done, all that may be done, in lesse time than I have proposed the doubt in) or whether that soule finde new light in the same roome, and be not carried into any other, but that the glory of heaven be diffused over all, I know not, I dispute not, I inquire not. Without disputing, or inquiring, I know, that when Christ sayes, *That God is not the God of the dead*, he saies that to assure me, that those whom I call dead, are alive. And when the Apostle tels me, *That God is not ashamed to be called the God of the dead*, he tels me that to assure me, That Gods servants lose nothing by dying.

He was but a Heathen that said, If God love a man, *Juvenis tollitur*,[149] He takes him young out of this world; And they were but Heathens, that observed that custome, To put on mourning when their sons were born, and to feast and triumph when they dyed. But thus much we may learne from these Heathens, That if the dead, and we, be not upon one floore, nor under one story, yet we are under one roofe. We think not a friend lost, because he is gone into another roome,[150] nor because he is gone into another Land; And into another world, no man is gone; for that Heaven, which God created, and this world, is all one world. If I had fixt a Son in Court, or married a daughter into a plentifull Fortune, I were satisfied for that son and that daughter. Shall I not be so, when the King of Heaven hath taken that son to himselfe, and maried himselfe to that daughter, for ever? I spend none of my Faith, I exercise none of my Hope, in this, that I shall have my dead raised to life againe.

This is the faith that sustaines me, when I lose by the death of others, or when I suffer by living in misery my selfe, That the dead, and we, are now all in one Church, and at the resurrection, shall be all in one Quire.

But that is the resurrection which belongs to our other part; That resurrection which wee have handled, though it were a resurrection from death, yet it was to death too; for those that were raised again, died again. But the Resurrection which we are to speak of, is for ever; They that rise then, shall see death no more, for it is (sayes our Text) *A better Resurrection*.

2

Beloved, There is nothing so little in heaven, as that we can expresse it; But if wee could tell you the fulnesse of a soul there, what that fulnesse is; the infinitenesse of that glory there, how far that infinitenesse goes; the Eternity of that happinesse there, how long that happinesse lasts; if we could make you know all this, yet this *Better Resurrection* is a heaping, even of that Fulnesse, and an enlarging, even of that Infinitenesse, and an extention, even of that eternity of happinesse; For, all these, this Fulnesse, this Infinitenesse, this Eternity are in all the Resurrections of the Righteous, and this is a *better Resurrection;* We may almost say, it is something more than Heaven; for, all that have any Resurrection to life, have all heaven; And something more than God; for, all that have any Resurrection to life, have all God; and yet these shall have a better Resurrection. Amorous soule, ambitious soule, covetous soule, voluptuous soule, what wouldest thou have in heaven? What doth thy holy amorousnesse, thy holy covetousnesse, thy holy ambition, and voluptuousnesse most carry thy desire upon? Call it what thou wilt; think it what thou canst; think it something that thou canst not think; and all this thou shalt have, if thou have any Resurrection unto life; and yet there is a *Better Resurrection*. When I consider what I was in my parents loynes (a substance unworthy of a word, unworthy of a thought) when I consider what I am now, (a Volume of diseases bound up together, a dry cynder, if I look for naturall, for radicall moisture, and yet a Spunge, a bottle of overflowing Rheumes, if I consider accidentall; an aged childe, a gray-headed Infant, and but the ghost of mine own youth) When I consider what I shall be at last, by the hand of death, in my grave, (first, but Putrifaction, and then, not so much as putrifaction, I shall not be able to send forth so much as an ill ayre, not any ayre at all, but shall be all insipid, tastlesse, savourlesse dust; for a while, all wormes, and after a while, not so much as wormes, sordid, senslesse, namelesse dust) When I consider the past, and present, and future state of this body, in this world, I am able to conceive, able to expresse the worst that can befall it in nature, and the worst that can be inflicted upon it by man, or fortune; But the least degree of glory that God hath prepared for that body in heaven, I am not able to expresse, not able to conceive.

That man comes with a Barly corn in his hand, to measure the compasse of the Firmament, (and when will he have done that work, by that way?) he comes with a grain of dust in his scales, to weigh the whole body of the world, (and when will he have done that work, that way?) that bids his heart imagine, or his language declare, or his wit compare the least degree of the glory of any good mans Resurrection; And yet, there is a *Better Resurrection*. A *Better Resurrection* reserved for them, and appropriated to them *That fulfill the sufferings of Christ, in their flesh,* by Martyrdome, and so become witnesses to that Conveyance which he hath sealed with his blood, by shedding their blood; and glorifie him upon earth (as far as it is possible for man) by the same way that he hath glorified them in heaven; and are admitted to such a conformity with Christ, as that (if we may have leave to expresse it so) they have dyed for one another.

Neither is this *Martyrdome,* and so this *Better Resurrection,* appropriated to a reall, and actuall, and absolute dying for Christ; but every suffering of ours, by which suffering, he may be glorified, is a degree of Martyrdome, and so a degree of improving, and bettering our Resurrection. For as S *Jerome* sayes, *That chastity is a perpetuall Martyrdome,* So every war maintained by us, against our own desires, is a Martyrdome too. In a word, to do good for Gods glory, brings us to a Good, but to suffer for his glory, brings us to a *Better Resurrection;* And, to suffer patiently, brings us to a Good, but to suffer chearefully, and more than that, thankfully, brings us to a *Better Resurrection*. If all the torments of all the afflicted men, from *Abel,* to that soul that groanes in the Inquisition, or that gaspes upon his death-bed, at this minute, were upon one man at once, all that had no proportion to the least torment of hell; nay if all the torments which all the damned in hell have suffered, from *Cain* to this minute, were at once upon one soul, so, as that soul for all that, might know that those torments should have an end, though after a thousand millions of millions of Generations, all that would have no proportion to any of the torments of hell; because, the extention of those torments, and their everlastingnesse, hath more of the nature of torment, and of the nature of hell in it, than the intensnesse, and the vehemency thereof can have. So, if all the joyes, of all the men that have had all their hearts desires, were con-centred in one heart, all that would not be as a spark in his Chimney, to the generall conflagration of the whole world, in respect of the least joy, that that soule is made partaker of, that departs from this world, immediatly after a pardon received, and reconciliation sealed to him, for all his sins; No doubt but he shall have a good Resurrection; But then, we cannot doubt neither, but that to him that hath been carefull in all his wayes, and yet crost in all his wayes, to him whose daily bread hath been affliction, and yet is satisfied as with marrow, and with fatnesse, with that bread of affliction, and not only contented in, but glad of that affliction, no doubt but to him is reserved a *Better Resurrection;* Every Resurrection is more than we can think, but this is more than that more. Almighty God inform us, and reveale unto us, what this *Better Resurrection* is, by possessing us of it; And make the hastening to it, one degree of addition in it. Come Lord Jesus, come quickly to the consummation of that Kingdome which thou hast purchased for us, with the inestimable price of thine incorruptible blood. *Amen.*

42. FROM A SERMON PREACHED TO THE KING, AT WHITE-HALL, 1 APRIL 1627[151]

I

God is said to have come to *Eliah* in that still small voice, and not in the *strong wind,* not in the *Earth-quake,* not in the *fire.* So God says, *Sibilabo populum meum,* I will but hisse, I will but whisper for my people, and gather them so. So Christ tells us things in *darknesse;* And so Christ speakes to us in our *Ear;* And these low voices, and holy whisperings, and halfe-silences, denote to us, the inspirations of his Spirit, *as his Spirit beares witnesse with our Spirit;* as the Holy Ghost insinuates himselfe into our soules, and workes upon us so, by his *private motions.* But this is not Gods ordinary way, to be whispering of secrets. The first thing that God made, was *light;* The last thing, that he hath reserved to doe, is the manifestation of the light of his Essence in our Glorification. And for Publication of himselfe here, by the way, he hath constituted a *Church,* in a Visibility, in an eminency, *as a City upon a hill;*[152] And in this Church, his Ordinance is Ordinance indeed; his Ordinance of preaching batters the soule, and by that breach, the Spirit enters; [153] His Ministers are an *Earth-quake,* and shake an earthly soule; They are the *sonnes of thunder,* and scatter a cloudy conscience; They are as the fall of waters, and carry with them whole Congregations; 3000 at a Sermon, 5000 at a Sermon, a whole City, such a City as Niniveh at a Sermon; and they are as the roaring of a Lion, where the Lion of the tribe of Juda, cries down the Lion that seekes whom he may devour; that is, Orthodoxall and fundamentall truths, are established against clamorous and vociferant innovations. Therefore what Christ tels us in the darke, he bids us speake in the light; and what he saies in our eare, he bids us preach on the house top. Nothing is Gospell, not *Evangelium,* good message, if it be not put into a Messengers mouth, and delivered by him; nothing is conducible to his end, nor available to our salvation, except it be avowable doctrine, doctrine that may be spoke alowd, though it awake them, that sleep in their sinne, and make them the more froward, for being so awaked.

God hath made all things in a *Roundnesse,* from the round superficies of this earth, which we tread here, to the round convexity of those heavens, which (as long as they shal have any beeing) shall be our footstool, when we come to heaven, God hath wrapped up all things in Circles, and then a Circle hath no *Angles;* there are no *Corners* in a Circle. Corner Divinity, clandestine Divinity are incompatible termes; If it be Divinity, it is avowable. *The heathens* served their Gods in Temples, *sub dio,* without roofs or coverings, in a free opennesse; and, where they could, in Temples made of *Specular stone,* that was transparent as glasse, or crystall, so as they which walked without in the streets, might see all that was done within. And even nature it self taught the naturall man, to make that one argument of a man truly religious, *Aperto vivere voto,* That he durst pray aloud, and let the world heare, what he asked at Gods hand; which duty is best performed, when we joyne with the Congregation in publique prayer.

2

This whisperer wounds thee, and with a stilletta of gold, he strangles thee with scarfes of silk, he smothers thee with the down of Phœnixes, he stifles thee with a perfume of Ambar, he destroys thee by praising thee, overthrows thee by exalting thee, and undoes thee by trusting thee; By trusting thee with those secrets that bring thee into a desperate perplexity, *Aut alium accusare in subsidium tui,* (as the Patriarch, and Oracle of States-men, *Tacitus,*[154] says) Either to betray another, that pretends to have trusted thee, or to perish thy selfe, for the saving of another, that plotted to betray thee. And therefore, if you can heare a good Organ at Church, and have the musique of a domestique peace at home, peace in thy walls, peace in thy bosome, never hearken after the musique of sphears, never hunt after the knowledge of higher secrets, than appertaine to thee; But since Christ hath made you *Regale Sacerdotium,* Kings and Priests, in your proportion, *Take heed what you hear,* in derogation of either the State, or the Church.

43. FROM A SERMON OF COMMEMORATION OF THE LADY DANVERS, 1 JULY 1627[155]

I

It is a fearefull thing to fall into the hands of the living God, if I doe but fall into his hands, in a fever in my bed, or in a tempest at Sea, or in a discontent at home; But, *to fall into the hands of the living God,* so, as that, that *living God,* enters into *Judgement,* with mee, and passes a finall, and irrevocable Judgement upon mee, this is a Consternation of all my spirits, an Extermination of all my succours. I consider, what *God* did with one word, with one *Fiat* he made all; And, I know, he can doe as much with another word; With one *Pereat,* he can destroy all; As hee *spake, and it was done, he commanded and all stood fast;* so he can *speak,* and all shall bee *undone; command,* and all shall *fall in peeces.* I consider, that I may bee surpriz'd by *that day,* the *day of Judgement.* Here Saint *Peter* saies, *The day of the Lord wil come as a Thiefe.* And Saint *Paul* saies, we cannot be ignorant of it, *Your selves know perfectly, that the day of the Lord so commeth as a Thiefe.* And, as the *Judgement* it selfe, so the *Judge* himselfe saies of himselfe, *I will come upon thee as a Thiefe.* He saies, *he will,* and he *doe's it.* For it is not, *Ecce veniam,* but *Ecce venio, Behold I doe come upon thee as a Thiefe;* There, the *future,* which might imply a *dilatorinesse,* is reduc't to an infallible *present;* It is so sure, that he *will* doe it, that he is said, to *have* done it already. I consider, *hee will come as a Thiefe*, and then, *as a Thiefe in the night;* And I doe not only not know *when* that night shall be, (For, himselfe, as he is the Son of man, knowes not that) but I doe not only not know *what* night, that is, *which* night, but not *what* night, that is, *what kinde* of night he meanes. It is said so often, so often repeated, that *he will come as a Thiefe in the night,* as that hee may meane all kinde of *nights.* In my night of *Ignorance* hee may come; and hee may come in my night of *Wantonnesse;* In my night of inordinate and sinfull *melancholy,* and *suspicion* of his *mercy,* hee may come; and he may come in the night of so *stupid,* or so *raging* a *sicknesse,* as that he shall not *come* by *comming;* Not come so, as that I shall receive him in the *absolution* of his *Minister,* or receive him in the participation of his *body* and his *bloud* in the *Sacrament.* So hee may come upon mee, as *such a Thiefe,* in *such a night;* nay, when all these nights of *Ignorance,* of *Wantonnesse,* of *Desperation,* of *Sicknesse,* of *Stupiditie,* of *Rage,* may bee upon mee all at once. I consider, that the *Holy Ghost* meant to make a deepe impression of a great *terror* in me, when he came to that expression, *That the Heavens should passe away,* Cum stridore, *with a great noise, and the Elements melt with fervent heat, and the earth, and the workes that are therein,* shall be burnt up; And when he adds in *Esay, The Lord will come with fire, and with his Chariots, like a whirlewind, to render his anger, with fury; for by fire, and by his sword will the Lord plead with all flesh.* So when hee proceeds in *Joel, a day of darknesse, and gloominesse; and yet a fire devoureth before them, and a flame burneth behind them.* And so in *Daniel* also, *His Throne a fiery flame, and his wheeles a burning fire, and a fiery streame issuing from him.* I consider too, that with this *streame of fire,* from him, there shall bee a *streame,* a deluge, a floud of teares, from us; and all that *floud,* and *deluge* of teares, shall not put out one coale, nor quench one sparke of that fire. *Behold, hee commeth with clouds, and every eye shall see him;* And, *plangent omnes, All the kindreds of the earth shall waile and lament,* and weepe and howle *because of him.* I consider, that I shall *looke* upon him then, and see all my *Sinnes, Substance,* and *Circumstance* of sin, *Waight,* and *measure* of sinne, *hainousnesse,* and *continuance* of sinne, all my sinnes imprinted in his wounds; and how shall I bee affected then, confounded then to see him so mangled with my sinnes? But then I consider againe, that I shall looke upon him againe, and not see all my sinnes in his wounds; My *forgotten* sinnes, mine *un-considered, unconfest, unrepented* sinnes, I shall not see there; And how shall I bee affected then, when I shall stand in *Judgement*, under the guiltinesse of some sins, not buried in the wounds, not drown'd in the bloud of my *Saviour? Many*, and *many*, and *very many*, *infinite*, and *infinitely infinite*, are the *terrours* of that day.

2

Our first word, *Neverthelesse*, puts us first upon this consideration, That shee liv'd in a Time, wherein this *Prophecie* of Saint *Peter*, in this *Chapter*, was over-abundantly perform'd, That there should bee *scoffers, jesters* in divine things, and matters appertaining to *God*, and his *Religion*. For, now, in these our dayes, excellency of *Wit*, lies in *prophanenesse;* he is the *good Spirit*, that dares abuse *God;* And hee *good company*, that makes his company the worse, or keepes them from goodnesse. This being the Aire, and the Complexion of the *Wit* of her Times, and her inclination, and conversation, naturally cheerfull, and merry, and loving facetious-nesse, and sharpnesse of wit, *Neverthelesse*, who ever saw her, who ever heard her countenance a *prophane speech*, how sharpe soever, or take part with *wit*, to the prejudice of *Godlinesse?* From this I testifie her *holy cheerfulnesse*, and *Religious alacrity*, (one of the best *evidences* of a *good conscience*) That as shee came to this place, *God's house of Prayer*, duly, not onely every *Sabbath*, when it is the house of other exercises, as well as of *Prayer*, but even in those *weeke-dayes*, when it was onely a house of *Prayer*, as often as these doores were opened for a *holy Convocation;* And, as she ever hastned her *family*, and her *company* hither, with that cheerful provocation, *For God's sake let's go, For God's sake let's bee there at the Confession:* So her selfe, with her whole family, (as a *Church* in that *elect Ladie's* house, to whom *John* writ his second *Epistle*) did, every Sabbath, shut up the day, at night, with a generall, with a cheerfull *singing of Psalmes;* This *Act of cheerfulnesse*, was still the last *Act* of that family, united in it selfe, and with *God*. *God loves a cheerfull giver;* Much more a cheerfull giver of himselfe. Truly, he that can close his eyes, in a holy cheerfulnesse, every night, shall meet no distemper'd, no inordinate, no irregular sadnesse, then, when *God*, by the hand of *Death*, shall close his eyes, at last.

But, returne we againe to our *Neverthelesse;* You may remember, that this word in our former part, put us first upon the consideration of *Scoffers* at the *day of judgement*, and then, upon the consideration of *Terrours*, and sad *Apprehensions* at that *day*. And for her, some sicknesses, in the declination of her yeeres, had opened her to an overflowing of *Melancholie;* Not that she ever lay under that *water,* but yet, had some-times, some high Tides of it; and, though this distemper would some-times cast a cloud, and some halfe damps upon her naturall cheerfulnesse, and sociablenesse, and sometimes induce darke, and sad apprehensions, *Neverthelesse,* who ever heard, or saw in her, any such effect of *Melan-choly* as to murmure, or repine, or dispute upon any of *Gods* proceedings, or to lodge a Jelousie, or Suspition of his mercy, and goodnesse towards her, and all hers? The *Wit* of our time is *Prophanenesse; Neverthelesse,* shee, that lov'd *that,* hated *this;* Occasionall *Melancholy* had taken some hold in her; *Neverthelesse,* that never Ecclipst, never interrupted her cheerfull confidence, and assurance in *God.*

Our second word denotes the *person; We, Neverthelesse We;* And, here in this consideration, *Neverthelesse shee.* This may seeme to promise some picture, some Character of her *person.* But shee was no stranger to them that heare me now; nor scarce to any that may heare of this hereafter, which you heare now, and therefore, much needes not, to that purpose. Yet, to that purpose, of her *person,* and *personall circum-stances,* thus much I may *remember* some, and *informe* others, That from that *Worthy family,* whence shee had her originall extraction, and birth, she suckt that love of *hospitality,* (*hospitality,* which hath celebrated that *family,* in many Generations, successively) which dwelt in her, to her end. But in that *ground,* her Fathers *family,* shee grew not many yeeres. Transplanted young from thence, by mariage, into another *family of Honour,* as a flower that doubles and multiples by transplantation,[156] she multiplied into *ten Children; Job's* number; and *Job's* distribution, (as shee, her selfe would very often remember) *seven sonnes,* and *three daughters.* And, in this ground, shee grew not many yeeres more, than were necessary, for the producing of so many plants. And being then left to chuse her owne ground in her *Widow-hood,* having at home establisht, and increast the estate, with a faire, and noble Addition, proposing to her selfe, as her principall care, the education of her *children,* to advance that, shee came with them, and dwelt with them, in the *Universitie;*[157] and recompenc't to them, the losse of a *Father,* in giving them *two mothers;* her owne personall care, and the advantage of that place; where shee contracted a friendship, with divers reverend persons, of eminency, and estimation there; which continued to their ends. And as this was her greatest *businesse,* so she made this state, a large *Period;* for in this state of *widow-hood*, shee continued *twelve yeeres*. And then, returning to a *second mariage*, that *second mariage* turnes us to the consideration of another *personall circumstance*; that is, the *naturall endowments of her person*; Which were such, as that, (though her *vertues* were his principall *object*) yet, even these her *personall* and *naturall endowments*, had their part, in drawing, and fixing the affections of such a person, as by his *birth*, and *youth*, and *interest in great favours in Court*; and *legall proximity* to great possessions in the world, might justly have promist him acceptance, in what *family* soever, or upon what *person* soever, hee had directed and plac't his Affections. He plac't them here; neither *diverted* then, nor *repented* since. For, as the well tuning of an *Instrument*, makes *higher* and *lower* strings, of one sound, so the inequality of their yeeres, was thus reduc't to an evennesse, that shee had a *cheerfulnesse*, agreeable to his *youth*, and he a *sober staidnesse*, conformable to her *more yeeres*. So that, I would not consider her, at so much more than *forty*, nor him, at so much lesse than *thirty*, at that time, but as their *persons* were made *one*, and their *fortunes* made one, by *mariage*, so I would put their *yeeres* into *one number*, and finding a *sixty* betweene them, thinke them *thirty* a peece; for, as twins of one houre, they liv'd. *God*, who joyn'd them, then, having also separated them now, may make their *yeres* even, this other way too; by giving him, as many yeeres after her going out of this World, as he had given her, before his comming into it; and then, as many more, as *God* may receive *Glory*, and the World, *Benefit* by that Addition; That so, as at their first meeting, she was, at their last meeting, he may bee the *elder person*.

To this consideration of her *person* then, belongs this, that *God* gave her such a *comelinesse*, as, though shee were not *proud* of it, yet she was so content with it, as not to goe about to mend it, by any *Art*. And for her *Attire*, (which is another *personall circumstance*) it was never *sumptuous*, never *sordid*; But alwayes agreeable to her *quality*, and agreeable to her *company*; Such as shee might, and such, as others, such as shee was, did weare. For, in such things of *indifferency* in themselves, many times, a *singularity* may be a little worse, than a fellowship in that, which is not altogether so good. It may be *worse*, nay, it may be a *worse pride*, to weare worse things, than others doe. Her *rule* was *mediocrity*.[158]

And, as to the consideration of the *house*, belongs the consideration of the *furniture* too, so, in these *personall circumstances*, we consider her *fortune*, her *estate*. Which was in a faire, and noble proportion, deriv'd from her *first husband,* and fairely, and nobly dispenc'd, by her selfe, with the allowance of her *second.* In which shee was one of *Gods* true *Stewards,* and *Almoners* too. There are dispositions, which had rather *give presents,* than *pay debts;* and rather doe good to *strangers,* than to those, that are *neerer* to them. But *shee* alwayes thought the care of her family, a *debt,* and upon that, for the *provision,* for the *order,* for the *proportions,* in a good largenesse, shee plac't her first thoughts, of that kinde. For, for our *families,* we are *Gods Stewards;* For those without, we are his *Almoners.* In which office, shee gave not at some *great dayes,* or some solemne goings abroad, but, as *Gods true Almoners,* the *Sunne,* and *Moone,* that passe on, in a continuall doing of good, as shee receiv'd her *daily bread* from God, so, *daily,* she distributed, and imparted it, to others. In which office, though she never turn'd her face from those, who in a strict inquisition, might be call'd idle, and vagrant Beggers, yet shee ever look't first, upon them, who *labour'd,* and whose *labours* could not overcome the *difficulties,* nor bring in the *necessities* of this life; and to the *sweat of their browes,* shee contributed, even her *wine,* and her *oyle,* and any thing that was, and any thing, that might be, if it were not, prepar'd for her owne table. And as her house was a *Court,* in the conversation of the best, and an *Almeshouse,* in feeding the *poore,* so was it also an *Hospitall,* in ministring releefe to the *sicke.* And truly, the love of doing good in this kind, of *ministring to the sicke,* was the *hony,* that was spread over all her bread; the *Aire,* the *Perfume,* that breath'd over all her house; The disposition that dwelt in those her children, and those her kindred, which dwelt with her, so bending this way, that the *studies* and *knowledge* of *one,* the *hand* of another, and *purse* of all, and a *joynt-facility,* and *opennesse,* and *accessiblenesse* to persons of the meanest quality, concur'd in this blessed *Act of Charity,* to *minister releefe to the sicke.* Of which, my selfe, who, at that time, had the favour to bee admitted into that *family,* can, and must testifie this, that when the late heavy *visitation* [159] fell hotly upon this *Towne,* when every doore was shut up, and, lest *Death* should enter into the house, every house was made a *Sepulchre* of them that were in it, then, then, in that time of *infection,* divers persons visited with that *infection,* had their releefe, and releefe *appliable to that very infection,* from this house.

Now when I have said thus much (rather thus little) of her *person,* as of a *house,* That the *ground* upon which it was built, was the *family* where she was *borne,* and then, where she was *married,* and then, the time of her *widowhood*, and lastly, her *last mariage*, And that the *house* it selfe, was those faire *bodily endowments*, which *God* had bestow'd upon her, And the *furniture* of that *house*, the *fortune*, and the *use* of that *fortune*, of which *God* had made her *Steward* and *Almoner*, when I shall also have said, that the *Inhabitants* of this *house*, (rather the *servants*, for they did but wait upon *Religion* in her) were those married couples, of *morall vertues*, *Conversation* married with a *Retirednesse*, *Facility*[160] married with a *Reservednesse*, *Alacrity* married with a *Thoughtfulnesse*, and *Largenesse*[161] married with a *Providence*, I may have leave to depart from this consideration of her *person*, and *personall circumstances*, lest by insisting longer upon them, I should seeme to pretend, to say all the good, that might bee said of her; But that's not in my *purpose*; yet, onely therefore, because it is not in my *power*; For I would doe her all *right*, and all you that good, if I could, to say all. But, I haste to an end, in consideration of some things, that appertaine more expresly to me, than these *personall*, or *civill*, or *morall* things doe.

In those, the next is, the *Secundum promissa*, That shee govern'd her selfe, *according to his promises;* his promises, laid downe in his *Scriptures.* For, as the *rule* of all her *civill Actions*, was *Religion*, so, the *rule* of her *Religion*, was the *Scripture;* And, her *rule*, for her particular understanding of the *Scripture*, was the *Church.* Shee never diverted towards the *Papist*, in undervaluing the *Scripture;* nor towards the *Separatist*, in undervaluing the *Church.* But in the *doctrine*, and *discipline* of that *Church*, in which *God* seal'd her, to himselfe, in *Baptisme*, shee brought up her children, shee assisted her family, she dedicated her soule to *God* in her life, and surrendered it to him in her death; And, in that forme of *Common Prayer*, which is ordain'd by that *Church*, and to which she had accustom'd her selfe, with her family, twice every day, she joyn'd with that company, which was about her *death-bed*, in answering to every part thereof, which the Congregation is directed to answer to, with a *cleere understanding*, with a *constant memory*, with a *distinct voyce*, not two houres before she died.

According to this promise, that is, the will of *God* manifested in the *Scriptures*, She *expected*; Shee expected this, that she hath received; *Gods Physicke*, and *Gods Musicke*; a *Christianly death*. For, *death*, in the *old Testament* was a *Commination;* but in the *new Testament, death* is a *Promise;* When there was a *Super-dying*, a *death* upon the *death*, a *Morte* upon the *Morieris*, a *Spirituall* death after the *bodily*, then wee died *according to*

Gods threatning; Now, when by the *Gospell* that *second death* is taken off, though wee die still, yet we die *according to his Promise;* That's a part of his *mercy,* and his *Promise,* which his *Apostle* gives us from him, That wee shall *all bee changed;* For, after that *promise,* that *change,* follow's that triumphant *Acclamation, O death where is thy sting, O grave where is thy victory?* Consider us fallen in *Adam,* and wee are miserable, that wee must die; But consider us restor'd and redintegrated in *Christ,* wee were more miserable if wee might not die; Wee lost the *earthly Paradise* by death then; but wee get not *Heaven,* but by *death,* now. This shee expected till it came, and embrac't it when it came. How may we thinke, shee was joy'd to see that face, that *Angels* delight to looke upon, the face of her *Saviour,* that did not abhor the face of his fearfullest *Messenger,* Death? Shee shew'd no feare of his face, in any change of her owne; but died without any change of *countenance,* or *posture;* without any *strugling,* any *disorder;* but her *Death-bed* was as quiet, as her *Grave.*[162] To another *Magdalen, Christ* said upon earth, *Touch me not, for I am not ascended.* Being ascended now, to his glory, and she being gone up to him, after shee had awaited his leisure, so many yeeres, as that more, would soone have growne to bee *vexation,* and *sorrow,* as her last words here, were, *I submit my will to the will of God;* so wee doubt not, but the first word which she heard there, was that *Euge,* from her *Saviour, Well done good and faithfull servant; enter into thy masters joy.*

Shee expected that; dissolution of body, and soule; and rest in both, from the incumbrances, and tentations of this world. But yet, shee is in *expectation* still; Still a *Reversionarie;* And a *Reversionary* upon a long life; The whole world must die, before she come to a *possession* of this *Reversion;*[163] which is a *Glorified body in the Resurrection.* In which *expectation,* she return's to her former *charity;* shee will not have that, till *all wee* shall have it, as well as shee; She eat not her morsels alone, in her life, (as *Job* speakes) Shee lookes not for the *glory* of the *Resurrection* alone, after her death. But when *all we,* shall have beene mellow'd in the earth, many yeeres, or chang'd in the *Aire,* in the twinkling of an eye, (*God* knowes which) That *body* upon which you tread now, That *body* which now, whilst I speake, is mouldring, and crumbling into lesse, and lesse dust, and so hath some *motion,* though no *life,* That *body,* which was the *Tabernacle* of a *holy Soule,* and a *Temple* of the *holy Ghost,* That *body* that was eyes to the blinde, and hands, and feet to the lame, whilst it liv'd, and being dead, is so still, by having beene so *lively* an example, to teach others, to be so, That *body* at last shall have her last expectation satisfied, and dwell *bodily*, with that *Righteousnesse,* in these *new Heavens,* and *new Earth,* for *ever,* and *ever,* and *ever,* and *infinite,* and *super-infinite evers.* Wee end all, with the *valediction* of the *Spouse* to *Christ: His left hand is under my head, and his right embraces mee,* was the *Spouses valediction,* and *goodnight* to *Christ* then, when she laid her selfe downe to sleepe in the strength of his *Mandrakes,*[164] and in the power of his *Spices,* as it is exprest there; that is, in the *influence* of his *mercies.* Beloved, every good *Soule* is the *Spouse* of *Christ.* And this good *Soule,* being thus laid downe to sleepe in his peace, *His left hand under her head,* gathering, and com-posing, and preserving her *dust,* for *future Glory, His right hand embracing her,* assuming, and establishing her *soule* in present *Glory,* in his *name,* and in her *behalfe,* I say that, to *all you,* which *Christ* sayes there, in the behalfe of that *Spouse, Adjuro vos, I adjure you, I charge you, O daughters of Jerusalem, that yee wake her not, till she please.* The words are directed to the *daughters,* rather than to the *sons of Jerusalem,* because for the most part, the aspersions that women receive, either in *Morall* or *Religious* actions, proceed from women themselves. Therfore, *Adjuro vos,* I charge you, O ye daughters of *Jerusalem,* wake her not. Wake her not, with any *halfe calumnies,* with any *whisperings;* But if you wil wake her, wake her, and keepe her awake with an active imitation, of her *Morall,* and her *Holy vertues.* That so her *example* working upon you, and the number of *Gods Saints,* being the sooner, by this blessed *example,* fulfil'd wee may all meet, and meet quickly in that *kingdome,* which *hers,* and *our* Saviour, hath purchac't for us all, with the inestimable price, of his incorruptible bloud. To which glorious Sonne of God, &c.

44. FROM A SERMON PREACHED AT THE EARL OF BRIDGEWATERS HOUSE IN LONDON AT THE MARIAGE OF HIS DAUGHTER, 19 NOVEMBER 1627[165]

I

As in all other states and conditions of life, so in all mariages there will be some encumbrances, betwixt all maried persons, there will arise some unkindnesses, some mis-interpretations; or some too quick interpretations may sometimes sprinkle a little sournesse, and spread a little, a thin, a dilute and washy cloud upon them; Then they mary not, till then they may; then their state shall be perfect as the Angels, till then it shall not; These are our branches, and the fruits that grow upon them, we shall pull in passing, and present them as we gather them.

First then, Christ establishes a Resurrection, *A Resurrection there shall be,* for, that makes up *Gods circle.* The *Body* of Man was the first point that the foot of Gods Compasse was upon: First, he created the body of *Adam:* and then he carries his Compasse round, and shuts up where he began, he ends with the *Body of man* againe in the glorification thereof in the Resurrection.[166] God is *Alpha* and *Omega,* first, and last: And his *Alpha* and *Omega,* his first, and last work is the *Body of man* too. Of the Immortality of the *soule,* there is not an expresse *article* of the *Creed:* for, that last article of *The life everlasting,* is rather *de praemio, & poena,* what the soule shall suffer, or what the soule shall enjoy, being presumed to be *Immortall,* than that it is said to be *Immortall* in that article; That article may, and does presuppose an Immortality, but it does not constitute an Immortality in our soule, for there would be a life everlasting in heaven, and we were bound to beleeve it, as we were bound to beleeve a God in heaven, though our *soules* were not immortall. There are so many evidences of the immortality of the soule, even to a naturall mans *reason,* that it required not an Article of the Creed, to fix this notion of the Immortality of the soule. But the Resurrection of the *Body* is discernible by no other light, but that of *Faith,* nor could be fixed by any lesse assurance than an *Article* of the *Creed.* Where be all the splinters of that Bone, which a shot hath shivered and scattered in the Ayre? Where be all the Atoms of that flesh, which a *Corrasive* hath eat away, or a *Consumption* hath breath'd, and exhal'd away from our arms, and other Limbs? In what wrinkle, in what furrow, in what bowel of the earth, ly all the graines of the ashes of a body burnt a thousand years since? In what corner, in what ventricle of the sea, lies all the jelly of a Body drowned in the *generall flood?* What coherence, what sympathy, what dependence maintaines any relation, any correspondence, between that arm that was lost in Europe, and that legge that was lost in Afrique or Asia, scores of yeers between? One humour of our dead body produces worms, and those worms suck and exhaust all other humour, and then all dies, and all dries, and molders into dust, and that dust is blowen into the River, and that puddled water tumbled into the sea, and that ebs and flows in infinite revolutions, and still, still God knows in what *Cabinet* every *seed-Pearle* lies, in what part of the world every graine of every mans dust lies; and, *sibilat populum suum,* (as his Prophet speaks in another case) he whispers, he hisses, he beckens for the bodies of his Saints, and in the twinckling of an eye, that body that was scattered over all the elements, is sate down at the right hand of God, in a glorious resurrection. A Dropsie hath extended me to an enormous corpulency, and unwieldinesse; a Consumption hath attenuated me to a feeble macilency and leannesse, and God raises me a body, such as it should have been, if these infirmities had not interven'd and deformed it.

2

We are come, in our order proposed at first, to our second Part, *Erimus sicut Angeli, we shall be as the Angels of God in heaven;* where we consider, first, what we are compared to, those *Angels;* And then *in what* that Comparison lies, wherein we shall be like those Angels; And lastly, the Proposition that flowes out of this proposition, In the Resurrection we shall be like them, *Till the Resurrection we shall not,* and therefore, in the meane time, we must not looke for *Angelicall perfections,* but beare with one anothers infirmities. Now when we would tell you, what those *Angels* of God in heaven, to which we are compared, are, we can come no nearer telling you that, than by telling you, we cannot tell. The Angels may be content with that *Negative* expressing, since we can express God himselfe in no clearer termes, nor in termes expressing more Dignity, than in saying we cannot expresse him. Onely the Angels themselves know one another; and, one good point, in which we shall be like them then, shall be, that then we shall know what they are; we know they are *Spirits* in *Nature,* but what the nature of a spirit is, we know not: we know they are *Angels* in *office,* appointed to execute Gods will upon us; but, *How* a spirit should execute those bodily actions, that *Angels* doe, in their owne motion, and in the transportation of other things, we know not: we know they are *Creatures;* but whether created with this world, (as all our later men incline to think) or long before, (as all the *Greeke,* and some of the *Latin* Fathers thought) we know not: we know that for their number, and for their faculties also, there may be one *Angel* for every man; but whether there be so, or no, because not onely amongst the Fathers, but even in the *Reformed* Churches, in both sub-divisions, *Lutheran,* and *Calvinist,* great men deny it, and as great affirme it, we know not: we know the Angels know, they understand, but whether by that way, which we call in the Schoole, *Cognitionem Matutinam,* by seeing all in God, or that which we call *Vespertinam,* by a clearer manifestation of the *species* of things to them, than to us, we know not: we know they are distinguished into Orders; the Apostle tells us so: but what, or how many their Orders are, (since S. *Gregory,* and S. *Bernard* differ from that Designe of their *nine orders,* which S. *Denis the Areopagite* had given before, in placing of those nine, and *Athanasius* addes more to those nine,) we know not; But we are content to say with S. *Augustine, Esse firmissime credo, quaenum sint nescio;* that there are distinct orders of *Angels,* assuredly I beleeve; but what they are, I cannot tell; *Dicant qui possunt; si tamen probare possunt quod dicunt,* saies that Father, Let them tell you that can, so they be able to prove, that they tell you true. They are Creatures, that have not so much of a Body as *flesh* is, as *froth* is, as a *vapor* is, as a *sigh* is, and yet with a touch they shall molder a rocke into lesse Atomes, than the sand that it stands upon; and a milstone into smaller flower, than it grinds. They are Creatures *made,* and yet not a minute elder now, than when they were first made, if they were made before all measure of time began; nor, if they were made in the beginning of Time, and be now six thousand yeares old, have they one wrinckle of Age in their face, or one sobbe of wearinesse in their lungs. They are *primogeniti Dei,* Gods eldest sonnes; They are super-elementary meteors, they hang between the nature of God, and the nature of man, and are of middle Condition; And, (if we may offencelessely expresse it so) they are *aenigmata Divina,* The Riddles of Heaven, and the perplexities of speculation.[167]

45. FROM A SERMON PREACHED AT WHITE-HALL, 29 FEBRUARY 1628[168]

I

He that will dy with Christ upon Good-Friday, must hear his own bell toll all Lent; he that will be partaker of his passion at last, must conform himself to his discipline of prayer and fasting before. Is there any man, that in his chamber hears a bell toll for another man, and does not kneel down to pray for that dying man? and then when his charity breaths out upon another man, does he not also reflect upon himself, and dispose himself as if he were in the state of that dying man? We begin to hear Christs bell toll now, and is not our bell in the chime? We must be in his grave, before we come to his resurrection, and we must be in his death-bed before we come to his grave: we must do as he did, fast and pray, before we can say as he said, that *In manus tuas,* Into thy hands O Lord I commend my Spirit. You would not go into a Medicinal Bath without some preparatives; presume not upon that Bath, the blood of Christ Jesus, in the Sacrament then, without preparatives neither. Neither say to your selves, we shall have preparatives enough, warnings enough, many more Sermons before it come to that, and so it is too soon yet; you are not sure you shall have more; not sure you shall have all this; not sure you shall be affected with any. If you be, when you are, remember that as in that good Custome in these Cities, you hear cheerful street musick in the winter mornings, but yet there was a sad and doleful bel-man, that wak'd you, and call'd upon you two or three hours before that musick came; so for all that blessed musick which the servants of God shall present to you in this place, it may be of use, that a poor bell-man wak'd you before, and though but by his noyse, prepared you for their musick.

2

For to suffer for God, man to suffer for God, I to suffer for my Maker, for my Redeemer, is such a thing, as no such thing, excepting only Gods sufferings for man can fall into the consideration of man. Gods suffering for man was the Nadir, the lowest point of Gods humiliation, mans suffering for God is the Zenith, the highest point of mans exaltation: That as man needed God, and God would suffer for man, so God should need man, and man should suffer for God; that after Gods general Commission, *fac hoc & vives,* do this and thou shalt live, I should receive and execute a new Commission, *Patere hoc & vives abundantius,* suffer this and you shall have life, and life more abundantly, as our Saviour speaks in the Gospel; that when I shall ask my soul *Davids* question, *Quid retribuam,* what shall I render to the Lord, I shall not rest in *Davids* answer, *Accipiam Calicem,* I will take the cup of salvation, in applying his blood to my soul, but proceed to an *Effundam Calicem,* I

will give God a Cup, a cup of my blood, that whereas to me the
meanest of Gods servants it is honor enough to be believed for Gods
sake: God should be believed for my sake, and his Gospel the better
accepted, because the seal of my blood is set to it; that that dew which
should water his plants, the plants of his Paradise, his Church, should
drop from my veines, and that sea, that red sea, which should carry up
his bark, his Ark, to the heavenly Jerusalem, should flow from me: This
is that that poures joy even into my gladness, and glory even into mine
honor, and peace even into my security; that exaltes and improves every
good thing, every blessing that was in me before, and makes even my
creation glorious, and my redemption precious; and puts a farther value
upon things inestimable before, that I shall fulfil the sufferings of Christ
in my flesh, and that I shall be offerd up for his Church, though not for
the purchasing of it, yet for the fencing of it, though not by way of
satisfaction as he was, but by way of example and imitation as he was
too. Whether that be absolutely true or no, which an Author of much
curiosity in the Roman Church saies, that *Inter tot millia millium,* amongst
so many thousand thousands of Martyrs in the Primitive Church, it
cannot be said that ever one lack'd burial, (I know not whence he raises
that) certainly no Martyr ever lack'd a grave in the wounds of his
Saviour, no nor a tomb, a monument, a memorial in this life, in that
sense wherein our Saviour speaks in the Gospel, That no man shall leave
house, or Brother, or wife for him, but he shall receive an hundred fold
in this life; Christ does not mean he shall have a hundred houses, or a
hundred wives, or a hundred Brethren; but that that comfort which he
lost in losing those things shall be multiplied to him in that proportion
even in this life. In which words of our Saviour, as we see the dignity
and reward of Martyrdome, so we see the extent and latitude, and
compass of Martyrdome too; that not only loss of life, but loss of that
which we love in this life; not only the suffering of death, but the
suffering of Crosses in our life, contracts the Name, and entitles us to
the reward of Martyrdome. All Martyrdome is not a *Smithfeild*
Martyrdome, to burn for religion. To suffer injuries, and upon advantages offered, not to revenge those injuries is a Court Martyrdome. To
resist outward tentations from power, and inward tentations from
affections, in matter of Judicature, between party and party, is a
Westminster Martyrdome. To seem no richer than they are, not to make
their states better, when they make their private bargains with one

another, and to seem so rich, as they are, and not to make their states
worse, when they are call'd upon to contribute to publick services, this
is an Exchange-Martyrdome. And there is a Chamber-Martyrdome, a
Bosome-Martyrdome too; *Habet pudicitia servata Martyrium suum,*
Chastity is a dayly Martyrdome; and so all fighting of the Lords battails,
all victory over the Lords Enemies, in our own bowels, all chearful
bearing of Gods Crosses, and all watchful crossing of our own immoderate desires is a Martyrdome acceptable to God,[169] and a true
copy of our pattern *Stephen,* so it be inanimated with that which was
even the life and soul and price of all *Stephens* actions and passions, that
is, fervent charity, which is the last contemplation, in which we propose
him for your Example; that as he, you also may be just paymasters in
discharging the debt, which you owe the world in the signification of
your Names; and early Disciples and appliers of your selves to Christ
Jesus, and humble servants of his, without inordinate ambition of high
places; and constant Martyrs, in dying every day as the Apostle speaks,
and charitable intercessors, and Advocates and Mediators to God, even
for your heaviest Enemies.

3

Here I shall only present to you two Pictures, two pictures in little: two
pictures of dying men; and every man is like one of these, and may know
himself by it; he that dies in the Bath of a peaceable, and he that dies
upon the wrack of a distracted conscience. When the devil imprints in a
man, a *mortuum me esse non curo,* I care not though I were dead, it were
but a candle blown out, and there were an end of all: where the Devil
imprints that imagination, God will imprint an *Emori nolo,* a loathness
to die, and fearful apprehension at his transmigration: As God expresses
the bitterness of death, in an ingemination,[170] *morte morietur,* in a con-
duplication of deaths, he shall die, and die, die twice over; So *aegrotando
aegrotabit,* in sicknesse he shall be sick, twice sick, body-sick and soul-
sick too, sense-sick and conscience-sick together; when, as the sinnes of
his body have cast sicknesses and death upon his Soule, so the inordinate
sadnesse of his Soule, shall aggravate and actuate the sicknesse of his body.
His Physitian ministers, and wonders it works not; He imputes that to
flegme, and ministers against that, and wonders again that it works not;
He goes over all the humors, and all his Medicines, and nothing works,
for there lies at his Patients heart a dampe that hinders the concurrence

of all his faculties, to the intention of the Physitian, or the virtue of the Physick. Loose not, O blessed Apostle, thy question upon this Man, *O Death where is thy sting? O Grave where is thy victory?* for the sting of Death is in every limb of his body, and his very body is a victorious grave upon his Soule: And as his Carcas and his Coffin shall lie equally insensible in his grave, so his Soule, which is but a Carcas, and his body, which is but a Coffin of that Carcas, shall be equally miserable upon his Death-bed; And Satan's Commissions upon him shall not be signed by Succession, as upon *Job,* first against his goods, and then his Servants, and then his children, and then himselfe; but not at all upon his life; but he shall apprehend all at once, Ruine upon himselfe and all his, ruine upon himselfe and all him, even upon his life; both his lives, the life of this, and the life of the next world too. Yet a drop would redeeme a shoure, and a Sigh now a Storme then: Yet a teare from the eye, would save the bleeding of the heart, and a word from the mouth now, a roaring, or (which may be worse) a silence of consternation, of stupe-faction, of obduration at that last houre. Truly, if the death of the wicked ended in Death, yet to scape that manner of death were worthy a Religious life. To see the house fall, and yet be afraid to goe out of it; To leave an injur'd world, and meet an incensed God; To see oppression and wrong in all thy professions, and to foresee ruine and wastefulnesse in all thy Posterity; and Lands gotten by one sin in the Father, molder away by another in the Sonne; To see true figures of horror, and ly, and fancy worse; To begin to see thy sins but then, and finde every sin (at first sight) in the proportion of a Gyant, able to crush thee into despair; To see the Blood of Christ, imputed, not to thee, but to thy Sinnes; To see Christ crucified, and not crucifyed for thee, but crucified by thee; To heare this blood speake, not better things, than the blood of *Abel,* but lowder for vengeance than the blood of *Abel* did; This is his picture that hath been Nothing, that hath done nothing, that hath proposed no *Stephen,* No Law to regulate, No example to certifie his Conscience: But to him that hath done this, Death is but a Sleepe.

Many have wondred at that note of Saint *Chrysostom's,* That till Christ's time death was called death, plainly, literally death, but after Christ, death was called but sleepe; for, indeede, in the old-Testament before Christ, I thinke there is no one metaphor so often used, as Sleepe for Death, and that the Dead are said to Sleepe: Therefore wee wonder sometimes, that Saint *Chrysostome* should say so: But this may be that which that holy Father intended in that Note, that they in the old-Testament, who are said to have slept in Death, are such as then, by Faith, did apprehend, and were fixed upon Christ; such as were all the good men of the old-Testament, and so there will not bee many instances against Saint *Chrysostome*'s note, That to those that die in Christ, Death is but a Sleepe; to all others, Death is Death, literally Death. Now of this dying Man, that dies in Christ, that dies the Death of the Righteous, that embraces Death as a Sleepe, must wee give you a Picture too.

There is not a minute left to do it; not a minutes sand; Is there a minutes patience? Bee pleased to remember that those Pictures which are deliver'd in a minute, from a print upon a paper, had many dayes, weeks, Moneths time for the graving of those Pictures in the Copper; So this Picture of that dying Man, that dies in Christ, that dies the death of the Righteous, that embraces Death as a Sleepe, was graving all his life; All his publique actions were the lights, and all his private the shadowes of this Picture. And when this Picture comes to the Presse, this Man to the streights and agonies of Death, thus he lies, thus he looks, this he is. His understanding and his will is all one faculty; He understands Gods purpose upon him, and he would not have God's purpose turned any other way; hee sees God will dissolve him, and he would faine be dissolved, to be with Christ; His understanding and his will is all one faculty; His memory and his fore-sight are fixt, and concentred upon one object, upon goodnesse; Hee remembers that hee hath proceeded in the sinceritie of a good Conscience in all the wayes of his calling, and he foresees that his good name shall have the Testimony, and his Posterity the support of the good men of this world; His sicknesse shall be but a fomentation to supple and open his Body for the issuing of his Soule; and his Soule shall goe forth, not as one that gave over his house, but as one that travelled to see and learne better Architecture, and meant to returne and re-edifie that house, according to those better Rules: And as those thoughts which possesse us most awake, meete us againe when we are asleepe; So his holy thoughts, having been alwaies conversant upon the directing of his family, the education of his Children, the discharge of his place, the safety of the State, the happinesse of the King all his life; when he is faln a sleepe in Death, all his Dreames in that blessed Sleepe, all his devotions in heaven shall be upon the same Subjects, and he shal solicite him that sits upon the Throne, and the Lamb, God for Christ Jesus sake, to blesse all these with his particular blessings: for, so God giveth his beloved sleep, so as that they enjoy the next world and assist this.

So then, the Death of the Righteous is a sleepe; first, as it delivers them to a present rest. Now men sleepe not well fasting; Nor does a fasting Conscience, a Conscience that is not nourish'd with a Testimony of having done well, come to this Sleepe; but *dulcis somnus operanti,* The sleepe of a labouring man is sweete. To him that laboureth in his calling, even this sleepe of Death is welcome. *When thou lyest downe thou shalt not be afraid,* saith *Salomon;* when thy Physician sayes, Sir, you must keepe your bed, thou shalt not be afraid of that sick-bed; And then it followes, *And thy sleepe shall be sweet unto thee;* Thy sicknesse welcome, and thy death too; for, in those two *David* seems to involve all, *I will both lay me downe in Peace, and sleep;* imbrace patiently my death-bed and Death it selfe.

So then this death is a sleepe, as it delivers us to a present Rest; And then, lastly, it is so also as it promises a future waking in a glorious Resurrection. To the wicked it is far from both: Of them God sayes, *I will make them drunke, and they shall sleepe a perpetuall sleepe and not awake;* They shall have no part in the *Second Resurrection.* But for them that have slept in Christ, as Christ sayd of *Lazarus, Lazarus Sleepeth, but I goe that I may wake him out of sleep,* he shall say to his father; Let me goe that I may wake them who have slept so long in expectation of my coming: And *Those that sleep in Jesus Christ* (saith the Apostle) *will God bring with him;* not only fetch them out of the dust when he comes, but bring them with him, that is, declare that they have beene in his hands ever since they departed out of this world. They shall awake as *Jacob* did, and say as *Jacob* said, *Surely the Lord is in this place, and this is no other but the house of God, and the gate of heaven,* And into that gate they shall enter, and in that house they shall dwell, where there shall be no Cloud nor Sun, no darkenesse nor dazling, but one equall light, no noyse nor silence, but one equall musick, no fears nor hopes, but one equal possession, no foes nor friends, but one equall communion and Identity, no ends nor beginnings, but one equall eternity. Keepe us Lord so awake in the duties of our Callings, that we may thus sleepe in thy Peace, and wake in thy glory, and change that infallibility which thou affordest us here, to an Actuall and undeterminable possession of that Kingdome which thy Sonne our Saviour Christ Jesus hath purchased for us, with the inestimable price of his incorruptible Blood. *Amen.*

46. FROM A SERMON PREACHED TO THE KING AT WHITE-HALL, UPON THE OCCASION OF THE FAST, 5 APRIL 1628[171]

This may be some Embleme, some useful intimation, how hastily Repentance follows sinne; *Davids* sinne is placed, but in the beginning of the night, in the Evening, (*In the evening he rose, and walked upon the Terase, and saw Bathsheba*) and in the next part of time, in the night, he falls a weeping: no more between the sweetnesse of sinne, and the bitternesse of repentance, than between evening, and night; no morning to either of them, till the Sunne of grace arise, and shine out, and proceed to a Meridionall height, and make the repentance upon circumstance, to be a repentance upon the substance, and bring it to be a repentance for the sinne it selfe, which at first was but a repentance upon some calamity, that that sinne induced.

He wept then, and wept in the night; in a time, when he could neither receive rest in himselfe, which all men had, nor receive praise from others, which all men affect. And he wept *Omni nocte;* which is not onely *Omnibus noctibus,* sometime every night, but it is *Tota nocte,* cleane through the night; And he wept in that abundance, as hath put the Holy Ghost to that Hyperbole in *Davids* pen to expresse it, *Liquefecit stratum, natare fecit stratum,* it drowned his bed, surrounded his bed, it dissolved, it macerated, it melted his bed with that brine . . . Tentations take hold of us sometimes after our teares, after our repentance, but seldome or never in the act of our repentance, and in the very shedding of our teares; At least *Libidinum pompa,* The victory, the triumph of lust breaks not in upon us, in a bed, so dissolved, so surrounded, so macerated with such teares. Thy bed is a figure of thy grave; Such as thy grave receives thee at death, it shall deliver thee up to Judgement at last; Such as thy bed receives thee at night, it shall deliver thee in the morning: If thou sleepe without calling thy selfe to an account, thou wilt wake so, and walke so, and proceed so, without ever calling thy selfe to an account, till Christ Jesus call thee in the Clouds. It is not intended, that thou shouldest afflict thy selfe so grievously, as some over-doing Peni-tents, to put chips, and shels, and splints, and flints, and nayles, and rowels of spurres in thy bed, to wound and macerate thy body so. The inventions of men, are not intended here; But here is a precept of God, implied in this precedent and practise of *David*. That as long as the sense of a former sinne, or the inclination to a future oppresses thee, thou must not close thine eyes, thou must not take thy rest, till, as God married thy body and soule together in the Creation, and shall at last crowne thy body and soule together in the Resurrection, so they may also rest together here, that as thy body rests in thy bed, thy soule may rest in the peace of thy Conscience, and that thou never say to thy head, Rest upon this pillow, till thou canst say to thy soule, Rest in this repentance, in this peace.

47. FROM A SERMON PREACHED AT S. PAULS, FOR EASTER-DAY, 1628[172]

First then we consider, (before we come to our knowledge of God) our sight of God in this world, and that is, sayes our Apostle, *In speculo, we see as in a glasse*. But how doe we see in a glasse? Truly, that is not easily determined. The old Writers in the Optiques said, That when we see a thing in a glasse, we see not the thing itselfe, but a representation onely; All the later men say, we doe see the thing it selfe, but not by direct, but by reflected beames. It is a uselesse labour for the present, to reconcile them. This may well consist with both, That as that which we see in a glasse, assures us, that such a thing there is, (for we cannot see a dreame in a glasse, nor a fancy, nor a Chimera) so this sight of God, which our Apostle sayes we have *in a glasse,* is enough to assure us, that a God there is.

This glasse is better than the water; The water gives a crookednesse, and false dimensions to things that it shewes; as we see by an Oare when we row a Boat, and as the Poet describes a wry and distorted face, *Qui faciem sub aqua Phoebe natantis habes,*[173] That he looked like a man that swomme under water. But in the glasse, which the Apostle intends, we may see God directly, that is, see directly that there is a God. And therefore S. *Cyrils* addition in this Text, is a Diminution; *Videmus quasi in fumo,* sayes he, we see God as in a smoak; we see him better than so; for it is a true sight of God, though it be not a perfect sight, which we have this way. This way, our Theatre, where we sit to see God, is the whole frame of nature;[174] our *medium,* our glasse in which we see him, is the Creature; and our light by which we see him, is Naturall Reason.

Aquinas calls this Theatre, where we sit and see God, the whole world; And *David* compasses the world, and findes God every where, and sayes at last, *Whither shall I flie from thy presence? If I ascend up into heaven, thou art there;* At *Babel* they thought to build to heaven; but did any men ever pretend to get above heaven? above the power of winds, or the impression of other malignant Meteors, some high hils are got: But can any man get above the power of God? *If I take the wings of the morning, and dwell in the uttermost parts of the Sea, there thy right hand shall hold me, and lead me.* If we saile to the waters above the Firmament, it is so too. Nay, take a place, which God never made, a place which grew out of our sins, that is Hell, yet, *If we make our bed in hell, God is there too.* It is a wofull Inne, to make our bed in, Hell; and so much the more wofull, as it is more than an Inne; an everlasting dwelling: But even there God is; and so much more strangely than in any other place, because he is there, without any emanation of any beame of comfort from him, who is the God of all consolation, or any beame of light from him, who is the Father of all lights. In a word, whether we be in the Easterne parts of the world, from whom the truth of Religion is passed, or in the Westerne, to which it is not yet come; whether we be in the darknesse of ignorance, or darknesse of the works of darknesse, or darknesse of oppression of spirit in sadnesse, The world is the Theatre that represents God, and every where every man may, nay must see him.

The whole frame of the world is the Theatre, and every creature the stage, the *medium,* the glasse in which we may see God. *Moses made the Laver in the Tabernacle, of the looking glasses of women:* Scarce can you imagine a vainer thing (except you will except the vaine lookers on, in that action) than the looking-glasses of women; and yet *Moses* brought the looking-glasses of women to a religious use, to shew them that came in, the spots of dirt, which they had taken by the way, that they might wash themselves cleane before they passed any farther.

There is not so poore a creature but may be thy glasse to see God. The greatest flat glasse that can be made, cannot represent any thing greater than it is: If every gnat that flies were an Arch-angell, all that could but tell me, that there is a God; and the poorest worme that creeps, tells me that. If I should aske the Basilisk,[175] how camest thou by those killing eyes, he would tell me, Thy God made me so; And if I should aske the Slow-worme, how camest thou to be without eyes, he would tell me, Thy God made me so. The Cedar is no better a glasse to see God in, than the Hyssope upon the wall; all things that are, are equally removed from being nothing; and whatsoever hath any beeing, is by that very beeing, a glasse in which we see God, who is the roote, and the fountaine of all beeing. The whole frame of nature is the Theatre, the whole Volume of creatures is the glasse, and the light of nature, reason, is our light, which is another Circumstance.

Of those words, *John* 1.9. *That was the true light, that lighteth every man that commeth into the World,* the slackest sense that they can admit, gives light enough to see God by. If we spare S. *Chrysostomes* sense, That *that light,* is the light of the Gospel, and of Grace, and that *that light,* considered in it self, and without opposition in us, *does enlighten,* that is, would enlighten, *every man,* if that man did not wink[176] at that light; If we forbear S. *Augustines* sense, *That light enlightens every man,* that is, every man that is enlightned, is enlightned by that light; If we take but S. *Cyrils* sense, that this *light* is the light of naturall Reason, *which,* without all question, *enlightneth every man that comes into the world,* yet have we light enough to see God by that light, in the Theatre of Nature, and in the glasse of Creatures. God affords no man the comfort, the false comford of Atheism: He will not allow a pretending Atheist the power to flatter himself, so far, as seriously to thinke there is no God. He must pull out his own eyes, and see no creature, before he can say, he sees no God; He must be no man, and quench his reasonable soule, before he can say to himselfe, there is no God. The difference betweene the Reason of man, and the Instinct of the beast is this, That the beast does but know, but the man knows that he knows. The bestiall Atheist will pretend that he knows there is no God; but he cannot say, that hee knows, that he knows it; for, his knowledge will not stand the battery of an argument from another, nor of a ratiocination from himselfe. He dares not aske himselfe, who is it that I pray to, in a sudden danger, if there be no God? Nay he dares not aske, who is it that I sweare by, in a sudden passion, if there be no God? Whom do I tremble at, and sweat under, at midnight, and whom do I curse by next morning, if there be no God? It is safely said in the Schoole, *Media perfecta ad quae ordinantur,* How weak soever those meanes which are ordained by God, seeme to be, and be indeed in themselves, yet they are strong enough to those ends and purposes, for which God ordained them.

48. FROM A SERMON PREACHED AT S. PAULS IN THE EVENING, UPON THE DAY OF S. PAULS CONVERSION, 25 JANUARY 1629[177]

Poore intricated soule! Riddling, perplexed, labyrinthicall soule! Thou couldest not say, that thou beleevest not in God, if there were no God; Thou couldest not beleeve in God, if there were no God; If there were no God, thou couldest not speake, thou couldest not thinke, not a word, not a thought, no not against God; Thou couldest not blaspheme the Name of God, thou couldest not sweare, if there were no God: For, all thy faculties, how ever depraved, and perverted by thee, are from him; and except thou canst seriously beleeve, that thou art nothing, thou canst not beleeve that there is no God. If I should aske thee at a Tragedy, where thou shouldest see him that had drawne blood, lie weltring, and surrounded in his owne blood, Is there a God now? If thou couldst answer me, No, These are but Inventions, and Representations of men, and I beleeve a God never the more for this; If I should ask thee at a Sermon, where thou shouldest heare the Judgements of God formerly denounced, and executed, re-denounced, and applied to present occasions, Is there a God now? If thou couldest answer me, No, These are but Inventions of State, to souple and regulate Congregations, and keep people in order, and I beleeve a God never the more for this; Bee as confident as thou canst, in company; for company is the Atheists Sanctuary; I respit thee not till the day of Judgement, when I may see thee upon thy knees, upon thy face, begging of the hills, that they would fall downe and cover thee from the fierce wrath of God,[178] to aske thee then, Is there a God now? I respit thee not till the day of thine own death, when thou shalt have evidence enough, that there is a God, though no other evidence, but to finde a Devill, and evidence enough, that there is a Heaven, though no other evidence, but to feele Hell; To aske thee then, Is there a God now? I respit thee but a few houres, but six houres, but till midnight. Wake then; and then darke, and alone,

Heare God aske thee then, remember that I asked thee now, Is there a God? and if thou darest, say No.

49. FROM A SERMON PREACHED UPON CHRISTMAS DAY [?1629][179]

I

God, who vouchsafed to be made Man for man, for man vouchsafes also to doe all the offices of man towards man. He is our Father, for he made us: Of what? Of clay; So God is *Figulus,* so in the Prophet; so in the Apostle, God is our Potter. God stamped his Image upon us, and so God is *Statuarius,* our Minter, our Statuary. God clothed us, and so is *vestiarius;* he hath opened his wardrobe unto us. God gave us all the fruits of the earth to eate, and so is *oeconomus,* our Steward. God poures his oyle, and his wine into our wounds, and so is *Medicus,* and *Vicinus,* that Physitian, that Neighbour, that Samaritan intended in the Parable. God plants us, and waters, and weeds us, and gives the increase; and so God is *Hortulanus,* our Gardiner. God builds us up into a Church, and so God is *Architectus,* our Architect, our Builder; God watches the City when it is built; and so God is *Speculator,* our Sentinell. God fishes for men, (for all his *Johns,* and his *Andrews,* and his *Peters,* are but the nets that he fishes withall) God is the fisher of men; And here, in this Chapter, God in Christ is our Shepheard. The book of *Job* is a representation of God, in a Tragique-Comedy, lamentable beginnings comfortably ended: The book of the Canticles is a representation of God in Christ, as a Bridegroom in a Marriage-song, in an Epithalamion: God in Christ is represented to us, in divers formes, in divers places, and this Chapter is his Pastorall. The Lord is our Shepheard, and so called, in more places, than by any other name; and in this Chapter, exhibits some of the offices of a good Shepheard. Be pleased to taste a few of them. First, he sayes, *The good Shepheard comes in at the doore,* the right way. If he come in at the window, that is, always clamber after preferment; If he come in at vaults, and cellars, that is, by clandestin, and secret contracts with his Patron, he comes not the right way: When he is in the right way, *His sheep heare his voyce:* first there is a voyce, He is heard; Ignorance doth not silence him, nor lazinesse, nor abundance of preferment; nor indiscreet, and distempered zeale does not silence him; (for to induce, or occasion a silencing upon our selves, is as ill as the ignorant, or the lazie silence) There is a voyce, and (sayes that Text) it is his voyce, not alwayes another in his roome; for (as it is added in the next verse) *The sheep know his voyce,* which they could not doe, if they heard it not often, if they were not used to it. And then, for the best testimony, and consummation of all, he sayes, *The good Shepheard gives his life for his sheep.* Every good Shepheard gives his life, that is, spends his life, weares out his life for his sheep: of which this may be one good argument, That there are not so many crazie, so many sickly men, men that so soon grow old in any profession, as in ours.

2

There is Ayre enough in the world, to give breath to every thing, though every thing doe not breath. If a tree, or a stone doe not breathe, it is not because it wants ayre, but because it wants meanes to receive it, or to returne it. All egges are not hatched that the hen sits upon; neither could Christ himselfe get all the chickens that were hatched, to come, and to stay under his wings. That man that is blinde, or that will winke, shall see no more sunne upon S. *Barnabies* day, than upon S. *Lucies;* no more in the summer, than in the winter solstice. And therefore as there is *copiosa redemptio,* a plentifull redemption brought into the world by the death of Christ, so (as S. *Paul* found it in his particular conversion) there is *copiosa lux,* a great and a powerfull light exhibited to us, that we might see, and lay hold of this life, in the Ordinances of the Church, in the Confessions, and Absolutions, and Services, and Sermons, and Sacraments of the Church: Christ came *ut daret,* that he might bring life into the world, by his death, and then he instituted his Church, *ut haberent,* that by the meanes thereof this life might be infused into us, and infused so, as the last word of our Text delivers it, *Abundantius, I came, that they might have life more abundantly.*

Dignaris Domine, ut eis, quibus debita dimittis, te, promissionibus tuis, debitorem facias; This, O Lord, is thine abundant proceeding; First thou forgivest me my debt to thee, and then thou makest thy selfe a debter to me by thy large promises; and after all, performest those promises more largely than thou madest them. Indeed, God can doe nothing scantly, penuriously, singly. Even his maledictions, (to which God is ever loth to come) his first commination was plurall, it was death, and death upon death, *Morte morieris*. Death may be plurall; but this benediction of life cannot admit a singular; *Chajim*, which is the word for *life*, hath no singular number. This is the difference betweene Gods Mercy, and his Judgements, that sometimes his Judgements may be plurall, complicated, enwrapped in one another, but his Mercies are alwayes so, and cannot be otherwise; he gives them *abundantius, more abundantly*.

3

Humiliation is the beginning of sanctification; and as without this, without holinesse, no man shall see God, though he pore whole nights upon the Bible; so without that, without humility, no man shall heare God speake to his soule, though hee heare three two-houres Sermons every day. But if God bring thee to that humiliation of soule and body here, hee will emprove, and advance thy sanctification *abundantius*, more abundantly, and when he hath brought it to the best perfection, that this life is capable of, he will provide another *abundantius*, another maner of abundance in the life to come; which is the last beating of the pulse of this text, the last panting of the breath thereof, our anhelation, and panting after the joyes, and glory, and eternity of the kingdome of Heaven; of which, though, for the most part, I use to dismisse you, with saying something, yet it is alwaies little that I can say thereof; at this time, but this, that if all the joyes of all the Martyrs, from *Abel* to him that groanes now in the Inquisition, were condensed into one body of joy, (and certainly the joyes that the Martyrs felt at their deaths, would make up a far greater body, than their sorrowes would doe,) (for though it bee said of our great Martyr, or great Witnesse, (as S. *John* calls Christ Jesus) to whom, all other Martyrs are but sub-martyrs, witnesses that testifie his testimony, *Non dolor sicut dolor ejus*, there was never sorrow like unto his sorrow, it is also true, *Non gaudium sicut gaudium ejus*, There was never joy like unto that joy which was set before him, when he endured the crosse;) If I had all this joy of all these Martyrs, (which would, no doubt, be such a joy, as would worke a liquefaction, a melting of my bowels) yet I shall have it *abundantius*, a joy more abundant, than even this superlative joy, in the world to come. What a dimme vespers of a glorious festivall, what a poore halfe-holyday, is *Methusalems* nine hundred yeares, to eternity? what a poore account hath that man made, that saies, this land hath beene in my name, and in my Ancestors from the Conquest? what a yesterday is that? not six hundred yeares. If I could beleeve the transmigration of soules, and thinke that my soule had beene successively in some creature or other, since the Creation, what a yesterday is that? not six thousand yeares. What a yesterday for the past, what a to morrow for the future, is any terme, that can be comprehended in Cyphar or Counters?[180] But as, how abundant a life soever any man hath in this world for temporall abundances, I have life more abundantly than hee, if I have the spirituall life of grace, so what measure soever I have of this spirituall life of grace, in this world, I shall have that more abundantly in Heaven, for there, my terme shall bee a terme for three lives; for those three, that as long as the Father, and the Son, and the holy Ghost live, I shall not dye. And to this glorious Son of God, and the most almighty Father, &c.

50. FROM A LENT-SERMON PREACHED TO THE KING, AT WHITE-HALL, 12 FEBRUARY 1630[181]

I have seen Minute-glasses; Glasses so short-liv'd. If I were to preach upon this Text, to such a glass, it were enough for half the Sermon; enough to show the worldly man his Treasure, and the Object of his heart (*for, where your Treasure is, there will your Heart be also*) to call his eye to that Minute-glass, and to tell him, There flows, there flies your Treasure, and your Heart with it. But if I had a Secular Glass, a Glass that would run an age; if the two Hemispheres of the World were composed in the form of such a Glass, and all the World calcin'd and burnt to ashes, and all the ashes, and sands, and atoms of the World put into that Glass, it would not be enough to tell the godly man what his Treasure, and the Object of his Heart is. A Parrot, or a Stare,[182] docile Birds, and of pregnant imitation, will sooner be brought to relate to us the wisdom of a Council Table, than any *Ambrose,* or any *Chrysostome,* Men that have Gold and Honey in their Names, shall tell us what the Sweetness, what the Treasure of Heaven is, and what that mans peace, that hath set his Heart upon that Treasure. As Nature hath given us certain Elements, and all Bodies are compos'd of them; and Art hath given us a certain Alphabet of Letters, and all Words are compos'd of them: so, our blessed Saviour, in these three Chapters of this Gospel, hath given us a Sermon of Texts, of which, all our Sermons may be compos'd. All the Articles of our Religion, all the Canons of our Church, all the Injunctions of our Princes, all the Homilies of our Fathers, all the Body of Divinity, is in these three Chapters, in this one Sermon in the Mount: Where, as the Preacher concludes his Sermon with Exhortations to practice, (*whosoever heareth these sayings of mine, and doth them*) so he fortifies his Sermon, with his own practice, (which is a blessed and a powerful method) for, as soon as he came out of the Pulpit, as soon as he came down from the Mount, he cur'd the first Leper he saw, and that, without all vainglory: for he forbad him to tell any man of it.

51. FROM A SERMON PREACHED AT S. PAULS, UPON EASTER-DAY, 1630[183]

I

Our first consideration is upon the persons; and those we finde to be Angelicall women, and Evangelicall Angels: Angels made Evangelists, to preach the Gospell of the Resurrection, and Women made Angels, (so as *John Baptist* is called an *Angel,* and so as the seven Bishops are called *Angels*) that is, Instructers of the Church; And to recompence that observation, that never good Angel appeared in the likenesse of woman,[184] here are good women made Angels, that is, Messengers, publishers of the greatest mysteries of our Religion. For, howsoever some men out of a petulancy and wantonnesse of wit, and out of the extravagancy of Paradoxes, and such singularities, have called the faculties, and abilities of women in question, even in the roote thereof, in the reasonable and immortall soul,[185] yet that one thing alone hath been enough to create a doubt, (almost an assurance in the negative) whether S. *Ambroses* Commentaries upon the Epistles of S. *Paul,* be truly his or no, that in that book there is a doubt made, whether the woman were created according to Gods Image; Therefore, because that doubt is made in that book, the book it self is suspected not to have had so great, so grave, so constant an author as S. *Ambrose* was; No author of gravity, of piety, of conversation in the Scriptures could admit that doubt, whether woman were created in the Image of God, that is, in possession of a reasonable and an immortall soul.

The faculties and abilities of the soul appeare best in affaires of State, and in Ecclesiasticall affaires; in matter of government, and in matter of religion; and in neither of these are we without examples of able women. For, for State affaires, and matter of government, our age hath given us such a Queen, as scarce any former King hath equalled; And in the Venetian Story, I remember, that certain Matrons of that City were sent by Commission, in quality of Ambassadours, to an Empresse with whom that State had occasion to treate; And in the Stories of the Eastern parts of the World, it is said to be in ordinary practise to send women for Ambassadours. And then, in matters of Religion, women have evermore had a great hand, though sometimes on the left, as well as on the right hand. Sometimes their abundant wealth, sometimes their personall affections to some Church-men, sometimes their irregular and indiscreet zeale hath made them great assistants of great Heretiques; as S. *Hierome* tels us of *Helena* to *Simon Magus,*[186] and so was *Lucilia* to *Donatus,*[187] so another to *Mahomet,* and others to others. But so have they been also great instruments for the advancing of true Religion, as S. *Paul* testifies in their behalf, at *Thessalonica, Of the chiefe women, not a few;* Great, and Many. For, many times women have the proxies of greater persons than themselves, in their bosomes; many times women have voices, where they should have none; many times the voices of great men, in the greatest of Civill, or Ecclesiasticall Assemblies, have been in the power and disposition of women.

Hence is it, that in the old Epistles of the Bishops of Rome, when they needed the Court, (as, at first they needed Courts as much, as they brought Courts to need them at last) we finde as many letters of those Popes to the Emperours Wives, and the Emperours Mothers, and Sisters, and women of other names, and interests in the Emperours favours and affections, as to the Emperours themselves. S. *Hierome* writ many letters to divers holy Ladies; for the most part, all of one stocke and kindred; and a stock and kindred so religious, as that I remember, the good old man saies, That if *Jupiter* were their Cousin, of their kindred, he beleeves *Jupiter* would be a Christian; he would leave being such a God as he was, to be their fellow-servant to the true God.

Now if women were brought up according to S. *Hieromes* instructions in those letters, that by seaven yeares of age, they should be able to say the Psalmes without book; That as they grew in yeares, they should proceed in the knowledge of Scriptures, That they should love the Service of God at Church, but not *sine Matre,* not goe to Church when they would, but when their Mother could goe with them, *Nec quaererent celebritatem Ecclesiarum,* They should not alwaies goe to the greatest Churches, and where the most famous Preachers drew most company; If women have submitted themselves to as good an education as men, God forbid their sexe should prejudice them, for being examples to others. Their sexe? no, nor their sins neither: for, it is S. *Hieromes* note, That of all those women, that are named in Christs pedegree in the Gospell, there is not one, (his onely Blessed Virgin Mother excepted) upon whom there is not some suspitious note of incontinency. Of such women did Christ vouchsafe to come; He canme of woman so, as that he came of nothing but woman; of woman, and not of man. Neither doe we reade of any woman in the Gospel, that assisted the persecutors of Christ, or furthered his afflictions; Even *Pilats* wife disswaded it. Woman, as well as man, was made after the Image of God, in the Creation; and in the Resurrection, when we shall rise such as we were here, her sexe shall not diminish her glory: Of which, she receives one faire beame, and inchoation in this Text, that the purpose of God is, even by the ministery of Angels, communicated to women.

2

If I awake at midnight, and embrace God in mine armes, that is, receive God into my thoughts, and pursue those meditations, by such a having had God in my company, I may have frustrated many tentations that would have attempted me, and perchance prevailed upon me, if I had beene alone, for solitude is one of the devils scenes; and, I am afraid there are persons that sin oftner alone, than in company; but that man is not alone that hath God in his sight, in his thought. *Thou preventedst me with the blessings of goodnesse,* saies *David* to God. I come not early enough to God, if I stay till his blessings in a prosperous fortune prevent me, and lead me to God; I should come before that. *The dayes of affliction have prevented me,* saies *Job.* I come not early enough to God, if I stay till his Judgements prevent me, and whip me to him; I should come before that. But, if *I prevent the night watches, and the dawning of the morning,* If *in the morning my prayer prevent thee O God,* (which is a high expression of *Davids,* That I should wake before God wakes, and even prevent his preventing grace, before it be declared in any outward act, that day) If before blessing or crosse fall upon me, I surrender my selfe intirely unto thee, and say, Lord here I lye, make thou these sheets my sheets of penance, in inflicting a long sicknesse, or my winding sheete, in delivering me over to present death, Here I lye, make thou this bed mine Altar, and binde me to it in the cords of decrepitnesse, and bed-ridnesse, or throw me off of it into the grave and dust of expectation, Here I lye, doe thou choose whether I shall see any to morrow in this world, or begin my eternall day, this night, Thy Kingdome come, thy will be done.

52. FROM A SERMON PREACHED UPON THE PENITENTIALL PSALMES [DATE UNKNOWN][188]

I

This whole world is one Booke; And is it not a barbarous thing, when all the whole booke besides remains intire, to deface that leafe in which the Authors picture, the Image of God is expressed, as it is in man? God brought man into the world, as the King goes in state, Lords, and Earles, and persons of other ranks before him. So God sent out Light, and Firmament, and Earth, and Sea, and Sunne, and Moone, to give a dignity to mans procession; and onely Man himselfe disorders all, and that by displacing himselfe, by losing his place.[189] *The Heavens and Earth were finished, Et omnis exercitus eorum,* says *Moses, All the Host thereof;* and all this whole Army preserves that Discipline, onely the Generall that should governe them, mis-governs himselfe. And whereas we see that Tygers and Wolves, Beasts of annoyance, doe still keepe their places and natures in the world; and so doe Herbs and Plants, even those which are in their nature offensive and deadly, (for *Alia esui, alia usui,* Some herbs are made to eat, some to adorne, some to supply in Physick) whilest we dispute in Schools, whether if it were possible for Man to doe so, it were lawfull for him to destroy any one species of Gods Creatures, though it were but the species of Toads and Spiders, (because this were a taking away one linke of Gods chaine, one Note of his harmony) we have taken away that which is the Jewel at the chaine, that which is the burden of the Song, Man himselfe. *Partus sequitur ventrem;* We verifie the Law treacherously, mischievously; we all follow our Mother, we grovell upon the earth, whose children we are, and being made like our Father, in his Image, we neglect him.

2

So then is Pride well represented in the Horse; and so is the other, Lust, licentiousnesse in the Mule. For, besides that reason of assimilation, that it desires, and cannot, and that reason, that it presents unnaturall and promiscuous lust, for this reason is that vice well represented in that Beast, because it is so apt to beare any burdens. For, certainly, no man is so inclinable to submit himselfe to any burden of labour, of danger, of cost, of dishonour, of law, of sicknesse, as the licentious man is; He refuses none, to come to his ends. Neither is there any tree so loaded with boughs, any one sin that hath so many branches, so many species as this. Shedding of blood we can limit in murder, and manslaughter, and a few more; and other sins in as few names. In this sin of lust, the sexe, the quality, the distance, the manner, and a great many other circumstances, create new names to the sin, and make it a sin of another kinde. And as the sin is a Mule, to beare all these loads, so the sinner in this kind is so too, and (as we finde an example in the Nephew of a Pope) delights to take as many loads of this sin upon him, as he could; to vary, and to multiply the kindes of this sin in one act, He would not satisfie his lust by a fornication, or adultery, or incest, (these were vulgar) but upon his own sex; and that not upon an ordinary person, but in their account, upon a Prince; And he, a spirituall Prince, A Cardinall; And all this, not by solicitation, but by force: for thus he compiled his sins, He ravished a Cardinall.[190] This is the sin, in which men pack up as much sin as they can, and as though it were a shame to have too little, they belie their own pack, they bragge of sins in this kinde, which they never did, as S. *Augustine* with a holy and penitent ingenuity confesses of himselfe.[191]

53. DEATHS DUELL, OR, A CONSOLATION TO THE SOULE, AGAINST THE DYING LIFE, AND LIVING DEATH OF THE BODY, 25 FEBRUARY 1631[192]

TO THE READER.

This Sermon was, by Sacred Authoritie, stiled the Authors owne funeral Sermon.[193] *Most fitly: whether wee respect the time, or the matter. It was preached not many dayes before his death; as if, having done this, there remained nothing for him to doe, but to die: And the matter is, of Death; the occasion and subject of all funerall Sermons. It hath beene observed of this Reverend Man, That his Faculty in Preaching continually encreased: and, That as hee exceeded others at first; so, at last hee exceeded himselfe. This is his last Sermon; I will not say, it is therefore his best; because, all his were excellent. Yet thus much: A dying Mans words, if they concerne our selves; doe usually make the deepest impression, as being spoken most feelingly, and with least affectation. Now, whom doth it not concerne to learn, both the danger, and benefit of death? Death is every mans enemy, and intends hurt to all; though to many, hee be occasion of greatest goods. This enemy wee must all combate dying; whom hee living did almost conquer; having discovered the utmost of his power, the utmost of his crueltie. May wee make such use of this and other the like preparatives, That neither death, whensoever it shall come, may seeme terrible; nor life tedious; how long soever it shall last.*

Buildings stand by the benefit of their *foundations* that susteine and *support* them, and of their *butteresses* that comprehend and *embrace* them, and of their *contignations*[194] that knit and *unite* them: The *foundations* suffer them not to *sinke*, the *butteresses* suffer them not to *swerve*, and the *contignation* and knitting suffers them not to *cleave*. The body of our building is in the former part of this verse: It is this, hee that *is our God* is the *God of salvation; ad salutes,* of salvations in the plurall, so it is in the originall; the *God* that gives us spirituall and temporall salvation too. But of this *building*, the *foundation*, the *butteresses*, the *contignations* are in this part of the *verse*, which constitutes *our text*, and in the three divers *acceptations* of the words amongst our expositors, *Unto God the Lord belong the issues of death.* For *first* the *foundation* of this *building*, (that our *God* is the *God of all salvations*) is laid in this; That *unto* this *God the Lord belong the issues of death,* that is, it is in his power to give us an *issue* and deliverance, even then when wee are brought to the jawes and teeth of death, and to the lippes of that whirlepoole, the grave. And so in this acceptation, this *exitus mortis*, this *issue of death* is *liberatio a morte*, *a deliverance from death*, and this is the most obvious and most ordinary acceptation of these words, and that upon which our *translation* laies hold, the *issues from death*. And then *secondly*, the butteresses that comprehend and settle this building, That hee that is *our God*, is the *God of* all *salvation*, are thus raised; unto *God the Lord belong the issues of death*, that is, the disposition and *manner of our death:* what kinde of *issue*, and *transmigration* wee shall have out of this world, whether prepared or sudden, whether violent or naturall, whether in our perfect senses or shaken and disordered by sicknes, there is no condemnation to bee argued out of that, no Judgement to bee made upon that, for howsoever they dye, precious in *his sight is the death of his saints*, and with him are the *issues of death*, the *wayes* of our *departing* out of this *life* are in his *hands*. And so in this *sense* of the *words*, this *exitus mortis*, the *issue of death*, is *liberatio in morte*, *A deliverance in death;* Not that God will *deliver* us *from dying*, but that hee will *have a care* of us in the *houre of death*, of what kind soever our passage be. And this *sense* and acceptation of the *words*, the naturall frame and contexture doth well and pregnantly administer unto us. And then *lastly* the *contignation* and knitting of this building, that hee that is *our God* is the *God of all salvations*, consists in this, *Unto this God the Lord belong the issues of death*, that is, that this *God* the *Lord* having *united* and knit *both natures in one*, and being *God*, having also *come* into this *world*, in our *flesh*, he could have no other meanes to save us, he could have no other *issue* out of this world, nor *returne* to his former *glory*, but by *death;* And so in this sense, this *exitus mortis*, this *issue of death*, is *liberatio per mortem*, a *deliverance by death*, by the death of this *God* our *Lord Christ Jesus*. And this is Saint *Augustines* acceptation of the words, and those many and great persons that have adhered to him. In all these three lines then, we shall looke upon these words; *First*, as the *God of power*, the *Almighty Father* rescues his servants from the jawes of death: *And then*, as the *God of mercy*, the glorious *Sonne* rescued us, by taking upon himselfe this *issue of death: And then* betweene these two, as the *God of comfort*, the *holy Ghost* rescues us from all discomfort by his blessed impressions before hand, that what manner of death soever be ordeined for us, yet this *exitus mortis* shall bee *introitus in vitam*, our *issue in death*, shall be an *entrance into everlasting life*. And these three considerations, our deliverance *a morte, in morte, per mortem, from death*, *in death*, and *by death*, will abundantly doe all the offices of

the *foundations*, of the *butteresses*, of the *contignation* of this our *building;*
That he that is our *God*, is the *God of all salvation*, because *unto* this *God*
the Lord belong the issues of death.

First, then, we consider this *exitus mortis*, to bee *liberatio a morte*, that
with *God*, the *Lord* are the *issues of death*, and therefore in all our deaths,
and deadly calamities of this life, wee may justly *hope* of a good *issue* from
him; and all our *periods* and *transitions* in this life, are so many passages
from death to *death*. Our very *birth* and entrance into this life, is *exitus a*
morte, an *issue from death*, for in our mothers *wombe* wee are *dead so*, as
that wee doe *not know* wee *live*, not so much as wee doe in our *sleepe*,
neither is there any *grave* so close, or so *putrid* a *prison*, as the *wombe*
would be unto us, if we stayed in it *beyond* our time, or dyed there *before*
our time. In the *grave* the *wormes* doe not kill us, wee *breed* and *feed*, and
then *kill* those wormes which wee our selves produc'd. In the *wombe*
the dead *child* kills the *Mother* that conceived it, and is a murtherer, nay a
parricide, even after it is dead. And if wee bee not dead so in the *wombe*,
so as that being dead, wee kill her that gave us our first life, our life of
vegetation, yet wee are dead so, as *Davids Idols* are dead. In the *wombe*
wee have *eyes and see not, eares and heare not;* There in the wombe wee
are fitted for *workes of darkenes*, all the while deprived of light: And
there in the *wombe* wee are taught *cruelty*, by being *fed with blood*, and
may be *damned*, though we be *never borne*.[195] Of our very making in the
wombe, *David* says, *I am wonderfully and fearefully made*, and, *Such know-*
ledge is too excellent for me, for even that *is the Lords doing, and it is*
wonderfull in our eyes. Ipse fecit nos, it is hee that hath made us, and not wee
our selves, no, nor our parents neither; *Thy hands have made me and*
fashioned me round about, saith *Job*, and, (as the *originall word* is) *thou hast*
taken paines about me, and *yet*, says he, *thou doest destroy me*. Though I
bee the *Master peece* of the greatest *Master* (*man* is so,) yet if thou doe no
more for me, if thou leave me where thou madest mee, destruction will
follow. The *wombe* which should be the *house of life*, becomes *death* it
selfe, if *God* leave us there. That which God threatens so often, the
shutting of the womb, is not so *heavy*, nor so discomfortable a *curse* in the
first, as in the *latter* shutting, nor in the shutting of *barrennes*, as in the
shutting of *weakenes*, when *children are come to the birth*, and there is not
strength to bring forth.

It is the *exaltation* of *misery*, to *fall* from a *neare hope* of *happines*. And
in that vehement imprecation, the *Prophet* expresses the highth of *Gods*

anger, *Give them O Lord, what will thou give them? give them a mis-carying wombe.* Therefore as soone as wee are men, (that is, inanimated, quickned in the womb) thogh we cannot our selves, our parents have reason to say in our behalf, *wretched man that he is, who shall deliver* him *from this body of death?* for even the *wombe* is a *body of death,* if there bee no deliverer. It must be he that said to *Jeremy, Before I formed thee I knew thee, and before thou camest out of the wombe I sanctified thee.* Wee are not sure that there was no kinde of shippe nor boate to fish in, nor to passe by, till *God* prescribed *Noah* that absolute *form* of *the Arke.* That word which the *holy Ghost* by *Moses* useth for the *Arke,* is common to all kinde of *boates, Thebah,* and is the same word that *Moses* useth for the *boate* that he was *exposed* in, that *his mother layed him in an arke* of *bulrushes.* But we are sure that *Eve* had no *Midwife* when she was *delivered* of *Cain,* therefore shee might well say, *possedi virum a Domino, I have gotten a man from the Lord,* wholly, entirely from the Lord; It is the *Lord* that *enabled* me to *conceive,* The *Lord* that *infus'd* a *quickning soule* into that conception, the *Lord* that *brought into the world* that which himselfe *had quickened;* without all this might *Eve* say, My *body had bene* but *the house of death,* and *Domini Domini sunt exitus mortis,* to *God the Lord belong the issues of death.*

But then this *exitus a morte,* is but *introitus in mortem,* this *issue,* this deliverance *from* that *death,* the death of the *wombe,* is an *entrance,* a delivering over to *another death,* the manifold deathes of this *world.* Wee have a winding sheete in our Mothers wombe, which growes with us from our conception, and wee come into the world, wound up in that *winding sheet,* for wee come to *seeke a grave;* And as prisoners discharg'd of actions may lye for fees;[196] so when the *wombe* hath discharg'd us, yet we are bound to it by *cordes* of flesh, by such a *string,* as that wee cannot goe thence, nor stay there. We celebrate our owne funeralls with cryes, even at our birth; as though our *threescore and ten years of life* were spent in our mothers labour, and our circle made up in the first point thereof. We begge one Baptism with another, a sacrament of tears; And we come into a world that lasts many ages, but wee last not. *In domo Patris,* says our blessed *Saviour,* speaking of *heaven, multae mansiones,* there *are many mansions,* divers and durable, so that if a man cannot possesse a *martyrs* house, (he hath shed no blood for *Christ*) yet hee may have a *Confessors,* he hath bene ready to glorifie *God* in the *shedding of his blood.* And if a woman cannot possesse a *virgins* house (she hath embrac'd the *holy state* of *mariage*) yet she may have a *matrons* house, she hath brought forth and brought up *children in the feare of God. In domo patris, in my fathers house,* in heaven there *are many mansions;* but here upon earth *The Son of man hath not where to lay his head,* sayes he himselfe. *Nonne terram dedit filiis hominum?* how then hath *God given this earth* to the *sonnes of men?* hee hath *given* them *earth* for their *materialls* to bee made of earth, and he hath given them *earth* for their *grave* and sepulture, to *returne* and resolve to *earth,* but not for their *possession: Here wee have no continuing citty,* nay no *cottage* that continues, nay no persons, no bodies that continue. Whatsoever moved Saint *Jerome* to call the journies of the *Israelites,* in the *wildernes,* Mansions, the *word* (the word is *Nasang*) signifies but a *journey,* but a peregrination. Even the *Israel of God* hath no mansions; but journies, pilgrimages in this life. By that measure did *Jacob* measure his life to *Pharaoh, The daies of the years of my pilgrimage.* And though the *Apostle* would not say *morimur,* that, whilest wee *are in the body* wee *are dead,* yet hee sayes, *Peregrinamur,* whilest wee are *in the body,* wee are but in *a pilgrimage,* and wee are *absent from the Lord;* hee might have sayd *dead,* for this whole *world* is but an *universall church-yard,* but our *common grave;* and the life and motion that the greatest persons have in it, is but as the shaking of buried bodies in their graves by an *earth-quake.* That which we call life, is but *Hebdomada mortium, a week of deaths,* seaven dayes, seaven periods of our life spent in dying, *a dying seaven times over;* and there is an end. *Our birth dyes* in *infancy,* and our *infancy* dyes in *youth,* and *youth* and the rest dye in *age,* and *age* also dyes, and *determines all.* Nor doe all these, youth out of infancy, or age out of youth arise so, as a *Phoenix* out of the *ashes* of another *Phoenix* formerly *dead,* but as a *waspe* or a *serpent* out of a *caryon,* or as a *Snake* out of *dung.* Our *youth* is *worse* than our *infancy,* and our *age worse* than our *youth.* Our *youth* is *hungry and thirsty,* after those *sinnes,* which our *infancy knew not;* And our *age* is *sory* and *angry,* that it *cannot pursue* those *sinnes* which our *youth* did. And besides, al the way, so many deaths, that is, so many deadly calamities accompany every condition, and every period of this life, as that death it selfe would bee an ease to them that suffer them. Upon this sense doth *Job* wish that *God had not given him* an *issue* from the *first death,* from the *wombe, Wherefore hast thou brought me forth out of the wombe? O that I had given up the Ghost, and no eye had seen me; I should have been, as though I had not been.*

And not only the impatient *Israelites* in their murmuring (*would to*

God wee had dyed by the hand of the Lord in the land of Egypt) but *Eliah* himselfe, when he *fled* from *Jesabell*, and went for his life, as that text sayes, under the juniper tree, requested that *hee might dye*, and sayd, *It is enough, now O Lord, take away my life.* So *Jonah* justifies his impatience, nay his anger towards *God* himselfe. *Now O Lord take, I beseech thee, my life from mee, for it is better for me to dye than to live.* And when *God* asked him, *doest thou well to be angry for this,* and after, (about the Gourd) *dost thou well to be angry for that,* he replies, *I doe well to be angry, even unto death.* How much worse a death than death, is this life, which so good men would so often change for death? But if my case bee as Saint *Paules* case, *quotidia morior,* that *I dye dayly,* that something heavier than death fall upon me every day; If my case be *Davids* case, *tota die mortificamur, all the day long wee are killed,* that not onely every day, but every houre of the day some thing heavier than death fall upon me, though that bee true of me, *Conceptus in peccatis, I was shapen in iniquity, and in sinne did my mother conceive me,* (there I dyed one death,) though that be true of me (*Natus filius irae*) I *was borne* not onely the child of sinne, but *the child of wrath,* of the wrath of God for sinne, which is a heavier death; Yet *Domini Domini sunt exitus mortis,* with *God the Lord are the issues of death,* and after a *Job,* and a *Joseph,* and a *Jeremie,* and a *Daniel,* I cannot doubt of a deliverance. And if no other deliverance conduce more to his glory and my good, yet he hath the *keys of death,* and hee can let me out at that dore, that is, deliver me from the manifold deaths of this world, the *omni die* and the *tota die,* the *every dayes death* and *every houres death,* by that *one death,* the *final dissolution* of body and soule, the end of all.

But then is that the end of all? Is that dissolution of body and soule, the last death that the body shall suffer? (for of spirituall death wee speake not now) It is not. Though this be *exitus a morte,* it is *introitus in mortem:* though it bee an *issue from* the manifold *deaths* of this *world,* yet it is an *entrance* into the *death of corruption* and *putrefaction* and *vermiculation*[197] and *incineration,* and dispersion in and from the *grave,* in which every dead man dyes over againe. It was a *prerogative* peculiar to *Christ,* not to dy this death, *not to see corruption.* What gave him this priviledge? Not *Josephs* great proportion of *gummes* and *spices,* that might have preserved his body from corruption and *incineration* longer than he needed it, longer than *three dayes,* but it would not have done it for ever. What preserved him then? did his exemption and *freedome from originall*

sinne preserve him from this corruption and *incineration?* 'Tis true that
original sinne hath induced this corruption and *incineration* upon us; If
wee had not sinned in *Adam, mortality had not put on immortality,* (as the
Apostle speakes) nor *corruption had not put on incorruption,* but we had had
our *transmigration* from this to the other world, without any *mortality,*
any *corruption at all.* But yet since *Christ* tooke *sinne* upon him, so farre
as made him *mortall,* he had it so farre too, as might have made him see
this corruption and *incineration,* though he had no *originall sinne* in
himself. What preserv'd him then? Did the *hypostaticall union* of both
natures, *God* and *Man,* preserve him from this corruption and *incineration?* 'tis true that this was a most powerfull *embalming,* to be embalmd
with the *divine nature* it selfe, to bee embalmd with *eternity,* was able to
preserve him from corruption and *incineration* for ever. And he was
embalm'd so, embalmd with the *divine nature* it selfe, even in his *body* as
well as in his *soule;* for the *Godhead,* the *divine nature* did not depart, but
remained still *united* to his *dead body* in the *grave;* But yet for al this
powerful *embalming,* this *hypostaticall union* of both natures, we see *Christ*
did *dye;* and for all this *union* which made him *God* and *Man,* hee
became no man (for the *union* of the *body* and *soule* makes the man, and
hee whose soule and body are separated by death, (as long as that state
lasts) is properly no man.) And therefore as in him the dissolution of
body and *soule* was no *dissolution* of the *hypostaticall union;* so is there
nothing that constraines us to say, that though the *flesh* of *Christ* had
seene corruption and *incineration* in the grave, this had bene any *dissolution*
of the *hypostaticall union,* for the *divine nature,* the Godhead might have
remained with all the *Elements* and *principles* of *Christs* body, as well as it
did with the two *constitutive* parts of his *person,* his *body* and his *soul.* This
incorruption then was not in *Josephs gummes* and *spices,* nor was it in
Christs innocency, and *exemption* from *originall sin,* nor was it (that is, it
is not necessary to say it was) in the *hypostaticall union.* But this *incorruptiblenes* of his *flesh* is most conveniently plac'd in that, *Non dabis, thou
wilt not suffer thy holy one to see corruption.* We looke no further for *causes*
or *reasons* in the *mysteries of religion,* but to the *will* and pleasure of *God:
Christ* himselfe limited his *inquisition* in that *ita est, even so Father, for so it
seemed good in thy sight. Christs* body did *not see corruption,* therefore,
because *God* had *decreed* it shold not. The humble soule (and onely the
humble soule is the religious soule) rests himselfe upon *Gods* purposes,
and his decrees; but then, it is upon those purposes, and decrees of *God,*

which he hath declared and manifested; not such as are *conceived* and imagined in our selves, though upon some probability, some *veri-similitude*. So, in our present case, *Peter* proceeded in his *Sermon* at *Jeru-salem*, and so *Paul* in his at *Antioch*. They preached *Christ* to have *bene risen* without seeing *corruption*, not onely because *God* had *decreed* it, but because he had *manifested* that *decree* in his *Prophet*. Therefore doth Saint *Paul* cite by special number the *second Psalme* for that *decree;* And there-fore both Saint *Peter* and S. *Paul* cite for it that place in the 16. *Psalme*, for when *God* declares his *decree* and purpose in the expresse words of his *Prophet*, or when he declares it in the reall execution of the decree, then he makes it ours, then he manifests it to us. And therfore as the *Mysteries* of our *Religion*, are *not* the *objects* of *our reason*, but *by faith we rest* on *Gods decree* and purpose, (It is so, O *God*, because it is *thy will*, it should be so) so *Gods decrees* are ever to be considered in the *manifestation* thereof. All *manifestation* is either in the *word* of *God*, or in the *execution* of the *decree;* And when these two concur and meete, it is the strongest *demonstration* that can be: when therefore I finde those *markes* of *adoption* and *spirituall filiation*, which are delivered in the *word* of *God*, to be upon me, when I finde that reall *execution* of his *good purpose* upon me, as that *actually* I doe *live* under the *obedience*, and under the *conditions* which are *evidences* of *adoption* and *spirituall filiation;* then, and so long as I see these *markes* and live so, I may safely comfort my selfe in a *holy certitude* and a *modest infallibility* of my *adoption*. *Christ* determines himself in that, the purpose of *God;* because the purpose of *God* was manifest to him: S. *Peter* and S. *Paul* determine themselves in those two wayes of knowing the *purpose* of *God*, the *word* of *God* before, the *execution* of the *decree* in the *fulnes of time*. It was *prophecyed before*, say they, and it *is performed now*, *Christ is risen* without seeing corruption.

Now this which is so singularly peculiar to him, that *his flesh should not see corruption*, at his *second coming*, his coming to *Judgement*, shall extend to all that are then alive, their *flesh* shall not *see corruption*, because (as the Apostle saies, and saies as a secret, as a mystery, *behold I shew you a mystery*) *wee shall not all sleepe*, (that is, not continue in the state of the dead in the grave,) *but wee shall all be changed*.[198] In an instant we shall have a *dissolution*, and in the *same instant* a *redintegration*, a *recompacting of body* and *soule*, and that shall be truely a death and truely a resurrection, but no sleeping, no corruption. But for us that dye now and sleepe in the state of the dead, we must al passe this *posthume* death, this *death* after *death*, nay this death after buriall, this *dissolution* after *dissolution*, this *death* of *corruption* and *putrifaction*, of *vermiculation* and *incineration*, of *dissolution* and *dispersion* in and *from* the grave. When those bodies that have beene the *children* of *royall parents*, and the *parents* of *royall children*, must say with *Job*, to corruption thou art my father, and *to the Worme thou art my mother and my sister*. *Miserable riddle*, when the *same worme* must bee *my mother*, and *my sister*, and *my selfe*. *Miserable incest*, when I must bee *maried* to my *mother* and my *sister*, and bee both *father* and *mother* to my *owne mother* and *sister*, *beget*, and *beare* that *worme* which is all that *miserable penury*; when my *mouth* shall be *filled* with *dust*, and the *worme* shall *feed*, and *feed sweetely* upon me, when the *ambitious* man shall have *no satisfaction*, if the *poorest alive* tread upon him, nor the *poorest* receive any *contentment* in being made *equall* to *Princes*, for they *shall bee equall* but *in dust*. One dyeth at his full strength, being wholly at ease and in quiet, and another dyes in the *bitternes of his soul*, and never *eates* with *pleasure*, but they lye downe *alike* in *the dust*, and the *worme covers them*; The worm covers them in *Job*, and in *Esay*, it *covers them and is spred under them*, the worme is spred *under thee*, and the worme *covers thee*; There's the *Mats* and the *Carpets* that *lye under*, and there's the *State* [199] and the *Canapye*, that *hangs over* the greatest of the sons of men. Even those bodies that were *the temples of the holy Ghost*, come to this *dilapidation*, to ruine, to rubbidge, to dust: even the *Israel of the Lord*, and *Jacob* himselfe hath no other specification, no other denomination, but that *vermis Jacob*, thou *worme of Jacob*. Truely the consideration of this *posthume death*, this death after buriall, that after *God*, (with whom are the *issues of death*) hath delivered me from the *death* of the *wombe*, by bringing mee into the *world*, and from the manifold *deaths* of the *world*, by laying me in the *grave*, I must dye againe in an *Incineration* of this *flesh*, and in a dispersion of that dust: That that *Monarch*, who spred over many nations alive, must in his dust lye in a corner of that *sheete of lead*, and there, but so long as that lead will laste, and that privat and *retir'd man*, that thought himselfe his owne for ever, and never came forth, must in his dust of the grave bee published, and (such are the *revolutions* of the *graves*) bee mingled in his dust, with the dust of every high way, and of every dunghill, and swallowed in every puddle and pond: This is the most inglorious and contemptible *vilification*, the most deadly and peremptory *nullification* of man, that wee can consider. *God* seemes to have caried the declaration of his *power* to a great height, when hee sets the *Prophet Ezechiel* in the *valley of drye bones,* and sayes, *Sonne of man can these bones live?* as though it had bene impossible, and yet they did; The *Lord* layed *Sinewes upon them, and flesh,* and breathed into them, and *they did live:* But in that case there were *bones* to bee *seene,* something visible, of which it might be sayd, can this thing live? But in this death of *incineration,* and dispersion of dust, wee see *nothing* that wee can call *that mans;* If we say, can this dust live? perchance it *cannot,* it may bee the meere *dust* of the *earth,* which never did live, nor never shall. It may be the dust of that mans worms which did live, but shall no more. It may bee the dust of *another* man, that concernes not him of whom it is askt. This death of *incineration* and dispersion, is, to naturall *reason,* the most *irrecoverable death* of all, and yet *Domini Domini sunt exitus mortis, unto God the Lord belong the issues of death,* and by *recompacting* this *dust* into the *same body,* and *reanimating* the *same body* with the *same soule,* hee shall in a blessed and glorious *resurrection* give mee such an *issue from* this *death,* as shal never passe into any other death, but establish me into a life that shall last as long as the *Lord of life* himselfe. And so have you that that belongs to the *first acceptation* of these words, (*unto God the Lord belong the issues of death*) That though from the *wombe* to the *grave* and in the grave it selfe wee passe from *death* to *death,* yet, as *Daniel* speakes, *The Lord our God is able to deliver us, and hee will deliver us.*

And so wee passe unto our *second accommodation* of *these words* (*unto God the Lord belong the issues of death*) That it *belongs* to *God,* and *not* to *man* to *passe a judgement* upon us at our death, or to conclude a dereliction on *Gods* part upon the manner thereof.

Those *indications* which the *Physitians* receive, and those *presagitions* [200] which they give for *death* or *recovery* in the *patient,* they receive and they give out of the grounds and the *rules of their art:* But we have no such rule or art to give a *presagition* of *spirituall death* and damnation upon any such *indication* as wee see in any *dying man;* wee see often enough to be sory, but not to despaire; for the *mercies* of God worke *momentarily* in minutes, and many times *insensibly* to *bystanders* or any other than the party departing, and wee may bee deceived both wayes: wee use to comfort our selves in the death of *a friend,* if it be testified that he went away like a *Lambe,* that is, without any *reluctation.* But, *God* knowes, that may bee accompanied with a *dangerous damp* and *stupefaction,* and *insensibility* of his *present state.* Our blessed *Saviour* suffered *colluctations* [201]

with *death*, and a *sadnes even in his soule to death*, and an *agony* even to a
bloody sweate in his *body*, and *expostulations* with *God*, and *exclamations*
upon the crosse. He was a *devout man*, who said upon his death bed, or
death-turfe (for hee was an *Heremit*) *septuaginta annos Domino servivisti*,
*& mori times? hast thou served a good Master threescore and ten yeares, and
now art thou loath to goe into his presence?* yet *Hilarion* [202] was loath. He
was a *devout* man (an *Heremit* too) that sayd that day hee died, *Cogita te
hodie coepisse servire Domino, & hodie finiturum. Consider this to be the first
days service that ever thou didst thy Master*, to glorifie him in a Christianly
and a constant death, *and if thy first day be thy last day too, how soone dost
thou come to receive thy wages?* yet *Barlaam* could have beene content to
have stayd longer for it: Make no *ill conclusions* upon any mans *loathnes*
to *dye*. And then, upon *violent deaths* inflicted, as upon malefactors,
Christ himselfe hath forbidden us by his owne death to make any *ill
conclusion;* for his owne *death* had those impressions in it; He was *reputed*,
he was *executed* as a *malefactor*, and no doubt many of them who concurred to his death, did beleeve him to bee so. Of *sudden death* there are
scarce examples to be found in the *scriptures* upon *good men*, for *death* in
battaile cannot be called *sud[d]en death;* But *God* governes not by
examples, but by *rules*, and therefore make no *ill conclusion* upon *sudden
death* nor upon distempers neyther, though perchance accompanied with
some *words of diffidence* and distrust in the *mercies of God*. The *tree lyes as
it falles;* 'Tis true, but yet it is *not the last stroake* that *fells* the *tree*, nor the
last word nor *gaspe* that *qualifies* the *soule*. Stil *pray* wee for a *peaceable life*
against *violent death*, and for *time of repentance* against *sudden death*, and
for *sober* and *modest assurance* against *distemperd* and *diffident death*, but
never make *ill conclusions* upon persons overtaken with such deaths;
Domini Domini sunt exitus mortis, to God the Lord belong the issues of death.
And *he* received *Sampson*, who went out of this world in *such a manner*
(consider it *actively*, consider it *passively*, in his *owne death*, and in those
whom he *slew* with himselfe) as was subject to interpretation hard
enough. Yet the *holy Ghost* hath moved S. *Paul* to celebrate *Sampson* in
his *great Catalogue*, and so doth all the *Church*. Our *criticall* day is *not the
very day* of our *death:* but the whole course of our life. I thanke him that
prayes for me when my bell tolles, but I thank him much more that
Catechises mee, or *preaches* to mee, or *instructs mee how to live. Fac hoc &
vives, there's* my securitie, the mouth of the *Lord hath sayd it, doe this and
thou shalt live:* But *though I doe it*, yet I *shall dye too*, dye a bodily, a

naturall death. But *God* never mentions, never seems to consider that death, the bodily, the naturall death. *God* doth not say, Live well and thou shalt dye well, that is, an easie, a quiet death; But *live well here*, and thou shalt *live well for ever*. As the first part of a sentence peeces wel with the last, and never respects, never hearkens after the *parenthesis* that comes betweene, so doth a *good life* here flowe into an *eternall life*, without any consideration, what *manner* of *death* wee dye: But whether the *gate* of *my prison* be *opened* with an *oyld key* (by a gentle and *preparing sicknes*) or the gate bee *hewen downe* by a *violent death*, or the gate bee *burnt downe* by a *raging* and *frantique feaver, a gate into heaven* I shall have, for *from* the Lord is the *cause* of *my life*, and *with God the Lord are the issues of death*. And further wee cary not this *second acceptation* of the *words*, as this *issue of death* is *liberatio in morte, Gods care* that the *soule* be *safe*, what *agonies* soever the *body suffers* in the *houre* of death; but passe to our *third part* and last part; as this *issue of death* is *liberatio per mortem*, a *deliverance by the death* of another, by the *death* of *Christ*.

Sufferentiam Job audiistis, & vidistis finem Domini, sayes Saint *James* 5.11. *You have heard of the patience of Job*, says he, All this while you have done that, for in every man, calamitous, miserable man, a *Job* speakes; Now *see the end of the Lord*, sayth that *Apostle*, which is not that end that the *Lord* propos'd to himselfe (*salvation to us*) nor the end which he proposes to us (*conformitie to him*) but *see the end of the Lord*, sayes he, The end, *that the Lord* himselfe came to, *death*, and a painefull and a shamefull death. But why did he dye? and why dye so? *Quia Domini Domini sunt exitus mortis* (as Saint *Augustine* interpreting this *text* answeres that question) because *to* this *God our Lord belong'd the issues of death*. *Quid apertius diceretur?* sayes hee there, what can bee more obvious, more manifest than this sense of these words? In the former part of this verse, it is sayd, *He that is our God, is the God of salvation, Deus salvos faciendi*, so hee reads it, the *God* that must save us: Who can that be, sayes he, but *Jesus?* for *therefore* that *name* was *given him*, because he was to *save us*. And to this *Jesus*, sayes he, this *Saviour, belongs the issues of death; Nec oportuit eum de hac vita alios exitus habere quam mortis*. Being come into this life in our mortal nature, he could not goe out of it any other way than by Death. *Ideo dictum*, sayes he, *therefore it is sayd, To God the Lord belong the issues of death; ut ostenderetur moriendo nos salvos facturum, to shew that his way to save us was to dye*. And from this *text* doth Saint

Isiodore prove, that *Christ* was *truely Man,* (which as many *sects* of *heretiques denyed,* as that he was *truely God*) because to him, though he were *Dominus Dominus* (as the *text* doubles it) *God* the *Lord,* yet to *him,* to *God the Lord belong'd the issues of death. Oportuit eum pati,* more can not be sayd, than *Christ* himselfe sayes of himself, *These things Christ ought to suffer;* hee had no other way but by death. So then *this part* of our *Sermon* must needes be a *passion Sermon;* since all his *life* was a *continuall passion,* all *our Lent* may well bee a *continuall good Fryday. Christs* painefull life tooke off none of the *paines* of his death, hee felt not the lesse then for having felt so much before. Nor will any thing that shall be sayd before, lessen, but rather inlarge your devotion, to that which shall be sayd of his passion at the time of the due *solemnization* thereof. *Christ* bled not a droppe the lesse at the last, for having bled at his *Circumcision* before, nor wil you shed a teare the lesse then, if you shed some now. And therefore bee now content to consider with mee how to *this God the Lord belong'd the issues of death.*

   That *God,* this *Lord,* the *Lord* of *life could dye,* is a strange contemplation; That the *red Sea* could bee *drie,* That the *Sun* could *stand still,* That an *Oven* could be *seaven times heat* and *not burne,* That *Lions* could be *hungry* and *not bite,* is strange, *miraculously strange,* but *supermiraculous* that *God could dye;* but that *God would dye* is an *exaltation* of that. But even of that also it is a *superexaltation,* that God *shold dye, must dye,* and *non exitus* (said *S. Augustin*) *God* the *Lord had no issue but by death,* and *oportuit pati* (says Christ himself) all this *Christ ought to suffer,* was bound to suffer. *Deus ultionum Deus* says *David, God* is the *God of revenges,* he wold *not passe* over the sin of man unrevenged, unpunished. But then *Deus ultionum libere egit* (sayes *that place*) The *God of revenges workes freely,* he *punishes,* he *spares whome he will.* And wold he *not spare himselfe?* he would not: *Dilectio fortis ut mors, love is strong as death,* stronger, it drew in death that naturally is not welcom. *Si possibile,* says *Christ, If it be possible, let this Cup passe,* when his *love expressed in a former decree* with his *Father,* had *made* it *impossible. Many waters quench not love, Christ* tryed many; He was *Baptized* out of his *love,* and his love determined not there; He wept over *Jerusalem* out of his love, and his love determined not there; He *mingled blood* with *water* in his *agony* and that determined not his love; hee *wept pure blood,* all his blood at all his eyes, at all his pores, in his *flagellation* and *thornes* (to the Lord our God *belong'd the issues of blood*) and these *expressed,* but these did *not quench his love.*[203]

Hee *would not* spare, nay he *could not spare himselfe*. There was nothing more free, more voluntary, more spontaneous than the death of *Christ*. 'Tis true, *libere egit*, he *dyed voluntarily*, but yet when we consider the *contract* that had passed betweene his *Father* and *him*, there was an *oportuit*, a kind of *necessity* upon him. All this *Christ ought to suffer*. And when shall we *date* this *obligation*, this *oportuit*, this *necessity?* when shall wee say *that* begun? Certainly this *decree* by which *Christ was to suffer* all this, was an *eternall decree*, and was there any thing before that, that was eternall? *Infinite love, eternall love*, he pleased to follow this home, and to consider it seriously, that what liberty soever wee can *conceive* in *Christ*, to dye or not to dye; this *necessity of dying*, this *decree* is as *eternall* as that *liberty;* and yet how small a matter made hee of this *necessity* and this *dying?* His *Father* cals it but *a bruise*, and but a *bruising of his heele* (*the serpent shall bruise his heele*) and yet that was, that the *serpent should practise* and *compasse* his *death*. Himselfe calls it but a *Baptisme*, as though he were to bee the better for it. *I have a Baptisme to be Baptized with*, and he was in paine till it was accomplished, and yet this *Baptisme* was *his death*. The *holy Ghost* calls it *Joy* (*for the Joy which was set before him hee indured the Crosse*) which was not a *joy* of his reward after his passion, but a joy that filled him even in the middest of those torments, and arose from them. When *Christ* calls his passion *Calicem, a Cuppe*, and no worse, (*Can ye drink of my Cuppe?*) he speakes not odiously, not with detestation of it: Indeed it was a *Cup, salus mundo, a health to all the world*. And *quid retribuam*, says *David, what shall I render to the Lord?* answere you with *David, accipiam Calicem, I will take the Cup of salvation;* take it, that *Cup of salvation*, his *passion*, if not into your *present imitation*, yet into your *present contemplation*. And behold how that *Lord* that was *God*, yet *could dye, would dye, must dye*, for your *salvation*.

That *Moses* and *Elias talkt with Christ* in the *transfiguration*, both Saint *Mathew* and Saint *Marke* tel us, but what they talkt of, onely S. *Luke, Dicebant excessum eius*, says he, *they talkt of his decease, of his death* which *was to be accomplished* at *Jerusalem*. The *word* is of his *Exodus*, the very word of our Text, *exitus*, his *issue by death*. *Moses* who in his *Exodus* had *prefigured* this *issue of our Lord*, and in passing *Israel* out of *Egypt* through the *red Sea*, had foretold in that actual *prophesie, Christs passing of mankind through* the *sea* of his *blood*, and *Elias*, whose *Exodus* and *issue out of* this *world* was a *figure* of *Christs ascension*, had no doubt a great satisfaction in *talking* with our *blessed Lord de excessu eius*, of the *full consummation* of *all this* in *his death*, which was to bee *accomplished* at *Jerusalem*. Our *meditation* of his *death* should be more *viscerall* and affect us more because it is of a thing already done. The ancient *Romanes* had a certain tenderness, and detestation of the name of death, they cold not name death, no, not in their wills. There they could not say *Si mori contigerit*, but *si quid humanitus contingat*, not if, or when I dye, but when the course of nature is accomplished upon me. To us that speake dayly of the *death* of *Christ*, (he was *crucified, dead and buried*) can the memory or the mention of our owne *death* bee yrkesome or bitter? There are in these latter times amongst us, that name death freely enogh, and the death of *God*, but in *blasphemous oathes* and *execrations*. Miserable men, who shall therefore bee sayd never to have named *Jesus*, because they have named him *too often;* and therfore heare *Jesus* say, *Nescivi vos, I never knew you*, because they made themselves *too familiar* with him. *Moses* and *Elias* talkt with *Christ* of his *death*, only in a *holy* and *joyfull sense* of the *benefit* which *they* and *all* the world were to *receive by that. Discourses* of *Religion* should not be *out* of *curiosity*, but to *edification*. And then they talkt with *Christ* of his *death* at that time, when he was in the greatest *height* of *glory* that ever he admitted in this world, that is, his *transfiguration*. And wee are afraid to speake to the *great men* of this world of their *death*, but nourish in them a *vaine imagination* of *immortality*, and *immutability*. But *bonum est nobis esse hic* (as Saint *Peter* said there) *It is good to dwell here*, in this *consideration* of his *death*, and therefore *transferre* wee our *tabernacle* (our *devotions*) through some of those *steps* which *God* the *Lord* made to his *issue of death* that *day*.

Take in the *whole day* from the *houre* that *Christ received* the *passeover* upon *Thursday*, *unto* the *houre* in which hee *dyed* the *next day*. Make *this* present *day* that *day* in thy *devotion*, and consider what *hee did*, and remember what *you have done*. Before hee *instituted* and *celebrated* the *Sacrament*, (which was *after* the *eating of the passeover*) hee proceeded to that *act* of *humility*, to *wash his disciples feete*, even *Peters, who* for a while *resisted* him; In thy *preparation* to the holy and blessed *Sacrament*, hast thou with a sincere *humility* sought a *reconciliation* with all the *world*, even with those that have beene *averse* from it, and *refused* that *reconciliation* from thee? If so (and not else) thou hast spent that *first part* of this his *last day*, in a *conformity* with him. After the *Sacrament* hee spent the time till night in *prayer*, in *preaching*, in *Psalmes;* Hast thou considered that a *worthy receaving* of the *Sacrament* consists in a *continuation* of *holinesse after*, as well as in a *preparation* before? If so, thou hast therein also *conformed* thy selfe to him, so *Christ* spent his time till night. *At night* hee *went into the garden* to *pray*, and he prayed *prolixius;* he spent *much time* in prayer. How much? Because it is literally expressed, that he *prayed there three severall times*, and that *returning to his Disciples* after his *first prayer*, and *finding them a sleepe* sayd, *could ye not watch with me one houre*, it is collected that he *spent three houres* in *prayer*. I dare scarce aske thee *whither* thou *wentest*, or *how* thou *disposedst* of *thy self*, when it *grew darke* and after *last night:* If that time were spent in a *holy recommendation* of thy selfe to *God*, and a *submission* of *thy will* to *his*, it was spent in a *conformity* to him. In that *time* and in those *prayers* was *his agony* and *bloody sweat*. I will *hope* that thou didst *pray;* but not *every ordinary* and *customary prayer*, but *prayer actually* accompanied with *shedding of teares*, and *dispositively* in a readines to *shed blood* for *his glory* in *necessary cases*, puts thee into a *conformity* with him. About midnight he was *taken* and *bound with a kisse*, art thou not *too conformable* to him in that? Is not that *too literally*, too exactly *thy case?* at *midnight* to have *bene taken* and *bound with a kisse?* From thence he was *caried back* to *Jerusalem*, first to *Annas*, then to *Caiphas*, and (as late as it was) then hee was *examined* and *buffeted*, and *delivered over* to the custody of those *officers*, from whome he received all those *irrisions*, and *violences*, the *covering of his face*, the *spitting upon his face*, the *blasphemies of words*, and the *smartnes of blowes* which that *Gospell* mentions. In which compasse fell that *Gallicinium*, that *crowing of the Cock* which *called up Peter* to his *repentance*. How thou passedst all that time last night, thou knowest. If thou didst any thing then that needed *Peters teares*, and hast *not shed them*, let me be thy *Cock*, doe it now, Now thy *Master* (in the unworthiest of his servants) *lookes back upon thee*, doe it now. *Betimes*, in the morning, so soone as it was day, the *Jewes held a counsell* in the *high Priests hall*, and *agreed upon their evidence* against him, and then caried him to *Pilate*, who was to be his *Judge*. Diddest thou *accuse* thy selfe when thou *wakedst this morning*, and wast thou content to admit even *false accusations* (that is) rather to *suspect actions* to have beene sin, which were not, than to *smother* and *justify* such as were *truly sins?* then thou spentst that *houre* in *conformity* to him. *Pilate* found *no evidence against him*, and therefore to ease himselfe, and to passe a *complement* upon *Herod, Tetrarch of Galilee*, who was at that time at *Jerusalem* (because *Christ* being a *Galilean* was of *Herods juris-diction*) *Pilat sent him* to *Herod*, and rather as a *madman* than a *malefactor*,

Herod remaunded him (*with scornes*) to *Pilat* to proceed against him; And this was about *eight* of the *clock*. Hast thou been content to come to this *Inquisition*, this examination, this agitation, this cribration,[204] this pursuit of thy *conscience*, to *sift* it, to follow it from the *sinnes* of thy *youth* to thy *present sinnes*, from the *sinnes* of thy *bed*, to the *sinnes* of thy *boorde*, and from the *substance* to the *circumstance* of thy *sinnes*? That's *time spent* like thy *Saviours. Pilat* wold have *saved Christ*, by using the *priviledge* of the *day* in his behalfe, because that *day* one *prisoner was to be delivered*, but they chose *Barrabas;* hee would have *saved* him *from death*, by *satisfying their fury*, with *inflicting* other *torments* upon him, *scourging* and *crowning with thornes*, and *loading* him with many *scornefull* and *ignominious contumelies;* But this redeem'd him not, they pressed a *crucifying*. Hast thou gone about to *redeeme thy sinne*, by *fasting*, by *Almes*, by *disciplines* and *mortifications*, in the way of *satisfaction* to the *Justice* of *God?* that will not serve, that's not the right way, *wee presse* an utter *Crucifying* of that *sinne* that governes thee; and that *conformes* thee to *Christ*. Towards *noone Pilat* gave *judgement*, and they made such *hast* to execution, as that *by noone* hee was *upon the Crosse*. There now hangs that *sacred Body* upon the *Crosse, rebaptized* in his owne *teares* and *sweat*, and *embalmed* in his *owne blood alive*. There are those *bowells of compassion*, which are so conspicuous, so manifested, as that you may *see them through his wounds*. There those *glorious eyes* grew faint in their light: so as the *Sun ashamed* to survive them, *departed with his light too*. And then that *Sonne of God*, who was *never from us*, and yet had now come a *new way unto* us in *assuming our nature*, delivers that *soule* (which was *never out* of his *Fathers hands*) by a *new way*, a *voluntary emission* of it into his Fathers hands; For though to this *God our Lord, belong'd these issues of death*, so that considered in his owne contract, he *must* necessarily *dye*, yet at *no breach* or *battery*, which they had made upon his *sacred Body*, issued his soule, but *emisit*, hee *gave up the Ghost*, and as *God breathed a soule into* the *first Adam*, so this *second Adam breathed his soule into God, into the hands of God*. There wee leave you in that *blessed dependancy*, to *hang* upon *him* that *hangs* upon the *Crosse*, there *bath* in his *teares*, there *suck* at his *woundes*, and *lye downe in peace* in his *grave*, till hee vouchsafe you a *resurrection*, and an *ascension* into that *Kingdome*, which hee *hath purchas'd for you*, with the *inestimable price* of his *incorruptible blood*. AMEN.

NOTES

There are obvious difficulties in annotating the work of a learned author for a selection of this kind, and I have deliberately left many stones unturned. I have assumed that the reader's interest will be essentially a literary one, and I have compiled the notes on that basis. My chief aims have been to illustrate some of the main themes of Donne's prose by pointing to parallels elsewhere in his work and in that of other Renaissance and, occasionally, Classical writers; to provide some necessary biographical and historical information; to gloss obsolete words and phrases, and to offer translations of the Latin. In the case of the Sermons I have given no biblical references other than the initial texts, and I have rarely commented on Donne's quotations from the Church Fathers; to do otherwise would have produced a quite massive volume of annotation. (The references will be found in Potter and Simpson, here referred to as *Sermons*.) Nor have I glossed the Latin quotations in the Sermons, as Donne himself provides paraphrases; while these are not always accurate, they do at any rate show what he intended the Latin to mean. In the case of *Biathanatos,* since Donne himself worried that he might be accused of showing off, on account of the 'multiplicity of not necessary citations', I have deliberately ignored all but the most familiar of his authorities. References to Donne's poems are to *The Complete English Poems,* ed. A. J. Smith (Penguin, 1971).

In preparing these notes I have, of course, been greatly assisted by the large amount of secondary material on Donne, which it would be impossible to acknowledge fully here. I have found the following particularly helpful: R. C. Bald, *John Donne: A Life* (1970); John Carey, *John Donne: Life, Mind and Art* (1981); E. R. Curtius, *European Literature and the Latin Middle Ages* (1953). Potter and Simpson provide only textual notes to the Sermons, but I have gleaned useful information from their Introductions to the individual volumes in the California edition. I would also like to thank my colleagues in the Departments of English, Humanity and Ancient History at St Andrews for their patient help with my enquiries, and Phillip Mallett for his penetrating reading of the introduction.

PARADOXES

1. Donne refers to the Aristotelian doctrine of the three souls: vegetable (of plants), sensible (of animals), and rational (of human beings). The idea appears frequently in his writing, cf. *Devotions* 18; Sermon 13.1; 'To the Countess of Salisbury', ll. 52–4.

2. The argument is reminiscent of Nature's claim in Spenser's *Mutabilitie Cantos* that all things 'Doe worke their owne perfection so by fate' (VII.58). But this is presented as a means of transcending change or 'mutability', which instead desires its own decay (59). Here, as throughout the *Paradoxes*, Donne deploys arguments in ways which are philosophically inconsistent.

3. Cf. Sermon 8 on the text 'And though after my skin worms destroy this body, yet in my flesh shall I see God'.

4. Cf. 'To Sir Henry Wotton' l. 1, 'Sir, more than kisses, letters mingle souls . . .'.

5. Donne uses the term variously to mean 'fanciful', 'capricious' and 'ridiculous'.

6. Fancifully inventing.

7. Cf. *Biathanatos,* I.i.7, 'So that originall sinne is traduced by nature onely, and all actuall sinne issuing from thence, all sinne is naturall.'

8. The custom of dividing a dead man's property equally among his sons.

9. Temperaments; literally, the balance of humours in the body.

10. 'You will say and do nothing against Minerva's will' (Horace, *Ars Poetica*, l. 385).

11. Cf. *As You Like It*, I.ii.46–8, 'Indeed, there is Fortune too hard for Nature, when Fortune makes Nature's natural the cutter-off of Nature's wit'. The 'natural' is distinct from the artificial or professional fool.

12. The notion of the 'golden mean' derives from Aristotle. Donne's two extremes are illustrated by the 'forward' Pyrochles and the 'froward' Cymochles in *The Faerie Queene*, Book II.

13. 'He acts bravely who is miserable and can endure' (Martial, *Epigrams*, XI.56).

14. Donne makes the same point, suitably modified, in a sermon of 1621: 'The dead (men civilly dead, allegorically dead, dead and buryed in an uselesse silence, in a Cloyster, or Colledge) may praise God, but not in words of edification . . .' (*Sermons*, III, p. 259). He frequently expresses a hatred of solitude elsewhere: see Letter 3, *Devotions* 5, and Sermon 51.2.

15. Cf. 'Air and Angels', ll. 7–10 and 'The Ecstasy', ll. 61–8; also *Sermons*, IV, p. 358, 'Never go about to separate the thoughts of the heart, from the Colledge, from the fellowship of the body . . . All that the soule does, it does in, and with, and by the body.' Donne is quoting Tertullian.

16. In alchemy the elixir was the essence or 'quintessence' which could transmute base metals into gold.

17. Martial, *Epigrams*, II.41.

18. Cf. *The Praise of Folly*, I.

19. 'What is your Canius doing? He is laughing' (adapted from Martial, *Epigrams*, III.20).

20. Greek philosophers of the fifth century B.C., referred to from late antiquity as the laughing and weeping philosophers.

21. Tapestries.

22. A mythical lizard supposed to be able to live in fire, which it could quench by the chill of its body. Pliny tried the experiment, but the creature was soon burnt to a powder (see *Natural History*, X.67; XXIX.4).

23. At the core of this Paradox is the entirely serious point (cf. St Augustine, *City of God*, XII.3) that evil has no separate existence and can only inhere in good; thus there can never be a time when 'nothing shal be good'. Donne alludes to the paradox that sin is 'nothing' in the last line of 'The Litany' and in *Sermons*, VI.238. The world's 'dotage' refers to the popular belief that the world was in an advanced stage of decay; cf., especially, the *Anniversaries*.

24. ' "There are no gods: heaven is empty", Selius asserts – and proves it for while he denies these things, he sees himself made rich' (Martial, *Epigrams*, IV.21).

25. The judgement of Paris, which took place on Mount Ida, sparked off the Trojan war. He presented Aphrodite, as the most beautiful of the three goddesses, with an apple (or 'ball').

26. 'Worst of wives, worst of husbands, I'm surprised you get along so badly' (Martial, *Epigrams*, VIII.35).

27. Cf. *Sermons*, III, p. 244, 'Now this institution of mariage had three objects: first . . . it was given as a remedy against burning . . . Let him then that takes his wife in this first and lowest sense, *In medicinam*, but as his Physick, yet make her his cordiall Physick, take her to his heart' (Peters).

28. 'To give to each his own.'

29. 'As if it were not permitted, no girl says "no" ' (Martial, *Epigrams*, IV.71).

30. Peters has 'the lawes to entrap them', which does not seem to make sense. I have restored the reading of the first edition.

31. Peters regards this Paradox to be of doubtful authorship. I have included it because it is the best known of the Paradoxes ascribed to Donne, and its theme is entirely characteristic of him; cf. 'Change', 'Confined Love', 'Variety' and 'Woman's Constancy'. (The motto on his youthful portrait, however, is *Antes muerto que mudado*, 'Sooner dead than changed'.)

32. Cf. 'Good Friday, 1613. Riding Westward', ll. 1–10.

33. A child's first primer, but with a pun on the cuckold's horns.

PROBLEMS

1. The river Oxus in Russia.

2. Sprinklings.

3. Cf. Satire 3, 'Of Religion'.

4. Whether women had souls had been seriously debated on the basis of I Corinthians 11.1–12. Donne attacks those who propose such 'Paradoxes' in Sermon 51.1.

5. Montanists, whom Donne presents as being advocates of female ordination.

6. Tawdry (figurative).

7. Cf. 'The Ecstasy', ll. 61–2, 'As our blood labours to beget/Spirits, as like souls as it can'.

8. In a sexual sense cf. 'Love's Alchemy', ll. 1–2, 'Some that have deeper digged love's mine than I,/Say, where his centric happiness doth lie'.

9. 'The occupier has the rights.'

10. The subject of this Problem is discussed in Kepler's *De Stella Nova* (1606). A copy of this book marked by Donne survives.

11. The 'colours of rhetoric' was a common Renaissance metaphor for figurative language, as in Bacon's *The Advancement of Learning* (1605), Book II, where he contrasts the 'dry light' of reason.

12. Sexual transactions.

13. 'And the spectator pleases you more than the adulterer' (adapted from Martial, *Epigrams*, I.34).

14. From Suetonius's *Life of Horace*. Ben Jonson borrowed the idea for Mammon's sexual fantasy in *The Alchemist* (1610), II.ii. It reappears in a more pious context in Donne, *Sermons*, III, p. 57.

15. The famous sixteenth-century doctor and alchemist (considered a charlatan by many) who had challenged the classical doctrine of the four humours. Donne refers to him throughout his writings, including the Sermons, and his attitude towards him is typically ambivalent; he refers approvingly to Paracelsus in *Biathanatos*, III.iii.3 and the Conclusion. See also *Devotions*, notes 3 and 20.

16. Cf. *Devotions*, 12. Syphilis is 'Indian Vermine' because it was introduced to Europe by Columbus's voyages to the West Indies.

17. Donne refers to the nautical practice of using flags to indicate danger.

18. Peters notes an alternative reading, *straw* (i.e. 'strew'); it was thought that people's noses were liable to drop off with the cold in Russia.

19. Donne refers, respectively, to the Roman emperor, the teacher of St Thomas Aquinas, and the poet, Ovid.

20. Puritan reaction to Donne's own sermons is described in the elegy 'In memory of Doctor Donne: By Mr. R. B.': 'They humm'd against him; And

with face most sowre/Call'd him a strong lin'd man, a Macaroon . . .' (*Donne's Poetical Works*, ed. H. J. C. Grierson, I.386–7).

21. Long and short notes in music.

BIATHANATOS

1. For the contemporary debate on suicide see William Vaughan, who added a section on the subject to *The Golden Grove* (2nd edn, 1608), chaps. 14–29; Thomas Beard, likewise, in *The Theatre of God's Judgements* (2nd edn, 1612), II.xii; and Robert Burton, *The Anatomy of Melancholy* (1621), I.iv.1. Beard's line is closest to that of Donne: 'both charitie and conscience inhibites resolutely to judge all such to be damned that seeme to have made havocke of their owne lives . . .' (p. 307). (Beard also argues that apparently impossible suicides, such as those who drown in puddles or hang themselves from twigs, must in fact have been killed by the devil – a point which eluded Donne.)

2. A leading Calvinist theologian (1519–1605).

3. Donne had been brought up a Catholic. Both his uncle and brother were persecuted for their faith.

4. The idea is a Stoic commonplace, as in Seneca, *Moral Epistles*, 70. Donne's expression may come from Montaigne, *Essays*, II.iii, 'nature . . . hath left us the key of the fields', trans. Florio, who evidently did not know the idiomatic expression *avoir la clef des champs,* to be free to leave at any time. (For 'any affliction' the MS reads 'my affliction').

5. To stir up or harass.

6. 'A mean spirit and an unfortunate disposition' (*Natural History*, Preface).

7. The sin of despair, as in *Dr Faustus*, V.i.

8. 'The desires of the flesh.'

9. 'Punishment for sin.'

10. Cf. *Sermons*, V, pp. 93–4, 'for presumption takes away the feare of God, and desperation the love of God'.

11. Proves.

12. As if natural.

13. Transmitted. Cf. Paradox 4, 'That Nature is our worst Guide'.

14. 'Let us make man in our image, that is, a law unto himself' (Genesis I.26).

15. 'Not against universal law, but against the universality of the law.'

16. A well-known saying of Tertullian, a Father of the early Church (A.D. c. 160–c. 220). On the martyrs, cf. 'A Litany', ll. 82–9.

17. 'An athlete does not immediately win a race by taking off his clothes; nor do swimmers reach the other side just because they have stripped.'

18. 'With a mind worthy of a philosopher.'

19. 'That I will die voluntarily . . . caress the beasts with flatteries.'

20. 'Because death will be beneficial to me.'

21. 'Over the bridge.'

22. Cf. Montaigne, 'A Custom of the Isle of Cea' (*Essays*, II.3).

23. Donne's grandmother was Joan Rastell, More's niece. Euthanasia is discussed in *Utopia*, trans. Turner (Penguin, 1965), p. 102.

24. See *Laws*, IX.873.

25. A point where Donne does seem to come close to Montaigne's position on the law. The relevant essays are I.22 and 23 ('Of custom, and how a received law should not easily be changed'). The gist of the second essay is the power of custom and the fact that it precedes law.

26. Brought back from error.

27. 'It is expedient for states to be deceived in matters of religion.'

28. Donne is referring to Scipio's dream at the end of Cicero's *De Republica* and Macrobius's commentary on it.

29. 'From the mind.'

30. 'A decision once made cannot be revoked.'

31. The virgin martyrs of the early Church were the most famous example of apparently legitimate suicides. Vaughan (see note 1 above) argues that Pelagia and others did sin; chap. 28, 'An answere to the objection of the Virgins of the primitive Church'.

32. 'Other Latin [writers].'

33. 'We do not have anything to say about this.'

34. 'With most honoured veneration' (*City of God*, I.26).

35. 'For the commandment is a lamp; and the law is light' (Proverbs 6.23).

36. Cf. 'A Valediction: forbidding Mourning', l. 24, 'Like gold to aery thinness beat'.

37. 2 Peter 1.20.

38. 'Of the stricter bond.'

39. 'Divine law cannot be amended unless the amendment itself conforms with divine law.'

40. A hardening of the heart.

41. Blindness.

42. Romans 3.8.

43. A right to a possession acquired by long usage. *Malae fidei* = 'in bad faith'.

44. 'Of the general public.'

45. The canon deals with the lesser of two evils.

46. Ephesians 4.15,16.

47. John 10.15.

48. Emptying.

49. *Summa Theologica*, 3.47.1.

50. Cf. *Sermons*, V, p. 121, 'First then, *Ille dedit*, He gave, it was his own act; as it was he, that gave up the ghost, he that laid down his soule, and he that took it again; for no power of Man had the power, or disposition of his life'.

51. Acts 1–18.

52. Psalms 69 and 109.

53. 'He left the noose to such people.'

54. See Sermons, note 143.

55. Syphilis, cf. Problem 5. Donne is referring to Paracelsus's *Chirurgia Magna* (Strassburg, 1573), a copy of which he owned.

56. A Greek physician called 'the Father of Medicine' (*c*. 460–*c*. 377). Donne is referring to *Aphorisms*, 2.38.

57. 'Loss of reputation.'

58. Paracelsus and Pomponazzi. The latter was an Italian philosopher who had denied the immortality of the soul; see *Devotions*, note 68.

59. 'In a situation of great profit or loss, or in humility when vainglory is to be avoided.'

60. See *The Republic*, III.389. Donne has already cited authorities who have claimed that lying is a worse sin than suicide in I.i.7.

61. 'Let the man who does not digest his food sleep.'

LETTERS

1. The distinction is between an improvisation and a formal composition.

2. Philip Howard, Earl of Arundel (1557–95). After an extravagant youth he became a Catholic, and on trying to flee the country in 1585 was arrested and imprisoned in the Tower until his death.

3. Rebounded.

4. Probably Petruccio Ubaldini (*c*. 1524–*c*. 1600), illuminator and man of letters. The twelfth Earl of Arundel, Philip Howard's grandfather, had been his patron.

5. Pope Celestine V abdicated in 1294. Dante places him not in Purgatory, but at the gate of Hell, for having 'made the great refusal out of cowardice' (*Inferno*, III.59–60).

6. Donne may be referring to *Moral Epistles*, 39, 'they even love their own vices, and that is the worst vice of all'.

7. Sir Christopher Hatton (1540–91), Lord Chancellor from 1587.

8. 'To your worship' (Spanish). Goodyer (1571–1627), an easy-going spendthrift courtier, was possibly Donne's closest male friend. He is the subject of two epigrams by Ben Jonson.

9. Donne had secretly married Ann More, his employer's niece, in 1601. The enraged father had Donne imprisoned and his career prospects were blighted.

This letter was written from the cottage in Mitcham, Surrey, where the couple lived from 1606 to 1612.

10. Cf. *Sermons*, I, p. 203, 'Adam did not believe Eve, nor was not overcome by her reasons, when she provoked him to eat the Apple . . . he was affected by that near interest between them. And *ne contristaretur delicias suas*, lest by refusing he should put her, whom he delighted in, to a desperate sadness, and sense of her sin, he eat for company'.

11. Jane Meautys, lady-in-waiting to Lucy, Countess of Bedford (1581–1627). Bartlett was Carver to Queen Anne and later ended up in the Tower for bad language. Magdalen Herbert, later Lady Danvers, was another close friend of Donne's; see Sermon 43.

12. Gaping.

13. Cf. the Holy Sonnet, 'Batter my heart . . .'. The shipwreck also anticipates 'A Hymn to Christ, at the Author's last going into Germany'.

14. Swollen with water, yet insatiably thirsty. Donne frequently refers to this condition in his poems; cf. 'A Nocturnal upon S. Lucy's Day', l. 6, 'The Second Anniversary', ll. 46–7, and the Holy Sonnet, 'Since she whom I loved . . .', l. 8.

15. 'Cheerfully' (Italian).

16. See *Devotions*, note 15 and *Sermons*, note 95.

17. 'Moments of lucidity.'

18. Fancy foodstuffs, 'kickshaws'.

19. The Countess of Bedford. The verses in the garden (her home was at Twickenham) may have prompted Donne's poem, 'Twicknam Garden'.

20. The Earl of Ancrum (1578–1654). He accompanied Prince Charles on his visit to Spain to woo the Infanta in 1623.

21. A favourite image, cf. Sermon 5.2 and note 14.

22. Sermon 24. There is a close parallel to the passage on the 'flat map'; see *Sermons*, VI, p. 59.

DEVOTIONS

1. Taken in sequence the Latin headings or *stationes* form a poem of twenty-two lines. Despite Donne's use of the term *stationes* it is difficult to see how these 'stages' might correspond to the Stations of the Cross – a pictorial aid to meditation – as is sometimes claimed.

2. Slight symptom of approaching illness.

3. The notion that man is a microcosm of the world is the principle behind the entire sequence of Meditations. It was, of course, a very common idea in Renaissance literature: 'because in the little frame of mans body there is a representation of the Universall, and (by allusion) a kind of participation of all

the parts thereof, therefore was Man called *Microcosmos*, or the little world', Sir Walter Ralegh, *The History of the World* (1614), I.2.5. (Ralegh's subsequent analogies between veins and rivers, rocks and bones, are similar to Donne's in Meditation 4.) Cf. also the Holy Sonnet, 'I am a little world made cunningly'. The central importance of this idea in *Devotions,* with its system of universal analogies, may also indicate the influence of Paracelsus (see note 20): 'Man . . . is the Microcosm, the lesser world, and for his sake, the Macrocosm, the greater world, was founded, that he might be its Spectator', *Hermetical and Alchemical Writings,* trans. A. E. Waite (1894), I.161.

4. Anticipate.

5. Cf. the Holy Sonnet, 'Oh, to vex me, contraries meet in one', l. 7, 'As riddlingly distempered, cold and hot . . .'.

6. Cf. St Augustine, *Confessions,* I.6.

7. Genesis 28.16.

8. Matthew 13.15.

9. The circle is a favourite image in the Sermons; see Sermons, note 15.

10. The register of the elect; the other 'Book of Life' is the Bible.

11. 2 Kings 4.40.

12. Proverbs 13.17.

13. Isaiah 58.8.

14. Genesis 28.15.

15. Donne follows the old Ptolemaic system of the universe in which the stars and planets were thought to revolve around a fixed earth. The stars moved more quickly because they occupied the sphere furthest from the centre.

16. Genesis 3.19. Cf. also 'Hymn to God my God, in my sickness', ll. 23–5.

17. Images of confinement, and the term 'close prison' in particular, are frequent in Donne's prose, perhaps most memorably in *Deaths Duell* where the womb itself is seen as a dank and potentially lethal cell.

18. Diogenes the Cynic, *fl.* 380 B.C.

19. A 'type' in this sense is a foreshadowing equivalent. It is a favourite device in Herbert's poetry, cf. 'Mortification'.

20. Cf. *Sermons,* I V, p. 104, 'The Philosopher draws man into too narrow a table when he says he is the *Microcosmos,* an abridgement of the world in little . . . [he is] *Mundum Magnum,* a world to which all the rest of the world is but subordinate'. Donne is trying to place the Paracelsian notion that man is a microcosm of the world in the context of Christian humanism; Francis Bacon, his contemporary, was more thoroughly sceptical: 'The ancient opinion that man was *Microcosmus,* an abstract or model of the world, hath been fantastically strained by Paracelsus and the alchemists, as if there were to be found in man's body certain correspondences and parallels, which should have respect to all varieties of

things, as stars, plants, minerals, which are extant in the great world' (*The Advancement of Learning*, ed. G. W. Kitchin (1973), p. 209). Such correspondences are the very fabric of *Devotions*. Cf. also 'To the Countess of Bedford' ('To have written then . . .'), ll. 61–4.

21. The distinction is, roughly, between infections, cancers and fevers.

22. Medical preparations consisting of a single substance.

23. Transmitters of disease.

24. John 14.2. Plurality is the theme of Sermon 26.

25. A growing belief that there might be life on other planets was a consequence of the new cosmology of Copernicus. The idea is associated particularly with the Hermetic philosopher Giordano Bruno (1548–1600) and his work, *De L'infinito universo e mondi* (1584).

26. The idea that the Old and New Testaments are God's wills appears in the Holy Sonnet, 'Father, part of his double interest'; cf. also *Sermons*, IX, p. 232.

27. Probably Simeon Foxe (1568–1642).

28. The spleen was supposed to be the seat of melancholy. Donne ponders the psychosomatic nature of his illness in Meditation 12.

29. A noxious exhalation, as in 'The Dampe'.

30. The Sicilian tyrant Dionysius the Elder (*c.* 430–367 B.C.) drank himself to death while celebrating the award of first prize for his play *The Ransom of Hector* at the Athens drama festival. Donne is confusing him with his son who was deposed in 356.

31. At his death in Rouen in 1087 William's body was stripped and abandoned by his attendants, who then fled to the security of their estates.

32. A recipe or prescription.

33. Lists of recent deaths were posted in each parish of London.

34. A syrup used to cool fevers. Bezoar, an antidote against poison, was a kind of stone found in the intestines of goats.

35. One who enjoys the use of somebody else's property.

36. Son of Apollo, and mythical medical expert.

37. A mushroom used as a cathartic. Choler and phlegm were two of the four humours.

38. 2 Samuel 24.12–13; Job 1.16–19.

39. Epilepsy, as in *Julius Caesar*, I.ii.251–3.

40. Types of cancer; cf. Webster, *The White Devil*, V.iii.55.

41. Open, public.

42. The light is the empyrean, the heavenly realm beyond the fixed stars. Beneath the stars everything is subject to mutability and decay; cf. 'The Anniversary', ll. 6–7, 'All other things, to their destruction draw,/Only our love hath no decay'.

43. Cf. 'To the Countess of Bedford', ll. 57–8, 'For, bodies shall from death

redeemed be,/Souls but preserved, not naturally free', and *Sermons*, V, p. 385, 'And for the Immortality of the Soule, It is safelier said to be immortall, by preservation, than immortall by nature . . .'.

44. Sirius ascendant in July/August, and thought to spread plague; hence the term 'the dog-days'.

45. Donne is making a distinction between 'natural law' and the condition in which man lived before he constructed a politically organized society; cf. Cicero, 'There is, however, no such thing as private ownership established by nature . . .' (*De Officiis*, I.vii.21). '*Meum & Tuum*' ('mine and thine') was proverbial.

46. Cf. 2 Samuel 14.26.

47. The pigeons were applied to the soles of the feet; cf. Webster, *The Duchess of Malfi*, II.i.41–2.

48. A gas generated by an imbalance of humours in the body – in this case a preponderance of melancholy – which rises to the head.

49. Small change.

50. Pliny the Elder (A.D. 23–79) died of fumes while investigating Vesuvius (not Etna) after the destruction of Pompeii.

51. A 'channell' is a gutter, a 'shambles' a slaughterhouse.

52. Coming alternately.

53. An indisputable fact.

54. For his reflections on the nature of time Donne is partly indebted to St Augustine, *Confessions*, XI. Augustine considers 'whether happiness is in the memory' in X.20–21. But the despondent sense of time as meaningless flux is reminiscent of many of the *Songs and Sonnets*, and of Montaigne; see *Essays*, II.i, 'Of the Inconstancy of our Actions'.

55. A long sentence of some grammatical complexity.

56. The death knell.

57. Pre-Christian writers. On sleep as a figure of death, cf. Sermon 45.

58. Day of preparation for the Jewish Sabbath.

59. Meditations 16, 17 and 18 centre on the three bells rung upon the occasion of a death in the parish – the passing bell, the death knell and the funeral bell. Donne begins with the last, and then in 17 and 18 reflects upon the end of a specific, unknown individual. See also Sermon 45.

60. Gerolamo Maggi (1523–72) wrote *De Tintinnabulis* in Constantinople; it was published in Hanau in 1608.

61. Released.

62. Donne's marginal gloss refers to Antwerp and Rouen. He probably visited Antwerp with Sir Robert Drury in 1612; see Bald, p. 261.

63. Told by Angelo Rocca (1545–1620) in *De Campaniis* (Rome, 1612).

64. In medicine, the deadening of a part of the body.

65. The implication here that man instinctively desires death is the substance of the first part of *Biathanatos*.

66. Cf. Dante, *Paradiso*, XXXIII.85–7. The translation quoted in the Introduction is from the Temple Classics Dante (1899). There is a further parallel in St Bernard, 'There will be a time when heaven will be folded just like a book, in which certainly no-one should ever have to read again, because they will all be able to be taught by God' (*Sermones de diversis*, IX). Cf. also Sermon 15.3 and note 47, below.

67. Lawsuit. Donne refers to a dispute in Catholic canon law.

68. Donne is probably referring to the treatise by the Paduan philosopher Pietro Pomponazzi (1462–1525), *On the Immortality of the Soul* (1516). The Elizabethan poet Sir John Davies disputed these arguments in verse in *Nosce Teipsum*.

69. Cf. Paradox 4, 'For we cannot say that we derive our inclinations, our minds, our soules, from our parents by any way'. The doctrine of traduction, that souls are propagated from one generation to another, derives from Tertullian and found support from Sir Thomas Browne in *Religio Medici*, I.36 and Milton, *De Doctrina Christiana*, I.7. On this and the question of 'immediate infusion' see Carey, pp. 275–6.

70. See Sermons, note 96.

71. Gutter.

72. On the three souls, see *Paradoxes*, note 1.

73. Here, a 'ripening' of the matter producing the disease to the stage where it can be safely eliminated. More generally, a 'bringing to perfection', as in 'The Ecstasy', l. 27. On 'ripening', cf. Sermon 28.

74. Terms in law (which cannot, of course, interfere with the process of nature).

75. Censured in the ecclesiastical courts.

76. The *Herm* or *Herma* was a bust placed on a quadrangular pillar. Donne's symbolic reading of the statues would probably have surprised the Greeks, who used them as milestones and signposts.

77. The clenched fist and open hand as symbols of the arts of logic and rhetoric was a commonplace of Renaissance rhetoric books. It derives from Zeno the Stoic.

78. John 3.35.

79. The three stages of purgation.

80. Prisoners who refused to plead guilty or not guilty were crushed to death by having heavy weights piled on them.

81. See Sermons, note 95.

82. The orbits of the planets.

83. A wood on the side of a steep hill.

84. A soil consisting chiefly of clay and lime, used as a fertilizer.

85. Dead flesh preserved in bitumen and used for medicinal purposes. Cf. 'Love's Alchemy', ll. 23–4.

86. The image of God as physician (and sin as sickness) is particularly frequent in St Augustine. The promise of a glorified body in the Resurrection (1 Corinthians 15.39–42) is a theme which Donne returns to again and again in his sermons.

87. Donne's illness has been diagnosed as 'relapsing fever'; see Bald, p. 450.

88. The 'curfew' literally means 'cover the fire' (French: *couvrir le feu*).

89. A 'natural day' was a period of twenty-four hours (as in *Dr Faustus*, V.ii.150). A combination of the longest day and the longest night would total thirty-six hours.

SERMONS

1. On Ecclesiastes 8.11, 'Because sentence against an evil work is not executed speedily, therefore the heart of the sons of men is fully set in them to do evil'. (*Sermons*, I.2.)

2. Hard-heartedness.

3. On Proverbs 22.11, 'He that loveth pureness of heart, for the grace of his lips the king shall be his friend'. Paul's Cross was an outdoor pulpit next to St Paul's Cathedral. (*Sermons*, I.3.)

4. Cf. 'Good Friday, 1613. Riding Westward', ll. 40–42, 'Burn off my rusts, and my deformity,/Restore thine image, so much, by thy grace,/That thou mayst know me . . .'.

5. Cf. the 'Dull sublunary lovers' of 'A Valediction: forbidding Mourning'.

6. Earlier in the sermon Donne had said: 'Love is so noble, so soveraign an Affection, as that it is due to very few things, and very few things worthy of it. Love is a Possessory Affection, it delivers over him that loves into the possession of that that he loves; it is a transmutatory Affection, it changes him that loves, into the very nature of that that he loves, and he is nothing else'.

7. On Proverbs 8.17, 'I love them that love me; and those that seek me early shall find me'. Donne's wife, Ann, had died four months earlier on 10 August 1617; cf. the Holy Sonnet, 'Since she whom I loved . . .'. (*Sermons*, I.5.)

8. 'Spiritual covetousness' is a theme of the Holy Sonnets 'Batter my heart . . .' and 'Since she whom I lov'd . . .', though the words here echo the secular 'Lovers' Infiniteness'.

9. Cf. 'The Canonisation', l. 39, 'You, to whom love was peace, that now is rage . . .'.

10. St Augustine, *Confessions*, II.2.

11. Cf. 'Love's Alchemy', ll. 11–12, 'So, lovers dream a rich and long delight,/But get a winter-seeming summer's night'.

12. On Psalms 38.2, 'For thine arrows stick fast in me, and thy hand presseth me sore'. Donne was a Reader at Lincoln's Inn (where he had also been a student) from 1616 to 1622. (*Sermons*, II.1.)

13. On Psalms 89.48, 'What man is he that liveth, and shall not see death?' (*Sermons*, II.9.)

14. Cf. 'Hymn to God my God, in my sickness', ll. 13–15, 'As west and east/In all flat maps (and I am one) are one,/So death doth touch the resurrection', and Letter 5 above.

15. Donne frequently uses the circle as an image both of human life and of God himself; cf. Sermons 15.1, 27.2, 33, 42.1 and 44.1; it is also implicit throughout *Deaths Duell*.

16. On Ecclesiastes 12.1, 'Remember now thy Creator in the days of thy youth'. Donne was chaplain to the embassy, led by Lord Doncaster, which tried unsuccessfully to avert a war between Catholics and Protestants in central Europe (the Thirty Years' War). (*Sermons*, II.11.)

17. Lotions by which gold or silver particles could be recovered from earth or other matter.

18. Hebrew for 'in the days of thy youth', or 'choice' as Donne glosses it here.

19. The Spanish Armada (1588); the 'Vault' refers to the Gunpowder Plot (1605).

20. Cf. 'The Storme', l.43, 'Lightning was all our light . . .'.

21. Donne takes a similarly moderate line on predestination in Sermon 40.3, but his position is ambiguous, as he also believed in 'the first judgement, before all times'. (*Sermons*, II, p.319.)

22. A collective term for the medieval scholastic philosophers and theologians, the greatest of whom was St Thomas Aquinas (1225–74).

23. Panting, aspiration.

24. Cf. 'A Hymn to Christ, at the Author's last going into Germany', ll. 1–6.

25. On Romans 13.11, 'Now is our salvation nearer than when we believed'. (*Sermons*, II.12.)

26. On Job 19.26, 'And though after my skin worms destroy this body, yet in my flesh shall I see God' (*Sermons*, III.3.)

27. Metaphors of imprinting (of a wax seal) or stamping (of a coin) are used frequently by Donne to express the relationship between body and soul, God's image in man. The impression gives form to the wax and is inseparable from it. See note 32, below, on coins. Sacraments such as baptism are also 'seals' in the sense that they are pledges for man's redemption.

28. The 'exhausting' or 'emptying' of earthly life.

29. On Proverbs 25.16, 'Hast thou found honey? Eat so much as is sufficient for thee, lest thou be filled therewith and vomit it'. (*Sermons*, III.10.)

30. In Greek legend Zeus (Jupiter) impregnated Danae in the form of a shower of gold; the offspring was Perseus.

31. On Hosea 2.19, 'And I will marry thee unto me for ever'. (*Sermons*, III.11.)

32. The soul, the image of God in man, is corroded by sin like the image on a coin. In heaven, or at ordination, it will be 'restamped'; cf. Sermon 15.2 and 'To Mr. Tilman after he had taken orders', ll. 13–18.

33. The spheres were a series of concentric globes, each occupied by a planet, which were believed to revolve around the earth; their motion was directed by a lower order of angels called 'intelligences'; cf. 'The Ecstasy', ll. 49–52.

34. On I Corinthians 16.22, 'If any man love not the Lord Jesus Christ, let him be Anathema Maran-atha'. (*Sermons*, III.14.)

35. Sent back.

36. On John I.8, 'He was not that Light but was sent to bear witness of that Light'. This was the first sermon which Donne preached as Dean of St Paul's. (*Sermons*, III.17.)

37. Donne refers to the story of the tomb of Cicero's daughter; cf. 'Eclogue 1613. December 26', ll. 215–16, 'Now, as in Tullia's tomb, one lamp burnt clear,/Unchanged for fifteen hundred year . . .'.

38. The Koran.

39. Cf. 'To the Countess of Bedford', ll. 1–2, 'Reason is our soul's left hand, Faith her right,/By these we reach divinity . . .'.

40. On I Corinthians 15.26, 'The last enemy that shall be destroyed is death'. Cf. Donne's more famous, but blander, treatment of this theme in the Holy Sonnet, 'Death be not proud . . .'. (*Sermons*, IV.1.)

41. 'Death is a law, a debt to nature, and an obligation for mortals' (adapted from Seneca, *Natural Questions*, VI.32).

42. Hospitals for paupers.

43. On I Thessalonians, 4.17, 'Then we which are alive and remain shall be caught up together with them in the clouds, to meet the Lord in the air: and so shall we ever be with the Lord'. Cf. the Holy Sonnet on the Last Day, 'At the round earth's imagined corners . . .'. (*Sermons*, IV.2.)

44. Donne's reflections on 'nothing' derive from St Augustine's argument that all creation is essentially good, and that sin is therefore 'nothing', see *Paradoxes*, note 23. But cf. also 'A Nocturnal upon S. Lucy's Day'.

45. On II Corinthians 4.6, 'For God, who commanded the light to shine out of darkness, hath shined in our hearts, to give the light of the knowledge of the glory of God in the face of Jesus Christ'. The Spittle was the cross by the Hospital of St Mary, Bishopsgate. (*Sermons*, IV.3.)

46. Cf. 'Obsequies to the Lord Harrington', ll. 81–100.

47. The Book of Nature written by God at the Creation, and a more eloquent

testament of the divine author than the Bible itself. As a microcosm of the world man is a book within a book, an epitome of the Creation, and even the lowliest creatures are miniature books (in *Decimo sexto*) inscribed by God's hand. The theme is continued in Sermon 16. Donne was especially fond of the metaphor of the world as a book; cf. Sermons 38.4, 47, 52.1, and 'A Valediction: of the Book'. See also *Devotions*, 17 and note 66.

48. On Job 36.25, 'Every man may see it; man may behold it afar off'. Carlisle was Lord Doncaster, see note 16 above. (*Sermons*, IV.6.)

49. Virgil's poem on farming and rural life.

50. On Romans 8.16, 'The Spirit itself beareth witness with our spirit, that we are the children of God'. (*Sermons*, V.2.)

51. I.e. Jewry, the Jews. Sancerre was a Protestant stronghold besieged by the Catholics for nine months in 1573; cf. Elegy 8, l. 10. Geneva was the centre of Calvinism in Europe.

52. On Mark 16.16, 'He that believeth not shall be damned'. (*Sermons*, V.13.)

53. Defiled, polluted (figurative; in the Old Testament menstrual blood was referred to as the type of horrible pollution).

54. Cf. the opening of 'The Sun Rising'.

55. On Psalms 51.7, 'Purge me with hyssop, and I shall be clean: wash me, and I shall be whiter than snow'. (*Sermons*, V.15.)

56. Donne's terminology is borrowed from alchemy (see also *Sermons*, VII, p. 191). Similar processes of refinement and purification are described by Paracelsus in *Concerning the Transmutation of Natural Objects*, trans. Waite, I.151–60. Cf. also *The Alchemist*, II.v.22.

57. On Acts I.8, 'But ye shall receive power, after that the Holy Ghost is come upon you: and ye shall be witness unto me both in Jerusalem, and in all Judaea, and in Samaria, and unto the uttermost part of the earth'. This, Donne's first published sermon, appeared separately in 1622. The occasion was a feast at the Merchant Taylors' Hall. The first attempts at colonizing Virginia had been made in 1585–7 by Sir Walter Ralegh, and the Company was founded in 1606; Donne himself had sought the post of secretary in 1609, and in summer 1622 he was made an honorary member of the Company and its Council. (*Sermons*, IV.10.)

58. See *City of God*, XX.7.

59. Those who believe that Christ will reign in person on earth for a thousand years (the millennium).

60. The legal guardianship of a minor.

61. Earlier in the year Indians had attacked settlements on the James River, killing about 350 settlers and destroying a new ironworks.

62. 'Lust.'

63. The notorious house of correction where vagrants and prostitutes were whipped. The founding of the colony enabled the first sentences of transportation to be passed.

64. Spain, which had a large stake in the Americas. The proposed marriage of Prince Charles to the Spanish Infanta, which came to nothing the following year, obliges Donne to be cautious.

65. A bomb.

66. Spanish theologian (1534–83).

67. Spanish theologian (1540–1600). After posts in Peru and Mexico he wrote *De Procuranda indorum salute* (1588) about evangelism in the Americas.

68. Colossians I.29–30, 'For it pleased the Father that in him should all fulness dwell; And, having made peace through the blood of his cross, by him to reconcile all things unto himself; by him, I say, whether they be things in earth, or things in heaven'. (*Sermons*, IV.11.)

69. Ben Jonson, a friend of Donne's, was converted to Catholicism in 1598. The 'traitor' in question may have been Thomas Wright, author of *The Passions of the Minde* (1601).

70. On Romans 13.7, 'Render therefore to all men their dues'. (*Sermons*, IV,12.)

71. See *Biathanatos*, note 16. Tertullian has been claimed as the main patristic influence on Donne's prose style; see W. F. Mitchell, *English Pulpit Oratory from Andrewes to Tillotson* (1932), pp. 189–91.

72. A narrow strip.

73. Zero.

74. On John 11.35, 'Jesus wept'. (*Sermons*, IV.13.)

75. The general point is that the elements of heat and cold must be corrected by their opposites; cf. the Holy Sonnet, 'Oh, to vex me, contraries meet in one'. On the salamander, see *Paradoxes*, note 22.

76. On Psalms 6.8, 9, 10, 'Depart from me, all ye workers of iniquity; for the Lord hath heard the voice of my weeping. The Lord hath heard my supplication; the Lord will receive my prayer. Let all mine enemies be ashamed and sore vexed: let them return and be ashamed suddenly'. (*Sermons*, VI.1.)

77. See *Confessions*, III.5.

78. Collections of Papal decrees on points of doctrine or ecclesiastical law.

79. Suspicious.

80. Cf. the Holy Sonnet, 'Oh my black soul!'

81. A small, thin disc used for decorating material.

82. On Revelation 20.6, 'Blessed and holy is he that hath part in the first resurrection'. This was the first sermon which Donne preached after the severe illness recorded in *Devotions*. (*Sermons*, VI.2.)

83. Preachers had traditionally adopted the 'four-fold method' of biblical

exegesis by which the Scriptures were interpreted on the literal, the moral, the allegorical and the anagogical (spiritual) levels. In contrast with St Augustine, Donne emphasizes the primacy of the literal sense: 'We have a Rule . . . which is, Not to admit figurative senses in interpretation of Scriptures, where the literal sense may well stand' (*Sermons*, VII, p. 193). However, in many sermons Donne clearly concentrates on moral and spiritual meanings, and he had a poet's admiration for the figurative language of the Bible, as the previous sermon (24) indicates. Cf. also *Devotions*, Expostulation 19.

84. An Alexandrian biblical critic (*c.* 185–*c.* 254), chiefly remembered for his heretical belief that Satan would eventually be saved.

85. On Revelation 7.9, 'After this I beheld, and lo, a great multitude, which no man could number, of all nations, and kindreds, and people, and tongues, stood before the throne, and before the Lamb, clothed with white robes, and palms in their hands'. (*Sermons*, VI.7.)

86. Cf. *Devotions*, 5.

87. On Isaiah 7.14, 'Therefore the Lord himself shall give you a sign; Behold, a virgin shall conceive, and bear a son, and shall call his name Immanuel'. (*Sermons*, VI.8.)

88. Cf. 'The Sun Rising', ll. 9–10; the phrase anticipates the culminating passage on the seasons. The theme is continued in Sermon 28.

89. A Jewish high priest who formed a company of strolling exorcists.

90. Cf. 'A Lecture upon the Shadow'.

91. The term 'hieroglyphick' was used frequently in the early seventeenth century to mean a symbol or epitome (cf. *Devotions*, 20 and Sermon 40.4). A circle bisected by a 'direct line' is a symbol of mortality: 'Circles and right lines limit and close all bodies, and the mortall right-lined circle, must conclude and shut up all' (Sir Thomas Browne, *Hydriotaphia*, 5). The figure so formed is equivalent to the Greek *theta*, initial letter of *thanatos*, death.

92. On Acts 9.4, 'And he fell to the earth, and heard a voice saying unto him, Saul, Saul, why persecutest thou me?'. (*Sermons*, VI.10.)

93. St Augustine.

94. On John 5.28, 29, 'Marvel not at this: for the hour is coming, in the which all that are in the graves shall hear his voice, And shall come forth; they that have done good, unto the resurrection of life; and they that have done evil, unto the resurrection of damnation'. (*Sermons*, VI.13.)

95. Donne had read Kepler, as Problem 4 shows, and Copernicus is rather uncertainly satirized in *Ignatius his Conclave* (1611). He refers to the 'new philosophy' in 'To the Countess of Bedford', ll. 37–42, 'The First Anniversary', ll. 205–8, *Devotions*, 21 and Sermon 38.4, but he seems to have remained sceptical. His fascination with the circle and microcosm suggest that he found the old philosophy more imaginatively appealing.

96. Donne usually insists that at death the soul travels directly to heaven, for example, *Sermons*, III, p. 112, 'We shall see the Humanity of Christ with our bodily eyes, then glorified; but, that flesh, though glorifyed, cannot make us see God better, nor clearer, than the soul alone hath done, all the time, from our death, to our resurrection'. But the Holy Sonnet 'At the round earth's imagined corners . . .' implies that the soul dies with the body, and Sermon 38.1 refers to such 'out-places' as a green bed 'in *Abrahams bosome*'.

97. See *City of God*, XIX.6.

98. Roman jurist, died A.D. 223.

99. On Canticles 3.11, 'Go forth, O ye daughters of Zion, and behold King Solomon with the crown wherewith his mother crowned him in the day of his espousals, and in the day of the gladness of his heart' (The Song of Solomon). King James had died on the 27 March. (*Sermons*, VI.14.)

100. I.e. jet, a hard black substance which takes a brilliant polish.

101. The king was believed to have the power of curing scrofula (the 'King's Evil') by touch (cf. *Macbeth*, IV.iii.140–59).

102. On Psalms 62.9, 'Surely men of low degree are vanity, and men of high degree are a lie: to be laid in the balance, they are altogether lighter than vanity'. This is the first of Donne's five Prebend sermons on Psalms 62–6. He had been appointed prebendary of Chiswick in 1622 and was one of thirty prebendaries in the Chapter of St Paul's. (*Sermons*, VI.15.)

103. Cf. 'The Second Anniversary', ll. 491–4.

104. On Exodus 12.30, 'For there was not a house where there was not one dead'. Donne had been granted the living of St Dunstan's in the West by the Earl of Dorset in 1624. This sermon was preached shortly after the worst outbreak of plague since the Black Death: about forty thousand Londoners died, roughly one sixth of the city's population. Donne had spent the period at Lady Danvers's house in Chelsea. (*Sermons*, VI.18.)

105. Donne refers to the practice of grave-sharing in 'The Relic', ll. 1–2.

106. On Psalms 63.7, 'Because thou hast been my help, therefore in the shadow of thy wings will I rejoice'. (*Sermons*, VII.1.)

107. A cerecloth was a bandage smeared with soothing ointment; 'souple' = 'supple', to soften.

108. A late fourth-century collection of ecclesiastical regulations known as the *Apostolical Constitutions*.

109. An omer is a measure equivalent to five pints.

110. The distinction is between threatening and reminding.

111. Pliny, *Natural History*, XXVII.98 describes the lithospermum or 'Jupiter's corn'.

112. Lack of confidence; mistrust; doubt.

113. 'Thou hast, O God, denied even to Angells, the ability of arriving from

one Extreme to another, without passing the mean way between' (*Essays in Divinity*, ed. E. M. Simpson (1952), p. 37).

114. Recusants were Roman Catholics who refused to attend Church of England services; Separatists were Protestant non-conformists. Donne describes himself in terms of being 'halfe-present' in Sermons 8.2 and 38.3.

115. A Stoic philosopher (A.D. *c.* 55–135) who greatly influenced Emperor Marcus Aurelius.

116. A Platonic doctrine which Donne derives from St Augustine; cf. *Sermons*, IV, p. 98, 'God had no external pattern in the Creation, for there was nothing extant; but God had from all Eternity an internal pattern, an *Idaea*, a preconception, a form in himself, according to which he produc'd every Creature'; also *Sermons*, VIII, p. 120.

117. Beginnings.

118. Shield.

119. Reproof; rebuke.

120. See note 96 above. The description of the soul's journey to heaven, here denied, is similar to that in *The Second Anniversary*, ll. 185–206.

121. On I Corinthians 15.29, 'Else what shall they do which are baptized for the dead, if the dead rise not at all? Why are they then baptized for the dead?'. (*Sermons*, VII.3.)

122. A Neoplatonic philosopher and populariser of Plotinus (A.D. 234–after 301). He wrote fifteen books against the Christians.

123. On John 14.2, 'In my Father's house are many mansions: if it were not so, I would have told you'. (*Sermons*, VII.4.)

124. A temporary place of shelter erected on a journey.

125. 'The meadows are green, the crops flourish.'

126. The Schoolmen may have been wild, but their views on the crush in Hell were tenacious, as Joyce's hell-fire sermon illustrates: 'In earthly prisons the poor captive has at least some liberty of movement, were it only within the four walls of his cell or in the gloomy yard of his prison. Not so in hell. There, by reason of the great number of the damned, the prisoners are heaped together in their awful prison, the walls of which are said to be four thousand miles thick: and the damned are so utterly bound and helpless that, as a blessed saint, Saint Anselm, writes in his book on similitudes, they are not even able to remove from the eye a worm that gnaws it' (*A Portrait of the Artist as a Young Man* (Penguin, 1960), pp. 119–20). Donne's marginal gloss refers to Sebastian Munster.

127. Assyrian, Persian, Macedonian and Roman. The fifth monarchy will be the millennium.

128. On John 16.8–11, 'And when he is come, he will reprove the world of sin, and of righteousness, and of judgement: Of sin, because they believe not on

me; Of righteousness, because I go to my Father, and ye see me no more; Of judgement because the prince of this world is judged'. (*Sermons*, VII.8.)

129. On Psalms 64.10, 'And all the upright in heart shall glory'. (*Sermons*, VII.9.)

130. Donne makes a similar point about circles and corners in Sermon 42.1.

131. Cf. 'Good Friday, 1613. Riding Westward', ll. 23-5, 'Could I behold that endless height which is/Zenith to us, and to'our antipodes/Humbled below us?'

132. On John 11.21, 'Lord, if thou hadst been here, my brother had not died'. Cockayne was a rich London merchant, first governor of Ulster, and a member of the Merchant Adventurers Company. (*Sermons*, VII.10.)

133. A doctrine associated with Pythagoras which is the basis of Donne's unfinished satirical epic, *The Progress of the Soul*.

134. See note 96, above, on the state of the soul after death.

135. Galen and Ptolemy (both second century A.D.) were the standard authorities on physiology and astronomy respectively up to the seventeenth century. Donne is being distinctly old-fashioned in claiming them as authorities in 1626.

136. See *Devotions*, note 85.

137. A favourite topic of Donne's; see *Devotions*, note 20 and Sermons, note 47. It was a popular notion in the early seventeenth century; cf. Sir Thomas Browne, 'Wee carry with us the wonders, we seeke without us: There is all *Africa*, and her prodigies in us; we are that bold and adventurous piece of nature, which he that studies, wisely learns in a *compendium*, what others labour at in a divided piece and endlesse volume' (*Religio Medici*, I.15).

138. Literally, 'earth embossed with figures'. Simpson comments, 'Here the poet and the preacher are one. It was the poet who brought in amber and that magical and medicinal *terra sigillata* to suggest something rich and strange about the dust of these who had to die'. (*Sermons*, VII.23.)

139. Adapted from Catullus's famous lyric, '*Vivamus mea Lesbia atque amemus . . .*'.

140. Legal summons.

141. On Luke 2.29, 30, 'Lord, now lettest thou thy servant depart in peace, according to thy word: For mine eyes have seen thy salvation'. (*Sermons*, VII.11.)

142. On Isaiah 65.20, 'For the child shall die an hundred years old; but the sinner being an hundred years old shall be accursed'. (*Sermons*, VII.14.)

143. Donne entertained different views on the nature of shadows (see Letter 4). Here the notion is similar to Shakespeare's 'Light thickens; and the crow/ Makes wing to th' rooky wood' (*Macbeth*, III.ii.50-51).

144. The idea that man is a plaything of the gods probably derives from Plato, *Laws*, I.644, 'Let us suppose that each of us living creatures is an ingenious puppet

of the gods, whether contrived by way of a toy of theirs, or for some serious purpose'. Here Donne attacks the Calvinist belief that God has predestined a part of His creation to Hell, as he also does in *Sermons*, VII, p. 241. See note 21 above.

145. Cf. the horrific portrait of the atheist in Sermon 48.

146. The German astronomer Christopher Clavius published a computation of this kind in 1607. Donne refers to it frequently; see Carey, p. 129.

147. On Hebrews 11.35, 'Women received their dead raised to life again: and others were tortured, not accepting deliverance; that they might obtain a better resurrection'. (*Sermons*, VII.15.)

148. Cf. the end of the second Prebend sermon (33).

149. More familiarly, 'He whom the gods love dies young' (Plautus, *Bacchides*, IV.816, based on a line of Menander).

150. Cf. 'Hymn to God my God, in my sickness', l. 1, 'Since I am coming to thy holy room . . .'. Donne's daughter, Lucy, had died in January.

151. On Mark 4.24, 'Take heed what ye hear'. The political object of the sermon was to attack those who were seditiously 'whispering' against Charles I. Donne wrote to Sir Robert Ker, 'I hoped for the Kings approbation heretofore in many of my sermons; and I have had it. But yesterday I came very near looking for thanks; for, in my life, I was never in any one peece, so studious of his service' (*Letters* (1651), p. 305). Charles, however, was displeased with the sermon. (*Sermons*, VII.16.)

152. Cf. Satire 3, ll. 79–83, 'On a huge hill,/Cragged, and steep, Truth stands . . .'.

153. Cf. the Holy Sonnet, 'Batter my heart, three-personed God . . .', where the soul is also likened to a besieged town.

154. Donne may be referring to a speech by a friend of Sejanus in *Annals*, V.6.

155. On 2 Peter 3.13, 'Nevertheless we, according to his promise, look for new heavens and a new earth, wherein dwelleth righteousness'. Lady Danvers, formerly Mrs Magdalen Herbert, and mother of the poet George Herbert, had been a friend of Donne's for twenty years. She married Sir John Danvers, who was considerably younger than herself, in 1609. (*Sermons*, VIII.2.)

156. Cf. 'The Ecstasy', ll. 37–40.

157. Her eldest son, Edward, later Lord Herbert of Cherbury, matriculated at Oxford in 1596. Mrs Herbert stayed there in 1599–1600 and again in 1607–8 when her son William was up; see Bald, p. 119.

158. Moderation.

159. The plague epidemic of 1625 when Donne stayed with Lady Danvers.

160. Affability; openness.

161. Generosity.

162. Izaak Walton, who claimed to have been present at this sermon, seems to have modelled his account of Donne's own death on this passage; see *Lives* (Oxford, 1927), pp. 81–2.

163. In law, the return of an estate to its donor after the expiry of the grant.

164. Mandragora, a plant with narcotic properties (as in *Othello*, III.iii.327). No reference is intended to the plant's humanoid features, as in 'Go, and catch a falling star,/ Get with child a mandrake root'.

165. On Matthew 22.30, 'For in the resurrection they neither marry, nor are given in marriage, but are as the angels of God in heaven'. The occasion was the marriage of Mary Egerton, granddaughter of Sir Thomas Egerton, Donne's former employer, to Richard Herbert, grandson of Lady Danvers. (*Sermons*, VIII.3.)

166. Cf. 'A Valediction: forbidding Mourning', ll. 33–6.

167. Angelology was one of Donne's favourite subjects; cf. Sermons 15.3 and 31. Unlike Milton (*Paradise Lost*, V.469–500), he imagined angels to be entirely incorporeal, as he does in 'Air and Angels'.

168. On Acts 7.60, 'And when he had said this, he fell asleep'. (*Sermons*, VIII.7.)

169. Cf. Sermon 41.2. The exclamation in 'A Litany', ll. 89–90, '. . . for Oh, to some/Not to be martyrs, is a martyrdom' seems appropriate here.

170. Repetition.

171. On Psalms 6.6,7, 'I am weary with my groaning; all the night make I my bed to swim; I water my couch with my tears. Mine eye is consumed because of grief; it waxeth old because of all mine enemies'. (*Sermons*, VIII.8.)

172. On 1 Corinthians 13.12, 'For now we see through a glass, darkly; but then face to face: now I know in part; but then shall I know even as also I am known'. (*Sermons*, VIII.9.)

173. Martial, *Epigrams*, II.87. (In fact the text reads *Sexte* not *Phoebe*.)

174. The idea that the world is a theatre is similar to that of The Book of Nature, see note 47 above, and is not connected with the notion that 'All the world's a stage' or that 'Life is a dream'. 'Mirror' and 'Theatre' were used almost synonymously in sixteenth- and early seventeenth-century book titles to indicate a *display* of knowledge.

175. King of the serpents, hatched from a cock's egg, and reputed to be capable of staring a man dead.

176. To close one's eyes, not merely to blink.

177. On Acts 28.6, 'They changed their minds, and said that he was a god'. (*Sermons*, VIII.14.)

178. Cf. *Dr Faustus*, V.ii.163, 'Mountains and hills, come, come, and fall on me,/And hide me from the heavy wrath of God'.

179. On John 10.10, 'I am come that they might have life, and that they might have it more abundantly'. (*Sermons*, IX.5.)

180. Figures.

181. On Matthew 6.21, 'For where your treasure is, there will your heart be also'. (*Sermons*, IX.7.)

182. Starling.

183. On Matthew 28.6, 'He is not here: for he is risen, as he said. Come, see the place where the Lord lay'. (*Sermons*, IX.8.)

184. Cf. 'To the Countess of Bedford', ll. 30–32, '. . . for you are here/ The first good angel, since the world's frame stood,/That ever did in woman's shape appear'.

185. Cf. Problem 2 and 'To the Countess of Huntingdon', ll. 1–2, 'Man to God's image, Eve, to man's was made,/Nor find we that God breathed a soul in her . . .'. The dubious passage in St Paul is 1 Corinthians 11, 1–12.

186. A sorcerer who tried to buy the power of the Holy Spirit from the Apostles, hence the crime of 'simony'.

187. A Numidian bishop whose followers formed a schismatic body in the African Church in the fourth century.

188. On Psalms 32.9, 'Be ye not as the horse, or as the mule, which have no understanding: whose mouth must be held in with bit and bridle, lest they come near unto thee'. The sermon may belong to the winter of 1624–5. (*Sermons*, IX.17.)

189. I.e. in the 'chain of being', the hierarchy of creation which extends from the angels down to plants and stones.

190. Pier Luigi, son of Paul III, was supposed to have fatally raped the Bishop of Fano in 1537. Donne was fond of this tale and first used it in *Ignatius his Conclave* (1611). His version is somewhat inaccurate: he assumes, not un-reasonably, that the rapist was a Borgia.

191. *Confessions*, II.3.

192. On Psalms 68.20, 'And unto God the Lord belong the issues of death' ('i.e. from death' – Donne's note). The sermon was preached before the king at Whitehall; it was published the following year with a frontispiece based on the portrait of Donne in his shroud, which he commissioned on his death-bed. He died on 31 March. (*Sermons*, X.11.)

193. Donne had written to George Garrard in January, 'It hath been my desire, (and God may be pleased to grant it me) that I might die in the Pulpit; if not that, yet that I might take my death in the Pulpit, that is, die the sooner by occasion of my former labours' (*Letters* (1651), p. 243). Walton writes, '. . . when to the amazement of some beholders he appeared in the Pulpit, many of them thought he presented himself not to preach mortification by a living voice: but mortality by a decayed body and a dying face . . . Many that then

saw his tears, and heard his faint and hollow voice, professing they thought the Text prophetically chosen, and that Dr Donne *had preach't his own Funeral Sermon*' (*Lives*, p. 75).

194. Joints.

195. St Augustine did believe that the soul of an unborn infant could be damned, but Donne denies this elsewhere; see *Sermons*, IV, pp. 176–7. Simpson rather unconvincingly suspects a pun on 'dammed', as in the second Prebend sermon.

196. Remain in prison until the lawyer's bill has been paid.

197. The condition of being infested and consumed by worms.

198. This text (1 Corinthians 15.51) had a particular fascination for Donne: 'I scarce know of a place of Scripture, more diversely read' (*Sermons*, IV, p. 74). At one point he had hoped that he might be one of the lucky few who would be alive on the Last Day: 'Perchance I shall never die' (*Letters* (1651), p. 11). He discusses the question in *Sermons* (*Sermons*, II, pp. 198, 204–5; III, p. 103); see also Carey, pp. 227–9.

199. Canopy.

200. Predictions.

201. Struggles.

202. Founder of the Anchorite life in Palestine (A.D. *c.* 291–371). Under the influence of St Antony he was for a time a hermit in the Egyptian desert.

203. Cf. Herbert, 'The Agonie'.

204. Sifting.